The Brother's Twin

inspired by true events

by Carolyn Bennett-Hunter

Volume 5 of The Matter Series

Copyright 2024 by Carolyn Bennett-Hunter

INDEX

1. The Proposal 1
2. The Boys 11
3. The Girls 23
4. Deception 44
5. Apple Valley Memory Care 73
6. Kissin' Cousins 99
7. Special Blend 130
8. Christmas of '56 153
9. Comfort Zone 176
10. Leverage 223
11. Heavy Metal 239
12. Stray Cat 264
13. Hillview 283
14. Godspeed Island 307
15. For Whom the Bell Tolls 344
16. Epilogue 354

Other Books by Carolyn Bennett-Hunter:

City Beyond the Deep
The Widow's Four
The Oceanview Matter
The Powell Mountain Matter
The Killingham Matter
The Zarahemla Matter

ACKNOWLEDGMENTS

My heartfelt thanks to the family and friends who carefully proofed the pages of this book, including, but not limited to long-time dear friend and film producer Sherry Collins.

Special thanks to attorney friend Rachel Bertoni, and to paralegal friends Julie Cohen, Jacky Withem and Debbie Sword for their many hours spent proofing.

Thanks to my special friend and fellow writer Mardi Sayles-Smith, author of *Starseed: The Ripping of Innocence*, for her help proofing, as well.

Thanks to my dear friend Sandy Bunn, RN, for looking over the ventilator section of this story and for her valuable suggestions on how weaning from a breathing tube is accomplished.

I am particularly grateful to my wonderful husband David for his tireless hours of proofing, for his unique perspective on what some of the male characters in this story might have done under similar circumstances, and vital suggestions in regard to the plot sequence.

Thank you to friends Susan "Rives," Janette "Manza," and Sherry "Collingsworth" for agreeing to be featured as the characters bearing their names in this series.

Many thanks to former classmate and email friend Bert Higa for again sharing his aeronautic expertise, for looking over the helicopter sequence included in this book, and for agreeing to be featured as Bart Higbee again. Bert was a chief inspector at an aircraft repair station for commercial airliners, inspected propulsion systems for orbiting spacecraft, and worked for many years as an airplane mechanic. Bert is now semi-retired but actively participates in piloting small planes on humanitarian aid missions of mercy to third-world countries.

This fifth volume of The Matter Series required a lot more research than expected, including review of the many newspaper articles from The Fresno Bee about the case that inspired parts of this story.

My thanks to the Fresno County Sheriff's Office for sending me a copy of the Coroner's report upon which some of the details contained herein are based.

My gratitude to Senior Investigator Nick Zell from the Marion County Medical Examiner's Office for taking the time to discuss with me the significance of lead being found in a toxicology report. He explained to me that lead can accumulate in the human body over time and even contribute to altered mental states. Lead poisoning can also lead to possible heart, kidney, liver or other major organ failure, as the human body has no way of expelling it. There is no safe level of lead, and many older homes have aging water pipes that do contain lead.

Thanks to Danika Sekuloff from an organization called Rethink Mental Illness Advice Service of England for discussing the known causes of schizophrenia and for providing a useful link about them: www.rcpsych.ac.uk/mental-health/mental-illnesses-and-mental-health-problems/schizophrenia

My thanks to the volunteers at the Antique Powerland Car & Motorcycle Museum in Brooks, Oregon, for taking the time to show me step-by-step how to start up a 1936 Ford Sedan which, as I understand it, is not dissimilar to a 1939 version of that vehicle as portrayed in this book. They even let me sit in the driver's seat.

Heartfelt thanks to my dear friend Laurey Lee for helping me negotiate the nuances of my publishing program to prepare the final cover, and especially for all her help while I was incapacitated.

Cover photo by Cottonbro Studio as found at the website of royalty-free images (even for commercial use): https://www.pexels.com/royalty-free-images/

FOREWORD

Just as Jim Otterman sets out to help Carolyn and her cousin Leticia learn more about the results of a recent DNA test which reveals they might be half-sisters, Carolyn reluctantly asks him to look into an unsolved cold case in their family tree.

Was late Cousin Luke responsible for the mysterious death of his and Leticia's mother? Or could it have been someone else? What finally led a neighbor to peek through a particular window of the house where her skeleton was found?

Forbidden romance will pull at your heartstrings while mystery and suspense keep you reading until the end of this macabre thriller.

Fictitious names have been used when necessary to protect the identity of some characters in this book. And of course, any similarity to events, true crimes, places, organizations or persons either living or dead within the pages of this book is intentionally coincidental.

1. The Proposal

Carolyn slowly climbed from the white Dodge Dart convertible and began walking toward the two-story brick warehouse. Carolyn's long blonde hair perfectly matched her natural color and her daily exercise routine had helped her maintain a shapely physique, despite her age. Deeply saddened by the recent death of her mother, Carolyn was in no mood to endure much of Jim Otterman's usual verbosity.

"Is this Jim's warehouse?" questioned Janette. Her long auburn hair was neatly braided into a waist-length graying ponytail. Her irrepressible smile was often contagious. Janette had been Carolyn's long-time friend and confident for many years.

"That's what I understand," replied Carolyn.

"Carolyn!" came a familiar voice from behind them.

Carolyn was a bit more reserved in her response than Jim had hoped for as she and Janette turned to face him. *She'll come around*, vowed Jim. *I'm not about to give up on her yet.*

Jim Otterman was in excellent health for a man of 66 years, despite his slightly stooped shoulders and thin profile. While Jim's graying red hair was not as bright as in his younger years, it now had more of an iridescent quality. He had been trained in hand-to-hand combat during his years as a law enforcement officer and had surprisingly quick reflexes. Jim's ruddy complexion was still peeling from a recent sunburn obtained while in the lost city of Zarahemla. It was there that he, Carolyn, and the other members of their expedition to Colombia had discovered the ancient burial chamber of Queen Ariela, as well as many of the artifacts and other golden treasures slated to be housed in his new museum.

"Where's the reporters?" asked Carolyn. "I'm sure they're anxious to see some of the artifacts."

"That's not until tomorrow," grinned Jim. "Today's *your* day, ladies. A private tour of the collection."

Carolyn and Janette exchanged a surprised glance.

"Besides, we'll probably need some privacy anyway," Jim advised them as he motioned toward the building.

Carolyn frowned and thought, *Jim knows I'm happily married.*

"You did wanna talk to me about a cold case in your family history that needs solving," Jim reminded Carolyn as he raised an eyebrow and gave her a crooked smile.

"As I've told you before, we don't actually *know* if a crime was committed," recapped Carolyn. "Nothing was ever proven."

"Didn't you mention something about two cousins who recently took a DNA test and found out they're actually half-sisters?" prodded Jim with a sly wink as they followed him up the front steps of his warehouse.

"That's right," confirmed Carolyn.

When they reached the armor-plated security door, Jim pressed a hidden button on the outer edge of its doorjamb, causing the panel on a cleverly-disguised alarm keypad beside it to slide open.

"You also mentioned that the DNA test was recent, but that the crime took place several years ago," recounted Jim while he began entering a series of numbers into the alarm keypad.

"Alleged crime," corrected Carolyn.

"Of course," flirted Jim as the 15-foot-high steel door slid open and disappeared into the wall beside it.

"What I'm hoping for is to find out whether the circumstances behind those DNA results could have once been the motivation for someone else to commit a crime," elaborated Carolyn while she and Janette followed Jim inside.

"Let me get this straight," analyzed Jim. "The DNA test was recent, but the crime took place several years ago?"

"Yes, but like I said," reiterated Carolyn, "we don't even know if a crime was committed."

"Not to change the subject," interrupted Janette when Jim caused the entrance door to close again and lock behind them, "but can you tell us a little about the museum you plan to build?"

"Absolutely," responded Jim as he headed toward a rather elaborate glass display case in the main foyer. Inside was a conceptual design model of what the finished museum would look like. Beside it was a completed set of the architectural plans.

"Wow!" exclaimed Janette. "That'll really be something!"

"Indeed," agreed Carolyn. She did not seem enthused.

"Look familiar?" questioned Jim with a crooked grin.

Carolyn studied the model carefully. "A stepped pyramid? Won't that be rather costly to build?"

Jim merely shrugged. "It'll be just like the main pyramid in the City of Zarahemla."

"So, what is all this?" questioned Janette as she motioned toward stacks of crates lined up against the walls beside them.

"In a minute," responded Jim. He quickly pulled out an extendable pointer stick. "A little more about the design model first."

Carolyn sighed deeply. They had nearly been killed while at the pyramid. It was not a pleasant memory for her.

"First of all," indicated Jim, "you'll notice that natural light from the four upper windows will illuminate the interior, while at the same time being filtered to prevent degradation of the artifacts inside."

"Clever," nodded Janette.

"Another interesting fact," continued Jim while pointing at each of the four walls on the model, "is that each of these walls will be in direct alignment with a cardinal direction of the compass, just like the ancient pyramid this one is patterned after."

"The pyramid in Zarahemla had four staircases on both the inside *and* the outside walls," interjected Carolyn.

"For security reasons we plan to put them on the inside *only* on the museum," countered Jim while he tapped his pointer against one of the staircases. "You'll also notice that these have handrails. The ones in Zarahemla didn't."

"Now you've done it," Carolyn whispered to Janette.

"What about the artifacts? Aren't they in those crates?" inquired Janette. "It would be nice to see them."

"Patience," grinned Jim. "See the uppermost point of the room on the model? Notice how all four staircases spiral towards it."

Carolyn sighed deeply with frustration and shook her head. Like Janette, she was anxious to see the golden artifacts. "I take it you plan to display some of the artifacts in the display case on the main floor of the museum when it's finished?" questioned Carolyn while she studied the model more closely.

"Yes ma'am," grinned Jim while he reached for a five-inch binder setting on a small work table nearby. "I've even hired a company of artists to recreate exact replicas of the wall murals found in the main Zarahemla temple."

"Of course. Who would want to forget being held prisoner by the Colombians," muttered Carolyn.

"Regardless of that," countered Jim, "those wall murals are not only spectacular, but of great historical significance."

"I suppose," admitted Carolyn.

Jim opened the binder. "The wall murals will include scenes of ancient farmers sowing seed, picking crops, tending sheep; women spinning and weaving cloth on looms; beautiful young women dancing while people feast at tables full of food; and pictures of soldiers engaged in battle. On the upper portions of the walls will be pictures of the sun, the moon, the stars, and even other planets. Ancient hieroglyphics will also be chiseled into each wall, just like in the original temple."

"What language is this?" questioned Janette as she studied the blueprint.

"Sumerian," muttered Carolyn. "Just like on the artifacts he has stashed in those crates. Am I right?"

"Exactly," confirmed Jim. "Those will be the highlight of the museum, on display in the main lobby downstairs." He emphasized it by pointing again with his pointer.

"No doubt you plan to have adequate security?" asked Carolyn.

"Absolutely," Jim assured her. "Those artifacts are priceless."

"And irreplaceable," Carolyn reminded him.

"Remember how the pyramid in Zarahemla had a platform on its roof?" Jim grilled her.

"Yeah, I do," replied Carolyn. "It was accessed by the exterior staircases – the ones you don't plan to have here." Carolyn reached for Jim's pointer and used it for emphasis.

"Exactly," grinned Jim when he snatched the pointer back from her. "It was where ancient astronomers once studied the solar system. In fact, each staircase contained 91 steps, totaling 364 steps in all, the number of days in a solar year."

"Is that how many steps will be on each of these staircases?" asked Janette.

"Actually, yes," answered Jim. "There will also be a planetarium at the top of the stairs."

"A planetarium?" Carolyn suddenly laughed. "Really?"

"No joke," Jim was serious. "An overhead projection screen will slide into place. Next, a row of reclining seats will pop up from the floor. The guests will then be able to sit down and watch images projected by a Photon Simulator."

"A photon what?" asked Janette with a puzzled look on her face.

"Realistic astronomical images will appear on the screen above them, representative of the night sky over Zarahemla."

"Won't having this displayed on the ceiling kind of ruin it for anyone who hasn't come upstairs yet?" Carolyn grilled him.

"Not at all," smiled Jim. "It will be sealed off. Floor panels will slide shut before the simulation begins, isolating the viewing area from the lobby below.

"I take it customers will have to pay extra for this part of the tour," presumed Carolyn.

"Exactly," chuckled Jim.

"Ingenious," Janette complimented him.

"I was hoping to get a look at the artifacts before telling you about the possible cold case in my family tree," blurted Carolyn.

"I know," responded Jim from beside her. "Sorry if I got sidetracked."

"I'm glad you did!" exclaimed Janette. "Your museum will be spectacular."

"Thanks," responded Jim. "These plans were drawn up by the foremost architects in the world."

"In the world?" questioned Carolyn.

"Spare no expense," grinned Jim.

"I saw that movie," chuckled Janette.

"Let's hope you don't plan to have any dinosaurs in your exhibit," bantered Carolyn.

"Over here," indicated Jim, "are the crates." He grabbed a crowbar from his worktable and began prying up the lid on one of the crates. "Most of these you've already seen," he reminded them.

"Are these the same golden artifacts you had at the lighthouse?" inquired Janette.

"Yes, they are," confirmed Jim. Once the lid of the crate was removed, Jim carefully brushed aside the straw inside before pulling out the heavy object.

"The golden flower map," recognized Carolyn.

"I remember," acknowledged Janette. "Didn't you say the whole thing is a map of how to find the lost city of Zarahemla?"

"Correct," replied Jim. "The whole ensemble goes on to talk about following a higher path in life, living well and being in harmony with the universe."

"Did you ever find the missing piece?" inquired Janette. "Wasn't there a photo of it?"

Jim picked up a sealed pouch and carefully removed the photograph. "We will try to create a reproduction of it for the display."

"Wouldn't the original be better?" asked Janette.

"Perhaps you'd like to make a trip to Peru and ask Commander Nicolas González to turn it over to you," suggested Jim.

"Isn't he the one you filed a class action lawsuit against?" inquired Carolyn.

"That's right," confirmed Jim. "It includes the families of those whose loved ones were kidnapped and put into cryogenic storage containers at a hidden facility in the jungle."

"Oh, my God!" exclaimed Janette as she crossed herself.

"All so their body parts could be sold on the black market to illicit medical suppliers," added Carolyn.

"Obviously not a lawsuit we plan to drop," Jim advised them.

"I should think not," agreed Janette.

"Over in this crate," pointed out Jim, "is the golden book."

"Now you're talkin'," grinned Janette. "That should be the centerpiece in your display."

"Oh, it will be," responded Jim. He pried open the lid, brushed back the straw, and carefully pulled aside a black velvet cloth wrapped around the object.

"It must be worth a fortune," marveled Janette. It was even more impressive than she remembered.

"This is the artifact we found in Queen Ariela's burial chamber," nodded Carolyn.

"What language is that?" Janette suddenly asked. "Didn't you say it was Sumerian?"

"Yes. Last time you were at the lighthouse, we talked about the interpretation of it," recapped Jim.

"Remind me again what you said," requested Janette.

"Of course," agreed Jim. "The first part of the book talks about Queen Ariela, Giddianhi and Lachoneus. It then goes on to tell the story of Adam and Eve in the Garden of Eden and what happened there."

"Incredible," muttered Janette.

"It also talks about free agency and ends with Queen Ariela's testimony of the truthfulness of the gospel of Jesus Christ," concluded Jim.

"I'm glad it's safe," indicated Carolyn while she carefully leafed through the golden pages.

"Of course, visitors to the museum will not be allowed to touch it," teased Jim. "It will be housed in the glass display case."

"With guards on duty?" asked Janette.

"Every sort of security system you can imagine," Jim assured her. "Spare no expense."

Carolyn and Janette both chuckled at that.

"Not to change the subject or anything, but why don't we step into my office," invited Jim. "You can tell me about your cold case."

Carolyn and Janette followed Jim into his office.

"Soda?" offered Jim as he opened a small red refrigerator in the corner of the room and pulled out three cans of diet soda.

"Water for me," insisted Carolyn when she sat down in one of the overstuffed armchairs across from Jim's large mahogany desk.

"For you, anything," responded Jim while he put one of the sodas back and pulled out a bottle of water for Carolyn.

"Do you have one that hasn't been refrigerated?"

Jim nodded. He reached into a cupboard beside the refrigerator and pulled out an unrefrigerated bottle of water. He had forgotten Carolyn did not like cold beverages.

"Soda for me," mentioned Janette. "Cold, please."

"Ice?" questioned Jim.

Carolyn shook her head and smiled.

"Just cold," chuckled Janette when she took the can of soda from Jim and started to reach for the pull-tab on top.

"Allow me," insisted Jim. He grabbed the can back from her and opened it.

"Chilled glass?" asked Carolyn in a sarcastic tone.

"From the can's fine," grinned Janette.

"Look, I'm sorry, but this was a waste of time," apologized Carolyn as she got up to leave.

"Nothing doing," differed Jim while he opened Carolyn's water bottle for her. He carefully placed it on the desk near the chair she had just vacated. "Please, sit down."

After a moment of indecision, Carolyn finally complied and sat back down.

"You mentioned earlier that you and your cousin Leticia have taken DNA tests and believe you might be half-sisters," recounted Jim. "Is that correct?"

Carolyn merely shrugged.

Jim studied her with his piercing blue eyes.

"Her cousin Leticia was having doubts about it, too," interjected Janette. She shot Carolyn an inquisitive glance.

"Why?" Jim grilled her.

Janette nodded for Carolyn to respond.

"I'm just not so sure anymore," admitted Carolyn. "What if we're wrong? The facts just don't support us being half-sisters. For that matter, there may not be sufficient evidence to prove what really happened to my aunt, either."

"What about that front-page article in the *Ashton Times* all those years ago where the skeleton of a woman was found in the back room of a house where she lived with her son?" asked Janette.

"1997," recalled Jim. "That was only one of a series of news articles about it."

"A regular Norman Bates deal there," added Janette.

Jim gave Janette a warning look to be quiet and let Carolyn continue.

"Regardless of whatever else we find out, my cousin and I both want to know what really happened to her mother," continued Carolyn. "My aunt's skeletal remains had to be identified using her dental records. Little else was left."

"As I recall," responded Jim, "one of the newspaper articles said there was no indication of blunt force trauma found on her skeleton, nor were there any fractures or bullet holes, or other signs of violence, but they could not rule out smothering or subtle trauma to the body."

"That still doesn't tell us what really happened to her," frowned Carolyn. "Or who did it."

"Maybe she died of natural causes," opined Jim as he opened his laptop and searched for the pertinent news articles.

"The disturbing part is that her son Luke continued to live in the house like that," added Carolyn.

"With his mother's body locked away in the back room," Janette reminded them.

"Luke did have problems," acknowledged Carolyn, "but from what we know, he would never have done anything to deliberately harm his mother. He loved her. That's why this whole thing makes no sense."

"The newspaper article said they locked your cousin away in the Psych Unit of the Ashton Medical Center after that," mentioned Janette.

"For evaluation," clarified Carolyn.

"Isn't Luke about the same age as you?" asked Janette.

"Yes, he and I were born the same year," responded Carolyn. "I'm a month older. His sister Leticia is two years younger."

"Huh," nodded Janette.

"Could Luke have been placed in the Psych Unit of the Ashton Medical Center by someone to ensure his silence?" Jim grilled her.

"That's an interesting thought," pondered Carolyn.

"Isn't Luke dead now, too?" questioned Janette.

"Yes," confirmed Carolyn. "Luke was released several months before he became ill and died in 2019 on the steps of the Ashton Community Hospital."

"Wasn't he homeless at the time?" asked Janette.

Carolyn merely nodded.

"Perhaps you should begin by telling me everything you know about your dad and his brother," suggested Jim.

"What I can tell you is. My dad is dead, my Aunt Ruth is dead, and so is my Cousin Luke," recounted Carolyn. "Anything any of them knew is gone with them."

"Your dad and his brother were not exactly on speaking terms," recalled Janette.

"That's true," confirmed Carolyn. "Something happened between them when I was a baby that no one would talk about."

"Carolyn didn't even know she had an uncle until she was three years old," blurted Janette as she glanced at Jim.

"Let Carolyn tell it," Jim instructed her.

"It wasn't until my 18th birthday when they spoke again," revealed Carolyn. "And only a handful of times after that."

"Did you ever ask your dad why?" questioned Jim.

"Many times," replied Carolyn.

"I take it he never answered your question," surmised Jim.

"No," answered Carolyn while she sadly shook her head. "But, despite what Leticia and I suspected about being half-sisters, I'm just not so sure anymore. After reading several letters my mom wrote to her parents back then, it shows conclusively that my parents lived in another state and didn't even have a car during that time period."

"Start at the beginning and tell me everything you know," Jim directed her. "If there's a way to find out the truth, we will. Trust me."

2. The Boys

Walter and Willard were identical twins born in the aftermath of the Great Depression and were 12 years old during the summer of 1944. Their hard-working father was rarely home and usually out doing whatever work he could find. Their controlling mother kept them busy every moment doing menial tasks at home until they finally secured their first jobs. It was a paper route for the *Ashton Times*, but all money the twins earned was surrendered to their mother, Bell, in exchange for the privilege of living under their parents' roof. Failure to comply with any of Bell's demands often resulted in beatings from their father upon his return, at her behest to "keep them in line."

The white clapboard house they called home was in an economically depressed neighborhood and in desperate need of another coat of whitewash. Although both boys had hoped having the paper route might grant them a reprieve from the task of whitewashing the house that year, it was highly unlikely.

"Mother, is there any way we could keep some of the money from our paper route so we can buy baseball gloves?" asked Willard.

Bell pursed her lips as she slowly shook her head. "We just can't afford it."

"Please?" Walter chimed in.

Bell sighed deeply as she reconsidered but declined to give them a final answer.

"My chores are done for the day," mentioned Willard as he started for the door.

"It's a bit late to be out," objected Bell. "Your father will be home soon."

That always means be here when we eat or do without, Willard silently fumed.

"Just be back before supper," cautioned Bell. "And I don't want you hanging out with those Scaglioni boys. They're nothing but trouble. Just last week, Mrs. Beasley saw them stealing some of her chickens."

Willard rolled his eyes and nodded as he left. *Perhaps joining a gang might be for the best*, thought Willard. He was tired of being teased in school for his red hair and freckles. Almost daily as of late, he was called into the principal's office for fighting to defend himself.

It'll only be a matter of time before mother finds out anyway. By then, he could run away and stay with the gang at their fort, if they let him join. Or, maybe even leave to join the circus.

"You going with him?" Bell questioned Walter.

"No way," replied Walter as he thought of the dangerous gangs in their neighborhood.

"Good, you can help set the table," Bell instructed Walter as she nodded toward the dining room.

Goodie two shoes, thought Willard as he glanced through the window on his way past the house. *Always sucking up to her. Well, I'm tired of it!*

Two weeks later, there was a mysterious-looking box on the dining room table. The boys had just arrived home from school and were preparing to do their afternoon chores.

"Sit down," Bell instructed them. "I've got a surprise for you."

Waiting until both boys were seated, she slowly pushed the box toward Walter. "You open it."

Bell had a slight smile on her face as she watched. Her shoulder length blonde hair was neatly combed and pinned away from her face, swept into a large curl on top. Ruby red lipstick, blush and eye makeup stood in stark contrast to her alabaster complexion. Face powder heavily caked onto the open areas of her face meant one thing, she had been to town. Bell never went out without dressing up first. She still had on her black silk gloves and matching dress.

How does she afford such nice clothes and makeup if we're so poor? wondered Willard as he watched Walter open the box.

"Oh, wow!" exclaimed Walter. "A baseball glove!"

"And it's left-handed," pointed out Bell with a grin.

Willard frowned as he reached for the box to look inside. *Surely there must be a right-handed glove in there for me.* But alas, the box was now empty.

"Sorry, kid," Bell shrugged her shoulders. "There was only enough for one."

"That's not fair!" pouted Willard.

"You're right-handed," reminded Bell. "You can always just borrow one from somebody. Right-handed gloves are quite common."

"How could you afford this?" asked Walter, reluctant to accept the gift after seeing how upset his brother was.

"From your paper route money, of course," chuckled Bell.
"Mine, too?" demanded Willard.
"That's life," responded Bell unsympathetically.
"Well, it's not fair!" exclaimed Willard.
"Life rarely is," replied Bell. "Get used to it."

Jealous of his brother Walter for being their mother's favorite, Willard became withdrawn. Willard wanted more than anything to participate in a local softball tournament held at the community park near their home, but all boys participating were required to have their own baseball gloves.

It was not long before Willard managed to befriend the Scaglioni boys and be invited to join their gang. After listening to Willard's tale of how his mother had used his paper route money to buy his brother Walter a special left-handed baseball glove, but had not bothered to get him a glove, Tony Scaglioni's lips curled into an evil smile.

"There's only one thing to do," Tony advised him.
"That's right," agreed his brother Joey.
"Take some of Walter's paper route money to make up for it?" guessed Willard.
"No, stupid," laughed Tony. "You're gonna take all of it."
"He'll tell," objected Willard.
"Oh no, he won't. Come on!" yelled Joey as he and Tony headed for a nearby alley. "We'll wait for Walter here."
"What do you plan to do to him?" pressed Willard.
"First, we wait for Ronald," smirked Tony.
"And Ted," added Joey.
What are they planning? fretted Willard.
"Don't worry, we're not gonna hurt your brother," Tony assured Willard, as if able to read his mind.

No sooner had Ronald and Ted joined them than they saw Walter walking on the sidewalk towards them with his shoulder sack of newspapers, carefully placing one onto each porch as he passed.

"Surprise!" yelled Joey and Tony as they leapt from the alley and suddenly grabbed Walter by each of his arms before dragging him toward a nearby culvert.

"You'll never get away with this!" screamed Walter as Ronald stuffed a bandana into his mouth before tying it behind his head.

"We already have," assured Tony as he ripped off Walter's shoulder sack and tossed it to Willard.

"Get his money out and then toss the sack into the bushes," directed Joey.

Willard watched with trepidation as Ted tied Walter's hands behind his back while the entire gang surrounded them in the nearby culvert. Willard quickly removed Walter's money from the shoulder sack, put it into his pocket, and disposed of the shoulder sack as instructed. *I can't let the Scaglioni brothers know I'm having second thoughts about this.*

"Tie him to that ring," Tony commanded the others.

Without cavil, Willard's new cohorts worked together to secure Walter's ropes to a metal tie-down bracket welded onto the side of the culvert, just above water level.

"Now you won't have to explain a thing," hooted Tony as he and the other boys turned to leave.

"And if he rats on us," cautioned Joey, "we might just do something worse."

What will Walter do if the water level rises any higher than it is? worried Willard as it began to rain outside. *I'll just have to sneak back later to untie him. Besides, Walter would never dare tell, not after being threatened by the gang.*

It seemed as if hours had passed. Walter's wrists were raw from struggling to try and free himself. Unexpectedly, a young black boy approached, cautiously glancing in every direction to be sure he wasn't seen.

Walter felt tears of relief flow down his cheeks as the bands securing his hands to the metal tie-down bracket were untied by the stranger. His arms were becoming numb and he felt chilled from the cold water in which he stood.

Turning to bolt without bothering to untie the bandana around Walter's head, the young black boy started to make a run for it.

"Wait!" hollered Walter as soon as he was able to pull the bandana from his mouth. "Please come back."

Hesitating at first, the stranger cautiously returned but kept his distance. "You okay?"

"I'll live," muttered Walter as he tossed the bandana aside. "Hey, what's your name?"

"Montu."

"I owe you," pledged Walter.

Montu shook his head in the negative. "Dem boys're bad. Never tell 'em I helped ya."

"I won't tell," Walter promised Montu. "But if you ever need anything, anything at all, you just say the word."

Without further discussion, Montu made a run for it.

Walter guardedly exited the culvert, glancing in every direction to be sure his brother and the other boys were nowhere in sight before retrieving his shoulder sack of soggy newspapers from the bushes. *What would I have done if Montu hadn't freed me? And just how would Willard have explained my demise to our mother?*

Drenched and cold as he made his way home, Walter knew in his heart that things would never be the same between him and his brother after this. *Willard can never be trusted again,* decided Walter.

"There you are!" Bell scolded Walter through the window when she saw him approach the front door. Without wasting a moment, she hastily went outside to be there when he arrived. "Where have you been?"

Willard's worried face could be seen glancing outside from behind the parted curtains beside the front door.

"I was attacked," replied Walter. *Should I tell mother the truth? And what will Willard do to me if I do?*

"He's lucky to be alive," interjected Willard as he joined them on the porch. "Those same boys attacked me, too. Stole all my money."

"And you're just mentioning this *now*?" fumed Bell. *What did the boys really do with their paper route money? Was this some clever scam they cooked up to try and make me believe it was taken? I'll definitely get to the bottom of this,* she vowed.

"I was afraid of what you'd do if you found out I didn't help him," responded Willard. *That much is actually true.* "I ran away when I saw them tie Walter up, and was gonna go back after they left."

"You liar!" yelled Walter. "You just stood there and watched while the Scaglioni brothers and their friends tied me up!"

"Then how did *this* happen?" questioned Willard as he showed them a place on his wrist that looked like a rope burn.

"You probably did it to yourself to make your story more believable," Walter challenged him. "And just so you could take my paper route money!"

"Well, I don't have it!" screamed Willard.

"One of you is lying, that much is certain," snapped their mother. "Perhaps your father can find out who."

Both boys knew what that meant. They would each be mercilessly beaten with their father's leather belt when he got home from work. Their things would be searched and they would be sent to bed without any supper.

"To your room, *now!*"

Willard will be sorry, once I tell our father what really happened, determined Walter.

"Even if you tell Father what happened, he'll never believe you," whispered Willard as they headed for their room and closed the door behind them. "So, don't even think about it!"

How had Willard known what I was thinking? "Why did you let them do it?" Walter questioned him. "I could have died."

"You obviously didn't."

"No thanks to you!"

"I was gonna come back, but Mother wouldn't let me go back out again."

"You expect me to believe that?" Walter shook his head.

"It's true," assured Willard. "Who cut you loose?"

"No one *you* need to worry about."

"They better hope the Scaglioni brothers didn't see 'em."

"They didn't," responded Walter. "And once Dad finds that money, then he'll *know* who's telling the truth."

"He won't find it here."

"Where is it?"

"It's in a safe place."

Needless to say, both Walter and Willard received the beating of their lives that night, something neither of them would ever forget or fail to hold against each other.

* * *

Jim Otterman shook his head and stood to stretch before turning to study Carolyn's expression more closely. "What about before that? There *must* have been something else that happened between them. It just isn't feasible that Willard would suddenly join a gang and have them tie up his twin brother in a culvert over a baseball glove."

"The baseball glove was a pretty big deal," responded Carolyn.

"There had to be something else," surmised Janette.

"From what I know," continued Carolyn, "there was a constant rivalry between them. Walter always seemed to do better in school, too, and Willard was envious because his brother got a penny for every A from their dad."

"But not from the mother?"

"Oh, heck no! He probably told 'em not to tell her."

"Didn't Willard get any As?" asked Janette.

"I believe he did, but just in his welding class, not in anything else," recalled Carolyn. "I do know that my dad's report cards had mostly As on them, so that could have been another reason for Willard to be jealous."

"Pennies were worth quite a bit in those days," nodded Jim.

"Still, you're right," responded Carolyn. "That's hardly reason for Willard to tie up his brother in a culvert like that. There *must* have been something else."

"What else did your dad tell you about his childhood?" Jim pressed Carolyn.

"He was actually very secretive about it," replied Carolyn. "Most of what I learned about his early life was from my mom, while she was still able to tell me."

Jim scowled but then noticed a warning glance from Janette.

"I did find a group photo of my dad with the Cadet Corps in the bottom of a drawer after my mother died, along with a certificate showing he excelled and became a Cadet Corporal in his unit," elaborated Carolyn. "Oddly, he was only 15 years old at the time."

"What about his brother, Willard?" pressed Jim.

"I learned from Leticia that he was sent to the Cadet Corps at the same time as Walter, but to a different unit; Willard never achieved more than just Cadet."

"Interesting," nodded Jim.

"Isn't that where they sent teenage boys as an alternative to juvenile hall back then?" prodded Janette.

"No," interjected Jim. "The Cadet Corps is a military prep program for kids from ages 9 through 18. Today it includes girls, but back then only boys were allowed to join."

"You're kidding," frowned Janette.

"In 1973, North Georgia was the first of six senior military academies to accept girls into the Cadet Corps," elaborated Jim. "It was not until 1974 that girls were generally free to join the Cadet Corps following a federal court ruling in Texas. Then, in 1980 . . .."

"We get the idea," interrupted Carolyn as she rolled her eyes. *Once Jim got going on any topic, there was no stopping him.*

"What do they actually do in the Cadet Corps?" pressed Janette.

Jim raised one eyebrow at Carolyn before responding to Janette's question. "Well, they promote good citizenship, ethical values, leadership, community services, and try to provide military organizations with the best recruits possible. They also teach life skills and instill a sense of being a part of something greater than themselves. Some courses include culinary arts, medical training, law enforcement, and of course basic military skills."

"My dad did join the Air Force after that," acknowledged Carolyn. "It just seems odd that he never even told me about being in the Cadet Corps."

Janette pulled up their website on her phone. "It says here that all applicants must be United States citizens or legal residents. Must meet military standards. Must have good moral character, drug free and gang free, physically capable of participating in military oriented training, a full-time student with at least 'C' (2.0) Grade Point Average. Additionally, they must be committed to attending drills and other activities whenever necessary."

"Enough already!" snapped Carolyn as she got up and walked over to the doorway of Jim's office.

"Sorry," apologized Jim and Janette in unison.

Just then Carolyn's smartwatch began to chime. "It's Leticia. I'll be right back."

"Something's sure bothering her," remarked Jim as they watched Carolyn leave.

"Did you know about her mother passing?" asked Janette.

"No," responded Jim. *Strange that Carolyn hasn't mentioned it.*

"I'm sure she'll tell you when she's ready."

Jim merely nodded. *No wonder Carolyn is so preoccupied.*

"Anyway," continued Carolyn when she returned, "I think we may have finally located my uncle."

"They've been trying to find him for several years now," Janette chimed in.

"Leticia said he's in some nursing home somewhere up in Rosewood, but they won't even let her talk to him."

"That seems odd," commented Jim.

"Apparently his fourth wife has had him moved to more than a dozen different facilities just this year alone," elaborated Carolyn. "We need to get there before she decides to move him again."

"Good point," nodded Janette.

"He certainly might have some answers," remarked Jim.

"If he even remembers anything," opined Janette. "What if he's got dementia or something?"

"We need to try and find a way to see him," determined Carolyn. "Even people with dementia can recall more than you might imagine."

"You're going there now?" asked Jim.

"Yes, now," confirmed Carolyn as she headed for the front door of the warehouse.

"Hold it," called Jim. "Let's fly there in my Learjet."

"Nice," grinned Janette.

"Do we need to pick Leticia up on the way?" asked Jim.

"She'll meet us there," responded Carolyn while they exited the warehouse together and headed for the white Dodge Dart parked out front.

"We can take my Jeep to the airport," offered Jim. "It's right out back."

"MIRA's been through enough," insisted Carolyn as she opened the driver's side door to the white Dodge Dart.

"Isn't that the computer thing on his jet?" questioned Janette as she approached the passenger side door.

"MIRA is the Modulated Interfacing Resonance Assistant and onboard computer system on Jim's Learjet," explained Carolyn.

"Personally programmed by me," Jim proudly added as he motioned for them to follow him.

"Very impressive," complimented Janette.

"MIRA's all fueled up and ready to go," Jim persuaded Carolyn. "Come on. You can leave the Dodge Dart here. Save your gas. Let's take the Jeep to the airport."

"You've got a point," conceded Carolyn. "Okay, let's take the Jeep to the airport. Why not?"

Once onboard Jim's Learjet, Carolyn and Janette made themselves comfortable in the first seats available behind the cockpit area.

"Buckle up," instructed Jim as he glanced at them in the rearview mirror. "MIRA, please proceed with takeoff sequence."

"Roger that," responded MIRA while she powered up the aircraft before suddenly accelerating down the runway.

As soon as they were airborne, Jim commanded, "MIRA, continue to flight level four seven zero."

"Course plotted for Rosewood," confirmed MIRA. "Winds aloft checked, weather en route and destination checked. Flight plan filed and release time within your timeframe, Jim. Squawk code entered. Fuel load is adequate with a generous reserve. Estimated arrival time in 45 minutes."

"Thank you, MIRA," added Jim.

"You are welcome, Jim," responded MIRA.

"Four seven zero is pilot talk for 47,000 feet," Jim informed his passengers. "The extra zeros are not spoken in altitudes of 18,000 or above, which are called flight levels."

"You mention that every time I fly with you," Carolyn reminded him as she rolled her eyes and shook her head.

Jim merely shrugged his shoulders.

"Leveling off for cruising altitude now," verified MIRA.

"Nice view," admired Janette as she glanced outside. Glimmers of sunlight danced across the ocean waves below while they delicately licked the shoreline. "Won't we be flying over Oceanview Academy pretty soon, where you guys went to high school?"

"Lots of memories there," reminisced Carolyn.

"Not this time," lamented Jim as a fleeting expression of longing crossed his face but then disappeared as quickly as it had appeared. "We're headed the other direction."

"Cruising altitude attained," added MIRA.

"You may now unbuckle your seatbelts and feel free to move about the aircraft," Jim announced when he unbuckled his seatbelt, came back to where they were, and headed for the couch seat. Jim then grabbed and pulled out a retractable table from the wall and pressed a button on the edge of it. The surface of the table suddenly became a computer display.

"Uh, wow!" Janette was impressed.

"Now, let's see what else we can find out before we arrive at our destination," offered Jim. "We need to order a copy of the Ashton County Coroner's Report so we can find out who investigated the death of Carolyn's aunt."

"I did write to them two years ago but never heard back," related Carolyn. "Guess I need to follow up on that."

"No need, but it could take a few days, even with my connections," Jim advised her. "Most people have to wait six to eight weeks for one."

"Not surprising," responded Carolyn with a deep sigh of frustration.

"Meanwhile, tell us what you know about your aunt. Like how she first met your uncle, that kind of thing," Jim encouraged her.

"Well . . .," began Carolyn.

"Oh wait, here's something," interrupted Jim. "It appears that not only were your dad and his brother sent to military academy when they were only 15 years old, but both were basically on their own after that."

"What do you mean?" demanded Carolyn.

"The Census records for that year show Walter lived in a boarding house in Ashton and worked as a forklift driver and stock clerk at the Ashton Bell Telephone Company, until finally joining the military when he was 19 years old," revealed Jim.

"I'd always assumed they went back to live with their parents after their stint as cadets," mumbled Carolyn.

"Guess that old mother of theirs didn't get any more paper route money from 'em after that," chuckled Janette.

"Not likely," agreed Jim. "And, it shows that Willard found a welding job at the Ashton Valley Welding & Supply Company after he came home from military academy."

"That's incredible," marveled Carolyn. "I had no idea."

"Both brothers attended the Ashton City College Technical Program and obtained their high school diplomas through night school," elaborated Jim as he scrolled through the items pulled up on his tabletop computer screen. "That's pretty much it on their childhood."

"Wouldn't they have already received their high school diplomas from the cadet academy they went to?" questioned Janette.

"No, they didn't," replied Carolyn. "The training there was strictly to prepare them for going into the military, those who chose to."

"Huh," responded Janette.

"I also remember my dad telling me his parents never took them to see the doctor, as they thought it was a waste of money," recalled Carolyn. "Except the time my dad had appendicitis, and they took him to some old country doctor who literally had to rip him open to save his life. He had a jagged scar from it."

"Not even to the dentist?" pressed Janette.

"Oh heck, no," confirmed Carolyn. "The first time my dad ever saw a dentist in his life was after he joined the military, and ended up having half his teeth pulled. I can only imagine his brother must have gone through something similar."

"The parents obviously were not big on unnecessary expenses," concluded Jim.

"Like their children," sniggered Janette.

"That's true," agreed Carolyn. "In fact, when my parents were first married, they tried to get a loan to buy their first automobile but were turned down because his parents wouldn't cosign the loan."

"Why would they have to, if he already had a good job with the military?" asked Janette. "That doesn't make sense."

"During that time period, it was mandatory for any man under 25 years of age to have his parents cosign an auto loan, no matter how good a job he might have," interjected Jim.

"That's ridiculous," frowned Janette.

"Almost as ridiculous as them not allowing my mom's parents to cosign the loan, even though they offered," recalled Carolyn.

"Unbelievable," Janette shook her head with disapproval.

"Okay, tell us about your aunt," insisted Jim.

3. The Girls

Carolyn glanced through the Learjet window for several moments as she collected her thoughts.

"What about your aunt's childhood?" queried Jim. "Before she met your uncle? What was that like?"

"Well, Ruth and my mom were best friends since grade school," began Carolyn. "They double-dated most of the time during their teens, and even landed their first jobs together after graduating from high school. Both were telephone operators together at the Ashton Bell Telephone Company, and were roommates at a local boarding house within walking distance of where they worked."

"What about before that?" Jim quizzed Carolyn.

"Ruth's parents owned a grape vineyard and an activity hall, often renting it out for weddings and other celebrations," informed Carolyn. "They also loved the outdoors, fished, rode horses, and especially enjoyed camping."

"Anything significant happen during her childhood?"

"There was one thing for sure," responded Carolyn. "It was during a pack trip to Graveyard Meadows one fateful weekend when lightning struck. She was with her father, older sister, and brother-in-law. When an unexpected storm came up, they all gathered under a big tree for shelter."

"In a lightning storm?" Jim's eyebrows were raised.

"Yes, and all four of them were electrocuted," added Carolyn.

"That's horrible," muttered Janette.

"Ruth was only 16 years old at the time," described Carolyn. "When her father regained consciousness, he checked the others and assumed they were all dead. It must have been terrifying for him to just leave their bodies there like that when he left to get help."

"How far did he have to go?" asked Janette as she thought of the time that she and Carolyn had been on a pack trip of their own.

"It was a 12-mile hike to the Ranger Station," recounted Carolyn. "Ruth's father was cold, wet and hungry, but immediately returned with them by mule to retrieve the bodies of his loved ones."

"That had to be hard," Janette shook her head.

"Much to their surprise, Ruth was not where he'd left her," continued Carolyn. "At first, he assumed that some wild animal had dragged her body away, but the Ranger with him was an excellent tracker. So, in no time, they managed to locate her."

Janette shook her head as she thought of what it must have been like for them.

"And of course, Ruth was still dazed when they found her," added Carolyn. "The only other thing I really know about it was that she had been aimlessly wandering through the forest. She apparently had little memory after that of the 12-mile mule ride home, or of the subsequent funeral for her sister and brother-in-law."

"She undoubtedly suffered from PTSD after such a traumatic experience," opined Jim.

"Indeed," nodded Janette.

"Ruth was never the same," confirmed Carolyn. "My mom told me once that Ruth's entire personality was different after that."

"What about your mom's childhood?" Jim finally asked. *Is it too soon to ask Carolyn to talk about it?*

After a deep sigh, Carolyn went on. "My mom's father was a carpenter who did custom remodeling jobs for those who could afford it, and her mother owned a dress shop. Her older brother was on the football team in high school, and quite popular with all the girls. Her younger brother was more the studious type, leaning toward life as an architect. And of course, my mom was a tomboy during most of her childhood. She loved to climb fences and trees, played with toy cars in the dirt with her older brother, and truly enjoyed the outdoors."

"Anything traumatic happen during her childhood?" asked Jim.

"Not really," replied Carolyn. "Unless you consider a school bus crash to be a traumatic event?"

"Was it very serious?" probed Jim.

"Some guy ran a red light. The school bus driver swerved so hard to miss him that the bus flipped onto its side," recalled Carolyn.

"Drunk driver?" asked Jim.

"No, just some guy in a hurry on his way to work," replied Carolyn. "Probably late. I have a newspaper clipping about it at home. Only seven of the kids were hurt. I think all my mom had was a skinned knee, but one of the kids hit his head and had to go to the hospital. Anyway, most of their injuries were minor."

"Sounds like your mom had a fairly traditional family life, then," assumed Jim.

"Pretty much," nodded Carolyn.

"Exactly when was it that your mom and Ruth first met your dad and his brother?" Jim quizzed her.

"That would have been when they were working as telephone operators," answered Carolyn. "I believe it was in 1952."

* * *

Both Ruth and Charlotte were 22 years old, fair complexioned, and had dark brown, shoulder-length hair. It was lunch time at the Ashton Bell Telephone Company and their relief had just taken over.

"Let's go eat our sandwiches in the park today," suggested Charlotte. "I'm tired of that smokey old break room."

"Have you seen the new forklift driver?" asked Ruth with a sly smile. "He certainly seems to have noticed you."

"The one with the red hair?" grinned Charlotte. *Yes, I noticed him,* she thought.

"No, the old guy with the droopy shoulders and big gut," teased Ruth as she playfully slapped Charlotte on the arm. "Of course, the one with the red hair!"

Charlotte merely giggled as they sat down on the park bench. "He is rather good looking."

"Well, here he comes," whispered Ruth.

"Hello ladies," greeted Walter. "It's a lovely day."

"Yes, it is," agreed Charlotte with an irrepressible smile.

"I was wondering," began Walter, who ordinarily was rather shy and rarely spoke to people he didn't know.

"Wondering what?" pressed Charlotte.

"Well, I, I have a twin brother," stammered Walter, "and I was just wondering if you two ladies would be interested . . . ."

"Yes!" Ruth cut him off. "We would."

"Let him finish," blushed Charlotte.

"Perhaps we could all go to the movies on Saturday," suggested Walter. "*Treasure Island* is showing at the Ashton Cinema."

Charlotte and Ruth giggled with excitement.

"I'd love to," beamed Charlotte as her hazel eyes captured Walter's admiring gaze.

"Me, too," interjected Ruth, who could not help but notice the immediate attraction between Walter and Charlotte. *Hopefully, his brother will find me as attractive.*

Walter could not hide his flushed cheeks but managed to maintain his composure as he smiled and nodded. "It's a date then?"

"Absolutely," flirted Charlotte.

"We can meet you there," suggested Ruth.

"We'll pick you up," Walter informed her.

"Where?" asked Ruth with a coy grin.

Ignoring Ruth's question, Walter turned to Charlotte. "May we pick you up at your place?"

"How about at my parents' house?" suggested Charlotte. "The boarding house has very strict rules about male visitors."

"I'll still need directions," smiled Walter as he maintained eye contact with Charlotte.

Charlotte blushed before continuing. "Just go down Sunnyslope to Willowbrook until you get to the third house on the left; it's the olive green one."

"There's a huge willow tree out front, too," interjected Ruth. "You can't miss it."

"I think we can find it," replied Walter without looking at her; his attention was focused on Charlotte.

"Besides, I'm sure my parents will want to meet you," added Charlotte.

"You been on your own long?" questioned Walter.

"Just a couple of years," volunteered Charlotte.

"Her job at the bakery down in Los Angeles didn't seem to pay the rent," mentioned Ruth. "That's why we decided to be roommates here in Ashton. Plus, she missed being near her folks, and me."

"True," shrugged Charlotte. "Also, it's within walking distance of where we work now. Unless I find something better."

"Think you will?" probed Walter as he studied her more closely.

"You never know," Charlotte blushed again and looked away to avoid the intense gaze of Walter's piercing blue eyes.

"The matinee begins at 2:00," described Walter. "Can you be ready by 1:30?"

"We'll *both* be there waiting," volunteered Ruth.

Charlotte merely nodded.

"It's a date," flirted Walter as he waited for Charlotte to look back up at him before he winked and turned to leave.

Charlotte and Ruth held off until Walter was hopefully out of hearing distance before clasping hands and letting out shrieks of delight.

"Oh, no!" Ruth suddenly became serious.

"What?" asked Charlotte.

"My poodle skirt is still at the cleaners, and I won't be able to get it back until payday," fretted Ruth.

"I can help with that," promised Charlotte.

"Are you sure?"

"Not a problem," Charlotte assured Ruth as they opened their lunch sacks and pulled out their sandwiches.

Willard loved his welding job at the Ashton Valley Welding & Supply Company, but had little time for much of anything else while attending night school three nights each week to obtain his high school diploma through the Ashton City College Technical Program.

Meanwhile, his brother Walter had somehow convinced him to go in together on a 1939 Ford 4-door sedan they were purchasing from their parents. *How did I ever let Walter talk me into such a commitment? Our parents never part with anything worth keeping anymore, especially an old car like that one! Worse still, we don't even live in the same boarding house, and now I have to check with my brother each time I want to use our car. And heaven only knows what our mother might do if either of us fails to make the payments on time! No doubt, she would repossess the car outright and call it good.*

In a hurry to get to the welding shop where his brother worked before lunch hour was over, Walter decided to go ahead and drive there. *Will there still be enough gas left for our date on Saturday? I hope so. Meanwhile, I need to make sure Willard will agree to come, especially since I already made the commitment for him.*

Wheel of Fortune by Kay Starr was loudly playing on the car radio as Walter pulled up in front of the Ashton Valley Welding & Supply Company. The blue and white striped awning hanging over its entrance was mounted on wrought-iron support brackets with leafy-branch designs cleverly welded onto its sides.

Not wanting to risk the engine dying again, Walter left the car running while he jumped out and dashed inside.

Immediately spotting his brother, who was working through lunch again, Walter made a beeline for his work station.

"Hey, you need to be wearing goggles," shouted the receptionist as she grabbed an extra pair from a wall hook near the entrance and hurried after him. "And you can't just go in there like that without checking in."

"Sorry," apologized Walter while he grabbed the goggles from her and put them on before continuing to where Willard was busy welding.

"You can sign in when you leave," called the receptionist as she returned to her desk by the entrance.

"Willard!" shouted Walter. "Stop a minute!"

Finally noticing his brother standing there, Willard turned off his equipment and took off his goggles. "What is it?" *Has something happened to one of our parents?*

"We have a double date for Saturday afternoon," Walter informed him. "I already promised the other girl you'd come."

Willard shook his head. "No, I need to finish a paper for one of my classes."

"Listen to me," persisted Walter as he grabbed his arm. "You don't understand. She's an absolute doll; if you don't come, the whole date might get called off."

Willard smiled a crooked grin. "The one you're going out with must be a doll, too."

Walter merely nodded. "Please?"

"I'll tell you what," bargained Willard. "You pay all expenses on the car this month, and you got a deal."

"*All* expenses?"

"Yep, including the payment to our mother," stipulated Willard.

Walter hesitated but only for a moment. "Okay, you got a deal."

It was Saturday, June 14, 1952, and the thermometer read 105° in the shade. Humidity was high, too.

"Maybe we should wait until this evening and just take 'em to the drive-in," suggested Willard as he and Walter climbed into the shiny black Ford and rolled down its front windows. "My shirt is already soaked with sweat."

"Nothin' doing," countered Walter. "Especially since I already made our monthly payment to Mother."

"You made the July payment already? Seriously?"

"I did," promised Walter.

"What about gas? Did you remember to fill it up?" Willard grilled him.

"Sorry, but I had to save *some* money for popcorn and sodas," pointed out Walter as he put the car in neutral, turned the ignition, pulled out the choke, set the throttle, depressed the clutch, and pushed in the start button. As the engine sputtered to life, he quickly pushed the choke back in to avoid flooding it and gently pulled the throttle forward for more power while warming up.

"What about oil?" Willard grilled him.

"It's fine," shrugged Walter. "We're only driving a few blocks."

"You'd better hope so."

"Waxed her, too," pointed out Walter while he turned on the car radio. *You Belong to Me* by Jo Stafford was playing.

"Looks nice," responded Willard as he watched Walter put the car into drive and pump the gas pedal.

The brothers became silent when they headed down Sunnyslope and turned onto Willowbrook. *Will we make it?*

Patchy shade from mature oak trees beside the curb strip made their bright red hair almost seem to glow in the intermittent sunlight, especially after being slathered with Vaseline Hair Tonic.

Even without consulting one another, Walter and Willard had managed to wear the same Old Spice After Shave Lotion, and each had on a medium brown baggy suit, highly polished brown penny loafers, white shirt and narrow green tie.

"Do you think the insurance is still good?" Willard suddenly asked.

"Like I said," chuckled Walter, "We're only driving a few blocks. Relax."

"What if Mother hasn't had a chance yet to put our names on her policy?" worried Willard.

"She probably wouldn't even bother to have a policy, not after selling it to *us*."

"But it's mandatory by law to have it now," persisted Willard.

"Ever since World War II ended," acknowledged Walter.

"We need to ask her about it."

"Especially considering what we're paying her for it," agreed Walter as they slowly pulled up in front of the third house on the left-hand side of Willowbrook.

"Nice pad," approved Willard before letting out a low whistle.

Walter nodded. *Much nicer than I'd expected, too.*

"No wonder she wanted to meet us here," added Willard. He nodded toward a sign on the front lawn that read *Custom Carpentry by Kalvin*. "Impressive."

"We'd better leave the car running," opined Walter.

"What if they're not even ready yet?" differed Willard. "Do you really want to run out of gas *here*?"

"Good point," nodded Walter while he pushed in the clutch, put it into first and then turned it off.

Before the brothers even had a chance to knock, the front door of the two-story olive-green house swung open.

"Please come in," beamed Ruth. She stood aside and motioned for them to come inside.

"Nice place," complimented Walter.

"Thanks, my folks seem to like it," blushed Charlotte when she joined them.

"This is my brother Willard," introduced Walter.

"Pleased to meet you," beamed Ruth while she enthusiastically shook Willard's hand. "I'm Ruth."

"Hello," greeted Charlotte as she shook Willard's hand after Ruth. "And I'm Charlotte."

"We can always switch dates," offered Willard while he flirted with Charlotte. He was immediately attracted to her and made no effort whatsoever to hide it.

"Sorry, but this one's taken," Walter informed him as he extricated his brother's hand from Charlotte's and offered her his arm.

"I'm sure we'll all have a wonderful time," commented Ruth. She quickly took Willard's arm to distract him from gaping at Charlotte.

"My parents are in there," pointed out Charlotte as she smiled at Walter and blushed. "I'm sure they want to meet you."

Charlotte's bright red poodle skirt had a black poodle on it, and her top and cummerbund were black. Her matching red scarf was even brighter than Walter's hair.

Her friend Ruth's poodle skirt was sky blue and also had a black poodle on it. The cummerbund and top were white, and its scarf was sky blue with white silk flowers embroidered onto it.

Both women had on silk stockings and slip-on shoes with handbags that matched their skirts.

"Lead the way," flirted Walter as he accompanied Charlotte to her parents' family room where they were busy watching a comedy show on their new Viking Console television set.

"CBS is the only station that broadcasts this time of day," explained Charlotte when they entered the room. "It's a brand-new set and my father is anxious to make sure everything works."

"It seems to be," observed Willard. *How can anyone afford a television set? Her parents must have lots of money. Perhaps I can still convince my brother to trade dates.*

"What are they watching?" asked Walter.

"*The Garry Moore Show*," revealed Ruth. "It's a comedy show starring Garry Moore, Carol Burnett, and Durward Kirby."

Neither Walter nor Willard had ever heard of any of them but nodded to be polite. This was also the closest either of them had ever been to an actual television set, other than seeing one through the front window display at Sears Department Store in downtown Ashton.

Charlotte's father motioned for all of them to sit down in the overstuffed leather chairs, or on the couch next to them.

"We really can't stay," Walter apologized to her father, "but it is nice to meet you, sir." Walter approached and extended his hand.

"Father, this is Walter," introduced Charlotte.

Kalvin merely nodded but clearly did not like having his television program interrupted.

"The movie we're going to see starts at 2:00," announced Ruth rather loudly. "Perhaps we can come back to visit afterwards?"

"It was very nice to meet both of you," beamed Charlotte's mother when she got up and shook Walter's hand and then Willard's. "Kalvin just got his new television set today."

"Understandable," nodded Walter as she accompanied them back to the foyer to see them off.

"And please, do come back afterwards," invited Charlotte's mother. "I'll have some pie and ice cream waiting for you."

"Now you're talking," grinned Willard.

"Until then," nodded Walter as they left.

* * *

After landing at the Rosewood Airport, Jim and his passengers disembarked.

"I suppose you have a rental car arranged?" Carolyn sighed deeply as she thought of her white Dodge Dart. *If only we had it now.*

"Already taken care of by MIRA," grinned Jim while he motioned for Carolyn and Janette to follow him toward the small terminal nearby.

"Do we even know what their visiting hours are at the facility?" Janette suddenly asked. "Maybe we should go there first?"

"Actually, we should probably try to call," mentioned Carolyn. "In fact, we need to call Leticia, too."

"I'm not getting any service here at all," realized Janette.

"What's Leticia's number?" asked Jim. "Just read it to me."

Janette gave Carolyn a worried look.

"I don't have any service here, either," revealed Carolyn. She then read Leticia's number out loud for Jim to put into his contacts.

"Are you sure that's a good idea?" Janette whispered to Carolyn.

"Jim's smartwatch is a satellite one, so he's probably the only one of us who can make the call."

"That's right," grinned Jim, who had somehow managed to sneak up close behind them and was privy to their conversation. "MIRA, call Leticia."

"That MIRA thing on your jet runs your smartwatch, too?" Janette was genuinely surprised.

"Of course," grinned Jim as he put it on speaker so all of them could hear it ring.

"Hello?"

"Leticia?"

"Yes, who is this?"

"Leticia," Carolyn spoke up. "I'm here with Jim and Janette, and we are at the Rosewood Airport. Where should we meet?"

"I'm running late, but should be there by 2:00," calculated Leticia. "Can I just meet you outside the facility?"

"Have you tried again to call them?" Carolyn quickly asked. "I haven't been able to get anyone to answer the phone there and now I don't have any service."

"Guess they'll just have to be surprised," interjected Jim.

"What if he's not there anymore?" inquired Janette. "What if they've moved him somewhere else?"

"Then we keep looking," determined Carolyn.

"Okay, I'll call you guys back at this number when I get to Rosewood, probably from the facility," responded Leticia.

"Sounds good. Drive safely," bid Jim before pressing a button on his smartwatch to disconnect the call. "Right now, ladies, we all need to eat."

"We do," agreed Carolyn as they walked across the tarmac.

"Tell me more about the boys' mother," Jim instructed her.

"That's a tough one," sighed Carolyn.

"How so?" asked Jim when they reached the terminal.

"I wouldn't even know where to begin," Carolyn shook her head with dismay.

"Here are your keys, Mr. Otterman," offered a handsome young attendant who approached and handed them to Jim. "It's the black Lamborghini on the side of the building."

Janette and Carolyn exchanged a surprised look.

"Thank you, sir," smiled Jim when he took the keys and headed in the direction indicated.

"Now we're styling," approved Janette.

"I wouldn't get too used to it," interjected Carolyn as the three of them approached and climbed into the sleek, four-seated vehicle.

"What do these run for?" Janette grilled him.

"If a person were to buy one," stipulated Jim, "Lamborghini's entry-level model has prices topping out at $331,000 for the STO coupe. The absolute cheapest of the group is a new base Huracán EVO RWD Coupe with an MSRP of $209,409."

"You asked," chuckled Carolyn as she watched Janette's shocked expression.

"Not much on leg room, are they?" frowned Janette while she climbed into the back seat and buckled up her seatbelt.

"I'm surprised they even make four-seaters," admitted Carolyn. "Most of the ones I've seen are smaller than this and are strictly used for racing. At least there's plenty of leg room up here."

"Some of the faster models require helmets," Jim informed them with a crooked smile.

"You're kidding, right?" Janette shook her head.

"Jim doesn't kid," Carolyn assured her.

"The 2024 Lamborghini Revuelto is the fastest from 0 to 60 with a time of 2.4 seconds, but those are strictly two-seaters," elaborated Jim.

"How fast can this thing go?" inquired Janette while she ran her hand across the expensive leather seat beside her.

"She can do 217 mph," described Jim, "though I'm certain Carolyn wouldn't want me to do that."

"You would be correct," responded Carolyn with a worried look on her face.

"Is it self-driving?" pressed Janette.

"While there's no fully self-driving Lamborghini, the 2022 Urus model was probably the first to incorporate advanced driver-assistance technology," rambled Jim. He had considered buying one once, but really didn't have a need since he already had his Learjet.

"It must have SIRI, then?"

"Absolutely."

"Good, cause even if I had service here, the battery on my cellphone is getting low," explained Janette.

"Hey SIRI, any good restaurants nearby?" asked Jim.

"There are two Mexican restaurants, one Italian restaurant, and one Thai food restaurant," responded SIRI.

"Thai sounds good to me," indicated Carolyn.

"Me, too," agreed Janette.

"Hey SIRI, show us the quickest route to the Thai food place," directed Jim.

A map with the route suddenly appeared on SIRI's screen.

"Well, she ain't MIRA, but she'll do," grinned Jim as he revved up the engine, put it into gear and drove away from the terminal.

Janette crossed herself and reached for the nearest handgrip.

"Relax," flirted Jim when he winked at her in the rearview mirror. "We'll be there in no time. Trust me."

The Velvet Ginger Thai Food Restaurant was set back from the street in a quiet suburb of downtown Rosewood, surrounded by dense foliage. *Will the Lamborghini be safe here?* wondered Jim as he glanced around the isolated parking lot. Only two other cars were present. *Hopefully, they'll be open soon, if they aren't already.*

"Lunch is on me," announced Jim while he climbed from the sleek black Lamborghini and came around to open the passenger doors for Carolyn and Janette.

A brick walkway leading to its porch was bordered by basil, oregano, chives, rosemary and other culinary herbs. Intermingled between them were several lavender, jasmine and other fragrant plants. Small solar-powered torch lights were inserted into the ground every few feet along the pathway. The familiar song of a black-capped chickadee rang out overhead.

"This place looks expensive," worried Janette when they reached its front porch. Even its steep, multi-layered gable roof was richly ornamented with hand-painted golden spires.

On each of its elaborately decorated teakwood entrance doors were hand-carved scenes of elephants surrounded by dense jungle. Intricate detail included small monkeys climbing in its trees. Beside each of the tall oval-shaped doors stood a life-sized wooden statue of a Thai woman with her hands pressed together in front. Painstakingly painted in lifelike colors, each wore a golden sarong draped over one shoulder and carefully wrapped around her waist. Red velvet curtains with black silk fringe hung halfway down the tall narrow windows behind them. Golden-colored candleholders in the shape of lotus blossoms sat on their sills but clearly had not yet been lit for the day.

"Wow!" exclaimed Carolyn.

"They don't look like they're open yet," observed Janette as she noticed a small sign by its front door. "Opens at 11:00."

"It's only 10:45," muttered Carolyn.

"MIRA would have known that," mumbled Jim while he motioned with his head for them to get back into the car.

"What about Mexican food?" suggested Janette.

"No, wait!" called Carolyn, who remained on the porch of the restaurant. "By the time you get to another place, this one will be open. We may as well wait."

"She's right," agreed Janette before turning back to join Carolyn at its entrance. "Look, someone's lighting the candles now!"

Jim merely shrugged his shoulders as he returned to wait with them. "Carolyn, please tell us about the boys' mother."

"I'm not too sure about her childhood," began Carolyn, "or what made her the way she was, but she definitely had issues."

"What kind of issues?"

"Issues of every kind, with just about everyone she knew," clarified Carolyn. "For example, when I was a little girl, my grandparents would play cards with my great uncle and his wife Mary every week. One Saturday night after they left, Bell discovered that a penny was missing from a little gambling jar she kept on the card table and claimed that Mary had stolen it."

"Had she?" probed Jim.

"I doubt it," replied Carolyn. "But, it gave Bell an excuse to hold something against her."

"For a mere penny?" Janette shook her head.

"Pennies may have been worth more back then," added Carolyn, "but that was ridiculous, and she held it against Mary for the rest of her life."

"Were you living with your grandparents?" questioned Jim.

"No, but my parents would often leave me there for the weekend, or during the day when they worked," explained Carolyn.

"Both of them worked?" probed Jim.

"Yes."

"Sounds like you were there quite a bit, then," surmised Jim.

"Every kid dreams of getting to go play at their grandparents' house," interjected Janette. "My parents kept me so busy working at home that I almost never got to."

"It was just the opposite for me," continued Carolyn. "Playtime was at home with my parents. Grandma's house usually meant hard work, most of the time I was there."

"What kind of work?" Jim frowned with disapproval.

"Well, she had different days for different things," described Carolyn. "Once my grandpa had gone to work for the day, she would keep me busy vacuuming, mopping floors and cleaning the bathroom and kitchen on Mondays. Then, on Tuesdays, we would clean out the fireplace, and polish all the fireplace utensils; after that, we would polish her silverware, jewelry, and any other silver she had in the house, including an old cowbell that once had belonged to my great, great grandmother."

"Say, what?" Janette could not believe what she was hearing.

"On Wednesdays we would do all the laundry, change out the sheets, and take the curtains out back where we'd hang them on the clothesline and beat them with a broom to get the dust out."

"Oh, my God!" exclaimed Janette. "Are you kidding?"

"She obviously didn't have a dryer," presumed Jim.

"They probably didn't even make 'em yet," guessed Janette.

"*Au contraire*," differed Jim. "The first automatic washing machine built for domestic use was in 1937, closely followed by the first electrically powered dryer in 1938; both appliances turned out to be a common staple across households in most developed countries."

"Not hers," chuckled Carolyn. "In fact, her washing machine wasn't even electric. It was one of those Amish-style hand wringer jobs. In today's world, it would be ideal for homesteading and off-grid living."

Jim and Janette both laughed.

"When we were done," described Carolyn, "we'd hang all the clothes up on her clothesline with wooden clothespins. Sometimes crows would fly over while scoping out her vegetable garden, but she'd chase 'em away with her broom."

All of them chuckled at that.

"What about on Thursdays?" queried Jim.

"Ah yes, yardwork day," sighed Carolyn. "Learned to use the power mower when I was only seven years old."

"She actually had a *power* mower?" Janette was surprised.

"I think my parents got it for them for Christmas one year," recalled Carolyn. "My dad probably got tired of going over there and using the push mower each week, as that was his task before it finally fell upon me."

"Understandable," recognized Jim.

"And of course, she had a quarter of an acre in her backyard," revealed Carolyn. "Beyond the grass area and its many flowerbeds, which she had me weed each week, was the vegetable garden, the fruit tree area, and the blackberries growing along the ditch. In fact, I can still remember her paddling me with her wooden yardstick once for *goofing off* when I stopped to eat some. Broke it clean in half."

"That's not right," objected Janette.

"And of course, her next-door neighbors had a quarter acre grape vineyard, and one summer they went on vacation to Armenia for three weeks," reminisced Carolyn.

"Let me guess," interrupted Janette. "She had you taking care of all that, too?"

"Yes," responded Carolyn as she paused to visualize the huge yards and all the work that she had done in them.

"Greetings," came a voice behind them. "Please, come inside."

A middle-aged Asian woman dressed in traditional Thai attire motioned for them to follow her. "This way," she directed with a heavy accent. "Would you like a booth?"

"Yes, please," responded Jim.

Elaborate wood carvings hung on several of the walls, each depicting various scenes from Thai life; all were brightly painted in realistic colors. Prominently displayed near the front entrance was a golden-framed portrait of the Thai Royal Family. Custom-made Thai lanterns hung over every table, all of them illuminated by electrical candlelight. Beyond the table area were several cozy booths in a small alcove. A round skylight above the alcove revealed the uppermost branches of a mature cedar tree outside. Also visible was an azure blue sky dotted with fluffy white clouds. The red leather seats in each booth exactly matched the red velvet curtains that hung by the front entrance, and each highly shellacked black tabletop was inlaid with real seashells. In the middle of the booth area, directly below the skylight, was a medium-sized fountain in the shape of a lotus blossom. The continuous flow of water over its petals gently fell into a water basin below it; that was illuminated by waterproof electrical lights mounted under its rim. Inside the basin were two large koi fish swimming amongst blossoming lily pads.

"This place is amazing!" exclaimed Janette.

"Good thing it's *on me*," grinned Jim.

"Indeed," smiled Carolyn. The delicious aroma of food being prepared could already be detected.

"Mind if I order for everyone?" asked Jim as they sat down in the booth.

Carolyn furrowed her brows. She had hoped to order Pad Thai with tofu because she was allergic to shellfish.

"No worries," assured Jim. "No shell fish, and Pad Thai with tofu will be among the choices."

How did he know? wondered Carolyn.

Just as the waitress started to hand each of them a menu, Jim turned to her and advised, "Mí cåpĕn txng mī menū dı«."

Extremely surprised, the waitress nodded and took back the menus, but responded in English. "What you like to order?"

"Phad thiy kab têāhū såhrab reīyk nåỳxy læa mímī hxy sı̀ xari ley," began Jim. "Khāw phad khí khāwklxng kí sm px peīya."

The waitress was busy trying to keep up as she wrote down Jim's order on a little pad.

"Xx reā mā reìm kan thī sup pæng khí kan dī kẁā," added Jim. "Dwy chā mali."

"Is that all?" questioned the waitress.

"Phak thempura k chèn kan," smiled Jim.

"It's lot of food," commented the woman as she added it to the list and mumbled, "ready soon." She swiftly headed for the kitchen.

"You speak Thai?" Carolyn knew Jim spoke at least a dozen languages, but certainly hadn't known about that one.

"Is it true you have a photographic memory?" Janette suddenly asked him.

"So it's been said," responded Jim with a crooked grin. He thoroughly enjoyed unexpected opportunities to show off some of his linguistic skills.

"What will we be having?" Carolyn gave Jim a questioning look.

"Everything you mentioned and more," smiled Jim. "You'll just have to wait and see."

Just then the waitress returned with steaming-hot jasmine tea, carefully pouring some for each of them. The black ceramic teapot and matching teacups were adorned with drawings of red hummingbirds on lotus blossoms.

A second waitress suddenly arrived with egg flower soup for each of them in matching black and red bowls.

"Is there any pepper?" wondered Carolyn.

"Khx phrikthiy såhrab sup phūhying hnxy kha," inquired Jim.

"Pepper," acknowledged the woman as she hurried off to comply with Jim's request.

"We'll have to be sure and take you along if we ever go to Thailand," joked Janette.

"Any time," responded Jim as he glanced longingly at Carolyn. *Why has she never felt the same way about me? Can't she see I'm still in love with her, even after all these years?*

Seeming to sense what Jim was thinking, Janette suddenly inquired, "So, how's your wife Sheree?" Thankfully, Carolyn had been busy gazing at the fountain and hadn't noticed the way Jim was looking at her.

Slightly embarrassed by Janette's dose of reality, Jim shrugged and responded, "Ann's death was difficult for all of us, so it will be a while before Sheree is up to company again."

"Still, she must have her hands full dealing with guests at your bed and breakfast while you're away," presumed Janette.

"Susan and Hector must be there helping," supposed Carolyn.

Jim merely nodded. He did not like the way the conversation was headed. "So, Carolyn, anything else on Thursdays?"

Breathing a heavy sigh, Carolyn continued. "Sometimes it would involve picking fruit or nuts from her trees. I remember one time when she had me climb to the very top of her lemon tree, because she wanted every last one. I was only seven years old at the time. Unfortunately, I lost my balance and fell. And of course, lemon trees have lots of thorns on them."

"Ouch!" commented Janette.

"Indeed," agreed Carolyn. "You should have seen what happened when my mom came to pick me up that night on her way home from work. My grandpa had just gotten home from his job, so he overheard their conversation."

"And?" prompted Jim.

"The first thing my mom did was ask me why I had scratches on my face and arms," described Carolyn. "When I told her what happened, she was furious. She turned to my grandma and told her that was *not* what they paid her for!"

"Your parents *paid* her to watch you? Even while you were busy doing all that work for her?" Jim grilled her.

"Every week," clarified Carolyn. "Anyway, when my grandpa heard this, he erupted like Mount Vesuvius. He rarely lost his temper, but when he did, it certainly was not pleasant. Apparently, he had no idea Grandma Bell was being paid to watch me, or that she was squirreling away all the money somewhere, and demanded to know what she was doing with all of it."

"What'd she tell him?" asked Janette.

"She made some excuse about buying groceries with it," replied Carolyn, "but there's no way she was bringing home that much food."

"I wonder what she did with it?" queried Janette.

"That was where Fridays came into the picture," revealed Carolyn. "Shopping day."

The waitresses arrived just then with a huge platter of dishes of food and set them all onto the table in family style. Not only was there Pad Thai noodles with tofu, but also orange chicken, brown and white fried rice, cashew delight, basil eggplant, and tempura vegetables.

"Anything else?" questioned the waitress as she looked at Jim.

"Nàn ca pĕn thânghmd," Jim informed her as he pulled out and handed her three one-hundred dollar bills. "Cæng hı reā thrāb hāk nàn mí pheīyngphx."

"Khxbkhun!" beamed the waitress as she took the money, bowed her head, and left.

"Thank you!" exclaimed Janette. "Everything looks delicious."

"Yes, thank you," added Carolyn as she smiled cautiously at Jim. *Hopefully he won't get the wrong idea, especially with us accepting his generosity like this.*

For several moments, each of them consumed their food in silence. Carolyn, of course, had silently blessed her food first before eating any of it.

"Shopping day on Fridays," urged Jim as he turned to Carolyn.

"Well, Grandma Bell actually did buy *some* food," affirmed Carolyn, "but usually would go to more of the expensive department stores and pretty much buy whatever she fancied."

"Really?" Janette raised one eyebrow.

"One of her favorite stores was Roddericks," remembered Carolyn. "It was a high-end lingerie place for women of means, and all the employees seemed to know her by name. Even the gloves there cost more than an entire outfit would run at a regular department store. One time she bought a pair of black silk gloves, but once we got back to her place, she secreted them in a box way up on her closet shelf."

"Probably so your grandpa wouldn't see 'em," guessed Janette.

"Another time, she bought a black bra and matching slip," added Carolyn. "Same story; she would often buy expensive fingernail polish or makeup for herself, but grandpa never bothered to look in her makeup drawer where she kept 'em."

"Did she buy any for you?" queried Janette.

"Not makeup, no," answered Carolyn. "But, believe it or not, she would occasionally buy me sewing stuff, and fabric with which to make my own clothes."

"You're kidding," sniggered Janette.

"Saturdays were sewing days," continued Carolyn. "It was very important to her that I learn how to make my own clothes. In fact, she had me making my own coats by the time I was nine years old, including tailored buttonholes and all."

"So, she worked you all week, and then took you shopping?" Jim questioned her.

"I did see my mother giving her money once and specifically heard her mention that it was for buying material for me so I could learn how to sew," conceded Carolyn.

Jim nodded as he considered that.

"The sad part is that I grew three clothing sizes when I was in the eighth grade," recalled Carolyn. "And shot up 14 inches that year, too, making me the tallest person in my class."

"What happened to all those clothes you made for yourself?" pressed Jim.

"Donated to charity," revealed Carolyn. "I did a lot of sewing that year. My dad had no intention of allowing me to buy store-bought clothes once I knew how to make my own."

"What about Sundays?" Jim interrogated her.

"Baking day, of course," revealed Carolyn. "The only job Grandma Bell ever told anyone about was when she worked for 15 years at a bakery each Sunday."

"They usually start pretty early in the morning," commented Janette. "My sister used to get up at 3:00 a.m. every morning when she worked at one."

"Yep," acknowledged Carolyn. "And we got there by 4:00 a.m. She would take me with her. Sometimes, Grandma Bell would turn me loose with various tubes of frosting that she and I had made up together, and taught me how to decorate cardboard boxes to look like cakes for display in the front at the counter. It was work, but also fun."

"Huh," muttered Jim.

"Then when we got back to her place, she taught me how to make home-made cinnamon rolls and frosting," elaborated Carolyn. "It was very important to her that I learn everything involved in becoming a homemaker, so that I would never have to go out and work like my mother did. Working outside the home for any woman was considered as a failure back in those days, probably for not marrying well."

"Meaning into money," acknowledged Janette.

"Yep," confirmed Carolyn.

"She no doubt kept her twin sons busy working when they were living at home, too," surmised Jim.

"Every minute, I'm sure," confirmed Carolyn.

"No wonder they never came home again after military academy," commented Janette.

"Not by choice," stipulated Carolyn. "According to their mother, the family just couldn't afford it."

"Makes you wonder, though," pondered Janette.

"Not to change the subject," interrupted Jim, "but we need to find out more about that 1939 Ford Sedan your dad was standing by in that old photo."

"Perhaps my uncle will know more about it," speculated Carolyn. *Hopefully that car was not at the heart of whatever went wrong between them.* "If we get to see him."

"And if he remembers it," muttered Janette while she took another bite of the delicious Thai food on her plate.

4. Deception

The summer of 1952 passed quickly for Walter and Willard. Every spare moment they had was spent courting Charlotte and Ruth. In fact, the two couples had originally planned to have a double wedding ceremony at the end of August.

Deep in thought as he paused beside the gravel-covered hellstrip in front of his parents' house, Walter folded his arms while he studied the neatly-kept yard. *No one else in the entire neighborhood still puts a new coat of whitewash on their house each year,* considered Walter. *And there's no way Mother does this by herself. So, just how can she afford it? Is this a good time to ask her about the car insurance? What if there really isn't any?*

Mature camelia bushes on either side of the tiny wooden porch were in radiant bloom. Next to them were several red and yellow rose bushes, hydrangeas, chrysanthemums and a few late-blooming purple irises. A patch of sunflowers grew on the west side of the house, farthest away from the freestanding one-car garage. Raised garden beds near the hellstrip grew tomato plants, zucchini squash, green onions, carrots, garlic and mustard plants. *Is it really true that garlic and mustard can help keep pests away?*

Walter's footsteps echoed loudly on the creaky wooden porch as he stepped onto it. Pausing for courage and taking a deep breath, he carefully knocked on the front door.

"I thought I recognized those footsteps," came the voice of Bell from behind him. She was coming from the garage, carrying a heavy box of empty canning jars.

"Let me help you with that," offered Walter as he approached and took it from her.

"The only time you've been here to visit all summer was to make payments on that stupid car!" scolded Bell. She clearly was displeased.

Walter pursed his lips together while his mother opened the front door and motioned for him to go inside.

"That's probably the only reason you're here now," accused Bell as she followed him to the kitchen and watched him set down the box on the well-worn butcherblock counter before turning to face her.

"Not entirely," replied Walter. He pulled out a chair at the yellow formica dining table. It perfectly matched the red and yellow flowered kitchen curtains that were fluttering in the breeze from the open window, and the red vinyl asbestos floor tiles. "Can we sit down?"

Bell folded her arms and squinted her eyes at him. "Why?"

Even when working around the house, Bell would always wear a nice dress, makeup, and made sure her hair looked impeccable. Of course, she was always fastidious about wearing a full-body bib apron to protect her clothes while performing such tasks. *After all, one never knows when visitors might stop by unexpectedly. Or, when it might be necessary to go somewhere.*

"There's something I need to ask you," clarified Walter when he finally sat down. "Please?"

"I suppose you boys are planning to marry those two-bit hussies you've been shamelessly running around with all summer, and now you expect your father and me to drop everything and help you with it," snapped Bell.

"It's not like that at all," argued Walter.

"Then how is it?" Bell grilled him. "We go and let you buy the family car, and this is how you repay us? By not even bothering to come see us more often?"

"First of all, here's the payment for August," offered Walter as he pulled out an envelope and handed it to her.

"I suppose you're paying your brother's portion again this month, too?" Bell shook her head with frustration.

"No, just mine this time," clarified Walter.

"Well, you're a week late," retorted Bell when she finally sat down across from him and began counting the money. "And unless I get your brother's half by the end of this week, we may need to reconsider this whole arrangement."

"What do you mean?" Walter frowned as he glanced at his mother's new Wedgewood range and matching white General Electric refrigerator. *How in the world can she afford them?*

"We had an agreement that you boys would pay me a certain amount of money each month," Bell reminded him. "And on time."

"I can't make Willard come up with his half of the payment, nor can I afford to keep paying his half."

"Then it's clear you didn't think it through before you decided to buy the car from us," reasoned Bell. "Your father and I need that money each month to make payments on his new pickup truck. He needs it for work. I suppose we could always try and return it to the dealership, but then we'd be forced to take the Ford back from you. Frank's got to have a vehicle. That's all there is to it."

"Surely you can work with us," objected Walter. "This whole thing just isn't fair."

"Life's never fair," mentioned Bell with a smug look.

"I joined the Air Force today," blurted Walter as he maintained eye contact with her.

"You what!" exclaimed Bell. "What about the car?"

"I'm guessing you no longer have an insurance policy on the Ford?" probed Walter.

"Not unless *you* managed to get one," snapped Bell. "That car's your responsibility now. Don't tell me you boys have been driving it around without any car insurance? That's against the law, you know."

"Mother, I need to level with you," continued Walter. "Last week when Willard was out with Ruth, the engine blew up on him. We can't even drive it now."

"What?" Bell was positively livid. "And why isn't Willard here telling me about this himself?"

"The whole thing probably happened because he forgot to put oil in it," guessed Walter. "At any rate, now it will cost more than either of us has to repair it, let alone purchase car insurance. Plus, there's the fact that I'll be leaving for Basic Training in three weeks. I was thinking of signing over my half of the responsibility for the Ford to Willard."

Bell glared at him for several moments before responding. After shaking her head and pointing her finger at him in a menacing manner, Bell informed him, "This is what's going to happen, young man. Either you or that sorry brother of yours will pay me the rest of what you owe me on that car as agreed each month, or I will get an attorney and sue you both for breach of contract. Then when you lose – and you will – warrants will be issued for your arrest!"

"Mother, no," protested Walter. His face was flushed and he could no longer fight back the unmanly tears that had been straining to escape the corners of his eyes. "Please!"

"Please, what?" asked Bell, obviously unphased by his show of emotion. "The worst part is what your father will do when he finds about all of this. He'll be furious."

Walter was very afraid of his father Frank's thin leather belt and what would happen if the man lost his temper. One word from Bell was all it would take; regardless of the fact that he was now an adult and on his own, it would not matter.

"You have one week," Bell advised him as she nodded toward the door. "One of you had better be here by then with your brother's half of the payment for this month, or you'll both suffer the consequences."

"That still isn't fair," muttered Walter.

"No one ever said life is fair," Bell reminded him when she stood up to escort him to the door.

"I'll go see Willard right now," promised Walter as he hurriedly left and began walking away from the house.

Bell smugly nodded while she closed the door behind Walter and walked toward one of her wood-toned kitchen cupboards. On its top shelf in the back was what appeared to be a can of Hills Bros. coffee, though this particular can was devoid of coffee and filled instead with a thick stack of folded bills. *Perhaps I should hide this newest batch of money in the lining of my blue coat where the pink slips are? Diversify my hiding places. Then, by next month, I'll finally have enough saved up to buy that new sewing machine, and no one will be any the wiser.*

Bell thought of her secret job and how she had used the money to fully pay off both vehicles. A smirk crossed her lips. Meanwhile, Frank and the boys both could go on believing they were making the payments each month. *Yes, perhaps it is untruthful to let them believe otherwise, but the whole thing about making payments was intended to teach the boys responsibility.*

And marrying either of those no-good gold diggers? "Huh!" exclaimed Bell out loud. "Not if I have anything to do with it." *And how dare Walter join the Air Force without telling me first, especially while he's supposed to be making payments to me for that car.*

Despite the objection of his landlord at the boarding house where he now lived, Willard was busy working on the 1939 Ford Sedan in the alley behind it. Hopefully, the man wouldn't be by again until next week. Dressed in his overalls, Willard had the hood propped up; he was struggling to try and make the necessary engine repairs.

"I told her," came the voice of his brother from behind him.

Startled, Willard dropped his wrench in the dirt. After picking it up, he turned to face his brother. "How'd it go?"

"Terrible," Walter shook his head. "Mother says she's going to hire an attorney and sue us if we don't continue making payments. You've got one week to get your half to her for August or the whole deal is off."

"What do you mean?" frowned Willard.

"She probably plans to take back the car."

"Did you tell her about the engine and that it doesn't run?"

"Yes," confirmed Walter. "She was furious. But, in spite of everything, she said we have one week before she goes to Father or tries to hire an attorney."

"With what?" scoffed Willard. "Attorneys are expensive."

"I don't know," replied Walter, "but something tells me she's getting money from somewhere. Have you seen her new stove and refrigerator?"

"Really?"

"Or the new red and black Ford pickup truck Dad is driving these days? Those things aren't cheap."

Willard hesitated to say what was on his mind.

"This car is bad luck. The sooner we unload her, the better off we'll be," suggested Walter.

"You may be right," sighed Willard as he wiped off his hands on a shop rag.

"Mother wouldn't even consider letting me sign over my half of the responsibility to you," added Walter. "Even after I told her about leaving for Basic Training in three weeks."

"Did you tell her about the girls?"

"That we plan to marry 'em at the end of the month before I take off?" snorted Walter. "Not after what Mother said about us not coming to see her all summer. Her next remark, and I quote, was that she supposed we were planning on marrying those *'two-bit hussies we've been shamelessly running around with all summer'* and that now we probably expect her and Father to drop everything to help us with it."

"Wow!" exclaimed Willard.

"So, what now?"

"We have to find a way to get the pink slip from her," decided Willard. "Even if we have to break in and steal it."

"No way," objected Walter. "I'll have no part of something like that. She would have us arrested if we did."

"Well, we'll have to have it in order to sell the car," argued Willard. "Once we do, we can pay her the rest of what we owe her, split the remainder, and be done with it."

"I could use my half to get to Basic Training, take Charlotte with me, and marry her there," hoped Walter.

"Even if you got married here, they wouldn't come," pointed out Willard. "Nor would she bother sending any wedding gifts."

"She sure seems to come up with money to buy herself some pretty fancy clothes and things," commented Walter. "Have you seen all that stuff she hides up on her closet shelf so that Father won't see?"

"He's gotta know about it," presumed Willard.

"Not with him working all the time," differed Walter. "He's hardly ever there anymore, except just long enough to eat dinner and get a few hours of sleep."

"You know," hesitated Willard, "I probably shouldn't say anything, but I could swear I saw Mother walking toward town wearing her best black dress and matching silk gloves last Saturday night. Just like the ones she normally keeps up on her closet shelf."

"Father was out camping that weekend with Uncle Bill," recognized Walter.

"Indeed," Willard nodded as he began to smile.

"I know what we can do," planned Walter. "Perhaps, if you threaten to tell Father about what you saw, she might be willing to part with the pink slip?"

"You don't suppose she has a job somewhere, do you?"

"What, dealing blackjack at a local speakeasy?"

"They haven't called 'em that since the 1930s," laughed Willard. "But, there are several bars in downtown Ashton."

"It would have to be one with a back room," stipulated Walter. "The only place I know of where it's legal to gamble is in Vegas."

"This is what we're gonna do," decided Willard. "You get Father to take you fishing this weekend."

"But I have a date with Charlotte," objected Walter.

49

"Hear me out," instructed Willard. "We need to get Father out of the house so that one of us can follow Mother, should she happen to make another trip into town this Saturday night. Especially, since all we have left is one week to meet her demands."

Walter was silent for several moments before responding. "Then what?"

"Catch her in the act and confront her, right then and there," described Willard. "She'll no doubt be willing to make a deal."

"I sure wish there was another way," muttered Walter.

"Well, there isn't," responded Willard. "Not that you're willing to be a part of, so that's our only option at this point."

"I suppose you're right," relented Walter. "I'll try to call Father tonight."

"Don't just try. Make sure that you do," cautioned Willard as he smiled an evil smile. *It's about time someone put something over on Bell.*

Saturday afternoon showed up with the swiftness of a jackrabbit being pursued by a hungry coyote.

Bell waved at Frank and Walter as they drove off in the red and black Ford pickup. Their camping gear, a picnic basket, and two fishing poles could be seen laying in the truck bed. "Bring back plenty of fish!" she called.

Wasting no time, she hurriedly went inside, picked up the receiver to the black rotary dial phone, and began dialing.

On the third ring, a man's voice was heard on the other end of the line. "Hello?"

"This is Bell."

"Yer old man gone fishin' again?"

"Yes," answered Bell.

"Can ya come in early tonight?" asked the man.

"I'll need a ride," stipulated Bell. "I've got your order ready."

"A car'll be there at six o'clock."

"I'll be ready at six," promised Bell before hanging up.

Unknown to her, Willard had been hiding in the bushes outside the open dining room window and had overheard her part of the conversation.

I knew it! thought Willard as he stealthily made his way from the yard. *Six o'clock, huh? Well, I'll be here waiting, too.*

Knowing he would need a pretty fast bicycle in order to follow whatever car would be there to pick up his mother at six o'clock, Willard decided to pay a visit to his old friend Tony Scaglioni to see whether he might be willing to lend him his new one.

"What'll you give me if I let you borrow it?" Tony questioned Willard with a mischievous grin as he whipped out a comb from his back pocket and began combing back a stray lock of his greasy hair that had fallen onto his forehead.

"I just need to borrow it for the evening," responded Willard.

"Not until you tell me what for," smirked Tony. "You following someone? Maybe Ruth and some other guy?"

Recognizing that it was better to let Tony believe that story than the actual truth, Willard merely nodded.

"I knew it!" sniggered Tony. "Need any help?"

"Nah, this is something I must do alone."

"He anyone we know?" Tony pressed him. "If you're right about this, my brother Joey and I can help you teach him a lesson."

"I'll be sure to let you know," promised Willard when Tony motioned for him to go ahead and take the bike.

"Just make sure you bring her back in one piece," Tony cautioned Willard while he watched him reach for the 1952 Rollfast Hopalong Cassidy Boy's Bicycle propped against the railing of the Scaglioni porch. It was black and white with chrome trim.

"I'll guard it with my life," pledged Willard as he grabbed the bike, pushed up the kickstand, hopped on, and rode away.

Why are Tony and his brother still living at home with their folks? wondered Willard as he made his way toward his parents' house where he would hide in the bushes while he waited. *This bike is probably the only set of wheels he'll ever own; I'd best make sure nothing happens to it, that's for sure!*

Right at six o'clock sharp, a 1952 Buick Super Riviera pulled up in front of his parents' home. The highly waxed car was seaweed green with a white roof and side panels. Even its chrome trim seemed to glisten when tentacles of sunlight encircled it from above.

It must be right off the showroom floor, marveled Willard. *Will I be able to follow it undetected while it's still so light outside? I have no choice but to try.*

Bell opened the front door and emerged. She was adorned in a black and yellow paisley dress with a calf-length gored skirt, high waist-line, capped sleeves and bodice that was gathered beneath each side of the bust. Its v-shaped neckline reached up into a flared collar. Her black high-heeled shoes, clutch purse, and matching evening wrap were stunning. Needless to say, Bell's hair and makeup were impeccably done, as well.

Bell quickly motioned for the driver to come inside, which he did at once, leaving the motor running. The man was in his mid-thirties, tall and handsome with dark brown hair doused in tonic. His piercing blue eyes looked furtively in both directions. *Probably to be sure he isn't being followed,* fumed Willard.

The stranger's handlebar mustache was heavily waxed and curled up at both ends. He wore a black double-breasted silk suit and white shirt, with a black and red paisley necktie by Archivio. Stepping gingerly to avoid getting any dust on his black and white slip-on penny loafers, the man went inside.

It was all Willard could do to resist the urge to come charging out of the bushes and punch the guy right in the nose. *How dare this man come to the house like this while his father is away!*

Moments later, the man came back out, carrying a large box filled with what appeared to be jars of jam.

What in the world? wondered Willard. *Jam? Why in the world is Mother giving this man a box filled with jars of jam?* Bell hurried to open the trunk of the car for the man and waited while he carefully placed the box inside. Then both of them headed back for the house.

Is this the order she was referring to when she spoke on the phone earlier?

Without warning the man emerged from the house again, carrying yet another box filled with jars of something. Bell followed him out, pausing only long enough to secure the front door before making her way to the car. After the stranger had carefully placed the second box of jars into the trunk, he attempted to close it as quietly as possible. Then, almost as an afterthought, he opened the back door closest to the curb and took out yet another box of jars and handed it to Bell. It was clear by how she carried it toward the garage that the jars must be empty.

The man glanced guardedly in both directions while he grabbed what appeared to be a second box of empty jars and followed Bell to the garage to stash them inside.

What in the world? pondered Willard.

Bell and the man swiftly made their way back to the Riveria and climbed inside, both being careful not to slam the vehicle doors.

Are the jars filled with jam, or with something else? Willard began to wonder what was really going on and was deep in thought when he suddenly noticed the Riviera driving away.

Willard struggled to pull the bicycle from the bushes, but the spokes on the rear wheel were unexpectedly caught in the limbs of his mother's prized camelia bush. *Just great!*

By the time Willard finally managed to extricate the bicycle from the camelia bush, the Riviera was long gone. *The only thing I can do now is head for town and hope to spot it parked somewhere.*

As Willard rode the bicycle past the next-door neighbor's house, two of Mrs. Beasley's roosters were loudly competing for dominance over one another and for privileges with the various hens in her flock. *What a raucous those stupid birds are always making!*

Then as he rode past old man Jenkins' place, the vicious pair of Rottweilers he kept as guard dogs began snarling and barking, and chasing Willard from the other side of the fence. *Hopefully the fence will hold,* hoped Willard as he desperately began pedaling faster to get past them.

Perspiration dripped down Willard's face while he continued his ride to downtown Ashton in the 105° weather. *It has to be at least 90% humidity,* guessed Willard as he gingerly stepped on the bike's brakes and brought it to a stop on the side of the road. Carefully balancing it between his legs, he hurriedly took a handkerchief from his back pocket, unfolded it, and wiped the sweat from his face.

Willard squinted at the bright sun while he refolded and stuffed the handkerchief back into his pocket. *There can only be a handful of places where Mother might have gone,* he reasoned. Just then, several gnats flew toward his face. "Shoo!" cried Willard as he batted at them while hurriedly taking off on the bicycle again to try and get ahead of them. *This had better not be a wild goose chase!*

It was just after 2:00 a.m. on the morning of August 8, 1952. Despite the early hour, the humidity remained high in downtown

Ashton and the temperature outside was still an uncomfortable 97°. *If only there was a breeze to help cool it down,* wished Willard while he waited in the dark alley behind Sardini's Restaurant and Cocktail Lounge. The Riviera he sought was parked out front and had not moved all night. He was easily able to keep an eye on its left rear fender from his location. *Mother has to be inside.* Unfortunately, the bouncer at its entrance had turned him away due to not being properly dressed in a suit and tie.

Willard wrinkled his nose and shook his head. The odor of rotten food emanating from one of the large metal garbage receptacles beside him was nearly unbearable, not to mention the stench of something still smoldering in an incinerator next to it. *What if Bell was dropped off elsewhere before the man came here?* worried Willard.

Suddenly, the sound of inebriated patrons exiting the lounge could be heard around the corner. *It must be closing time,* assessed Willard. *If only I had a watch, or even the money to buy one.*

Deciding to leave the bike where it was as he skulked closer to the corner of the building for a better look, Willard carefully peeked at those laughing and talking on its front steps. One by one, they all disbursed and headed toward their parked cars out front or across the street. *Where is Mother?*

Unexpectedly, a door behind him opened and closed in the shadows. A lone woman had exited from the back door of the establishment and was headed towards him. *It's her!*

"Hello, Mother," greeted Willard when she neared his location.

Stunned to see him standing there but hiding it well, she demanded, "What are you doing here?"

"Where's all those jars of jam?" countered Willard with a smug look on his face. "Does Father know what you're doing here?"

"Do you?" demanded Bell as she turned to walk away.

"Wait," insisted Willard. He gently grabbed her arm to stop her. "You certainly must know it isn't safe for a woman to be out here alone at night like this."

"And so, you've come all this way, just to walk me home?"

"Actually, I followed you," admitted Willard as he darted over to where the bicycle was hidden and hurriedly wheeled it over to where his mother stood, watching him.

"A new bicycle?" she asked with a raised eyebrow.

"No, I borrowed it from Tony Scaglioni," Willard informed her.

"You were that desperate to follow me?" laughed Bell as she resumed walking toward the street.

"I'm sure Father will want to know why you gave all those jars of jam to that fancy man who came and picked you up earlier in that brand-new Riviera at our house," threatened Willard.

"Whose house?" sniggered Bell.

"Your house," corrected Willard. "Tell me, why isn't he giving you a ride back home?"

"Because I no longer have any jars for him to carry," explained Bell as she reached the street, turned the corner, and continued walking.

"Then what were you doing here so long like that, if all you were doing was selling the man your jars of jam? Or was something else in those jars?" demanded Willard while he steered the bicycle alongside her. "I'm sure Father will want to know what you were doing here and what kind of profit you made."

Bell gingerly pulled her black silk wrap around her waist and tied it on one side. It was much too hot out to wear over her shoulders.

"Walter and I are willing to make a deal with you," bargained Willard, choosing his words carefully.

"I'm listening," responded Bell as she continued walking.

"You hand over the pink slip to that car, and then we can sell it," described Willard.

"And just why should I do that?" Bell narrowed her eyes at him in the shadows.

"So we can get enough from it to pay you what we owe," explained Willard. "After we get it fixed, of course."

"Of course," sniggered Bell while she considered his proposition.

"I wonder who Father will be angrier with," suggested Willard. "With *us* for being a few days late paying you? Or with *you* for going downtown alone to a nightclub with some strange man while Father's away fishing?"

Bell stopped in her tracks and turned to face him. Even in the darkness, he could see she was livid. "Very well. I suppose we have a deal. But, if you *ever* breathe a word of *any* of this to your father, it will be the last deal you ever make. *Especially* about the jars. Do we understand each other?"

An evil smile crossed Willard's lips when they both began walking again. "Absolutely."

"And the fact that I was forced to sell those jars to help make the payment on your father's new pickup truck before it was due, is something for which you should be grateful, young man. Suppose the dealership had come to repossess it? Your father is well aware that your payments are what we use to meet that obligation."

Willard nodded. "That does make sense, but just exactly what was in those jars?"

"That's none of your business!" snapped Bell as she gave him a cautionary look.

"I take it they weren't filled with jam?"

"I'll allow your brother to sign over his responsibility for the car to you after this," elaborated Bell without answering his question, "but only if you can show me proof that the car has been repaired and fully insured before your next payment is due, or the vehicle is sold."

"Okay."

"On time," added Bell with a decisive nod.

"So, just what else were you doing in there all that time?" Willard grilled her while they walked along the street in the darkness.

"As I said, that's none of your business," answered Bell.

After several more minutes, Willard warned, "It's only a matter of time before Father finds out what you've been up to, whether we tell him or not."

"I wouldn't be so sure about that," smirked Bell.

* * *

The black Lamborghini rental Jim was driving rode smoothly and had nearly reached its destination. A green and white road sign indicating "2 miles to Rosewood" could be seen on the side of the road.

A sprawling grape vineyard on their right was filled with seasonal workers who were busy harvesting deep purple Concord grapes into white plastic buckets. When full, the buckets were then dumped into square vented harvest bins constructed of high-density polyethylene and mounted onto the back of a flatbed truck.

"That sure looks like a lot of work," assessed Janette.

"It is," confirmed Carolyn. "I still remember going out with my parents to pick grapes at some vineyard when I was about seven years old. Took me over an hour just to pick one bucketful."

Jim and Janette laughed at that.

On their left was an grove of Valencia oranges, though none of them were currently being picked. Farmland quickly gave way to the first sign of rural neighborhoods on the edge of Rosewood where a large sign read, "Welcome to Rosewood." Cleverly welded onto each side of the sign were brightly painted metal rosebushes, bearing realistic-looking metal roses decorated in pink, white, yellow and red, all with bright green leaves.

"Hey, I just got a text from Leticia, and she's staying at the Rosewood Hilton," Carolyn advised Jim and Janette. "She'll meet us in the lobby when we arrive, not at the facility."

"And, of course, we still don't know for sure if your uncle is in the same facility," Janette reminded her.

"Leticia should be able to find out by the time we get there," insisted Carolyn.

"Don't forget, I must be back by tomorrow for the ground breaking ceremony of my museum," described Jim. "But, if we're not finished by tonight, I can just leave you ladies here in Rosewood. If they have any more rooms there, of course."

"That's definitely not in the budget for me," declined Janette.

"Me, neither," agreed Carolyn.

"Then it's a good thing I'm paying for it," grinned Jim as he gave them each a mischievous look. "Don't worry, I'll come back to get you by tomorrow night."

"You're not even going with us to the facility today?" questioned Carolyn.

"Of course, I am," Jim assured her. "I just can't stay overnight."

Carolyn and Janette exchanged an apprehensive glance.

"Hey SIRI, plot a course for the Rosewood Hilton," directed Jim.

Almost instantaneously, it showed up on SIRI's screen.

"That reminds me of an old episode of *The Office*," remarked Janette. "They were using one of those GPS things to get somewhere and it led them straight into a lake."

Carolyn and Janette chuckled in response; Jim merely smiled and shook his head.

"Hey, there it is," indicated Janette while she pointed toward the huge hotel complex. "Nice place."

"Too bad we don't have our swimsuits," lamented Carolyn.

After pulling to a stop in one of the visitor spaces, Jim pulled out a Visa card and handed it to Carolyn. "Anything you ladies need while we're here, seriously. I won't take no for an answer."

"I can't," declined Carolyn.

Jim then handed the card to Janette. Speechless for a moment, she finally nodded and put it into her purse.

Carolyn took a deep breath and shot Janette a disapproving glance, which was deliberately ignored.

"It's gotta have at least 300 rooms," assessed Janette while they walked towards its covered entrance.

"Actually, it only has 120 rooms," Jim advised her when they went inside. "But, they are quite spacious."

"You've stayed here?" asked Janette.

"Not this specific one," clarified Jim, "but I have stayed at another one just like it in another city."

"How big are the rooms?" queried Janette.

"Huge," interjected a hotel greeter seated at the front reception desk. "Do you have a reservation?"

"How much to hold one of the rooms for tonight?" inquired Jim as he pulled out a roll of hundreds and gave the woman a pleasant wink.

"There's also a safe in each room," responded the woman. She tried not to stare at Jim's money. "Oh, sorry, will you all be staying in the same room?"

"Just the ladies," revealed Jim while he flirted shamelessly with the hotel greeter.

"Let me see what we have," blushed the woman as she turned to her computer. "We have a room with two queen-sized beds starting at $138. All guests have access to free parking and WiFi. The rooms have digital keys, are non-smoking, and some rooms are pet friendly."

"Sorry, but we left all the animals at home," teased Jim.

"Of course," smiled the woman. "There's also an on-site restaurant, indoor and outdoor pools, room service, and of course there is a business center with conference rooms available."

"What about the room we'll be staying in?" wondered Carolyn.

"That room will actually sleep up to four persons," described the greeter. "It has a mini fridge, portable shower chairs, scald-proof shower/tub, microwave, coffee maker, 400 thread count sheets, a 42-inch HDTV, hairdryer, iron with ironing board, and a whole range of bath amenities."

"I see you have vending machines, too," noted Janette as she glanced down one of the hallways where machines with various bottled drinks and fast meals could be seen."

"What about a gift shop where clothing items are for sale?" pressed Carolyn. "Do they sell bathing suits?"

"You're in luck," the woman assured her. "Anything else?"

"That oughta do it," grinned Jim while he peeled off two hundred-dollar bills and handed them to the woman. After glancing more closely at her name tag, he said, "Thank you, Marsha."

"I'll need your name, too, sir."

"Jim Otterman," came the response when he handed her his driver's license and business card.

"Are you *the* Jim Otterman?" Marsha was flabbergasted. "I obviously can't take your money."

"Why can't she take his money?" Janette whispered to Carolyn.

"Because he probably owns the place," revealed Carolyn.

"He actually does," confirmed Marsha after overhearing their conversation. "The entire chain."

"No way!" exclaimed Janette.

"Jim Otterman, the richest man in the world," gasped Marsha. "I never dreamed of actually meeting you."

"It's just another investment," Jim modestly shrugged his shoulders, to downplay it.

"Carolyn!" came the voice of Leticia from behind them.

"How are you?" asked Carolyn as she gave her cousin a hug. Then turning to the others, "This is my dear friend, Janette."

Leticia nodded politely at Janette. "Nice to meet you."

"And, my high school friend, Jim," added Carolyn.

"The pleasure is all mine," flirted Jim while he bowed and kissed Leticia on the hand.

"Charmed," stammered Leticia as she looked away to avoid his piercing blue eyes. Jim was not at all what she had expected.

"Leticia's room is on me, too," Jim informed Marsha. He handed her two more hundred-dollar bills.

"Yes, sir," Marsha nodded reservedly before handing him two digital keys to the room assigned to Carolyn and Janette.

"Do you need our IDs?" questioned Carolyn.

"Not necessary. The room is now booked by Mr. Otterman. We have his information already."

"Thank you!" exclaimed Leticia when she shook Jim's hand again.

"Yes, thank you very much!" beamed Janette.

"We do appreciate it," added Carolyn.

"My pleasure," beamed Jim as he handed the digital keys to Carolyn and Janette. "Now, let's all sit down over there, so we can decide where we're off to first."

"Just what is it like to have unlimited money and power at your disposal?" Janette asked Jim in hushed tones while they headed for the dining area. "It must be nice to have anything you want."

"Not anything," differed Jim as he glanced wistfully at Carolyn.

Janette understood immediately and merely nodded.

Once they were all seated, Leticia informed them, "I've already reached out to the place where I believe he is. They won't confirm or deny whether he's there."

"Why not?" Carolyn frowned.

"Because I'm not on their list," revealed Leticia with a sigh of frustration while she pushed her shoulder-length blonde hair out of the way towards her back. Bearing a strong resemblance to Carolyn, Leticia was also light complexioned but not as tall.

"That doesn't make sense," interjected Janette.

"His fourth wife apparently has complete say on who gets to see him and those people are unyielding," responded Leticia.

"The same thing happened two years ago when Leticia tried to see him before," Carolyn mentioned to the others.

"It was a 14-hour drive just to get there, too," recalled Leticia. "I can still see that woman's face as she stood at the door and told me my own father wanted nothing to do with me. She just sent me away, without even letting me talk to him."

"That's just what *she* says," pointed out Jim. "What about your dad? What does *he* say?"

"I haven't been able to get close enough to find out," admitted Leticia. "It's always just what *she* says."

"Not only that," added Carolyn, "there has been absolutely no response to any of the letters either of us has written to him."

"Assuming the letters ever made it to him," considered Jim.

"Sounds to me like she's waiting for him to die, and trying to keep the family away until it happens," opined Janette.

"We've got to try and see *him*, not her," determined Carolyn. "And the only way to do that is to go there. Plus, he's the only one who can tell us what we need to know about her mother, Ruth, and what really happened to her all those years ago."

"If he doesn't have dementia, and assuming he even knows anything," muttered Leticia while she sadly shook her head.

"Jim sometimes has a way of getting things done," interjected Janette as she gave him a wink.

"What's his fourth wife's name?" inquired Jim.

"Trixie," revealed Leticia.

Just then, Marsha approached with a hospitality tray on wheels filled with fruit, cheese, lunch meat, crackers, vegetables, pastries, bottled water, cups and a carafe of hot coffee. "Please let me know if you would like anything else. Obviously, it's on the house."

Jim gave her a crooked grin and another hundred-dollar bill. "Thanks."

"My pleasure!"

Once Marsha was gone, Jim turned to Leticia. "Tell me a little about your father's second, third and fourth wives."

"Oh my," sighed Leticia. "Well, his second wife was Beatrice, and his third wife was Matilda. Both were quite wealthy and both eventually died of cancer."

"Anything unusual about the circumstances in either case?" Jim interrogated her. "Foul play, for example?"

Leticia shook her head in the negative.

"How soon was it after your mother died when Willard married his next wife?" pressed Jim.

"Actually, my mother and him were divorced back in 1974," revealed Leticia. "I remember it well because he married Beatrice the very day it became final."

"That's awful," opined Janette.

"Intriguing," frowned Jim. "How long was he married to Beatrice?"

"She died in the 1980s," answered Leticia. "And again, it was not long before he married Matilda. He apparently didn't like being alone for very long, if you know what I mean."

"And when did Matilda pass away?" probed Jim.

"Not until after the turn of the century."

"So, Matilda was the one he was married to at the time his first wife, Ruth, passed away in 1996," considered Jim.

"I don't think there was any connection," opined Leticia. "They weren't even living in the same state."

"And what about the one he's married to now?"

"Well, shortly after Matilda died, my father moved into an independent living facility where he met Trixie," elaborated Leticia. "He quit having anything to do with the family after that."

"I told you she's a gold digger," assumed Janette.

"Money's not always all it's cracked up to be," responded Jim.

"I'd take my chances," Janette advised him.

"Seriously," interrupted Carolyn. "We need to accomplish two things here, which may or may not be connected in any way. First, we need to try and see my uncle so we can find out whether or not he knows anything about Ruth. Secondly, Leticia deserves the opportunity to see him again to find out for herself whether what Trixie says is really true about him not wanting to have anything more to do with her."

"And if so, *why*," added Leticia with a determined nod of her head. "I'd like to hear it from him."

"Dig in," offered Jim as he began passing around the food items. "Coffee, anyone?"

"I'll just have water," replied Carolyn. "No ice."

Jim merely nodded as he pulled out his laptop and turned to Leticia. "Name of the facility where you believe they have him now?"

"Apple Valley Memory Care," revealed Leticia. "The woman I spoke with was named Gertrude."

"That's who I spoke with, too," corroborated Carolyn.

"She hasn't heard my voice yet," volunteered Janette.

"I have a better idea," suggested Jim. "Have you ever volunteered as a candy striper?"

Janette appeared to be offended and shocked.

"Not a stripper," laughed Jim. "A candy striper, spelled with only one p. Someone who volunteers at a hospital as a nurse's aide."

"Oh," laughed Janette. "You had me there for a minute."

"They haven't called 'em candy stripers for 30 years," smiled Carolyn. "I did that one summer during junior high."

"But Gertrude knows your voice," Jim pointed out to Carolyn.

"Oh, wait a minute, no way," Janette shook her head. "You want *me* to try and bluff my way into that place as a nurse's aide?"

"A volunteer," corrected Jim with a sly smile.

"Sounds like a sure way to find out if he's there," agreed Carolyn. "I like it."

"It just might work," recognized Leticia.

* * *

Walter and Willard finally managed to sell the 1939 Ford to a man named Alex Buford on Saturday, August 16, 1952. Mr. Buford was an entrepreneur of sorts and one of his passions was collecting old cars that he felt were destined to become classics.

Fortunately for them, Mr. Buford also was a mechanic who owned his own auto shop. He quickly agreed to take the car *as is* so that he could get a better look under the hood when he made the repairs.

The brothers were seated on a bench behind the welding shop where Willard worked; it was their lunch hour.

"Not bad," nodded Willard as he counted his half of the profit. "Half of $1,000 comes to $500 for each of us."

"Especially when new Fords are selling anywhere from $1,500 to $2,300," agreed Walter. "Maybe now, Mother can finally finish making the payments on both vehicles."

"You know as well as I do that Mother's making money somewhere else on her own," pointed out Willard. "Knowing her, she's been pocketing the money. Heck, she probably has both vehicles paid off already."

"That's pure speculation," sniggered Walter.

"Maybe not," differed Willard. "What if I told you I think there's proof right there in her garage?"

"Of what?"

"That she has some sort of side business going on," claimed Willard with a knowing grin.

"How do you propose we get in there to find it?" wondered Walter. "Break in during the night?"

"No, nothing of the kind," replied Willard.

"Well, if we do pay her the $500 we still owe her, that brings our profit down to $500. Split in two, that's only $250 each."

"Certainly not enough to get another vehicle," lamented Willard.

"Or to take Charlotte with me when I leave," pointed out Walter. "Bus tickets alone are $45 each and renting an apartment will cost $280, not including utilities. Plus, we'll need to buy food."

"How soon do you get paid?" questioned Willard.

"I have the option of getting paid once or twice monthly," described Walter. "If I choose the second option, it would be at least two weeks before my first paycheck."

"Well, I'm going to need more than what's left of my half to rent an apartment with Ruth when we get married," asserted Willard. "And that's without traveling anywhere."

"You're the one who seems to know about some kind of proof in the garage," Walter reminded him. "I think I'll take my half now and then just send her what I owe her when I can."

"She'll be furious," warned Willard.

"You're the one she gave the pink slip to," recapped Walter as he pocketed his half of the profit and stood to leave. "Besides, Charlotte and I will be long gone by then anyway."

"You can't do that to me," argued Willard. "Mother will end up taking everything I have to make up for your portion!"

"I doubt it."

"What if you distract her while I search the garage?" proposed Willard.

"For what?" pressed Walter. "I still don't see what you think you're going to find in there."

Willard then hesitated as he thought of the night he and his mother had walked from town in the darkness and of her threat that he would be sorry if he *ever* mentioned anything about the incident to his father, especially about the jars. *Does that include my brother? I can't take a chance. What if Bell calls the police on us for stealing her part of the money?*

"Don't worry, she'll get over it," chuckled Walter as he clapped his hand onto Willard's shoulder for a brief moment before starting to walk away with $500 in his pocket.

"Wait!" commanded Willard. "I'll tell you what. Let me give her the $500 that I have here tonight. Then you can send me my $250 when you get your first paycheck."

Walter hesitated and then nodded assent. "Okay, you got a deal." The brothers shook on it.

It was Saturday evening on August 16, 1952. Frank was sitting in the kitchen drinking a bottle of beer, eating barbecue potato chips, and reading a newspaper while waiting for dinner to be ready. He was currently reading from the world events section where it reported "34 people were killed yesterday after a flood hit the English village of Lynmouth in north Devon."

"Looks like Harry Truman won't be running for reelection," mentioned Bell while she sliced the tomatoes for their salad.

Frank scowled when he turned to that page and read, "The polls predict Adlai Ewing Stevenson II will be the leading Democratic candidate in 1953, and he will be going against some Republican named Dwight D. Eisenhower."

"That's not until next year, though," laughed Bell as she gingerly placed the sliced tomatoes on top of the salad. "Dinner's ready."

Just then there was a knock at the door.

"I'll get it," volunteered Bell while Frank put down his newspaper and came to the table.

"Willard?" Bell did not seem pleased to see him.

"Is it a bad time?"

"We were just sitting down to eat," replied Bell.

"May I come in?" asked Willard.

"There really isn't enough for three," responded Bell with an even glare. *How dare he show up unannounced at dinner time like this!*

"I only wanted to give you this," offered Willard as he handed her a roll of bills. "It's the $500 we still owe you for the Ford."

"That's different," smiled Bell. She stood aside and motioned for him to enter. "Please, join us for supper. I'm sure we'll manage to squeeze out a third serving."

As Willard passed by her, Bell grabbed him by the arm, pulled him close and whispered, "Not a word about this to your father, do you hear me?"

"Yes, ma'am," promised Willard while he returned her even gaze.

Quickly stuffing the money into her brassiere to hide it from Frank, Bell then closed the door and followed Willard to the kitchen.

"What are we having for dinner?" asked Willard.

"Your favorite," grinned Bell. "Corned beef hash."

Deciding to make sure his brother had followed through on giving the $500 to their mother, Walter paid a surprise visit to his parents' house the next day.

Frank had gone fishing for the day, probably with one of his buddies from work.

"Mother," called Walter as he approached. Bell was busy hanging up clothes on the outdoor clothesline and securing them with wooden pins. As expected, she was dressed in a rather nice floral print dress but also had on a full-body bib apron over it for protection.

Bell paused to shake out a towel while he approached.

"I just came by to make sure Willard gave you the $500."

Bell gave him a puzzled look. "What are you talking about?"

"The $500 we owed you for the car," clarified Walter. *Did Willard change his mind and decide to keep the money?*

"No, he was never here," lied Bell as she hung up the towel.

"I don't understand," fumed Walter. "He promised to bring you that money last night!"

"Perhaps he plans to come over today?" speculated Bell with a coy expression on her face. "I haven't seen him."

"Okay, thanks," nodded Walter as he suddenly turned and left. *How dare Willard try and double cross me like this!*

Becoming angrier with every step while he made his way to the boarding house where Willard lived, Walter paid little attention to his surroundings. His main focus was on confronting his brother.

"Walter!" called Willard from across the street. He was walking hand-in-hand with Ruth.

There he is, seethed Walter as he changed directions and crossed over to where they were. *He'd better have a good excuse!*

"Where's Charlotte?" asked Ruth when he arrived at their location.

"We were just going for an ice cream," informed Willard. "Wanna join us?"

"Is something wrong?" questioned Ruth as she studied Walter's face. *Clearly, something is bothering him.*

"I need to speak with my brother alone for a moment," Walter advised her. "It won't take long."

"I'll wait for you at the ice cream shop," Ruth told Willard.

Waiting until she was out of hearing range, Walter turned to confront his brother. "How dare you double cross me like that!"

"What do you mean?" frowned Willard.

"You promised to give Mother that $500 last night," Walter reminded Willard while he glared at him.

"And I did," asserted Willard.

"According to her, you were never there," Walter challenged him. "She thought perhaps you might be planning on going there today. Hopefully that's true?"

"No, I swear," Willard promised him. "I gave Mother the $500 last night. She even had me join them for dinner. They had corned beef hash. You can ask Father if you don't believe me. He was there."

"Did he see you give her the money?"

"Well, no," admitted Willard. "Mother whispered to me that I was not to mention a word about the money to Father, and I think she stuffed it into her bra or something when he wasn't looking."

"You're a liar!" shouted Walter. He suddenly punched his brother right in the nose, knocking him down in the process.

Enraged, Willard stood and tried to punch him back but wasn't quick enough. Walter leaped out of the way. Willard wiped the blood from his nose and mouth on his sleeve and was ready to try again. Just then, Ruth rushed outside and grabbed Willard by the arms from behind to restrain him. "Stop! It isn't worth it, please don't fight."

Walter shook his head with disgust as he watched Ruth give her handkerchief to Willard to stop his nosebleed. Without another word, Walter turned and walked away. *It will be a cold day in hell when I send you that $250*, thought Walter.

The following morning began much like any other Monday for Bell. Frank had gone to work for the day and there would be no one to disturb her as she set up shop for her new job in the boys' old room. Making moonshine had been profitable while it lasted, but hiding the entire affair and its proceeds from Frank had not been easy. *Sewing for Madame Claudia and her girls is safer and will actually yield a more dependable profit,* she considered. Best of all, Frank would be none the wiser as to who her clients really were, only that any unexplained extra money would come from sewing she had taken in and was able to do at home. *Of course, I'll need to have some legitimate clients in order to maintain appearances,* smiled Bell when she thought of the new dishwasher and other modern conveniences that were ahead in her future. Maybe even one of those color televisions RCA was advertising for release by Christmas of 1953.

Should I spring for a taxi both to and from town? wondered Bell as she tucked the $500 cash into the top of her left silk glove and sat down for a moment to pour herself a shot of brandy.

Just then there was a knock on the door. *Oh, no, what now?* Bell sighed deeply while she set down the liquor decanter and answered the door. "Walter?"

"Before you say anything," blurted Walter, "here's the $500 we owe you for the car."

"Really?" questioned Bell. She raised one eyebrow and carefully took the money from him. "Are you sure about this?"

"Whatever else you might think about me, Mother, I'm a man of honor, and I pay my debts," explained Walter while he maintained eye contact with her.

"I appreciate your honesty," nodded Bell as she quickly put the money inside her black clutch purse, "but shouldn't your brother be paying his half?"

"He claims he already paid you for both of us," Walter reminded her.

Bell sadly shook her head to be convincing.

"Perhaps if Willard ever does decide to pay you his half, you can send me back my share?" proposed Walter.

"I'll need your new address," prompted Bell with a poker face.

"Of course," agreed Walter. "I'll be sure and send it to you as soon as I get there."

"Surely you're not still going to Texas?"

"That's the plan," responded Walter with a determined nod.

"How will you get there now?" queried Bell.

"I'll manage," Walter assured her.

"I see," frowned Bell. She was not pleased by the news.

"You and dad take care of yourselves," bid Walter as he turned and left. *There's no reason to tell her that Charlotte had given him money from her savings, or that their wedding had been postponed because of it.*

"You, too," muttered Bell while she closed the door, returned to the liquor table and poured herself a shot of brandy.

After downing the entire shot in one gulp, Bell picked up the receiver to her black rotary dial phone and dialed O for operator.

"Operator speaking, how may I help you?"

"I need a yellow cab sent to 143 Second Street," requested Bell.

"One should be there in 15 minutes," committed the operator.

"Thank you," replied Bell before hanging up.

Bell carefully cut out the newspaper advertisement showing new Singer sewing machine consoles complete with attachments for $175, neatly folded the article, and placed it inside her black clutch purse.

Pleased with herself when she returned from town with her new Singer sewing machine console, attachments, and several bolts of fabric, Bell decided to have the cab driver bring it all inside before agreeing to paying his fare.

"I normally don't move furniture for people," complained the man while he struggled to carry the heavy sewing machine console up the steps and into the house for her. He was a heavyset man in his mid-forties with a thick Italian accent, balding head, and panted heavily from the exertion.

"And the bolts of fabric, too?" Bell gave him a coy look.

"Yeah, yeah, the fabric, too," muttered the taxi driver as he made two more trips to get it all.

"I sure appreciate it," smiled Bell when she paid him.

"I'll just bet you do," snapped the man as he snatched the money from her. *No tip? That figures.*

The taxi driver had transported crates of moonshine for Bell in the past and now was afraid of getting into trouble for it if anyone found out. As a result, it hadn't been too difficult for Bell to persuade him to help her with the sewing machine and lavish bolts of fabric.

"Thank you!" called Bell, trying her best to be charming. *What luck to have gotten that particular taxi driver.*

"Yeah, save it for someone who cares," muttered the man while he climbed back into his taxi. *Hope to never see ya again, lady,* thought the man as he drove away.

Noticing the daily mail had been delivered, Bell decided to see what was there before setting up her new sewing machine.

Grabbing the stack from the mailbox as she headed back inside, Bell quickly flipped through the pile. Suddenly, she froze. *What's this? A wedding invitation?*

After tossing the rest of the mail onto a cabinet beside the liquor decanter, Bell took out her letter opener and slit open the invitation. She pursed her lips while she removed it from the envelope.

There it is, frowned Bell. Willard and Ruth were indeed to be married on August 31, 1952, during the morning church service. *Well, at least someone will be there,* snorted Bell as she tossed the invitation down onto the pile of mail. *Perhaps there's still a way to convince Ruth she's making a mistake? I already tried reasoning with Willard, but to no avail.*

Ruth brimmed with excitement while she looked forward to her wedding the following day. It was after 9:00 p.m. on Saturday night, August 30, 1952. She had just tried on her ballerina length dress of white embossed organdy over taffeta, styled with an oval neckline. Her close-fitting, white feather hat added to the effect. She would, of course, be wearing her mother's pearls, too.

If only Charlotte could be there, Ruth abruptly became sullen. They had planned for years to be each other's Maid of Honor. Now, with the feud going on between their prospective husbands, it would not be possible. Worse still, it was doubtful Willard's parents would be there, either.

At that moment, a popular song by Patti Page titled *"I Went to Your Wedding"* began playing on the radio. Ruth frowned as she realized she would not be at Charlotte's wedding, either.

The lyrics of the song clutched at her heart when they finally came to the part that said, "You came down the aisle, wearing a smile, a vision of loveliness. I uttered a sigh, and then whispered goodbye, goodbye to my happiness. Oh, your mother was crying, your father was crying, and I was crying too. The teardrops were falling. because we were losing you."

Am I really going to lose Charlotte as my friend? wondered Ruth when she shut off the radio.

There was a quiet knock on her door. *Who can be interrupting me at this hour?* wondered Ruth. *I can't allow Willard to see me in my dress before the wedding, it would be bad luck!*

"Ruth, it's me," came Bell's voice from behind the door.

Recognizing her voice at once, she was almost afraid to answer. Ruth cautiously opened the door a crack and peered through before opening it wider. "Bell, how nice to see you. Please, come in."

"Is *that* what you're wearing?" scowled Bell.

"Yes, why?" Ruth did not like the way she had asked.

"You should have come to me," explained Bell. "I could have made you something better than that."

"Well, this is what I'm wearing," informed Ruth while she frowned at her future mother-in-law. *Why did she come?*

"I want you to reconsider marrying Willard," Bell was direct. "I know you think this is the right thing to do now, but in time you'll come to regret it."

"I don't understand."

"Are you aware that Willard claims to have paid me $500 for the Ford?" questioned Bell.

"He *did* pay you that money!" shouted Ruth. "How dare you come here like this and accuse him of taking that money!"

"I could call the police, you know," threatened Bell with an even gaze of disapproval.

Ruth was visibly shaken. Her hands had begun to tremble as she pointed toward the door. "Get out!"

"Are you sure this is what you want to do?" Bell had a slight smirk on her face.

"Why are you doing this?" Ruth demanded. "You've hated me from the moment you met me. You haven't even given me a chance."

"I'm giving you a chance now, to change your mind," Bell informed Ruth while narrowing her eyes at her. "Otherwise, I can't guarantee what the consequences will be."

"Just wait until I tell Willard about this," Ruth warned her.

"He'll never believe you," snickered Bell when she turned to leave.

"We'll see about that," Ruth glared at Bell.

Without a further word, Bell sauntered from the room.

"Oooh!" exclaimed Ruth while she grabbed the door and slammed it shut behind Bell as hard as she could.

Ruth was somber while she waited with Charlotte for the Greyhound Bus that would take Charlotte to Texas, where she planned to finally marry Walter. It was a cold and blustery Monday morning on October 20, 1952. Charlotte's parents were there to see her off, as well.

With summer long gone, temperatures had started to become cooler. The mornings and evenings were darker. Fallen leaves carpeted driveways, lawns, pathways, and sidewalks. There was a fresh, earthy scent in the air. Rain threatened to fall at any moment.

Ruth wiped away tears with her handkerchief as the bus pulled up. *Will I ever be allowed by Willard to see my dear friend Charlotte again after this?*

"I guess this is it," mentioned Charlotte while she hugged Ruth and each of her parents farewell.

"I'm so sorry Willard couldn't be here," apologized Ruth.

"You mean *wouldn't*," grumbled Charlotte's father with a sidelong glance at Ruth while he gave his daughter Charlotte one last hug before her departure.

"Whatever happened between those boys?" asked Charlotte's mother when she hugged her daughter, too. "It seems such a shame that the twins won't even speak to one another now."

"I'll write you all about it," Charlotte promised her mother as she picked up her suitcase and climbed onto the bus.

Do I dare let my parents know I drained out most of my savings account to make this trip possible? wondered Charlotte.

After carefully placing her suitcase beneath her seat, Charlotte glanced through the bus window until spotting Ruth and her parents in the crowd, waving goodbye. Charlotte put her white-gloved hand up to the window and waved back while the bus pulled away.

5. Apple Valley Memory Care

Janette looked at herself in the mirror. The tight-fitting scrubs were definitely not her style.

"Turn around," encouraged Carolyn. "You look great."

"What if the facility requires its staff to wear certain colors there?" wondered Janette while she followed Carolyn from the dressing room of the uniform shop where Jim and Leticia were busy looking at nursing shoes and other footwear. "I've seen some places where they do that."

"Nice," approved Jim. "Same as the ones I saw 'em wearing when we popped by there just now to scout the place out."

"I wouldn't know," Janette was nervous. "You made us wait in the car."

"Trust me, it's an exact match," Jim assured Janette while he handed her a navy-blue pair of Skechers to try on. "Just like these."

"What size are they?"

"Size eight, same as your other shoes," Jim informed her.

"Jim is observant," commented Carolyn with a twinkle in her eye. *Sometimes too observant.*

"Must be the detective in me," laughed Jim.

"Seriously, Jim, what exactly did you say to those people at that place?" worried Janette when she sat down to try on the shoes.

"Nothing to blow your cover," promised Jim. "Just asked about someone I knew who wouldn't be there, and of course they weren't."

Carolyn chuckled and shook her head.

"And you're *sure* they all had on navy blue uniforms?" Janette asked again. "Won't they be suspicious if someone they've never seen before just shows up like this?"

"You look great," smiled Leticia.

"You'll probably need one of these, too," insisted Jim as he grabbed a new stethoscope from the wall display and began removing it from the package.

"Excuse me, Sir," objected the store clerk, "but you will need to make a purchase first before opening that item."

"Of course," apologized Jim. He pulled out a roll of bills and flirted with the woman. "How much?"

Speechless for several moments, the clerk finally regained her composure, went back to her station and pulled up the item on her touch screen cash register. "That particular stethoscope sells for $175, and since you've already removed it from the package . . .."

"That's fine," interrupted Jim while he handed her two hundred-dollar bills. "We'll take it. What about the other stuff?"

"Well, the Skechers are $85, the navy-blue scrub jacket is $50, and the bottoms are $48," mentioned the woman as she rung up the items. "Your total will be $358 plus tax. That comes to $383.95."

"That's almost $30 in taxes," Leticia whispered to Jim. "Are you sure we need all *new* stuff for this? That seems like an awful lot for an outfit Janette's only gonna wear one time."

"7.25% taxes to be exact, and yes, it is necessary," insisted Jim. "Besides, we really don't have time to be choosy at this point."

The clerk gave Jim a curious look.

"Keep the change," flirted Jim as he handed her two more hundred-dollar bills.

"Thank you, Sir," acknowledged the woman while she handed Jim a receipt for the purchase.

"My other clothes are still in there," Janette reminded them.

The clerk quickly handed her an empty bag.

"Thanks," acknowledged Janette as she took it from her and hurried back to the dressing room to gather her things.

"Did you happen to find out how late the Apple Valley Memory Care is open?" Carolyn suddenly asked Jim.

"Their main door is open until 4:00 p.m.," Jim advised her.

"I have 3:45 p.m. now," worried Leticia.

"Then we better not dally," urged Jim when Janette joined them. They hurriedly left the uniform shop.

"Hard to believe it's been a month already since our return from Zarahemla," commented Carolyn while they climbed into the sleek black Lamborghini.

"Yep," agreed Jim as he glanced at his smartwatch before starting up the Lamborghini, putting it into gear and driving away at an accelerated speed. "Hey, SIRI, show us the fastest route to Apple Valley Memory Care."

"Do we really need to go so fast?" scowled Carolyn.

"I'm afraid so," insisted Jim while he tore around a corner that came up faster than expected.

"Smooth ride," admired Janette as she crossed herself and reached for the closest handgrip.

"Indeed," grinned Jim when he glanced at her in the rearview mirror. "Handles like it's on rails."

"Next time I want to ride on rails, I'll be sure to take a train," commented Carolyn.

"Actually, it really is hard to believe it's the 7th of September already," muttered Jim while he made another abrupt turn.

"The complete date is September 7, 2023," volunteered SIRI, "and you are exceeding the posted speed limit by more than 25 mph."

"Guess she told you," snickered Carolyn. The ride was truly terrifying, to say the least.

"She's definitely not MIRA," sighed Jim while he slowed before turning onto a private road labeled "Apple Drive."

Apple trees lined the left side of the road and were fully loaded with Granny Smith apples, just waiting to be picked. Some had already fallen onto the ground where squirrels could be seen munching on them.

To their right was a bioswale of tall grasses growing in the long, channeled depression intended to funnel roadway runoff water during the rainy season. On the other side of the bioswale was a chain link fence separating it from a track and field on which several high school students were currently jogging. Beyond the track stood several similar-looking buildings, including what appeared to be a gymnasium. Bleachers and a baseball diamond at the far end of the track were empty.

A quarter of a mile down the scenic drive stood Apple Valley Memory Care. Jim pulled into the roundabout at its entrance and came to a stop beneath its tall covered carport by the front door. A custom-crafted granite brick wall on the bottom half of the entire building and also covering the square support columns of the carport gave the place a rustic touch of elegance. The upper half of the structure was painted in a desert sand color with red cedar trim, and its roof was completely done in red tile roofing. Ornamental flowerbed grasses swayed gently in the breeze while behind them grew neatly pruned barberry shrubs, rhododendrons and juniper bushes that hugged the granite brick wall.

"You have five minutes to report for your shift," Jim informed Janette as he hopped out and hurriedly opened her door.

"My shift?" questioned Janette with a raised eyebrow.

"Your name is Wanda and today is your first day," Jim quickly briefed her. "The Rosewood Healthcare Staffing Agency has sent you."

"And you're only telling me this *now*?" questioned Janette. "I thought I was supposed to be a volunteer."

"There's no time for further explanation," replied Jim with a wink. "A woman named Veronica will be there, waiting for you."

"Just how long is my shift?" Janette demanded of Jim.

"Until 4:00 a.m.," Jim informed her. "Sorry, but there was no other way to get you inside."

"And just what happens when they expect me back tomorrow?" queried Janette as she headed for the thick glass front door.

"The agency will send someone else, of course," promised Jim. "Now hurry!"

A loud buzzing sound indicated the entrance doors had been unlocked from inside, without the need of pressing a code into the keypad beside it.

"Tell Carolyn she owes me big for this one," Janette instructed Jim when she opened the door and started to go inside.

"I'll be sure to let her know," agreed Jim.

"And," added Janette, "they'd better have a dinner break pretty soon. I mean it."

"I'm sure they do," chuckled Jim as he returned to the Lamborghini and paused before getting back in. *It will be a long night for poor Janette, but well worth it if Willard is actually there.*

In the main lobby of Apple Valley Memory Care was a large couch and two matching overstuffed chairs covered in rust-colored leather. In front of them was a hand-crafted oak coffee table cleverly designed from gnarled tree limbs supporting a cross section of the tree from which they were created. Its surface was highly shellacked and inlaid with a pair of matching horseshoes; a stack of healthcare magazines sat on top. To one side of the area was a gas fireplace whose hearth and walls were paved with granite bricks similar to those on the outside of the building. On its butcherblock mantle stood a red ceramic vase, containing a bouquet of realistic-looking artificial yellow roses.

"Hello, you must be Wanda?" greeted a middle-aged Hispanic woman with long straight black hair neatly woven into a braid that hung to her waist.

"Uh, yeah, that's me," lied Janette as she nodded at the woman. "But, I usually go by my middle name. You can call me Janette."

"Janette," smiled the woman while she studied her new clothing. "Is this your first job as a Nurse's Aide?"

"Sorry, but yes, it is," replied Janette.

"No worries," chuckled Veronica. "Very few of the Nurse's Aides ever last very long around here, anyway. By the way, my name is Veronica. And that's what I go by."

"I understand my shift lasts until 4:00 a.m.," mentioned Janette.

"Don't worry, you'll have two 15 minutes breaks and a lunch hour half way through," promised Veronica.

"I don't get to eat lunch until 10:00 p.m.?" questioned Janette with a worried look on her face.

"That's correct, but you do get a break at 7:00 p.m. and could eat something then," suggested Veronica. "And, of course, your other break will be at 1:00 a.m. in the morning, if you need one."

"And I don't suppose you have a cafeteria?"

"There is a dining area for the patients," laughed Veronica, "but staff members either bring their own food or can call for delivery. Tony's Pizza isn't too far away and delivers 24/7."

Janette appeared relieved. *Hopefully, I have enough money on me to cover it, though I can probably just use Jim's credit card.*

"To your right is the Director's office, though she's already gone home for the day," mentioned Veronica, "and this other office is where the Business Manager sits when she's here."

"Let me guess, she's gone home for the day, too?" Janette hoped her question didn't sound too sarcastic.

"That's right," confirmed Veronica. "Same with the receptionist, whose counter is over there, by the security doors."

"Security doors?"

"One for each side," clarified Veronica. "The more violent patients are on the north side. Those are the ones who act out physically and occasionally have violent mood swings."

Janette's eyes opened wide with concern.

"Don't worry," Veronica assured her. "We'll be working the south side tonight. The majority of them are just confused most of the time, but rarely dangerous."

Janette suddenly spotted a sign-in sheet at the receptionist counter. "Am I supposed to sign in?"

"Yes, we all do," replied Veronica while she grabbed a pen from behind the counter and handed it to her. "Just the date, time in, your name and cell number for now, and the time out when you leave."

"What if I don't know my cell number?"

"You can leave that blank."

"And these other questions about whether I've been exposed to anyone with COVID?"

"Just leave that blank, too," answered Veronica. "That was mostly for during the pandemic. Masks are no longer required, either, but there is an expectation that any time you have a fever or are not feeling well, you call in sick and stay home."

"Understandable," agreed Janette.

"And, before we go inside the secured area," continued Veronica, "this is the laptop you will be using."

Janette watched while she pulled it out from behind the receptionist counter before handing it to her.

"All patients, their room numbers, what medications they take, or anything else you might need to know about them is on their electronic chart that can be pulled up on that laptop," described Veronica while she opened her own laptop and set it on the counter. "You might want to open yours so you can follow along."

Janette quickly opened her laptop and set it on the counter beside Veronica's. "All the patients' charts are here?"

"It's a secure system, and yes, they are," responded Veronica. "For example, patient number three is a woman named Lola. She was put here by her family five years ago, because she suffers from dementia. Lola is very sweet, kind, and other than being delusional about her reality, is little trouble."

"No physical problems to speak of, then?" asked Janette.

"Other than her dementia or the expected physical maladies for a person of her age, no," confirmed Veronica. "But, patient number 16 is a woman named Gayle, and she can be verbally abusive to the male workers."

"Verbally abusive?" Janette raised an eyebrow.

"Click here for a profile of the patient," demonstrated Veronica, "and here for a list of their medications."

"She gets donepezil?"

"Yes. Donepezil is an FDA-approved medication used for the treatment of dementia and Alzheimer's disease in mild, moderate, and even severe cases," described Veronica.

"Does it help?"

"Although there is currently no evidence to suggest donepezil can alter the progression of the disease, it can improve cognition and behavior, thereby alleviating certain symptoms," recapped Veronica.

"Making the patients easier to manage," assumed Janette.

"Exactly," smiled Veronica. "And, since you're medication certified, your job will be to assist me with whatever I need while we're on this shift together. I may ask you to help me count out pills or other supplies for the med cart, or to help me with emergencies."

"What kind of emergencies?" frowned Janette. *What has Jim gotten me into?* worried Janette. *He knows perfectly well I'm not medication certified!*

"Just about anything you can imagine," responded Veronica. "Helping me administer medication, and occasionally changing briefs or bedding, cleaning up messes, assisting with toileting, calling for extra help when needed, that type of thing."

"Isn't there a housekeeping staff for some of that?" pressed Janette. *This is definitely not something I'm prepared to do!*

"Of course, and part of their duties include laundry and cleaning the rooms, but they can only be in so many places at once. Any one of us must be prepared to cover for one another in any given situation," replied Veronica. "It is the cleanliness, comfort and well-being of the patient that comes first, after all."

"Understandable."

"There are also kitchen staff who prepare and serve all the meals, but as I mentioned, that food is strictly for the patients," elaborated Veronica. "Most of whom eat in the dining area when they are able."

"One last thing before we go inside the patient area," added Veronica. "The entire building is one large oblong rectangle, and the north and south sides are virtually identical in layout; there are 30 rooms on each side."

"That many," mused Janette.

"Yes, and you must always make sure none of the patients are standing just inside the door, waiting to try and escape."

"Just like at a maximum-security prison," joked Janette.

"Pretty much," acknowledged Veronica as she began entering numbers into the keypad. "The combination changes each day, but will always start with the month, then the day, and finally the last two digits of the year. For example, today is September 7, 2023, so the code would be 090723."

"Don't the patients ever figure that out?"

"Sometimes they do, which is why there is another keypad at the front door with an entirely different combination," described Veronica.

"Which is?" prompted Janette.

"Which is why one of our senior staff would need to let you back inside if you should go out during your lunch break," smiled Veronica.

"I see," nodded Janette. *The woman obviously isn't going to tell me what it is.*

"Just make sure you keep in contact with one of us at all times with your walkie if you leave your assigned area," added Veronica when she handed one to Janette. "Keep it in your pocket."

"Tell me again how the pizza guy is able to deliver here?" asked Janette as she glanced at the lobby one last time before following Veronica into the secure area.

"They call us and let us know it's out there when they leave it by the front door," replied Veronica.

"Looks like the residents are eating now," observed Janette while they walked into the dining area.

"Everyone, this is Janette," announced Veronica.

About a dozen wooden dining tables, each seating four people, were positioned in various locations within the room. Picture windows on one side of the space overlooked an outdoor garden surrounded entirely by the south end of the building.

Janette felt an unexpected wave of compassion for the elderly individuals gazing at her with mild curiosity. Some stared off into space while others picked aimlessly at their food. Swallowing was difficult for some of them.

"Hello," said Janette in a loud voice.

"It's about time you came to see me," scolded one woman as she struggled from her seat, grabbed her walker, and headed toward Janette.

"That's Hope," introduced Veronica. "She thinks everyone is her daughter."

"Oh honey, I love you so much," proclaimed Hope when she suddenly let go of the walker and gave Janette a hug.

Veronica mouthed the words *just play along* so Janette could see and understand.

"Me, too," replied Janette while she hugged Hope back. "I'm so glad I was able to come see you tonight."

"Everyone, this is my daughter," called Hope as she started pulling Janette toward the table to introduce her to the others.

"Hope," interrupted Veronica, "can we come and see you in your room after you finish eating your supper?"

"Of course," agreed Hope. She finally let go of Janette, grabbed onto her walker, and returned to her place at the table.

"Most of their family members never bother to come see them," Veronica explained to Janette. "They probably figure their loved one won't remember anyway."

"How sad!" Janette felt a tear escape the corner of her right eye.

"And the indoor garden over there is a place where residents can go if they wish without being able to wander off," continued Veronica.

"It's beautiful," admired Janette. *But still a prison.*

Just then, a male food worker began putting slices of apple pie in front of each resident in the dining area. When he got to Gayle, she suddenly punched him in the arm as hard as she could and warned him, "Get that away from me! You come near me again and I'll cut you up and feed you to the hogs."

"Oh my," whispered Janette while she followed Veronica from the dining area to a long hallway just beyond it.

"As you can see, there are individual rooms for each resident," motioned Veronica, "and their names are in holders mounted on the door outside their rooms."

"Where does that go?" queried Janette upon noticing an exit door at the far end of the hall.

"I'll show you," replied Veronica as she started down the hall.

"What if one of them tries to open an outside door?"

"Then an alarm will sound." Veronica demonstrated when they got there.

"It doesn't actually open then?"

"Only with one of these," smiled Veronica. She pulled out her name badge and swiped it by a kiosk near the door to make the alarm stop ringing.

"What if there's an actual fire and none of the workers is around to let them out?" inquired Janette.

"Hopefully that will never happen," responded Veronica when she turned the corner and headed down the next hallway.

"Do I get a badge?" asked Janette.

"Not on your first day," replied Veronica, "but hopefully they can have it ready for you by tomorrow."

"I see."

"And the recreation area here at this end of the south side is where residents are welcome to sit and watch television, or draw in coloring books at the table when our craft lady comes out each week," elaborated Veronica. "We also take some of the residents – at least those who are able – for bus rides in the country, or to see Christmas tree lane each year. Once in a while, they get to eat out someplace, or even ride a tram through the zoo."

"At least they have something to do," recognized Janette.

"We try," Veronica assured her as she turned yet another corner and headed down a third hallway.

"So, the hallways form a big oblong rectangle that completely surround the garden area," realized Janette.

"Precisely, and this one leads back to the dining room where we started out," confirmed Veronica. "And the woman heading this way is Joella; she's always trying to find a way out."

"Poor thing," sympathized Janette.

"Her husband comes every Saturday to visit her," described Veronica, "but Joella thinks every day is Saturday and often waits just inside the exit door. She also knows about the code, but since she never knows what day it is, almost never gets it right."

"I wonder why he doesn't keep her at home?" wondered Janette out loud.

"Sometimes dementia patients can get confused, wander off and get lost, and their caregivers can't possibly watch them 24/7.

Even they have to sleep at night," described Veronica. "Hi Joella, this is Janette."

"Hi Janette," nodded Joella while she shuffled past them without further comment and continued down the hallway toward the exit door.

"Another danger of having them at home," continued Veronica, "is that sometimes they will turn on a burner on the stove and forget they are cooking something. Many household fires are caused like that."

"What a scary thought," realized Janette.

"They also can be a danger to themselves or others when allowed to be around sharp objects or even simple household cleaners," added Veronica. "Here, we are able to make sure those things are not in their rooms, and occasionally have to send things home with family members that could pose a danger to them if left here."

Janette suddenly spotted a room with Willard's name on it. "What about this man? I don't recall seeing any men in the dining area."

"Some patients choose to eat in their rooms," clarified Veronica. "This man is in pretty bad shape, though, as you'll see when we do our rounds later on."

"What about nail grooming kits?" questioned Janette. "Does someone come in and give them pedicures?"

"Actually, they do," confirmed Veronica. "We also have a hair dresser and a barber for the men who shaves them when needed."

"Wouldn't you want them to try and do what they can for themselves for as long as they can?" Janette grilled her.

"One man's family smuggled in a shaving kit for him," recalled Veronica, "and later we found him trying to brush his teeth with a razor blade. Thankfully, his injuries were treatable."

"Oh, my God!" exclaimed Janette.

"We periodically do room searches, too, just in case anything dangerous might be in them," elaborated Veronica.

"Prudent," agreed Janette.

"Another thing we do in our spare time is make sure the room numbers are written on each piece of clothing or bedding that belongs to each resident."

"Why would you need to do that?" frowned Janette.

"You'd be surprised what can get lost in laundry," answered Veronica. "Joella is also a kleptomaniac, goes into other rooms and takes whatever she fancies. One time she stole another resident's white fleece blanket and it was not until it made its way to laundry that it was identified by the room number written on its tag and returned to its owner. Compression socks are the worst, always getting lost."

"And you let Joella get away with stealing stuff?"

"We try to stop her when we can, but it's not her fault. It's part of the disease and the way it affects her," clarified Veronica. "We also try to make sure the family members keep any jewelry or other valuables at home, as we can never guarantee something won't get lost here."

"Remind me to never get dementia!" exclaimed Janette while she followed Veronica through yet another set of locked doors on the other side of the dining area.

"Amen to that," agreed Veronica as she made sure the door was securely locked behind them. "Over there is the laundry area, and this is our pharmacy."

Two med carts could be seen parked in the middle of the room with their brakes engaged. On top of each one lay various first aid supplies, including Band-Aids, gauze, scissors, paper tape, cotton balls, hydrogen peroxide, tweezers, hand sanitizer, paper towels, a pitcher of water, small plastic cups, and packets of saltine crackers. Also, on top of each med cart was a small workspace, the size of a laptop. Numbered medication drawers covered their sides.

"Most of these are loaded up already," indicated Veronica, "but before we head out onto the floor to begin giving meds, we need to do one final check to be sure everything is here on our cart. Scott and McKayla are responsible for the other cart."

"I see, one cart for each side," acknowledged Janette.

"Exactly."

"How do we check it?" questioned Janette.

"You will look up each patient on your laptop and read to me the medications they are supposed to get," clarified Veronica, and then I will check that resident's drawer on the cart."

"Starting with number one?"

"That works," agreed Veronica. "Just the evening ones."

Janette located patient number one. "Okay, it says here that Alice is patient number one. Her nighttime medications include:

Donepezil, 10 mg; Memantine, 7 mg; Metopropol, 25 mg; Combigan and Latanoprost, 1 drop each eye; and Lavothyroxine, 25 mcg."

"There should be some vitamins listed there, too," encouraged Veronica. "Even those require a doctor's prescription when we administer them."

"Okay," sighed Janette. "Let's see. Alice gets Vitamin D3, 1000 IU; Vitamin C, 1000 mg; and a Vitamin B complex."

After making sure the other 29 drawers were correct, Veronica motioned for Janette to follow her back to the patient area. "And of course, once we're out there, the carts can never be left unattended."

"Understandable," mumbled Janette. "Break's not until 7:00?"

"That's right," smiled Veronica, "and if we're lucky we can get all the meds distributed by then. It's important to try and administer them as soon after they've eaten as possible."

"Of course," Janette rolled her eyes.

"Here," Veronica suddenly grabbed a packet of saltine crackers from the cart. "Normally we're not supposed to eat these, but if you're that hungry, I'm sure we can spare a couple of crackers."

"It shows, huh?"

"My first night working graveyard shift, I sat down for break and fell fast asleep," chuckled Veronica. "I wouldn't recommend it."

"Veronica, this is Scott," came a voice on their walkies. "We need immediate help with number 47."

Veronica quickly took out her walkie and responded. "We're just starting meds, can't McKayla help you?"

"She's busy changing number 32," replied Scott. "I need you to come and help me NOW."

"You remain here with the cart," Veronica instructed Janette. "Just make sure none of the patients take anything from it. I'll be back as soon as I can."

The moment Veronica was out of view, Janette started to wheel the cart toward Willard's room. *After all, I do need to keep the cart with me. Hopefully, I'll be able to speak with him.*

The plush red carpets with repeating golden paisley patterns on them reminded Janette of something that belonged on a cruise ship from the past, especially with the green and yellow braid designs along both edges. The thick carpet pile did not make it easy to wheel the med cart. Olive green and sage colored wall panels on either side of the hallway were adorned with paintings and enlarged photographs from the 1920s, most of people enjoying everyday life at its finest. Each wooden frame was hand-carved with floral patterns and looked expensive. Speakers mounted on the ceiling throughout the building continuously played music from that era, as well. At the moment, a song called *"Let Me Call You Sweetheart"* was playing.

I feel like I'm on the Titanic, smiled Janette as she shook her head. *Hopefully. this music will not be playing all night long.*

Once she reached the far end, Janette looked both ways to be sure the coast was clear before knocking on Willard's door. "Willard?"

"Come in," came a slurred voice.

Janette pushed open his door and pulled the med cart in behind her. "Time for your meds, Willard. My name is Janette."

Willard was unable to sit up without assistance, and was obviously in pain. "You're new." He sounded as if he might have had a stroke at some point, and was difficult to understand.

Janette quickly pulled up his profile on the laptop, which she had sitting on top of the med cart. Congestive heart failure, dementia, bed sores, and type two diabetes. *Oh no! He will need an insulin shot.*

"Willard, I see here that you get an insulin shot, but we are going to have to wait for the nurse to give you that."

"That's fine," muttered Willard. Speaking was difficult for him.

"Do you remember your daughter Leticia?"

Willard opened his eyes wider and looked at Janette with curiosity. "You know my daughter?"

"Yes, I do," Janette assured him.

"I thought she wanted nothing more to do with me."

"That's not true," Janette promised him. "In fact, she's been looking for you for quite some time, and wants very much to see you."

Unexpectedly, Willard began clutching his chest and mumbled, "I think I'm having a heart attack. Oooh! Oooh! Help me!" His words were slurred and difficult to understand.

Janette immediately took out her walkie and pressed the button. "I'm in room 23 and Willard is having a heart attack. Hurry!"

"Call 911 right now!" came the voice of Veronica on the other end of the walkie.

"On it," promised Janette while she took out her cellphone and dialed 911. It rang only once before being answered.

"911, what's your emergency?"

"We have a patient here at Apple Valley Memory Care in room 23, and he's having a heart attack," described Janette. "Hurry!"

"I need to verify your name and cellphone number," informed the operator.

"My name is Janette, but I'm not sure of my cellphone number."

"That's okay, I have you number, Janette. Someone is on the way," the operator advised her. "But I will need you to remain with the patient and stay on this line until they arrive."

"I'm not sure how they will get inside this place," wailed Janette. "I'm gonna need to go and let them in!"

"Don't worry, ma'am, our paramedics have override codes for all the doors there. Please stay where you are."

"Okay, okay," agreed Janette.

"What is the patient's name?"

"Willard Bennett," muttered Janette as she gently put one hand on his neck to feel for a pulse.

"Can you tell if Willard is still breathing?"

"I'm not sure," moaned Janette.

"Do you know CPR?"

"Not really," admitted Janette. Tears began to stream down her cheeks. "I do have a stethoscope, though."

"Do you know how to use it?" questioned the 911 operator.

"Yes!" screamed Janette as she put in the earpieces before placing the diaphragm of the stethoscope on Willard's chest so that she could listen. "I'm checking him for a heartbeat now."

After several moments, the 911 operator prompted, "Janette, are you getting anything?"

"Yes, he's still alive," responded Janette with a deep sigh of relief. "I think he's just unconscious."

"Try to wake him."

"Willard? Can you hear me?" hollered Janette. "Help is coming, please stay with me, Willard. Willard?"

Just then, the paramedics arrived. Janette gingerly wheeled her med cart out of their way. One of the paramedics began questioning her while the other paramedic checked on Willard.

"Willard, are you having chest pains?" asked the first paramedic.

"Oooh!" moaned Willard when his eyes fluttered open again; he nodded affirmatively.

After quickly doing an EKG to check Willard's heart rhythm and to confirm whether the symptoms were due to a heart attack, the paramedic spoke into a walkie clipped to his chest.

"I have an elderly male age 91 who's had a heart attack. Giving him oxygen now," described the paramedic.

Meanwhile, the other paramedic put an IV into Willard's arm, and advised into his walkie, "Administering morphine."

The first paramedic added, "putting a glyceryl trinitrate tablet under his tongue and an aspirin to chew on."

"We need to get you to the hospital, Willard," the other paramedic informed him while they carefully transferred him to a stretcher.

Veronica raced toward room 23, just in time to see Willard being wheeled away. Then, turning to Janette, she questioned, "What happened? What were you doing in his room?"

"I thought I heard him calling for help," lied Janette.

Veronica nodded and sighed deeply. "You did the right thing."

"And, where were *you*?" demanded Janette.

"Number 47 didn't make it," responded Veronica as she sadly shook her head. "Someone from Rosewood Mortuary will be here within the hour to retrieve her body."

"Does this kind of thing happen very often around here?" frowned Janette.

"Thankfully not," Veronica assured her while she put a comforting hand on Janette's shoulder, "but sometimes it does."

What will I tell Leticia? wondered Janette. *I have to call Jim as soon as possible to let him know what's happening.*

* * *

Charlotte woke with a start when the Greyhound bus pulled into the station at Wichita Falls, Texas. Stiff from riding for 2½ days on the bus, she stood and stretched before retrieving her suitcase from beneath the seat. It was already dark outside. *Hopefully Walter will be there waiting for me. What will I do if he isn't?*

Charlotte removed her suitcase from beneath the seat and watched for an opening in the aisle full of passengers waiting to disembark. *Oh, my purse!* Charlotte turned back to retrieve it from the seat. *Thank goodness! I wouldn't want to lose that!*

When she finally made her way to the front of the bus, Charlotte tried to see through the windows on either side, but it was too dark to make out the individual faces of those waiting for their loved ones to get off the bus.

Nearly tripping on the steep bus steps because of her high heeled shoes, Charlotte managed to climb off with her suitcase in one hand and was tightly clutching her purse in the other. Studying the crowd for Walter's bright red hair, she easily spotted him. Quickly tucking her purse under the arm carrying her suitcase, Charlotte began to wave with her other arm.

The moment Walter saw Charlotte's white gloved hand waving at him, he pushed his way through the crowd towards her. *Thank God she's safe,* thought Walter when he finally reached her. He looked handsome in his Air Force Uniform. After removing his hat, he threw his arms around her, pulled her close and declared, "I've missed you!"

"I've missed you, too," blushed Charlotte as Walter gave her a long, lingering kiss. He hadn't said anything about her two-piece white wool suit or how trim she looked in its form-fitting skirt, but this was the only thing she could find on short notice that was in her budget and it would have to serve as her wedding dress.

"Come on, you two," prompted a tall handsome black man who suddenly stepped from the shadows. He was also dressed in an Air Force Uniform.

"Charlotte, this is my friend Montu," Walter introduced him. *I'll have to tell Charlotte later about the incredible coincidence of running into Montu, and that he's the very same child who untied my wrists so long ago when I was left in a culvert by my brother Willard and the Scaglioni gang.*

"Nice to meet you, ma'am," grinned Montu.

"Same here. Are you two in the same unit?" asked Charlotte.

"We were in basic together," Walter informed her.

"That's right," declared Montu. "And 'twas in de summer of 1948 when President Truman signed an Order sayin' we could."

"That we could serve together," clarified Walter, "and that there would be equal treatment within the military services without regard to race, color, religion, or national origin."

"I see," nodded Charlotte as she shook Montu's hand. "Thank you for your service."

"My pleasure," beamed Montu.

"Montu's mother has an extra room where you can stay tonight," Walter mentioned to Charlotte.

"That's right, and tomorrow's your big day," Montu grinned even wider.

Yes, tomorrow is the big day, October 24, 1952. Walter and I will finally be married, thought Charlotte as she smiled, blushed and gazed lovingly at Walter.

Before Walter could pick up Charlotte's suitcase, Montu had already snatched it and was headed toward a nearby bus stop.

"Weren't you able to get a car yet?" Charlotte whispered to Walter with concern while they followed Montu toward the bus stop.

Walter shook his head in the negative. "It took everything I had left just to rent the apartment, but I get paid next week. Then, all we'll have to do is pick out a car and put a down payment on it."

"And still buy groceries," Charlotte reminded him, "but I'm sure I can get a job somewhere."

Walter nodded, but he clearly wasn't pleased about his new bride being forced to work. *A woman's place is in the home.*

Just then, it started to sprinkle; Charlotte pulled her sky-blue scarf up over her hair.

"The bus should be along most any minute, ma'am," hoped Montu when they joined him at the bus stop. Charlotte's suitcase was sitting by the bench. "Please, y'all sit down."

"I'd better not," declined Charlotte while she smoothed her white wool skirt and nervously fidgeted with her purse. "I've been trying to keep this outfit clean, as it's going to be my wedding dress."

"The bench does look pretty wet," apprised Walter while he put his arm around her. "I think I'll stand, too."

"And you know how 'em sergeants be if you gets your uniform dirty," grinned Montu, who also remained standing.

When the bus pulled up, Montu stood aside to wait for Walter and Charlotte to get on first.

Upon noticing Montu, the driver advised them, "There'll be a black bus along in another 45 minutes."

"This one will do just fine," Walter informed him while he and Charlotte climbed aboard with Montu closely following them.

"Fare's 8-cents apiece, 17-cents for two, or a quarter for three," mentioned the driver when he realized Montu was carrying a suitcase and appeared to be with them.

"Thank you," nodded Walter while he dug some change from his pocket and put a quarter into the fare box.

"On this bus, you three will need to sit in the back," stipulated the bus driver. "If you plan to sit together, that is."

The bus driver was an overweight, middle-aged white man with greasy blonde hair slicked back into a pompadour hairstyle. His bloodshot blue eyes and the ruddy tone of his face suggested he might be a heavy drinker. His bluish gray, double-breasted uniform jacket was rumpled and in desperate need of ironing; an unpleasant body odor emanated from his person.

Walter frowned at the man but nodded in acknowledgement before he and Charlotte proceeded towards the rear of the bus. *I don't want any trouble.*

"Y'all musta never heard o' President Truman," Montu said to the bus driver as he raised his eyebrows.

"This ain't the military, mister," growled the bus driver while he glared at Montu with disapproval. "It's a city bus."

Walter hurried up to the front of the bus and put a hand on Montu's arm. He gently shook his head as if to say, *it isn't worth it.*

Montu gave the bus driver a final glance of displeasure but refrained from continuing the conversation and followed Walter to the back of the bus where Charlotte was waiting for them.

"Thank you," said Charlotte when Montu placed her suitcase beneath the rear seat of the bus where they sat together.

"You're most welcome, ma'am," replied Montu. "Is it just me, or did that driver man smell like the rotten side of a stink bug?"

Charlotte, Walter and Montu suddenly began laughing together and couldn't stop for several minutes. *Good thing the driver didn't hear Montu's remark!* thought Charlotte.

Two weeks had passed since Walter and Charlotte's simple wedding ceremony before a Justice of the Peace. Montu and his mother had been their only witnesses.

Grateful for the black and white snapshot Montu's mother had taken of them on their wedding day, Charlotte proudly displayed her copy of the photo in a small frame that hung on the wall of their scantily furnished apartment.

The rundown single-story quadplex apartment was located near a set of railroad tracks where hobos sometimes wandered. Charlotte felt unsafe when there by herself, especially with no phone or car. It was a 1½ mile walk down the road from Sheppard Air Force Base where Walter spent most of his time. Occasionally, he was late getting home, like tonight. The dirt sidewalks in-between the two locations were bedecked with potholes that filled with mud and were slippery when it rained. Charlotte's 11-mile bus ride to Wichita Falls for her secretarial job each week day involved riding on the same bus they had ridden with Montu when arriving. Worse still, it was driven by that same bus driver. *What a horrible man,* thought Charlotte.

With pencil in hand, she sat down at the small kitchen table their landlord had lent them. He had also been kind enough to lend them two rickety wooden chairs. Otherwise, the two single beds, one dresser and a refrigerator were the only other furniture in the apartment. *At least there's indoor plumbing*, thought Charlotte. An electric single burner sat on the kitchen counter, purchased from their meager earnings, and was their only way of cooking.

"Dear Mom and Dad," wrote Charlotte. "Here is a copy of our wedding picture I want you to have. Wish you could have been there. Walter's friend Montu and his mother were our witnesses, and we were married by a Justice of the Peace."

Charlotte paused to consider what she would say next. *Should I tell them about the situation with Walter's brother?*

Sharpening her pencil before continuing, Charlotte wrote, "I'm not sure how to tell you this, but remember that 1939 Ford that Walter and his brother were buying from his folks? Well, his mother expected them to pay her half of the $1,000 they sold it for, so Willard gave her the whole $500 for both him and Walter. Once Walter got here, he was supposed to send $250 back to Willard as soon as he had it. That way, we would have enough to get settled first. Unfortunately, their mother claims Willard never paid her at all and accused him of keeping the money for himself, so Walter ended up giving his entire $500 to their mother, leaving him with nothing."

Charlotte absentmindedly tapped the pencil's eraser on the table for several moments before continuing the letter. "The question is," she wrote, "who is lying? His brother? Or their mother? Either way, I was forced to use what was left in my savings to get us established here, but I have a job now as a secretary at an insurance company, so am getting by. We hope to put a down payment on a car of our own soon, when we both have the day off. Love you lots, Charlotte."

Upon hearing Walter's footsteps on the wooden porch, Charlotte swiftly folded the letter she was writing and stuffed it inside her Bible. *Walter doesn't need to know what I wrote to my parents.*

"Hello," called Walter when he opened the door and came inside, took off his hat, and gave Charlotte a hug. "I missed you!"

"I missed you, too," smiled Charlotte as she hugged him back.

"What's for dinner?"

"Macaroni and cheese with canned peas again," apologized Charlotte. "I'm sorry."

"Beats starving," assured Walter while he sat down at the table and waited for Charlotte to serve him. "Reading the good book again?"

"I try to read the Bible as often as I can," replied Charlotte as she picked it up and moved it to the bedroom to make room for their dinner. She then brought the plates of food and put them on the table. "Sorry it's cold."

"No worries," responded Walter. "I'm sorry for being late."

After blessing the food, they began to eat. Neither of them was thrilled about the meal, but grateful for tap water to wash it down.

"Anything new?" questioned Charlotte.

Walter hesitated before responding. "I went to see the Chaplain today."

"The Chaplain? Whatever for?"

"What if Willard was telling the truth?" proposed Walter. "What if I really do owe him $250?"

Charlotte became quiet and picked at her peas.

"I got paid today and an E-1 with less than two years of service only gets $83.20 a month, before taxes."

Charlotte took a sip of water and swallowed hard.

"Rent here is $175 and we were lucky to find it," continued Walter. "Most places are $250 or more."

"My new job pays $200 a month," Charlotte reminded him before taking another bite of peas. "That'll give us $283.20."

"Before taxes," pointed out Walter as he took a bite of cold macaroni and cheese before making a face.

Charlotte went to a drawer in the kitchen, took out a piece of paper and a pencil, and returned to the table.

"Let's see, if we multiply $283.20 by 12, it comes to $3,387.40 that we make together before taxes," she continued while scribbling the estimate. "And, if I'm not mistaken, our tax bracket will be about 25% that goes to the government."

"24.6%," corrected Walter as he took the piece of paper from her and continued the calculations. "Taxes on that amount would be $883.30, leaving us with $2,504 income per year, and divided by 12 that give us $208.66 per month to live on."

Charlotte looked like she was going to be sick.

"$208.66 minus our rent of $175 comes to roughly $33.66 left each month for groceries or anything else we might need," concluded Walter. "I figure if we can put away at least $10.41 each month, there should be enough to pay Willard his $250 in 24 months."

"I hope you like macaroni and cheese," muttered Charlotte while she sadly shook her head. *What are we going to do?*

"Once I hit two years, they'll start paying me $91 per month," Walter informed her, "but if I work hard enough, perhaps I can get promoted to an E-2 or even an E-3, and with each promotion the pay rate goes up, too. An E-7 can get as much as $206.39 per month, even with less than two years of service."

"What's that, a General?" teased Charlotte to try and lighten the mood.

"An E-7 is a Master Sergeant," revealed Walter, "but I have no intention of being in for more than four years anyway. It's doubtful I'm going to make General."

"Jobs in the private sector pay a lot more," mentioned Charlotte while she finished off the last of her peas.

"My brother has a job welding and gets good money," added Walter. "He'll be okay, but I still feel bad that it will take me a couple of years to make this right with him. That's just the way it has to be."

It was September of 1954. Nearly two years had passed since Charlotte and Walter were married in Texas. Next month would be their second wedding anniversary.

Not only had Walter managed to become an E-4 in record time, but had just learned he was being transferred to Norton Air Force Base by the end of the week. *Charlotte will be pleased about moving closer to Ashton and to her parents*, thought Walter. *Sadly, that also means moving closer to my parents, as well.*

The 1½ mile walk down the road from Sheppard Air Force Base to their rundown quadplex apartment seemed to stretch into infinity. At the moment, it was dusty and dry. Leaves on several nearby trees had already started to turn colors. The bouquet of sunflowers he'd picked from a nearby field were starting to wilt so he was anxious to get them to Charlotte soon. *At least it isn't raining yet,* sighed Walter. *The last thing I need now is to step into some pothole and possibly sprain my ankle.* Nevertheless, dark gray anvil-shaped clouds with flattened tops were beginning to form overhead.

If I hurry, perhaps I can make it to the bus stop in time to greet Charlotte and walk her home, hoped Walter while he glanced at the angry-looking sky above. *Will there be another tornado?* The last one had come way too close for comfort!

Just as he was about to give up hope and head for home, Walter spotted the bus headed towards him. *That will be Charlotte,* smiled Walter as he tried his best to straighten up one of the wilted sunflowers that had a mind of its own. *At least Charlotte had the option of choosing the early bus, regardless of what category these Texans seem to feel it belongs in,* considered Walter.

Brakes squealed loudly as the poorly maintained bus came to a stop and opened its doors. *Ah, yes, there's that bus driver again. The same one who picked us up when we first arrived two years ago. Him, we won't miss,* chuckled Walter as Charlotte climbed down the steep bus steps.

"Walter!" she exclaimed while she gave him a hug and a kiss. "Are these for me?"

Walter's eyes twinkled when he handed her the bouquet of sunflowers and offered her his arm.

"Our anniversary's not until next month," mentioned Charlotte while she inhaled their fragrance.

Both of them suddenly turned away and covered their faces as the bus started forward again.

"Dusty one minute and raining the next," sputtered Walter while he and Charlotte each hurried to brush the dust off their clothes as raindrops began to fall.

"You certainly didn't get off early just to walk me home in the rain," teased Charlotte.

"I've got good news," Walter informed her with a crooked grin.

"You've been promoted?" guessed Charlotte with a hopeful gleam in her eyes.

"Even better," replied Walter. "We leave on Friday to move to Norton Air Force Base."

Charlotte came to a stop and turned to face him. "What?"

"I know it's short notice," apologized Walter, "but you know how the military is."

"Today is Tuesday," panicked Charlotte. "I'm pretty sure I need to give them two weeks' notice at my job."

"I'm sorry, but tomorrow will need to be your last day," Walter instructed her. "You're gonna need all day Thursday to get everything ready. Our bus to California leaves on Friday morning."

"What time?"

"5:00 a.m. sharp," revealed Walter. "You'll need to give our landlord notice, pack up our things, and put in a forwarding order at the post office. Thankfully, the utilities are in our landlord's name, so nothing to worry about there."

"And where will we live when we get there?" worried Charlotte.

"Montu is already there and has made all the arrangements for us," revealed Walter. "We'll be renting from a Dr. and Mrs. Shamrock."

"Shamrock?" questioned Charlotte. "Seriously?"

"That's their name, no kidding," Walter assured her. "And the best part is, the apartment is *fully* furnished with a refrigerator and stove included. It even has red vinyl asbestos floor tiles."

"What about the rent?"

"They've agreed to wait until my first paycheck after we get there," elaborated Walter.

"What will *you* be doing between now and Friday?" asked Charlotte as she furrowed her eyebrows.

"I'm sorry, but they have me training all day, every day, right up until COB on Thursday night," explained Walter.

"Certainly, they would give you a day to pack," protested Charlotte. "What do they expect you to do? Stay up all night the day before your bus leaves?"

"It'll be alright," Walter promised her. "And, that brings me to the best news of all."

Charlotte gave him a curious look.

"I'll be permanently stationed there as an airplane mechanic, strictly state-side," Walter revealed to her with a big grin. "I won't have to go to Korea after all!"

"Oh Walter!" exclaimed Charlotte while she threw her arms around him and hugged him tightly. "Thank God!"

"But," added Walter, "my training is very intense right now. Tomorrow they'll have me servicing the engine on a brand-new supersonic jet they just came out with this year. It's called the F-100 Super Sabre. It's imperative I get up-to-speed on that model."

"Supersonic?" queried Charlotte.

"Yes, it's the first Air Force jet fighter plane ever that's capable of supersonic speed in level flight," described Walter with excitement. "It's also fully armed with nuclear bombs able to fire from four 20 mm cannons. It can even be equipped to fire rockets and missiles, including the heat-seeking GAR-8 Sidewinder. And, it's got a service ceiling above 50,000 feet with a range of more than 1,000 statute miles."

"Nuclear bombs," muttered Charlotte with dismay. "Like the ones used to wipe out Hiroshima?"

"Actually, those were atomic bombs," clarified Walter, "but that was a different war."

"Enough!" exclaimed Charlotte. "I get the idea."

"We certainly want our pilots to have safe aircraft to fly," Walter mentioned when they arrived at their apartment.

"Ones with dangerous weapons on them," countered Charlotte. She did not approve of nuclear weapons and could not wait until the war was finally over.

"Hey, I'm not a weapons specialist," pointed out Walter while he took off his hat and followed her to the kitchen. "Aircraft mechanics in the Air Force simply coordinate airplane maintenance plans and schedules to meet operational goals. Sometimes supervisors help with the recovery and launching of aircraft. Mainly, they review aircraft maintenance logs and that sort of thing."

"How about we splurge then and open up a can of tuna tonight?" asked Charlotte with a slight smile.

"As long as there's a slice of bread to go with it," agreed Walter while he pulled Charlotte close to give her a comforting hug. "Don't worry, everything will be fine. Trust me."

6. Kissin' Cousins

Deciding to leave the Lamborghini for Carolyn and Leticia to use in his absence, Jim had taken a taxi to the airport. He was just getting ready to climb into his Learjet for the return trip to the Ocean Bay International Institute of Science and Anthropology. The ground breaking ceremony for his museum was scheduled for tomorrow.

Oh my, realized Jim as he glanced at his smartwatch. *That's today! It's after midnight already. It really is September 8, 2023. Hopefully, I'll be able to stay awake for my own ground breaking ceremony when I get there. It's certainly too late to postpone it now, especially with the press showing up.*

Unexpectedly, his smartwatch began chiming. *It's Janette,* noticed Jim as he answered it. "Is everything alright?"

"No, everything's not alright," Janette was quite upset. "Willard just had a heart attack and they've taken him to the hospital."

"You should have gone with him," mentioned Jim.

"Uh, *how*? Did you forget you've got me stuck working *here* until 4:00 a.m. and that I've got responsibilities I can't just walk away from?" demanded Janette. "By the way, some other patient just died and they're wheeling out her body as we speak."

"Slow down a minute," requested Jim. "Do you know where they've taken Willard?"

"To the hospital, I guess," snapped Janette. "I'm tired, I'm still hungry, and I'm trapped here! I feel like I'm on the frickin' Titanic."

"Let me try to find out if there's anyone who can come and finish your shift," offered Jim.

"Like *who*?" questioned Janette. "It's kind of late now."

"It is after midnight," acknowledged Jim.

"Just make sure someone's here to get me when my shift is over in four hours," Janette instructed him. "I've tried to call Carolyn and Leticia, but they aren't answering."

"Have you called the front desk to see if they can check on them?" Jim asked her.

"Yes, but they won't do anything to help," growled Janette. "Something about privacy laws, and not being able to confirm whether they're there or not, even though that stupid girl knows darned well who I am because you personally checked us all in as guests! But of course, it's under *your* name. They never even bothered to have us write down our names, and would have no way of . . .."

"I'll tell you what," Jim interrupted her. "I will get someone else to cover for me at the ground breaking ceremony. I'm coming back to Rosewood right now. I'll check on Carolyn and Leticia first, but will be personally waiting for you when you get off your shift."

"Are you sure?"

"I've got people," Jim assured her. *Besides, if something were to happen to Carolyn, I'd never forgive myself. What if she and Leticia were to get into an accident?*

"I'll see you then," bid Janette as she hung up her cellphone. *I'll need to find a place to recharge this thing before making any more calls.*

Before emerging from the taxi that had pulled up in front of the Rosewood Hilton, Jim handed the driver a hundred-dollar bill. "Keep the change."

"Gee, thanks! Do you need me to wait?" asked the taxi driver as he stuffed the bill into his shirt pocket.

"Uh, give me a moment," Jim instructed him as he got out and glanced around the parking lot. Upon seeing the black Lamborghini was safely parked in one of the guest parking spaces, Jim came to the driver's side window of the taxi. "That'll be all, thanks."

"Okay, then. Have a good day, Sir. Just ask for Mike if you need me again." The taxi driver then drove away.

Jim entered the empty lobby of the Rosewood Hilton. *Where's Marsha, the desk clerk? And why is the front door open with no one on duty at this time of night?* Jim was not pleased.

"Oh, Mr. Otterman!" exclaimed Marsha when she emerged from the ladies' restroom and rapidly returned to her station at the front counter. "Welcome back!"

Jim approached, leaned forward, and folded his arms on the counter while he studied her for a moment before saying anything. "Marsha, there needs to be someone here at all times whenever the outside door is unlocked after hours."

"I'm so sorry," apologized Marsha. "I didn't think . . .."

"That's right," Jim cut her off. "You didn't think. Nor did you bother to press a simple button to secure those doors when you left your post."

Marsha was clearly nervous. Her lips were quivering.

Jim had a slight smile but wanted to make a point. "When my friend Janette called here earlier, all she wanted to know was whether Leticia and Carolyn had made it safely back to the hotel. Why were you unable to give her that information?"

Marsha's face began to turn red; tears threatened to spring from her eyes. "That is our policy."

"Yes, it is," confirmed Jim, "when a perfect stranger wants to know who is staying here. Yet, Janette and Carolyn were here *with me* when I checked them in earlier. I can't believe you wouldn't remember them, or extend the courtesy of letting one of them know the other was safe when being asked."

"I'm sorry, Sir," apologized Marsha. Tears were creeping down her cheeks.

"So, *are* they here?" questioned Jim with a raised eyebrow.

"I'm not sure," replied Marsha as she glanced at the security monitor displays mounted beneath her counter.

"Could they have snuck in while you were in the ladies' room?"

Marsha swallowed hard. "Let me ring their rooms."

"You do that," muttered Jim while he stared at her with those piercing blue eyes of his.

Marsha tried the room where Carolyn and Janette were staying first, but there was no answer. Then she tried Leticia's room; still no answer.

Jim pursed his lips together while he waited, drumming his fingers on the counter with frustration.

Marsha glanced again at the security monitor displays and noticed two women swimming in the indoor pool. "Mr. Otterman, I think they're in the indoor pool. They must have been in the sauna before that, which is why they didn't show up on one of the monitors."

Jim breathed a deep sigh of relief. "Thank you, Marsha."

"I'm truly sorry, Mr. Otterman," Marsha apologized again when Jim started to leave.

"You're forgiven," Jim grinned and winked at Marsha before heading for the indoor pool.

"Thank you, Sir," called Marsha. "It won't happen again."

"I know it won't," Jim assured her before leaving the lobby.

Carolyn and Leticia had purchased swimsuits at the giftshop earlier, but waited until after resting up to go for some well-deserved time in the sauna, followed by a late-night swim.

There had been a lot to discuss, and many questions they each hoped to ask Willard, should they be lucky enough to get in to see him. The perfectly heated pool water was inviting.

Recessed lighting from the edges of the ceiling and beneath the rim of the pool were currently dimmed to night mode due to the lateness of the hour. Large palm ferns, anthuriums, philodendrons, bird-of-paradise and other tropical plants in large white marble pots on one end of the room were misted at 15-minute intervals by an overhead sprinkling system. Rectangular mirror tiles with beveled edges mounted to the opposing wall made the entire pool room appear much larger than it was. Innumerable stars in the heavens above were easily visible through the glass dome roof overhead. Picture windows with rounded tops along a side wall overlooked the outdoor garden and hot tub area. The final wall of the pool room housed clean, white folded towels on a woven rattan and bamboo table. Beside it was a matching towel hamper for used towels, and an antiqued bamboo bench with a seat woven from tortoise rattan and rush. Above it hung a 14-peg wooden wall rack, available for hotel guests to hang up bathrobes or other items as desired. A large sign that read "No Life Guard on Duty" was prominently displayed beside the room's rounded interior entrance doors. Modular-shaped blue, brown and aquamarine glossy mosaic tiles lined not only the interior of the pool but also the walking surfaces around it.

Jim's well-worn leather cowboy boots echoed loudly as he made his way across the pool room. Upon noticing his approach, Carolyn and Leticia swam toward the shallow end of the pool to meet him. Dark blue, adjustable lounge chairs along one side of the pool were inviting; two of them already sported clean white towels Carolyn and Leticia had helped themselves to before going into the pool.

Jim was caught off guard when he saw Carolyn emerge from the pool wearing a black one-piece swimsuit with a lowcut racer back. *She's breathtaking!* Embarrassed by the sudden tightness in his jeans, Jim quickly sat down on one of the lounge chairs to wait for them.

"Jim, what brings you back at this hour?" asked Carolyn while she carefully wrung out her hair, grabbed her towel and began to dry off. She knew full well the affect she had on him, but tried to keep a poker face as she put on her robe and sat down in the chair next to him.

"Willard had a heart attack and was taken to the local hospital," announced Jim. "I'm very sorry."

"Oh, no!" exclaimed Carolyn. "That's horrible!"

"We need to go there, right now," insisted Leticia while she finished drying off and put on her robe, but did not sit down. "Come on!"

"I'll meet you ladies out front," promised Jim. *I'll wait until they leave to get back up, just in case.*

Carolyn smiled imperceptibly at his predicament but merely nodded as she got up to follow Leticia.

"I'll see what I can find out while you ladies get dressed," volunteered Jim.

Carolyn turned back and approached. When she leaned forward to put her hands on the arms of Jim's chair, her bathrobe fell open in front and the top of her cleavage was visible. Fresh droplets of water from her wet hair seductively dripped down her chest. "What about the ground breaking ceremony for your museum?" asked Carolyn.

"Chip and Hector will be there," replied Jim as he tried to control his response to her closeness. *Doesn't she know how difficult she's making this for me?*

"Thank you, Jim," smiled Carolyn. She gently kissed him on the cheek. "I know what being at your opening means to you."

"You mean more," blurted Jim. He gazed at her with longing in his eyes.

Carolyn slowly shook her head when she stood to leave. "Jim, as much as I appreciate everything you are doing, we've been over this before. Your friendship means everything to me, but you know we can never be more than just friends."

Jim nodded without saying anything more while he watched her turn and walk away. He'd been in love with her since high school and could not help how he felt. It just wasn't fair that he could never have her, but that wasn't going to stop him from being there for her when she needed him most.

The medical unit clerk working the nurse's station at the cardiac unit of Rosewood Memorial Hospital was a tall willowy man in his early twenties with pale skin, deep brown eyes, long dark lashes, and jet-black hair pulled into a ponytail. His scrubs were traditional Brunswick green. Cole's closed-back clogs were iridescent blue with thick rubber soles. His clean-shaven face was pleasant and his large white teeth were prominent when he smiled.

"May I help you?" asked Cole while he studied the strangers.

"My name is Jim Otterman," informed the red-headed man at his counter. "This is Leticia and Carolyn."

"I understand our father has been brought here," embellished Leticia. "His name is Willard."

"Oh yes, room 3," noted Cole after checking his computer. "May I see some identification?"

Leticia hurriedly opened her purse, removed her driver's license, and handed it to Cole.

Cole typed the information from it into his console before returning it to her. "And your sister?" prompted Cole when he turned to Carolyn. "May I see yours, too?"

"Oh, of course," replied Carolyn as she pulled out and handed him her driver's license. *Hopefully, Cole won't find out I'm only Willard's niece, if indeed that's the case.*

Again, Cole entered the information into his computer console before returning it. "And you, Mr. Otterman?"

"I'm just a family friend," replied Jim.

"I'm sorry, then," apologized Cole, "but only family can see him in the cardiac unit."

"Understandable," nodded Jim.

"Very well, I'll be right back," Cole informed them.

"Wait! Before you go, can't you please tell us how he is?" pleaded Leticia.

"The nurse will have to do that," replied Cole. He paused to give Leticia a compassionate smile. "This may take some time. You three are welcome to wait over there." Cole motioned toward several straight-back orange plastic chairs with silver metal legs in the hallway.

"Is he conscious?" persisted Leticia with a pleading look.

"I'll be right back," Cole promised her without answering the question as he hurried away.

Jim put a reassuring arm around Leticia and led her to the hallway chairs. Carolyn silently followed.

Vending machines with bottled water and various snacks of an indeterminate age could be seen on the opposite wall, right beside the unisex restrooms.

"I need to see him," muttered Leticia. "What if he dies before I get the chance?"

"Ladies, I promised Janette I would be there at 4:00 a.m. sharp to pick her up," Jim informed them as he stood. "It's 3:45 a.m. now."

"Are you coming back?" queried Carolyn.

"Of course," smiled Jim as he winked at her. "Just call me if anything changes. Otherwise, I'll be back shortly."

"Thank you, Jim," sniffed Leticia.

"Yes, thank you," added Carolyn while they watched him leave. Jim's cowboy boots echoed loudly down the hall.

We're both tired, but don't dare fall asleep now, thought Leticia. *This might be our only chance to ever see Willard again, and we need to make the most of it.*

"Hello ladies, I'm Natalie," informed the nurse standing in front of them. "I know you ladies have been waiting for quite a while now, but we're still trying to stabilize Willard and are waiting for the doctor to decide whether he can have any visitors, even family."

"How much longer will that be?" Leticia grilled her.

"Well, usually Dr. Shotts does not come on duty until 8:30 a.m. It could be anytime between then and noon before he gets around to seeing all his patients," elaborated Natalie.

Not only was Natalie the head nurse at Rosewood Memorial Hospital, but was also in charge of the cardiac unit. She was a short, stout middle-aged woman in excellent shape from lifting and moving bedridden patients on a daily basis. In sharp contrast to her alabaster skin, Natalie's horn-rimmed glasses were black in color. Naturally flipped upward at the ends, her straight dishwater-blonde hair was chin-length. Extra short bangs were intentional, to keep them from her eyes. She wore no makeup whatever. It was clear from the expression on her face and the determined set of her jaw that Natalie was all business. Unlike the medical unit clerk or other hospital personnel working in the cardiac unit, Natalie's attire was entirely white. Her uniform was an old-school, knee-length dress that had been starched and ironed many times. Her stethoscope hung neatly around her neck with the diaphragm of the stethoscope tucked into one of her pockets.

Natalie's shoes, however, were a new style clog; nevertheless, they were also white.

"We've been here since 3:30 a.m.," mentioned Carolyn.

"And it's only 5:00 a.m. now," pointed out Leticia.

"I'm sorry, but we really need to wait," insisted Natalie.

"Can you at least tell us how he is?" questioned Leticia. "My father and I have been estranged for many years. This might be my last chance to ever see him again. There are things that need to be said."

"I see," nodded Natalie, though she was clearly unmoved.

"Same here," volunteered Carolyn with a pleading look.

"What I can tell you is this," Natalie advised them. "Right now, we are waiting for Willard to regain consciousness so he can be seen by our cardiologist. He's had a rather serious heart attack and possibly a mild stroke, as well."

"Is it likely to have both at the same time?" asked Leticia.

"Oh yes, very possible," Natalie assured her. "In your father's case, we will need to have him conscious before confirming whether or not he's also had a stroke, but he did receive CPR and defibrillation before arriving at the hospital. They also inserted a tube down his airways to assist with breathing. He is currently on a ventilator, receiving all of his medications and saline solution through an IV."

"Hello ladies," came the voice of Jim Otterman from behind them. Janette was with him, still in the navy-blue scrubs she had worn all night long at Apple Valley Memory Care.

"I'm so sorry about Willard," mentioned Janette as she threw her arms around Leticia and then Carolyn.

"We're family friends," Jim explained to Natalie. "I take it you're the nurse in charge?"

"I am," confirmed Natalie while she narrowed her eyes at him.

"I'm Dr. Jim Otterman," he informed her.

"He's also a doctor," Carolyn whispered to Leticia and Janette. "He really is."

"Of course, you are," snickered Natalie after easily overhearing Carolyn's remark.

"I'm also on the Board of Directors for this hospital," mentioned Jim in all seriousness.

"I see," sighed Natalie as she folded her arms in front of her. *The Board of Directors are responsible for hiring staff. I'd better take him seriously, at least for now.*

"You did say Willard has been intubated," Jim reminded her. "What these lovely ladies here might not be aware of is that being on a ventilator is not usually painful but can be uncomfortable. With a breathing tube, the patient will not be able to eat or talk. With a trach tube, they may be able to talk with a special device and eat some types of food. With a face mask, they will be able to talk and eat only if recommended by your healthcare team. So, we need to determine whether Willard is stable enough to use a face mask rather than being intubated."

"That would be up to Dr. Shotts," Natalie advised him evenly.

"Unless, of course, he's planning to do immediate surgery," countered Jim while he reached for Natalie's electronic tablet. "May I?"

Natalie hesitated but finally allowed Jim to have a look.

Jim studied it carefully and then nodded. "Please notify me the moment Willard is awake," Jim instructed Natalie when he returned her electronic tablet. "Can you please do that for me, Natalie? I would like to be present on behalf of the family when Dr. Shotts sees him," he added as he handed her one of his cards.

"He's also an attorney," Carolyn mentioned to Natalie.

"Of course, he is," responded Natalie. She rolled her eyes and shook her head with pursed lips.

"A fact I'm sure you'd stake your job on," commented Jim as he raised an eyebrow at Natalie.

"I'll notify you when Dr. Shotts arrives," promised Natalie. *I'm not going to take any chances.*

"Much appreciated," nodded Jim. "Come on ladies, let's go have some breakfast while we're waiting for Natalie to call."

Once they were a respectable distance down the hall, Janette leaned close to Jim and whispered, "Do you think she'll check that out?"

"I hope she does," answered Jim in a serious tone. "I really am on the Board of Directors."

"He really is an attorney, a doctor, and many other things, as well," confirmed Carolyn.

"And rich," added Janette while she gave Carolyn a meaningful look. "Just my type. Too bad he's already taken."

"I heard that," grinned Jim. He knew she was only teasing him.

"How is Sheree, anyway?" Carolyn questioned Jim as the four of them exited the hospital before walking toward the sleek black Lamborghini parked in the emergency lot.

"Is Sheree your wife?" asked Leticia.

"She is," confirmed Jim with a sideways glance at Carolyn.

"Will she be at the ground breaking ceremony for your museum?" queried Leticia.

"Unfortunately, no," replied Jim when he opened the doors of the Lamborghini for them. "Someone must remain behind to run the bed and breakfast."

"That's just a two-hour drive down the coastline from Ocean Bay, right next door to Oceanview Academy," Carolyn explained to Leticia.

"That's where Carolyn and I were classmates in high school," elaborated Jim while he started the engine. "SIRI, where's a decent nearby restaurant where we can have breakfast at this hour?"

"Please state range," answered SIRI.

"Five miles," clarified Jim.

"There is a 24-hour diner at Rosewood Truck Stop," declared SIRI. "Nothing else is open at this hour."

"Perhaps we should just eat here," proposed Carolyn.

"Even the hospital cafeteria is closed right now," differed Janette. "We saw a sign when coming in. It doesn't open until 7:00 a.m."

"What about the Rosewood Hilton?" suggested Leticia. "Their restaurant looked pretty decent. They open at 6:00 a.m."

"Sounds good to me," agreed Janette. "That way, I can go up to the room and get out of these scrubs."

Everyone nodded in agreement.

"The Rosewood Hilton it is," grinned Jim as he put the Lamborghini into gear before taking off at a high rate of speed.

"Jim, slow down!" exclaimed Carolyn while she reached for a handgrip.

"Sorry," apologized Jim as he complied.

"Tell me about the high school you went to," requested Leticia.

"It was a strict coed parochial boarding school where girls and boys were not even allowed to hold hands," reminisced Carolyn. "And if they were caught by a faculty member, they were put on *social*."

"Social? What's that?" prompted Leticia.

"It meant you were not allowed to speak to someone of the opposite sex for the rest of the semester after that," clarified Carolyn, "unless it was a teacher or other faculty member."

"Three strikes and you got expelled," interjected Jim with a mischievous grin.

"Say, *what*?" Janette's eyes opened wide with disbelief.

"That's right," corroborated Carolyn. "Three times on social and you got expelled for the rest of the semester. After that, you'd have to grovel before the principal with your parents present and beg him to let you return."

"That's ridiculous!" exclaimed Janette.

"You sound like you speak from experience," opined Leticia.

"Some of us just never got caught," Jim assured her with a wink.

"Were you and Carolyn ever an item?" inquired Leticia.

"Unfortunately, no," lamented Jim while he glanced at Carolyn. "Just wishful thinking on my part."

"We've always been friends, nothing more," added Carolyn with a shrug of her shoulders.

Janette and Carolyn had been close friends for many years and shared many secrets, including the fact that Jim had relentlessly pursued Carolyn during high school in the hope she might one day come to feel the same way about him as he felt about her. The fact that Carolyn was never romantically interested in Jim and never would be was also well known to Janette.

"That was also where I learned to fly and got my first pilot's license," revealed Jim when he pulled into the parking lot of the Rosewood Hilton and drove to the covered entrance.

"We'll meet you in the dining area at 6:00 a.m.," Carolyn advised Jim while he held her door open for her to get out of the vehicle.

"If you get there first, tell 'em I like my coffee like my women: hot, blonde and bitter," joked Jim.

Carolyn tried not to smile as she nodded. *Guess that counts Sheree out, since she's always been homely and has dark brown hair, but she's one of the sweetest persons you'd ever hope to meet.*

"Yep, we'll see you there," called Janette while she hurried inside. "I can't wait to have a shower!"

"That's not a bad idea," agreed Leticia as she followed after her.

"I was just kidding," Jim whispered to Carolyn.

"I'll be sure and have 'em put lots of creamer and sugar in your coffee then," teased Carolyn.

"Hot, some creamer, no sugar," clarified Jim with a slight smile. "Pancakes with bacon and eggs, sunny side up sounds good, too."

Carolyn made a face. "I like my eggs well cooked, thank you, but an omelet sounds good. No cheese, of course."

"See you soon," called Jim when Carolyn headed inside.

The dining area of the Rosewood Hilton was more utilitarian than anything, consisting of square wooden tables with matching hard wooden chairs in various areas of the room. There were some hexagon-shaped booths with dark brown padded seats at one end of the room. Mood lights of various colors suspended from the ceiling hung over each table. Down the middle of the room was an elongated half-moon shaped planter box filled with tropical plants, and an aquarium filled with saltwater fish at one end. Paintings of tropical resorts and people lounging at them hung on every available wall space. The low-pile carpet was chocolate brown in color, designed for easy maintenance and heavy traffic.

A self-service buffet table with pastries, croissants, muffins, slices of bread and a toaster spanned the interior wall. A pitcher of waffle batter and a waffle iron sat on one end of it. A small round table with a large bowl of bananas, oranges and apples sat in the corner. To their right was another table filled with several carafes, each labeled according to its contents, such as decaf, regular and hot water. Beside them was a serving tray with individualized compartments, one filled with packets of creamer, another filled with sugar packets, another with sugar substitutes, and yet another with various selections of herbal tea. Also on the table were small pitchers of syrup, and packets of butter and various flavors of jam.

A final table of condiments including packets of salt, pepper, hot sauce, soy sauce, mustard and mayonnaise were located beside stacks of clean dinner plates, bowls, saucers and cups. Drinking glasses, silverware and a paper napkin dispenser sat near the cold water and soda dispenser, which had a lever for ice.

"Oh, no," frowned Janette. "I thought it would be a full-service restaurant."

"It will be," promised Jim as he joined her. "But not until 6:00 a.m. Ten more minutes. That stuff over there is just for folks who wanna eat something after hours."

"Waffles sound pretty good to me right now," considered Leticia while she headed for the self-service table.

"Me, too," agreed Janette as she joined her.

"I can wait," differed Carolyn. "I kind of had my heart set on an omelet, with fresh slices of kiwi on the side."

"I'll wait with you," offered Jim, "but meanwhile, I think I'll help myself to something hot, blonde and bitter." He was referring to the coffee, of course.

"Herbal tea sounds good," decided Carolyn. She followed him to the self-service table.

Once their orders had been placed and they were waiting for everyone's food to be brought, Jim turned to Carolyn. "You've already told us about life with Bell when you were growing up. What was she like later on in life?"

"That's a tough one," sighed Carolyn as she blew on and then took a sip of jasmine tea. *Thank goodness we were able to get a booth with cushioned seating.*

"That old lady was one tough customer," opined Janette.

"Amen to that," vouched Leticia.

"Yes, she certainly was," agreed Carolyn. "As I might have mentioned at some point, things started on a particularly downward spiral for Bell once the house my grandparents had was condemned by the City of Ashton. It was for a freeway that cut right through the center of town, and their property became the southwest interchange where Simpson Street used to be."

"That would have been in 1978," recalled Jim, who had a photographic memory. "I remember reading about it. A lot of people lost their homes over that project."

"Naturally," continued Carolyn, "they refused to leave at first and were the only ones left living in the neighborhood for two years."

"That's kind of creepy," frowned Janette.

"It was," confirmed Carolyn, "but when they finally had no choice but to leave, they were compensated for considerably less than the original offer."

"I remember," nodded Leticia. "That was when they moved to a high crime neighborhood on the other end of town."

"Yep," muttered Carolyn. "They couldn't afford anything else for what they got, and after being burglarized twice – not to mention my grandpa being robbed at gunpoint while walking his elderly dog one evening – they ended up selling again and moving to a single-wide trailer over at the coast."

"Their lives were never the same after that," added Leticia.

"But," elaborated Carolyn, "once they learned my parents had retired and were planning to move up north to be closer to me, Bell insisted they be moved up there, too."

"Be moved?" questioned Jim.

"Yeah," replied Carolyn. "In other words, Bell expected my parents to arrange and pay for it, even though they were in the middle of trying to do their own move. My dad was not pleased with the task of selling both properties."

"She had rather high expectations, didn't she?" asked Jim.

"You have no idea," sighed Carolyn. She paused to take another sip of tea.

Just then, the waitress arrived with a huge tray of food and placed it on an empty table nearby. "Who has the chicken omelet with no cheese and slices of kiwi and strawberry on the side?"

"Me," smiled Carolyn as she placed the delicious-looking plate in front of her.

"The pancakes with bacon and eggs, sunny-side up?"

Jim grinned and winked at her, motioning for her to set it down in front of him, which she did.

"And the rest of you are eating from the self-service?"

"Can you please bring me an omelet, too?" Janette suddenly requested. "*With cheese!*"

"Fruit on the side?" the waitress grilled her. "Or, would you rather have hash browns?"

"Oh, hash browns, absolutely," grinned Janette.

"Very well," acknowledged the waitress while she made a note of it on her pad. "Anything else?"

"I could use some hash browns with a side of fruit," ordered Leticia. "And, do you have cappuccino?"

"Yes, we do," smiled the waitress as she wrote it down.

"Uh, how about a basket of muffins?" requested Jim.

"You got it," responded the waitress. "Is that it?"

Everyone nodded and then paused until the waitress left before continuing their conversation.

"I'm exhausted after being up all night," yawned Carolyn, "but I doubt any of us will be getting much rest today."

"At least you didn't have to spend the night on the Titanic!" exclaimed Janette before taking a sip of coffee.

"The Titanic?" Carolyn seemed puzzled.

"Jim understands," muttered Janette.

"Indeed," nodded Jim while he stuffed a crispy slice of bacon into his mouth. "So, Carolyn, once everyone got moved up north, what happened after that?"

Carolyn stopped to devour a bite of kiwi before answering. "Well, my Grandpa Frank died shortly afterward of a massive heart attack in 1994. That was when Bell suddenly decided that she no longer wanted to drive anymore. And of course, she expected my parents to take her *everywhere*, including her many medical appointments. So, to help lighten their load, I took on the responsibility of taking Bell shopping every single Saturday, for *years*. We would usually go to at least a dozen stores, sometimes more."

"Why so many?" Jim grilled her.

"For example," elaborated Carolyn, "if a can of peas was 19¢ cheaper at another store across town, Bell would insist on going there instead. Never mind that it might cost *me* an extra few-dollars in gas money to get her there."

"She never reimbursed you?" Jim seemed surprised.

Carolyn began laughing so hard she nearly choked. "Are you kidding? Bell never reimbursed *anyone*, not even my parents."

"Where was Willard during all of this?" questioned Jim.

"I have no idea," admitted Carolyn, "but I'm sure he was busy with his second, third or fourth wives, doing whatever it was they enjoyed. Probably golfing and country clubs, that kind of thing."

"Isn't Willard the one who showed up for Bell's funeral and got upset because we were having one?" asked Janette.

"Yep," confirmed Carolyn. "He apparently thought having a funeral for her was a complete waste of money."

"If Carolyn hadn't called me," added Leticia, "I would never have known that my Grandma Bell had died."

"I was there, too," Janette reminded her.

"Wow!" exclaimed Jim. "No love lost there."

"That's why we keep trying to figure out what happened between those boys and their mother to tear the family apart so much," explained Carolyn.

"And to keep them from speaking to one another for all those years," added Leticia. "Or to me!"

"Could it be because of what happened to your mother, Ruth?" Jim suddenly asked Leticia.

"I don't know," admitted Leticia while she sadly shook her head.

"And no one will tell us," bemoaned Carolyn as she took a bite of her omelet. "Walter and Bell are gone now. The only one left who would know anything is Willard."

"I still need to follow up with the Ashton County Coroner's Office to see what else we can find out from them," mumbled Jim.

"One time," recalled Carolyn, "Bell fell and broke her hip after tripping on a stack of newspapers. And of course, she blamed my husband for leaving them *right* where she had insisted he put them. Nevertheless, she said it was *his fault* she had fallen."

"I remember when that happened," said Janette. "And your husband wasn't even there at the time!"

"Oh, it gets better," Carolyn assured her. "When I went to visit Bell in the nursing home where she was recovering, she insisted I go back to her apartment, not only to *get rid of* the newspapers, but to clean out her refrigerator and throw out any bad food."

"Did you?" Jim prompted her.

"Oh yes, I certainly did," sighed Carolyn while she shook her head. "Good thing I took my friend Valerie with me as a witness."

"Why would you need a witness for cleaning out a refrigerator?" Jim seemed confused.

"Because later, after we had tossed all the science experiments into the garbage," continued Carolyn, "Bell came home, saw most of the things in her refrigerator were gone, and accused me of *stealing* her food."

"What a load of crap," snorted Janette. "Why would *you* want her rotten food?"

"Certainly *not* so I could get a call from a social worker telling me that Bell had filed a complaint against me for stealing *all her food*," revealed Carolyn. "Good thing my friend Valerie was able to go there with me to try and explain what really happened."

"That's horrible she did that to you," opined Janette.

"She was always threatening somebody," responded Carolyn as she shrugged her shoulders. "Manipulating people was what she did."

"I'm kind of scared to go see Willard," Leticia suddenly admitted. "What if he won't talk to us?"

"Don't worry," Carolyn reassured her. "I'll be there with you, and together we'll find out the truth about what happened."

Jim's smartwatch began chiming. "Hello? Yes, this is he." Jim became serious and set down his fork. "When?"

* * *

It was October of 1954. Nearly a month had passed since Charlotte and Walter's move from Texas to Norton Air Force Base.

Charlotte paused by the front door to see what mail had come. Thankfully, there was a mail slot in the front door, so it was no longer necessary to retrieve their mail from a mailbox on the street.

She paused upon seeing an envelope from Ashton. *It's from Frank and Bell. What can they possibly want?*

"Honey, I'm home," greeted Walter when he came inside, pulled Charlotte close, and gave her a lingering kiss. "And I just got paid."

Charlotte held up the envelope from his parents, causing him to frown. "Now what?"

"Could she be sending you back your $250?" asked Charlotte with a snorting laugh.

Walter shook his head as he opened the envelope and began to read. "Apparently she's inviting us to a backyard barbecue."

"That's a four-hour drive," objected Charlotte.

Walter sighed heavily. "I do need to give Willard the $250 he thinks I owe him."

"But *why*?" questioned Charlotte. "You know as well as I do that Bell probably took it."

"I know," replied Walter, "but it's still the right thing to do."

"How much did you just get paid?" asked Charlotte with a sly smile while she looked up at him.

"$122.20," grinned Walter. "Don't forget, I'm an E-4 now. Starting next month, I'll hit the two-year mark. That means I'll be getting $129.95 per month after that."

"Not bad, considering you were only getting $83.20 when you first started out as an E-1," admitted Charlotte while she put her cheek against his chest and pulled him close.

"And this will be the very last month we'll ever need to set aside $10.41 for the *Willard* fund again," Walter reminded her when he hugged her back and rested his chin on the top of her head.

"$250 would go a long way toward the down payment on that new car we were looking at on Saturday," mentioned Charlotte.

"No, it's all settled," differed Walter. "That money goes to Willard. Perhaps then, things can be right between us again."

"If he'll even take it," commented Charlotte. "He's a proud man, your brother."

"I can be very persuasive," flirted Walter as he pulled back just enough to put one hand under her chin to lift it and kissed her again.

After a long passionate kiss, Walter finally extricated himself from her grasp, winked at her, and made his way to the refrigerator to retrieve a bottle of Coca-Cola.

"There's a bottle opener in the top drawer on the left," Charlotte directed him.

"Thanks," smiled Walter while he used it to remove the lid.

"Oh, no!" exclaimed Charlotte when the soda began foaming up and out onto the floor.

"I got this," Walter assured her as he made a beeline for the sink.

"It sure would be nice to get that new car," wished Charlotte out loud while she grabbed a rag and began wiping up the mess on the floor.

"That's the other news," Walter informed her when the soda began to calm down enough for him to take a sip from it.

"What news?" questioned Charlotte with a puzzled look on her face. *Once the money is gone, we'll have to start saving all over again. It'll probably be another two years before we have enough to even consider buying a car.*

"Well," grinned Walter, "the Shamrocks have agreed to cosign for us on the car loan."

"What?" Charlotte was stunned. "You're kidding! Our new landlords? They hardly even know us. Why would they do something like that for us?"

"They're genuinely kind people," pointed out Walter. "And why look a gift horse in the mouth?"

Charlotte quietly went to the sink and rinsed out the rag.

"Say something," Walter urged her.

"I'm thinking," responded Charlotte. "Do we really have enough to make the payments?"

"Well, let's see," calculated Walter. "I'll be getting $129.95 per month, and the pay at your new job is $250, so that comes to $379.95."

"But our rent is $200 per month now," Charlotte reminded him.

"Including all utilities," described Walter, "so we would still have $179.95 left over to use for everything else."

"Including the car payment," realized Charlotte.

"Besides, it's not like we're gonna spend $1,900 on a brand new one," argued Walter.

"Especially with gasoline prices up to 22¢ a gallon," agreed Charlotte. "Plus, there's upkeep and insurance."

"I know, I know, but the guy at the dealership has a 1951 Ford sedan on sale right now for only $950," elaborated Walter. "Sure, it's used, but it's in excellent condition. I stopped by there on my way home tonight and looked it over. We're not gonna get a better deal."

"How much would the payments be?" Charlotte grilled him.

"If we pay it off in two years, the payments would be about $40 per month," revealed Walter, "and he said he'll give us until tomorrow to decide."

"Why so soon?" asked Charlotte while she furrowed her eyebrows.

"Because another couple is interested in it, too. We really need to move on this," Walter encouraged her.

"I guess that would leave us about $140 a month to live on after that," realized Charlotte.

"Actually, $139.95," Walter corrected her with a sly smile. "Don't worry, everything will work out. Trust me."

Anxious to show off their new Simpson Street home to her twin sons and their wives, Bell had worked quite hard making sure everything was clean and presentable in both the house and the yard. She had also been one of the few customers fortunate enough to obtain a new LazyMan portable gas grill before they ran out of stock. Sold only by the Chicago Combustion Corporation and shipped to its customers by UPS, it was the first of its kind to hit the market in July of 1954, though it had taken weeks to arrive.

Bell had just finished checking the weather prediction before neatly placing her copy of the *Ashton Times* for Sunday, October 24, 1954, onto the patio picnic table. "It says there's no rain in the forecast and that it could get up to 80° today," she called to Frank as she put on a pair of dark blue dress gloves that perfectly matched her blue and white flowered dress, purse and shoes. She also had a full-body bib apron neatly folded over a patio chair, ready to put on when it came time to finish up the food preparations. Bell had made it herself and it was navy blue, of course.

Wiping the sweat from his brow with the back of his hand, Frank had just finished assembling the new barbecue out on the narrow gravel area that separated the patio from the sprawling back lawn. "We're gonna need to fill this propane tank, too," Frank informed Bell while he walked onto the patio and took a big gulp from an open bottle of Sarsaparilla soda. Unlike Bell, Frank preferred to dress casually when at home and had on a pair of blue jeans, black and white Keds sneakers, and a white V-neck T-shirt. Being a heavy smoker, Frank always kept a pack of cigarettes rolled up inside one sleeve of his T-shirt for easy access. He had just switched from Camel cigarettes to a new brand called Winston and went through at least a pack and a half of cigarettes each day; only 20 cigarettes came in a pack. *Perhaps I should pick up a carton? That way, I'll be sure to have enough packs to last through the week.*

"I can get the propane," volunteered Bell. "Besides, we're going to need some other things from the store, too."

"I think we'd better watch our spending," Frank cautioned her when she started to head into the house to retrieve her purse. "Hold on while I put away my tools first. I'm coming with you."

"That's really not necessary," argued Bell. "Plus, you'll need time to take a shower and get cleaned up." She did not want Frank to find out about her secret stash of extra spending money, either.

"I'm fine like this," insisted Frank while he took out a cigarette and lit it up. "But I *am* coming with you. Besides, I need to get more cigarettes."

"Very well," pouted Bell. She folded her arms in front of her and sat down at the picnic table to wait for Frank to pick up his tools. "The sooner we get going, the sooner we'll be back."

"Yeah, yeah, keep your shirt on," muttered Frank while he grabbed the last of his tools, put them inside his big metal tool box, latched it shut, and headed for the garage with the lit cigarette hanging from his mouth. "I'll be back for the propane tank and then meet you at the car."

Has Frank forgotten that this was Walter and Charlotte's second wedding anniversary? wondered Bell when she dashed inside to grab her purse and some extra spending money from her secret stash. It was her hope to surprise them with a small celebration so everyone could bury the hatchet and be friends again, especially since they had not been able to attend either of their sons' weddings. *Besides, I'll need to be on better terms with both my sons if I'm going to persuade Walter to move back to Ashton. That way, they can both help me with this huge yard in the future. Frank sure isn't much help, especially with such long hours.*

Frank was already waiting for her out front in the red and black Ford pickup by the time she got there. The empty 20-pound propane tank was sitting in the back, tightly strapped in place with medium dark brown bungee cords.

Bell climbed into the pickup and slammed the door shut. *Apparently, Frank has no intention of coming around to open the door for me anymore!*

"What's wrong?" asked Frank while he took a puff from his cigarette before starting up the engine.

Bell folded her arms, pursed her lips, and glared out the passenger window without answering.

"Maybe you'll feel more like talking when our guests arrive," hoped Frank as he backed up the vehicle, put it into gear, and headed for the corner gas station so he could get the propane tank filled.

"Perhaps I can just run on to the store while you fill that thing up," suggested Bell when they pulled into the Texaco gas station.

Immediately, four gas station attendants hurried out to meet them, waiting for Frank to pull up to a pump so they could fill his tank with gasoline, wash the windshield, check the oil, tire pressure, or whatever else might be needed. Each was wearing a uniform consisting of a khaki peaked cap with a matching khaki two-piece suit over a white shirt and black bow tie.

When the red and black Ford pickup drove over to the propane station instead, one of the attendants came to Frank's window and asked, "How can we help today? Do you need some propane, Sir?"

"I just need to fill up the propane tank in the back," directed Frank while he took a puff from his cigarette.

"Sir, can you please put out your cigarette while you're here at the gas station?"

"Of course," agreed Frank as he snuffed it out in the ashtray.

Filthy habit, thought Bell. She made an involuntary face of disgust at the ashtray and its contents. "Perhaps they might be able to empty your ashtray, too?"

"Yes ma'am," came the voice of another attendant, who had just finished wiping off the side windows. "I'll come around to your husband's side for it."

"Hey, thanks," said Frank as he pulled out the ashtray and handed it to the attendant to dump.

"They do everything but give you a tune-up," smiled Bell while she nodded with approval.

Like a flash, the attendants had performed their duties and scurried over to help the next new customer who had pulled into the gas station. All but the one who came up to the driver's side window for payment. "Here you are, mister," indicated the man as he gave Frank back the ashtray. It had not only been dumped, but also wiped out and cleaned. "4.6 gallons of propane at 29¢ a gallon comes to $1.33 plus 3¢ tax, bringing your total for today to $1.36."

"Wouldn't a 20-pound tank hold 20 gallons?" asked Bell while she watched Frank hand the attendant a one-dollar bill and two quarters.

"Typically, ma'am," grinned the attendant, "a full 20-pound propane tank weighs 37 pounds because the weight of an empty cylinder, also called the Tare Weight, is only 17 pounds. It holds 20 pounds of fuel, which is called its Water Capacity, thus adding up to a total of 37 pounds."

"Keep the change," Frank indicated to the attendant while he shot Bell a glance of frustration. She had embarrassed him, and he didn't like it. The least he could do was give the man 14¢ for his trouble, especially the lengthy explanation.

"Thank you, Sir!" exclaimed the attendant as Frank started up the engine and drove away.

The olive-green house with dark brown trim on Simpson Street was particularly well kempt. Not a weed could be seen in any of its flowerbeds. Oleander shrubs, bamboo bushes, dwarf olive trees, bougainvillea and bottlebrush adorned the front yard; late-blooming hyacinths grew in a flowerbed hugging the driveway where daffodils had been earlier in the spring.

Sunlight streamed through the towering willow tree in Frank and Bell's backyard. Dormant flowerbeds that would later be graced with carnations lay beneath a row of heavily laden grapevines along the west side of the yard. The seedless green grapes were inviting and ready to pick and enjoy.

On the east side of the large yard was Bell's clothesline, beneath which Frank had recently poured a cement pad by himself. There was no fence on that side of the yard, but the Byrd family who lived next door had a beautifully landscaped yard where a giant acacia tree grew. Beneath it sat a white wrought-iron table and matching chairs.

To the rear of the sprawling green back lawn that Frank kept neatly mowed was a quarter-acre dirt area, complete with a vegetable garden of tomatoes, green onions, red onions, garlic, squash, eggplant, watermelon, cantaloupes, mustard plants, and poppies. Also, in the dirt area were various trees. The lemon, orange, plum, loquat, apricot, and almond trees were among Bell's favorites, all high yielders. Beyond them at the northerly end of the property was a blackberry patch that grew alongside a meandering city ditch that flowed behind all the properties on Simpson Street.

Immediately behind Frank and Bell's home was a covered cement patio with a picnic table, several folding chairs, a chaise lounge, and three card tables that had been set up for serving food.

Frank was busy barbecuing T-bone steaks. Bell had just finished spreading homemade tablecloths on each of the card tables and was bringing out trays of food. Deviled eggs, coleslaw, olives, pickles, radishes, and green onions awaited consumption. Potato salad, celery stuffed with peanut butter, and homemade beef jerky were tempting, as well. A huge bowl of potato chips and various bowls of homemade dip sat beside them. Paper plates, plastic silverware, and napkins sat on a separate table beside an ice chest filled with cans of soda and beer.

It was about 4:30 p.m. Overhead electrical lighting on the patio would keep it lit, even after sundown.

"Something smells good!" exclaimed Willard when he and Ruth emerged from beside the house and came to the backyard patio.

"Yes, everything looks delicious," agreed Ruth as she studied the feast spread before them. "Is there anything I can do to help?"

"Just make yourselves comfortable," grinned Bell, without bothering to come give either of them a hug. Public displays of affection were normally not her way.

"Are we late?" asked Walter when he and Charlotte joined them.

"Thank you so much for having us over," added Charlotte before coming over and attempting to give Bell a hug.

"It's the least we could do," responded Bell, but without hugging her back. "Especially since we were unable to attend either of your weddings. We wanted to have a special celebration for you."

"Today is our second wedding anniversary," blurted Charlotte as she affectionately slipped her arm through Walter's and gave him a kiss on the cheek, causing him to blush in front of his parents.

"There you are!" hollered Joanie when she and her sister Verna showed up. Turning to Ruth, Joanie informed her, "We're your hubby's *kissin' cousins*. I'm sure he's probably told you *all* about us." Joanie then gave Willard a hug and a lingering kiss on the mouth, causing him to turn red in the face.

Ruth was clearly upset by the boldness of this stranger, and *cousin or not, her behavior is unacceptable!*

Joanie was tall and slim, with curves in all the right places. Her tight, blue-jean pedal pushers were neatly folded up on the ends, revealing well-tanned, clean-shaven legs below them. Joanie's bright red toenail polish exactly matched her open-toed Italian heels; her long fingernails were also painted with bright red nail polish. Her sleeveless white blouse was tight fitting, low-cut in the front, and well ironed. With her face makeup heavily applied, including bright red lipstick, Joanie almost looked like a gypsy with her many rings, bracelets, necklaces, and hoop-style earrings that glistened in the sunlight when she moved her head. Joanie's strawberry blonde bangs hung down loosely on one side of her forehead while her perfectly done French braid ponytail reached the middle of her back.

"And I'm the other *kissin' cousin,*" announced Verna while she came over and gave Walter a hug and a kiss on the cheek, even with Charlotte still clinging to his arm. "I'll bet you boys never expected to see us again," grinned Verna as she gave Walter a wicked wink and a pinch on the butt.

The look of disgust on Charlotte's face was obvious, though she was too stunned by the woman's behavior to say anything just yet.

Like her sister Joanie, Verna was stunning to look at and clearly knew it. She was similarly dressed in tight, blue-jean pedal pushers with well-tanned, clean-shaven legs. Verna's sandals were more of a beige color but also appeared expensive, and her toenails were painted with bright pink polish. Her pale pink cotton blouse had capped sleeves and was also well ironed, tight fitting, and low-cut in the front. Above her cleavage hung a simple strand of iridescent pearls that perfectly matched her pearl-drop earrings and single pearl ring. Verna's strawberry blonde hair was parted in the middle and hung loosely about her shoulders in delicate curls she seductively pushed out of her way with one of her bright pink fingernails.

In stark contrast to Joanie and Verna, both Charlotte and Ruth were dressed in simple sleeveless cotton shifts in neutral tones, and each sported a plain white sweater in case it got cold. Both wore tennis shoes with bobby socks neatly folded down on top of their hosiery. Neither wore much makeup or jewelry, and were the epitome of modesty. It was almost as if they had called one another to coordinate outfits.

"Auntie Bell let us know her next-door neighbors needed someone to housesit for a few months," elaborated Joanie.

"And here we are," flirted Verna as she sauntered over to one of the card tables and helped herself to a handful of potato chips. "Barbecue's my favorite," she informed the others while she seductively licked one of the chips before putting it into her mouth and devouring it. She maintained eye contact with Walter as she did.

"The Byrds have gone to England and won't be back until Christmas," smirked Bell. *This is even better than I'd hoped for. It's about time those no-good gold diggers my sons are married to find out about their checkered past. Who knows, their wives might even send 'em packing after this. Undoubtedly, my sons will come running back to me for a place to stay,* assumed Bell. *In return for my generosity, I'll have all the help I need with the chores involved in keeping up a place like this.*

Frank lit up a cigarette and took a big puff, shaking his head with disapproval at the whole affair. "Looks like the meat is ready."

"Hey, how 'bout some music while we eat," suggested Joanie. "Ya still got that RCA record player, Uncle Frank?"

"It only plays 45s," responded Frank while he finished plating the beautifully-done T-bone steaks.

"We haven't got very many records, anyway," interjected Bell when she took the platter from Frank and carried it over to one of the serving tables.

"Oh, yours are yesterday's news, anyway," giggled Verna. "We got some brand-new records with us, right next door. I'll be right back."

"We do," confirmed Joanie. "Stuff by The Crew Cuts, like *Sh'Boom (Life Could Be a Dream)*, and *Crazy 'Bout Ya Baby*."

"What will the neighbors think?" objected Bell.

"Oh, Aunt Bell, don't be so stuffy," countered Joanie. "We *are* the neighbors now."

Willard and Walter both chuckled at her comment, but Charlotte and Ruth were not amused. Frank merely shook his head.

"We also got stuff like *Mr. Sandman* by the Chordettes, or *Sneakin' Around* by B.B. King." Joanie chose that moment to glance at Willard and smiled ever so slightly when he turned away.

"Here we are!" exclaimed Verna when she returned with a small stack of 45 records in hand. All were in individual paper sleeves.

"Okay, fine," conceded Frank as he shrugged his shoulders. "You all go ahead and dish up your food. I'll be right back with the record player. If I can find it."

"Whoo hoo!" hollered Verna while she set down the records, grabbed a paper plate and began filling it up with food.

"Dig in," indicated Bell as she glanced at the others.

"Don't mind if I do, Aunt Bell," beamed Joanie while she followed her sister Verna through the food line.

"Which side are your cousins from?" Charlotte whispered to Walter. "I don't recall you *ever* mentioning them to me!"

"Their mother Violet is Bell's older sister," explained Walter in hushed tones. "Hey, I'm really sorry I didn't mention them, but I didn't think it was important. Both of them came to stay with us during the summer once when we were in junior high school, and had terrible crushes on both of us."

"Which I assume was not reciprocated?" Charlotte grilled him.

"Not on *my* part," Walter assured her.

"What y'all talkin' about?" asked Verna when she came up behind them with a heavily-laden plate of food. "Better get ya some vittles 'fore they're all gone."

Walter gave Charlotte a look of apology and put his arm around her as they went over to get some food. When Charlotte wasn't looking, he gave Verna a stern look of displeasure and shook his head in the negative. He definitely was not interested!

Okay, fine, thought Verna. She made a face at Walter and shrugged her shoulders. Carefully setting down her plate of food on the picnic table, she made a beeline for Frank, who had just come outside carrying his RCA record player.

"I'll need to plug in the other end of this extension cord first," Frank informed Verna after carefully placing the record player on the side of the patio farthest away from the food so nothing would happen to it. After plugging the record player's cord into one end of his extension cord, Frank grabbed the other end of it and began walking toward the garage.

Without waiting for Frank to return, Verna had already taken a small stack of 45 records out of their paper sleeves and put them in place on the record player, ready to drop down automatically and play one at a time once the device was plugged in.

Just when Verna opened the ice chest to retrieve a beer for herself, the record player came to life, dropped down the first record, and began playing *Mr. Sandman*. Uncle Frank had obviously plugged it in.

"Ginchy," grinned Verna as she grabbed a bottle opener from the serving table and used the *church key* portion of it to make two triangular piercings into the top of the can, one for airflow and the other from which she could drink her beer.

"I'll have one of those, too," indicated Joanie while she put her plate of food down on the table across from Verna's.

"Help yourself, I'm busy," responded Verna as she began to sway back and forth to the music before joining in singing with it.

"How old did you say your cousins are?" Ruth whispered to Willard when they finished getting their food.

"Joanie's the same age as me and my brother," answered Willard as he headed for the picnic table.

"What about Verna?" asked Ruth while she followed him.

"She's a year younger," replied Willard as he set his plate of food down next to Joanie's.

"Can't we sit down *there*, with Walter and Charlotte?" requested Ruth. *I want nothing to do with the kissin' cousins,* she thought.

"Perhaps you should eat down there with them," suggested Willard. "You must have a lot to get caught up on."

"You need to make up with your brother sometime," insisted Ruth. "This is ridiculous, the two of you not speaking like this."

"I'll talk to you," flirted Joanie when she sat down next to Willard with her opened can of beer and set it by her plate of food. "Can I get one of these for you?"

"Thanks, I'd like that," smiled Willard.

"Fine!" snapped Ruth. She quickly scooted her plate down to the other end of the picnic table where Walter and Charlotte were eating.

Bell smiled imperceptibly after observing the exchange. *Perhaps these freeloader nieces of mine will finally earn their keep.*

Frank elected to sit in the middle, with Verna on one side and an empty place beside him where Bell could sit by Ruth. Instead, Bell chose to sit next to Willard, so she could keep an eye on things. On her other side sat Walter and Charlotte; she conveniently turned her back on them by sitting sideways toward Willard and Joanie.

After the gut-stuffing meal, Willard got up to go use the restroom. Unnoticed by the others, Joanie followed after him, seemingly for the same purpose.

Willard had just finished washing and drying his hands. He was ready to head back outside when Joanie came up from behind in the hallway outside the bathroom and put her arms around him. "I've missed you."

"I've missed you, too," admitted Willard while he turned around and allowed Joanie to kiss him full on the lips again. *Does she suspect I'm still in love with her, even after all this time?*

"I waited for you to write me," whispered Joanie as she pushed herself against him.

"I'm married now," explained Willard, when he started to pull away. "We were just teenagers, anyway."

"Hey, do you remember the time Mrs. Beasley caught us in her hen house?" asked Joanie while she pulled him close again and gazed seductively into his eyes.

"How could I forget? That was the day Mrs. Beasley marched us back home and told my mother what we'd been doing," remembered Willard as he shook his head at the memory.

"I'll never forget the whippin' Aunt Bell gave the both of us with that yardstick of hers, right before callin' my mom to come take me and Verna back home that very night," lamented Joanie.

"But you and I were supposed to be married," Willard reminded her. He put his hands on her shoulders while searching her face in earnest. "We had planned to run away and elope before your mother could get there. Don't you remember? And next thing I knew, you were gone. She had already taken you home!"

"Where would we have gone?" Joanie quizzed him. "How would we ever have made it? You're right, we were just kids."

"We could have at least tried," opined Willard.

"You're still in love with me, aren't you?" asked Joanie while she gave him a sultry once-over. "I can tell."

"What I don't get is why you would just go off and join the Navy like that," mentioned Willard. "And not once did you ever bother to write *me*!" *Why am I still so angry about it, even after all these years?* he wondered.

"I know, that's what my mother told Bell," admitted Joanie.

Willard narrowed his eyes at her. "Weren't you in the Navy?"

"For nine months?" questioned Joanie with a raised eyebrow. "And then they conveniently kicked me out so I could come back home? Where do *you* think I was?"

"What did you do to get kicked out?" Willard grilled her.

"You are rather thick in that noggin of yours, aren't you?" Joanie shook her head with dismay. "Never mind, forget I said anything." *There's no need for Willard to know about the baby I gave for adoption. Willard's baby.*

Unknown to them, Ruth had come inside to use the restroom and seen them in each other's arms in the hallway. Quickly ducking out of sight so they wouldn't notice her, Ruth hid in the guest bedroom until they were gone. Hot tears of anger, humiliation and sadness streamed down her cheeks. *Was marrying Willard a mistake?* Ruth had not overheard their entire conversation, but she had certainly heard enough.

Ruth tightly clutched the $250 to her chest that Walter had handed her to give to Willard. *What should I do now?*

After using the restroom, Ruth splashed some cold water on her face to try and hide the fact she had been crying. Realizing it was as good as it was going to get, Ruth carefully slipped the money into a secret compartment in her purse before heading back outside.

She was just in time to see Walter and Charlotte pulling away in a 4-door 1951 Ford sedan that was seafoam-green with a white top. *Very nice,* thought Ruth. *Especially compared to the used convertible Oldsmobile Willard bought from a buddy at the fab shop where he works as a welder.* She thought it might be a 1949, but wasn't sure. It suffered major body damage at one point, which was why Willard obtained it so cheaply. And of course, Willard's superior welding skills enabled him to easily perform the bodywork needed to repair the car's damage, after which he painted the whole thing a horrid steel gray.

Still out back on the patio, Willard was shamelessly flirting with Joanie while he waited for Ruth to return. Frank and Bell were visiting with Verna, who had finally managed to empty out the large bowl of barbecue chips and was snacking on a piece of homemade beef jerky.

Blowing her nose one more time on the handkerchief she kept in her pocket, Ruth took a deep breath before joining them.

"Are you ready to leave yet?" Ruth whispered to Willard.

"Joanie and I were in the middle of a conversation," Willard curtly responded to Ruth. He was not pleased about being interrupted.

"Hi, Ruth," greeted Joanie with an insincere smile. "I think we're about done. You can have him back."

"Oh please, don't hurry on my account," answered Ruth while she glared at her rival.

"We should be off," Willard apologized to everyone. "Mother, thank you for the nice meal."

"Thank you for helping us eat it," grinned Bell. She made no effort whatsoever to hug her son or his wife before they made their exit. Her niece Joanie had exceeded her wildest expectations. *Now, it's just be a matter of time,* she thought smugly.

"Don't be a stranger, now," called Joanie as she watched Willard and Ruth walk away.

"Yes, come back soon, and bring that handsome brother of yours," added Verna while she took a sip of beer.

Frank merely shook his head with antipathy. *One of these days, Bell will get her comeuppance for interfering in the lives of others.*

The ride home was silent, save for the sound of Willard's car engine. Ruth stared out the passenger side window with great anxiety. Just when they pulled up in front of the small white clapboard house that she and Willard called home, Ruth turned to Willard and tried to hand him the $250. "Walter said to give you this."

Willard was *not* pleased. "Well, it's a little late now! I don't want his money. You can just send it back. Actually, I don't care what you do with it, but I'm not taking charity from the likes of him!"

Ruth watched in astonished silence as Willard got out of the vehicle, slammed its door shut, and stomped toward the house.

7. Special Blend

Nearly a year had passed since the eventful barbecue party at Frank and Bell's house on Simpson Street. It was September of 1955.

Even though Walter and Charlotte continued to live near Norton Air Force Base, Willard and Ruth had chosen to continue renting the small white clapboard house in Ashton. They decided to remain together, despite the incident with his cousin Joanie, but things were never the same.

With Willard busy working most of the time, Ruth's time alone as a full-time housewife led to anxiety, depression and uncertainty about his fidelity. Not only that, her husband's ongoing feud with his brother Walter made it awkward for her to reach out to her long-time best friend Charlotte, who she historically turned to for emotional support during the most difficult times in her life. Even worse, Ruth still suffered from PTSD as a result of the incident as a teenager when she had been electrocuted during the same lightning strike that killed her older sister and brother-in-law.

Unexpectedly, Willard's mother Bell began coming around during the middle of the day on week days to see how Ruth was, seemingly to befriend her. Bell would often bring with her a special blend of homemade tea that actually seemed to alleviate some of Ruth's symptoms of depression, for a small fee of course.

The doorbell rang. It was Bell. Ruth had been crying again, so she quickly dabbed her cheeks on a handkerchief before answering the front door. "Please, come in."

Dressed in a smart-looking black and yellow flowered dress with black silk gloves, purse and heels, Bell also wore a black hat with a realistic yellow silk rose perched on its side. In the woven, black basket she carried over one arm, there were six mason jars containing her *special blend* of poppy seed tea. She arrived by taxi, as she normally did when not wanting Frank to know she had been somewhere. Upon finding Ruth at home, Bell waved for the taxi driver to go ahead and leave. *Besides, I still have one more customer in Ruth's neighborhood to see next after her. I can call for another taxi after that.*

"Hello," smiled Bell when she stepped inside and made her way to the kitchen counter so she could set down her heavy basket of goods. "I figured you'd probably be about out by now."

Ruth merely nodded. The $250 Willard had refused to accept from Walter last year was beginning to dwindle. *Would Willard be upset if he **ever** found out I kept it?* she wondered. *Still, at the time he said he didn't care what I did with it. Why should I feel such apprehension about it now? And, what will I do when it's gone?*

"I can only spare three jars today," clarified Bell while she carefully removed them from her basket and set them on Ruth's kitchen counter. "Your neighbor Tina has already spoken for the other three jars I have with me today, but I could come back with more later in the week."

"This is good for now," responded Ruth as she headed for the bedroom to retrieve some money. "I'll be right back."

"I saw in the paper today that a bottle of vodka is selling for $7.42," mentioned Bell when Ruth came back into the room. "Prices just keep going up, don't they?"

"You're not raising *your* prices on the poppy seed tea, are you?" questioned Ruth as she handed Bell three five-dollar bills, one for each jar.

"Of course not," grinned Bell while she swiftly put the $15 into her purse. "You're family. And poppy seed tea is easy enough to make, if you know how."

"Would you care for some tea cakes?" offered Ruth.

"That would be nice," replied Bell as she approached Ruth's kitchen table, but paused to brush off the chair with her handkerchief before sitting down. It was clear from her demeanor that Bell did not approve of Ruth's housekeeping skills.

Ruth retrieved a tin canister on her kitchen counter and brought it to the table. After removing the lid, she pushed it toward Bell. "Please, help yourself."

Made from simple cupboard ingredients of lard, sugar and flour, the oddly-shaped tea cakes were obviously homemade.

Bell frowned at the stale-looking creations in Ruth's tin canister and slowly shook her head. "Maybe another time. I wouldn't want to take the last of your tea cakes."

"It's no problem," countered Ruth. "I can wrap a couple of them up in some aluminum foil for you to take with you."

"I'd better not," declined Bell. *Food poisoning is the last thing I need now, especially with my special blend business picking up. Even the local madame and her girls have become loyal customers and swear it's not only good for natural pain relief, but also for a good high at the end of a busy evening.*

"Perhaps I can help you next time you make another batch of tea," suggested Ruth. *I'll need to learn how before my funds ran out. I can't afford to keep buying it from Bell.*

Bell smiled ever so slightly. "Perhaps, we'll see."

"I have some empty jars you might want to take with you," remembered Ruth. "Do you want to take them today?"

"How many?" asked Bell with a raised eyebrow.

"At least a dozen," guessed Ruth. "They're out in the shed."

"Next time," responded Bell.

"So, just what do you put in the poppy seed tea when you make it?" probed Ruth. "I'm curious."

"Lemon juice," revealed Bell with a sly grin.

"You do have lots of lemons on your lemon tree," acknowledged Ruth while she slowly nodded. "What else?"

"The rest is in the preparation," revealed Bell. "You know, many customers have told me it not only helps with depression and headaches, but also promotes digestion, boosts skin and hair health, and even treats coughs and asthma."

"I've seen poppies growing wild behind your garden area," mentioned Ruth. "Are those the ones you use?"

"Well, of course," smirked Bell. "It would be illegal to pick wild poppies somewhere else, or on public land."

"Is it true there's opium in them?" Ruth suddenly asked. She had been hesitant to find out.

"Who knows," grinned Bell while she shrugged her shoulders. "None of my customers seems to complain."

"Oh, I'm not complaining," assured Ruth. "I just wouldn't want Willard to find out and think I'm taking drugs, or anything like that."

"Have I ever mentioned our arrangement to him?" Bell grilled her with a questioning look.

"No, you haven't," acknowledged Ruth. "I just wouldn't want him to find out I've been paying you like this."

Bell smiled a crooked smile. "You can be certain he won't hear it from me." *Frank must never find out about my newfound steady source of income, either!*

* * *

Leticia and Carolyn sat silently by Willard's bedside, watching him struggle to breathe, even with the use of a ventilator. It was Saturday, September 9, 2023, and they had each slept around the clock in their rooms at the Rosewood Hilton while waiting for the call that Willard was conscious again. The call had never come, but they had returned to the Rosewood Memorial Hospital anyway to wait for an opportunity to finally speak with him, should he wake up unexpectedly. Jim and Janette were waiting in the hall, drinking cups of coffee from a nearby vending machine.

Seeming to be aware that he was not alone, Willard slowly opened his eyes. Everything appeared fuzzy at first.

Noticing at once, Carolyn touched Leticia on the arm and motioned toward Willard with her head.

"Dad?" Leticia gently took his hand and squeezed it. "Can you hear me?"

Unable to speak due to the breathing tube, Willard slowly nodded his head and squeezed her hand in return.

"He's smiling!" exclaimed Leticia. "I think he's glad to see us."

"Hi Uncle Willard, I'm your niece Carolyn," explained Carolyn while she gently took his other hand in hers. "I know we haven't seen each other for many years, but I'm so glad we finally found you again!"

Willard seemed troubled but was unable to respond. He simply squeezed Carolyn's hand to let her know he had heard her.

"Ladies," came the voice of Natalie when she entered the room. "Now that Willard is conscious, Dr. Shotts has ordered our respiratory therapist to begin weaning him from the ventilator by changing its settings to more *on demand* so he can breathe with a simple oxygen mask instead. You'll need to leave the room until this is accomplished."

"How long will it take?" questioned Carolyn.

"It can vary from a few minutes to several hours," described Natalie. "If he starts breathing on his own without any problems, it should go fairly quickly."

"How soon will we be able to talk to him?" Leticia grilled her.

"It all depends on him," replied Natalie. "If everything goes well and he tolerates breathing on his own, he should advance quickly to the mask, but may have a sore throat and a hoarse voice for a while afterward. If, on the other hand, he can't breathe on his own during a controlled test, we'll have to continue weaning later. If repeated weaning attempts are unsuccessful over time, he may need to use the ventilator long term."

Carolyn and Leticia exchanged a worried look.

Cole entered the room with a med cart filled with special equipment for the procedure. "Dr. Shotts is on his way and actually wants to do the extubation himself."

"Very well," nodded Natalie. "Ladies?" she motioned for Carolyn and Leticia to leave.

"We'll just be outside, in the hall," responded Carolyn while she and Leticia left the room.

"How is he?" asked Jim as they sat down beside him and Janette.

"They need to wean him from his breathing tube to a simple oxygen mask," explained Leticia. "Hopefully, he'll be able to talk to us afterwards, if it works."

"Of course, it will," Jim assured Leticia while he put a comforting arm around her.

"Oh good, you're still here," came the voice of Natalie when she approached. "Dr. Shotts had an emergency and won't be able to do the extubation until later."

"How much later?" asked Leticia.

"It will be at least a couple of hours," replied Natalie. "Besides, Willard needs his rest right now; the weaning process can be exhausting. May I suggest you come back after lunch?"

"Can't we just wait with him?" pleaded Leticia.

"I'm sorry," refused Natalie as she unemotionally adjusted the black horn-rimmed glasses on her nose. "It's also time to change his sheets right now."

"On it," acknowledged Cole while he hurried into Willard's room with a clean set of bedding.

"Well, as Arnold once said, *we'll be back,*" grinned Jim as he stood to leave.

Natalie was not amused by the anecdote and met his even gaze with annoyance.

"Alrighty then," muttered Janette when she got up, too.

"I wonder when someone else will take over *Nurse Ratched*'s shift," added Leticia in hushed tones once they were far enough down the hall to avoid being overheard.

The group walked in silence after that until reaching the Lamborghini.

"Where should we eat lunch?" questioned Janette while Jim unlocked and opened the doors for them.

"That Thai place was fabulous," opined Carolyn.

"Let's do Mexican this time," differed Janette while they climbed inside and buckled their seatbelts.

"Hey SIRI, show me directions to a good Mexican restaurant that is open and located within a five-mile radius of our current location," specified Jim.

"La Casa Del Pueblo," responded SIRI as the route materialized on her screen.

"Works for me," approved Janette.

Carolyn and Leticia nodded their heads in agreement.

La Casa Del Pueblo it is," announced Jim while he started up the vehicle and took off at a high rate of speed.

"Jim," cautioned Carolyn, who was sitting in the front passenger seat and reaching for a handgrip. "Can you *please* slow down?"

"Sorry," apologized Jim. "It isn't every day you get to drive something that corners like it's on rails."

"Well, if you *do* decide to drive on rails," stipulated Carolyn, "you can stop and let me out first."

"Oh, by the way, ladies," mentioned Jim, "the Coroner's report just arrived in my email this morning."

"What did it say?" asked Leticia. She was anxious to find out.

"I was hoping to get a look at it during lunch," replied Jim.

"He's probably a fast reader, too," chuckled Janette.

"Let's hope so," commented Leticia.

"He is," Carolyn assured her with a heavy sigh.

"Turn right on Evergreen Street at the next intersection," came the voice of SIRI.

The light was green, so Jim slowed and made the turn, being mindful of Carolyn's desire to travel at a reasonable speed.

"Continue on Evergreen Street for two miles, and then turn left on Larch Street," added SIRI.

The municipally-maintained road-verge located between the sidewalk and the road was planted with mature gingko trees interspersed with cherry trees on either side of the two-lane thoroughfare. St. John's Wort was planted beneath them as ground cover and to help keep weeds at a minimum. The gingko leaves were just beginning to turn a gorgeous yellow. It would be a few more weeks before the cherry tree leaves would start to metamorphosize into brilliant shades of orange, bronze and red. Most of the businesses along Evergreen Street were housed in well-kempt mid-century modern and Tudor-style homes now occupied by lawyers, dentists, hair dressers, doctors' offices, coffee shops, and other small businesses.

"I'll bet it's a mess to rake up all these leaves, once they start to fall," opined Carolyn.

"Good thing they're on city land," replied Jim.

"Like they're gonna bother to come out and rake 'em up each week," scoffed Janette. "They probably come out once a year with a recycling truck so the residents or small business owners can put all the leaves they've raked up into them, just like anywhere else."

"*Touché*," chuckled Jim.

"Turn left on Larch Street in 200 feet," announced SIRI.

"We should have just eaten at the hospital," lamented Leticia.

"We're almost there," Jim assured her as he winked at Leticia in his rearview mirror. "Would you like me to speed up?"

"No!" came the voices of his passengers in unison.

Jim responded with a crooked smile while he slowed for the turn onto Larch Street.

SIRI continued, "La Casa Del Pueblo is located at 135 Larch Street. You will reach your destination in 100 feet."

"Hey SIRI, stop navigation," Jim informed the device.

"Navigation stopped," confirmed SIRI before her screen suddenly went dark.

"At least MIRA would have said thank you, Jim, or something like that," chortled Carolyn.

"Indeed," agreed Jim when he turned into the parking lot of La Casa Del Pueblo and pulled into in a spot near its entrance.

Mature yucca trees lined the far end of the parking lot, providing minimal shade from the sun for the cars lucky enough to get there first. Surrounding the yucca trees were a series of low-lying sagebrush intended as groundcover. Silvery in color when backlit by the sun, the drought-tolerant plants were a perfect complement to the other full-sun selections on the property.

The jagged flagstone path leading to La Casa Del Pueblo's front entrance was surrounded by a huge cactus garden interspersed with large boulders and river rock. In fact, the entire establishment was encircled by cactus of every kind, including golden barrel, prickly pear, saguaro, blue flame, candelabra, claret cup, lemon ball, hedgehog, and several other less common varieties of cactus. A towering monkey puzzle tree stood in the very center of the garden, its distinctive spiky branches quite at home in the prickly garden. A black wrought-iron bench sat beside the front door.

"Definitely stay on the path!" exclaimed Janette while they made their way toward the entrance.

"How do they get these all to grow here in this climate?" questioned Carolyn as she studied the impressive cactus garden.

"Con mucho cariño y ternura," came the voice of a worker who had been hidden from view behind a large cactus on which he was working, cautiously trying to brace up one of its heavy limbs. "Welcome to La Casa Del Pueblo, I am Roberto."

"¿Estás abierto para el almuerzo?" asked Jim.

"Si, de esta manera," grinned Roberto while he carefully took off his thick leather welding gloves and came over to push open the door for them. "This way." Roberto's clean-shaven face and naughty smile were compelling, and he made intentionally flirtatious eye contact with each of the women.

"Thank you," smiled Carolyn as she and the others followed them inside.

"My pleasure, Señorita," flirted Roberto, causing her to blush while he undressed her with his eyes.

Janette and Leticia were both surprised by his boldness and attempted to avoid further eye contact with the man.

Roberto was around 30 years old, extremely handsome, about 6'5" tall, and obviously a weight lifter. His long black hair was neatly tied back into a ponytail, though his work boots, blue jeans and red flannel shirt seemed out of place inside the posh establishment. Roberto immediately removed and hung his sombrero and garden gloves on wall pegs inside the front entrance where they blended seamlessly with the other Mexican wall decorations. Large oil paintings depicting scenes from Mexican village life graced most of the walls. An accordion and a guitar were mounted on one wall beside highly decorated maracas, and a pair of castanets. A refurbished juke box sat beneath them. The 45 vinyl records it played were exclusively Mexican folk music, including polka, mariachi, ranchera, and others.

Each of the tables was hand painted with picturesque scenes from Mexican villages and heavily lacquered on top. The bench seat backs were likewise decorated.

"These are lovely," admired Janette as she stopped to study some of them while trying to follow Roberto and the others to the table he was leading them to.

"Fueron enviadas a Ecuador para ser pintadas a mano durante la pandemia," volunteered Roberto while he motioned toward a large table in the corner of the room.

"What did he say?" asked Janette as she turned to Jim. Her Spanish was rusty, so she didn't understand.

"My apologies, ma'am," flirted Roberto. "They were all sent to Ecuador to be hand painted during the pandemic, during our down time when we were closed."

"Very beautiful," complimented Carolyn when she and the others sat down on the hard, rounded wooden bench seat surrounding their table.

"Do you ladies mind if I order?" questioned Jim.

"Actually, I'd just like some carne asada tacos," mentioned Janette. "If that's okay?"

"Anything you want, it's on me," insisted Jim.

"Carne asada tacos for me, too," nodded Carolyn.

"I'd like a taco salad with shredded beef," requested Leticia.

"Las bellas damas ciertamente saben lo que quieren," grinned Roberto as he turned to Jim. "And you?"

"Fajitas de pollo," decided Jim.

"Gracias," acknowledged Roberto while he smiled again at each of the women. "What would you lovely ladies like to drink? Margaritas, perhaps? Vino de casa?"

"Water for me," indicated Leticia.

"Me, too," added Janette.

"Sí, por favor tráeme un vaso de agua," requested Carolyn. It was the only phrase from her high school Spanish class that she still remembered well enough to use.

"Estás llena de sorpresas, bella dama," flirted Roberto. He caused Carolyn to blush again.

"Water for everyone," added Jim, who unexpectedly felt a slight wave of jealousy at the way Roberto was interacting with Carolyn. "Un lanzador estaría bien."

"As you wish," responded Roberto when he left to go fill their order.

"So, about that autopsy report," prompted Leticia.

Jim pulled out his laptop and opened it.

"Won't you need a Wi-Fi password?" questioned Janette.

"I've got satellite," Jim assured her while he logged into his device.

"Of course, you do," chuckled Janette as Roberto returned with a large basket of tortilla chips and two kinds of salsa.

"Nuestra contraseña es cactus," volunteered Roberto when he saw Jim's laptop.

"Gracias, pero no es necesario. Tengo satélite," responded Jim with a sly smile.

"Impresionante," nodded Roberto when he left for the kitchen.

"Their password is cactus, if anyone needs it," chuckled Jim.

"Makes sense," acknowledged Leticia.

"Okay, this is what we know," began Jim. "Let's start by reviewing the newspaper articles."

"Do we have to?" asked Leticia. The entire subject was quite painful and she did not wish to relive it.

"We will need to review and compare all the facts as part of our investigation," replied Jim.

"Very well, go ahead," agreed Leticia.

Just then, a beautiful young woman resembling Roberto showed up with two pitchers of water and glasses for each of them. She wore an off-the-shoulder elastic Mexican dress hand-embroidered across the bodice and waistline with bright red flowers, green stalks and leaves. Her long dark hair was worn straight back and neatly braided. Her bright red lipstick and long red fingernails were complemented by a string of red beads and matching earrings. Even without the heavy makeup or long false eyelashes, the young woman was well-built and stunning to behold. She carefully placed silverware packets wrapped in paper napkins by each of them.

"Thank you," acknowledged Jim as he winked at her.

"De nada," responded the waitress while she flirted back at Jim.

Carolyn resisted smiling at the exchange, though Janette and Leticia could not help it.

"Okay, let's see what we have here," mumbled Jim when he refocused his attention on the laptop.

"We should probably look at them in chronological order," suggested Carolyn.

"Agreed," nodded Jim. "The first article is dated January 24, 1997, and appears in Section B of the *Ashton Times* for that day. It mentions that the skeletal remains of a 66 year old woman were found in the Ashton home she shared with her son, who reportedly had some mental problems."

"I'm not sure I'm comfortable with this," interrupted Leticia. "Do I have to be here when you go over this?"

"What do you suggest?" questioned Jim as he gave her an inquisitive look. "You and Carolyn are asking me to try and determine what happened to your mother, and the only way I can accomplish that is by starting out with a review of the facts."

"Perhaps I can wait in the car," replied Leticia.

"¿Hay algún problema?" asked Roberto when he returned with some bean dip.

"No problemo," Jim assured him with a slight smile. He loved using that phrase, even if it wasn't real Spanish or grammatically correct.

Roberto immediately recognized it and grinned. "Your food will be ready shortly."

"I'm sorry," apologized Leticia. "I know it's the only way. Please go ahead."

"As you wish," responded Jim. "Let's see. Oh yes, the article goes on to say that the decedent had apparently been dead for quite some time, possibly several years."

"No, it was more like 12 to 18 months," corrected Leticia. "It mentions that in a subsequent article."

"Wasn't she pretty much nothing but a skeleton by the time they found her?" queried Janette.

"That's what it says," confirmed Jim. "It also says that her son was still living there the entire time."

"No way," said Janette. "You mean to tell me he just left her there in the house like that and still kept living there?"

"That's exactly what he did," grimaced Leticia. The entire subject was very difficult for her.

"Exactly where in the house was she found?" Janette grilled Jim.

"It says her remains were found on a bedroom floor of the home," clarified Jim while he studied the tiny print in the newspaper article with squinted eyes. "It also says that her 40 year old son was taken away and hospitalized for mental health evaluation. It says he was delusional at the time but did admit to authorities that the remains were those of his mother."

"Oh, my God!" exclaimed Janette. "What was wrong with him?"

"Luke had schizophrenia with multiple personality disorder," described Leticia. She suddenly grabbed a tortilla chip, put some salsa onto it, and stuffed it into her mouth.

"The article continues by saying the police had to use flashlights when they went into the house, as the electricity had been turned off," related Jim.

"He undoubtedly ran out of money after she died," volunteered Leticia. "So, he was unable to pay the utility bill."

"How sad," opined Carolyn while she slowly shook her head before reaching for a tortilla chip.

Jim nodded as he read the next portion and hesitated before summing it up. "The Ashton County Coroner who came to the scene said that at first glance, there did not appear to be any sign of blunt force trauma, though the cause of death would be difficult to determine due to the advanced decomposition of the body."

Carolyn and Janette both frowned. Leticia was fighting back tears that threatened to erupt from her eyes.

Jim skipped over part of the article but then stopped. "Here's something. Looks like a neighbor had come into the yard looking for their cat when they noticed an open window."

"That's when they looked inside and saw my aunt's skeleton," Carolyn finished for him. "And was why they called the police."

"According to the neighbors, the home's exterior had been well maintained until the previous year," added Jim while he skimmed over the rest of the article.

The beautiful young Mexican woman arrived at their table with a folding tray stand. She quickly unfolded and placed it in the aisle beside them. Roberto was right behind her, carrying a huge tray filled with plates of food he carefully set down on top of the stand.

"Oh, everything looks delicious!" exclaimed Janette.

"Por favor, disfruta," smiled the waitress as she placed each of the plates in front of them. "Please enjoy."

"And don't hesitate to let us know if you need anything else," added Roberto while he flirted again with each of the women at the table.

"En realidad eso será todo," responded Jim as he pulled out his roll of hundreds and handed two of them to Roberto. "Conserve el cambio y revisaremos material confidencial, por lo que agradeceríamos que no lo desembolsen."

"Thank you very much!" exclaimed Roberto. "We will leave you to your meeting."

"What did you tell him?" questioned Carolyn in hushed tones.

"That we will be discussing confidential materials and would appreciate not being disturbed," revealed Jim.

"And to keep the change?" asked Carolyn with a knowing smile.

"Of course," grinned Jim while he gave her an unguarded glance filled with longing.

Carolyn quickly turned away, determined not to let Jim know she had noticed.

"Maybe we could go over the next article after lunch," suggested Leticia as she picked up a fork to begin eating her taco salad.

"Sure. We can wait until after eating," agreed Jim, "but do need to try and go over as much of this as we can while we have the chance."

"That works," agreed Leticia when she took a bite and began chewing. "Not bad."

Carolyn and Janette were already devouring their carne asada tacos in silence, and Jim hurried to eat his fajitas de pollo, so they could get back to the business at hand.

Upon finishing their food, Jim noticed Roberto heading for the door and motioned for him.

"¿Sí señor?" questioned Roberto as he approached.

"¿Puedes retirar estos platos y traernos más agua? Entonces podremos reanudar nuestra reunión," described Jim.

"Maria," called Roberto while he hurried over to retrieve the folding tray stand and set it up again. "Por favor, retira los platos sucios."

"Sí," nodded Maria. She hurried over with the serving tray, placed it on the stand, and began gathering up their dirty plates before quickly wiping off the table with a wet rag.

"Gracias," acknowledged Jim while he handed Maria a hundred-dollar bill. "¿Puedes traernos también jarras de agua fresca?"

"More water, sí," beamed Maria as she hurried off to comply with Jim's request.

"Now, where were we?" asked Jim when he reopened his laptop. "Oh yes, the next article was on the following day, January 25, 1997; it also appears in Section B of the *Ashton Times*."

"Aquí estás," indicated Maria as she placed the fresh pitchers of water on their table, along with clean glasses and a small pile of paper napkins. "¿Te traigo el cambio ahora o cuando hayas terminado?"

"No need for change," flirted Jim when he responded in English. "And we'll show ourselves out when we're done."

"¡Muchas gracias!" grinned Maria as she left to return to her other duties in the kitchen.

"This article seems to theorize as to why the window was open," mentioned Jim, "and the fact that a screen had been pried off. Possibly by a burglar."

"Even a burglar would've been frightened off after looking inside and seeing her skeleton lying there," assumed Janette.

"No doubt," agreed Carolyn.

"It reiterates much of what the previous article stated," continued Jim, "but interestingly, the window lock was stuck in the open position from being previously painted."

"Then it couldn't have been a burglar," surmised Carolyn.

"Strange that someone would paint a house with a window open like that," pondered Janette.

"Unless it was meant to stay open from that time on and pretty much proves it wasn't a burglar at all," guessed Jim. "Do we know when the house was last painted?"

"I have no idea," admitted Leticia as she shrugged her shoulders.

"The article goes on to reveal the identity of the deceased, and talks about Ruth being a public employee who finally retired in 1986 after 20 years with the Social Security office in Ashton," read Jim.

"That's correct," corroborated Leticia. "Mom was a claims examiner there and was respected and well-liked by everyone who knew her. The next article after this even has a photo of her with her coworkers there."

"How old was Ruth when she retired?" questioned Janette.

"I believe she was 56," responded Leticia.

"Ruth and Charlotte were both born in 1930," volunteered Carolyn, "so that sounds right."

"That means Ruth would have continued to live alone with her son Luke for about 10 years after retiring until the time listed as her approximate date of death in 1997," calculated Jim.

"Actually," interjected Leticia, "Luke went away to Bible College for only two years before coming back home to live with her. That was in 1976."

"Remind me again, what year were Willard and Ruth divorced?" Jim grilled her.

"Their divorce was final in 1974, the same day Willard married Beatrice, the woman who became his second wife," answered Leticia. "That was also the year Luke graduated from high school."

"Hmm," considered Jim as he slowly drummed his fingers on the table. "So, it was more like 20 years that Luke lived alone with Ruth."

"Except for the short time I came back to live with them after I graduated from college," explained Leticia, "but I couldn't wait to leave again and it was only a short time before I left to live on my own."

"Why?" probed Jim while he studied her closely.

Leticia became quiet and shook her head. "I couldn't stay there anymore."

"Let's finish looking over the newspaper articles," suggested Carolyn while she put a comforting hand on Leticia's shoulder.

Jim sighed heavily. "It says here Ruth was lying on her back on the floor of a bedroom between the foot of the bed and a wall, and that she had paper towels covering her. Both feet and one hand were propped up with plastic shopping bags that had rolls of toilet paper inside them."

"I wonder if she had edema," speculated Carolyn. "Wouldn't that be what someone would do to try and get the swelling down in someone's limbs? Perhaps caused by congestive heart failure?"

"A very real possibility," agreed Jim as he took a sip of water and considered Carolyn's theory.

"I believe she did have congestive heart failure," remembered Leticia. "That was another reason Luke refused to leave her alone."

"It also says here Ruth's other hand had a plastic drinking bottle by it, and an electric fan on a nearby stool was aimed toward her," considered Jim.

"That makes sense," opined Janette. "When my mother-in-law was dying of congestive heart failure, she would try and rip her clothes off because she was really hot and couldn't cool down."

"Hence nothing but the paper towels covering her, and the fan and bottle of water to try and cool her down," assessed Jim.

"If you read on," said Leticia, "you'll see that an empty vodka bottle lay by her feet, too, and Luke was a heavy drinker."

"Why didn't he just call for help?" questioned Janette.

"Luke wasn't well," Leticia reminded her. "Don't forget, not only did he have schizophrenia, but he also suffered from multiple personality disorder."

"Luke must have felt powerless to do anything but just sit there and watch her die," surmised Jim.

"While doing nothing but getting drunk!" exclaimed Leticia bitterly. "Not once did he bother to try and call me, or reach out for help. Perhaps one of the neighbors could have called 911 for him." She then broke into tears and began sobbing.

"It's okay," comforted Carolyn as she gave Leticia a hug. "We're going to try and figure out why."

"We can't rule out the possibility Luke was no longer able to bear watching her suffer and decided to take the matter into his own hands," Jim reminded them. "Both articles we've read so far indicate that they could not rule out smothering or other subtle trauma to the body."

"Didn't that particular article say something about there being a 70% chance they would prove it, if there was foul play involved?" asked Carolyn. "And that they still needed to test the remains for heavy metals and drugs?"

"Yes, and that's about it for that article," agreed Jim while he put on his Bluetooth to answer his chiming smartwatch. "It's the hospital."

Carolyn and the others became silent as Jim nodded his head.

"When will that be?" questioned Jim. "Okay, we'll plan to be there then. Thank you for letting us know."

"Well?" urged Leticia.

"The extubation went well," revealed Jim, "but Dr. Shotts has ordered that Willard not have any visitors, including family, until after his evening meal tonight."

"That's insane," objected Leticia.

"Nevertheless, it looks like we still have a couple more hours to finish going over this stuff," calculated Jim. "Unless you ladies would like to go back to the hotel first?"

"We may as well get it over with," snapped Leticia.

"The final article is dated February 11, 1997, and appears on the cover page of Section C in the *Ashton Times* for that day. In fact, the article is so long that it continues on the next page, and fills up two entire pages in the newspaper."

"They did interview me for parts of that article," revealed Leticia, "but Willard never spoke to me again after that. I don't think he ever forgave me for talking to the reporter."

"So, was today the first time your father has seen you since then?" questioned Jim.

Leticia merely nodded her head.

"I couldn't help but notice you called him by his name, rather than calling him Dad," observed Jim.

Leticia merely shrugged her shoulders.

"It was that way for me, too," interjected Carolyn. "I usually called my father by his first name until I was about seven years old."

"Hmm. Well, let's hope everything goes well tonight," wished Jim before taking another sip of water.

"Perhaps we can skip over parts of the article that cover what we've already discussed," Carolyn recommended to Jim.

"Precisely what I had in mind," agreed Jim as he gave Carolyn another one of those longing looks that she would deliberately ignore.

"Get on with it," urged Leticia. She was anxious to get it over with.

"This third and final article starts out by mentioning that Ruth and Luke kept to themselves and really didn't socialize with their neighbors," narrated Jim while he attempted to summarize the information. "Looks like Ruth had a hard time walking towards the end, too, but was always accompanied by her unkempt son Luke whenever they would leave the house or go to the store."

"It also tells how Luke would go outside in the yard drunk with only a towel wrapped around himself when he went out to get the newspaper," growled Leticia. "He obviously didn't care what the neighbors might think."

"Still, it seems like someone would have noticed when they didn't see Ruth with him anymore," opined Janette.

"Well, apparently they didn't," countered Leticia as more tears began to stream down her cheeks. "I just figured she wanted nothing more to do with me when she didn't answer my cards or letters. How was I to know all that was going on?" Leticia then began weeping again while Janette and Carolyn tried to comfort her.

"The police did have to kick in the door before taking Luke into custody," continued Jim, seemingly oblivious to how upset Leticia had become. "They also found a pile of mail that had not been opened since 1995, and a phone that had never been hooked up."

"Jim, that's enough," admonished Carolyn. "Can't you see how upset Leticia is? We really need to get back to the hotel now."

"But wait, you have to hear *this*," muttered Jim when he pulled up the Coroner's report and raised his eyebrows.

"Jim," cautioned Carolyn, as she gave him a warning glance.

"Okay, let's finish up at the hotel then," agreed Jim while he watched Carolyn and Janette help Leticia up and head for the door.

Having left Leticia to rest in her room at the Rosewood Hilton, Jim, Carolyn and Janette went down to the lobby to resume their discussion about the case.

"Let's use a conference room," suggested Jim. "That way we won't be disturbed."

"The hospital could call at any time," Carolyn reminded him.

"There is that," acknowledged Jim as he approached the front desk. "Marsha, was it?"

"Oh, Mr. Otterman, hello! What can I do for you?" responded Marsha with a nervous smile.

"We need to use the Redwood Room," Jim informed her.

"Absolutely," nodded Marsha. She grabbed a keycard from beneath the counter and handed it to him. "Do you need any beverages or anything else?"

"This'll do, thanks," winked Jim as he took the keycard from her and started down the hall with his laptop under one arm.

"I really could use a cup of coffee," Janette mentioned to Marsha. "If it's no trouble."

"Not at all. I'll bring you some right away," offered Marsha. "How do you take it?"

"With sugar, cream and an extra shot," answered Janette.

"I'll take one, too," decided Jim, who had turned back to wait for Janette, "but without the sugar."

"Oh, that's right," Janette teased him, "you like your coffee like your women: hot, blonde and bitter."

Jim blushed slightly as he gave Janette a crooked smile before turning to see Carolyn's reaction.

"If it's no trouble Marsha, I could use some mineral water," added Carolyn with a straight face, deliberately ignoring Janette's attempt at comic relief.

"You got it," said Marsha. She hurried off to fill their order.

"Okay, then," muttered Jim when he resumed his trek to the Redwood Room, slid the keycard through a slot at its entrance, and pushed open the thick wooden door labeled *Redwood Room*. The gold-colored plaque was neatly engraved in bold black letters and mounted at eye level. The simple but elegant conference room consisted of little more than a long wooden table surrounded by 12 plush office chairs. Each rose-colored chair had wheels, could swivel or be adjusted for height. The same low-pile, chocolate brown carpet found in the lobby also adorned the conference room floor, as well. A series of three overhead skylights gave its orange and beige walls a warm appearance.

A rectangular one-way window on its southern wall overlooked the outdoor garden area, though no one from outside could see in. The northern wall housed a huge retractable projection screen upon which images could be projected from state-of-the-art computer equipment kept on that end of the table. The east end of the room was adorned by a large oil painting of a redwood forest trail. The west end of the room was occupied by a small supply table, just inside the door. On it were tablets, pencils, pens, paperclips, a stapler, and a telephone.

"This will do nicely," approved Jim while he pulled out one of the chairs, sat down, and opened up his laptop. "Hold on while I plug it in, I think it's running low on juice."

"Jim, I'm not sure if you realize how hard all of this has been on Leticia," Carolyn informed him, "but we need to try and get our crime scene discussion out of the way before she rejoins us."

"I agree," nodded Janette. "None of this can be easy for her."

Jim finished plugging in his laptop just when Marsha entered the room with a small tray containing their beverages. She carefully placed coasters by each of them before setting down the mugs and bottle of mineral water.

"Thanks again," smiled Jim as he pulled out and handed her a hundred-dollar bill.

"Oh, I couldn't possibly take that much," declined Marsha.

Jim then folded the bill in half and tucked it into her pocket, flirting shamelessly with her while he did.

Marsha finally conceded. "Okay, if you insist. Thank you!" She then hurriedly left, being mindful not to let the door slam shut behind her.

I must be in the wrong line of work, thought Janette.

"So, where were we?" asked Jim.

"The third newspaper article," Carolyn reminded him again.

"The long one in tiny print," acknowledged Jim as he pulled it up and tried to enlarge it on his screen. "Apparently, the neighbors never questioned why they hadn't seen Ruth in recent months, except one neighbor who assumed she'd been put in a nursing home."

"I don't think we discussed that yet, but yes, that's what the article says," confirmed Carolyn.

"Let's cover our bases," replied Jim while he continued scanning the article. "It also talks about Luke looking disheveled and returning from the store quite often with a brown paper sack that appeared to have a bottle of alcohol inside, from all appearances."

"Leticia did say he drank a lot," interjected Janette.

"Okay, here's where we were when we left off," recognized Jim. "We were talking about how the police had to kick in the door and forcibly take Luke into custody."

"That was when they took him to the psych ward for further evaluation," added Carolyn.

"The police found that no mail had been opened since 1995," continued Jim, "and, of course, we already talked about the electricity being off and them having to go inside with flashlights."

"How creepy," shuddered Janette.

"We've already talked about how her body was found, the possibility she may have had congestive heart failure, and that being why her limbs were elevated with a fan pointed toward her," reiterated Carolyn.

"Tell me what you know about Luke," requested Jim. He gave Carolyn an inquisitive glance.

"Leticia could probably tell you more," sighed Carolyn, "but as it says in the article, it was unnatural how dependent Luke and his mother were upon each other. In fact, that was one of the reasons Leticia decided to distance herself from them; it was more than she could deal with at the time."

"You can't really blame her," muttered Janette. "She probably needed to consider the safety of her own family, too, especially if Luke was dangerous."

"It says here Ruth fought depression, and she was not only dealing with Luke's drunken fits of rage, but also with the fact that her own mother had Alzheimer's at the time," summarized Jim. "It's little wonder she had a complete collapse from depression and had to be hospitalized in 1992. Apparently, Luke had to be put in a care facility during that time, without Ruth there to take care of him."

"Wow," mumbled Janette while she took a sip of coffee.

"And just as soon as Ruth did go back home, Luke came right back, too," marveled Carolyn as she shook her head.

"The article goes on to say both of them were prescribed medication for their conditions, but stopped taking them," mused Jim.

"Didn't someone from social services look in on them?" asked Janette. "It seems like they would have."

"Apparently not," replied Jim while he frowned at the article. "It also says they continued to live on Ruth's retirement and Luke's Social Security disability benefits until the money finally ran out as a result of extravagant spending by Luke."

"Why didn't Ruth do something about it?" queried Janette. "How could she just let Luke take advantage of her like that?"

"It gets weirder," remarked Jim. "Probably due to his illness, Luke thought that Nazis and some other cult groups were *after him* and was very paranoid. He even thought he'd been injected with *cancerous warts*, but the article does not say by whom."

"Didn't it say something about him shadow boxing in the yard and talking to people that weren't there?" questioned Carolyn.

"That's what it says," confirmed Jim while he shook his head. "It also says he got straight As in school, went to Bible College and at one point wanted to become a pastor."

"You're kidding?" Janette could not believe it.

"The one real job Luke had was as a social worker for the State's Human Services Department, hired especially for his Spanish-speaking skills," reiterated Jim.

Janette continued to shake her head in disbelief.

"When that didn't work out, Luke tried to start his own mail-order business, and even tried his hand at being a professional gambler," summarized Jim.

"Now, that's probably where all his mother's money went," speculated Janette. "What a shame she didn't try to stop him."

"It says here she even bought him a car at one point, and Luke took a cross-country road trip *by himself*," mentioned Jim.

"Luke never married, and never had kids," Carolyn reminded them. "In fact, the only friend he did have was some guy he knew from Bible College, and they were going to get an apartment together, but Ruth put a stop to it and convinced Luke to remain at home with her. She didn't want to be left alone."

"It goes on to say they were only able to confirm her identity from her dental records," concluded Jim. "That's about all we're gonna get from the newspaper articles. What I'm most interested in is the results of the toxicology report and whether any heavy metals were found in what was left of her remains."

"Wouldn't that be in the autopsy report?" asked Janette.

"Yes," answered Jim. Just then his smartwatch began to chime. "It's the hospital again," muttered Jim as he put in his ear buds. "This is Jim."

After a brief silence, Jim nodded his head. "We'll be there shortly. Thank you for letting me know."

"Well?" questioned Carolyn.

"Let's get Leticia and go see him."

8. Christmas of '56

Despite their husbands' differences, Ruth and Charlotte had managed to reach out to one another and were excited to learn the other had just given birth to their first child.

Charlotte had given birth to Carolyn in August and was thrilled to finally have a baby of her own. She and Walter had moved back to Ashton shortly thereafter, to be closer to her parents.

Ruth had given birth to Luke in September, and was equally exuberant about being a new mother. Leticia would not be born for another two years.

After becoming pregnant, Ruth had refused to buy any more of Bell's poppy seed tea, and was convinced it might be harmful to her unborn child. Withdrawal had been difficult, and something Ruth had done completely on her own. Otherwise, her pregnancy had gone well. Now, she was focused on wrapping a set of bath towels that would be Christmas gifts for Walter and Charlotte. She had found them on sale at a price too good to refuse. Nevertheless, it was her hope to keep them hidden from Willard until the next morning. Just then the front door opened. *Willard is home early!*

"What's all this?" questioned Willard as he frowned at the partially wrapped presents on the kitchen table.

"Bell invited us to come over for Christmas dinner tomorrow," Ruth informed him while she swallowed uncomfortably.

"My mother's got plenty of towels, why would she need more?" Willard grilled her.

"Actually, the presents are for Walter and Charlotte," clarified Ruth. "They plan to be there, too."

Willard's nostrils flared with displeasure.

"Don't you think it's time the two of you made up?" asked Ruth as she glanced at the crib nearby where Luke was peacefully sleeping. "They have a baby now, too. Her name is Carolyn."

After pursing his lips together, Willard walked over to the refrigerator, took out a beer, removed the lid with a bottle opener, and took a sip before sitting down at the table.

"Please?" Ruth gave Willard a pleading look. "You know how important Charlotte is to me. We've been friends for years, and I miss her. It would be so nice to meet our new niece."

"And of course, my mother is already expecting us to be there?" Willard questioned her with a woeful expression on his face.

Ruth sheepishly shook her head. "I could always call and tell your mother we can't come."

"Not *now*," conceded Willard while he took another sip of beer. "Breaking a promise to that woman just isn't done."

"You're home early," observed Ruth as she scrambled to finish wrapping the last present so she could clear off the table.

"The boss gave everyone the rest of the day off with pay, since it's Christmas Eve," explained Willard while he wiped off his upper lip.

"How wonderful!" exclaimed Ruth as she whisked the wrapped presents and wrapping paraphernalia from the table and took them to the hall closet to get them out of the way.

"Does Walter know we'll be there?" Willard interrogated her.

"Charlotte was planning on letting him know tonight," admitted Ruth. She grabbed a bag of potato chips from her pantry and poured them into a big bowl for Willard. It was his snack of choice to eat while waiting for dinner each night.

"*Wah! Wah! Wah!*" screamed baby Luke when he woke from his nap.

"Can you check on him while I get your dinner started?" asked Ruth hopefully.

"He's *your* kid," snorted Willard as he stuffed a handful of potato chips into his mouth. "It's still early. Dinner can wait until you're done."

I thought as much! Ruth silently fumed. *It's clear Willard isn't going to help care for baby Luke in any way.*

Willard continued to drink beer and eat potato chips while Ruth changed and fed Luke before putting him back into his crib.

"Since tomorrow is Christmas, I thought you might like something simple for dinner tonight," explained Ruth while she filled a pot with water, put it on the stove, and lit the pilot light before adjusting the flame so it could come to a boil.

"Let me guess," snorted Willard. "Spaghetti again?"

"Actually, I was thinking of macaroni and cheese, canned peas, and tuna on the side," described Ruth as she scurried to get them ready.

Willard sighed deeply, shook his head, and then belched. "Well, at least we'll get something decent to eat tomorrow, I guess."

"Bell is an excellent cook," agreed Ruth while she opened the can of peas and put them into a second saucepan.

"You might wanna take those stinkers out to the garage," suggested Willard as he made a face.

"Of course," complied Ruth. She hurried to retrieve the dirty diaper bag and made a beeline for the garage. *Hopefully, the water on the stove won't boil over before I get back. Willard would no doubt sit there and let it happen. I'll just have to rinse out and wash the diaper after dinner.*

"Telephone," Willard informed her when she came back inside.

Ruth darted over to pick up the ringing phone. "Hello? Oh, how nice to hear from you. Can I call you back in a few minutes? I've got dinner on the stove."

Willard took another sip of beer while he strained his ears to hear Ruth's side of the conversation.

"Oh, that's wonderful," agreed Ruth. "We'll see you then."

"Who was it?" questioned Willard as he watched Ruth hang up the phone and hurry back over to the stove.

"It was your mother. Bell and Frank are both looking forward to seeing us tomorrow," revealed Ruth while she poured the macaroni noodles into the boiling water, stirred them, and turned down the flame. She then stirred the peas.

"Just out of curiosity," inquired Willard, "what will *we* be giving my parents for Christmas?"

"Several jars of homemade blackberry jam," responded Ruth rather proudly. *I've been trying to figure out a way to return the rest of Ruth's mason jars to her and this is the perfect opportunity.*

"That's it?" questioned Willard with a raised eyebrow.

"I could always make a loaf of bread," suggested Ruth. "Unless you think I should go out and buy something?"

"Bell always serves her homemade whole wheat bread for Christmas dinner," recalled Willard. "The jam should be enough."

I thought as much, supposed Ruth as she drained the noodles into a colander. Just then the phone rang again. Ruth turned off the burner on which the peas had been heating. *They're almost done, anyway,* she realized.

"I can get it," offered Willard, who had just finished eating all the chips in his bowl and was currently wiping his hands on his pantlegs.

"Thank you," Ruth smiled with relief while she continued making dinner. "I should have everything ready soon."

Willard set down his half-consumed bottle of beer and sauntered over to pick up the phone. "Hello?"

"Oh, Willard, how are you?" asked Charlotte from the other end.

"Ruth's busy making dinner," volunteered Willard.

"Willard, we're having to take baby Carolyn to the emergency room tonight," revealed Charlotte in a panicked voice. "She's quite sick with pneumonia. Can you please extend our apologies to your parents for us? I don't see any possible way we can be there tomorrow. Plus, we wouldn't want to expose anyone, just in case we have it, too."

"No problem," muttered Willard before hanging up.

"Who was that?" queried Ruth while she began placing dinner on the table.

"Nothing important," assured Willard as he sat down to eat.

It was Tuesday morning, December 25, 1956. Bell had spent hours making all the preparations for Christmas dinner. The turkey was in the oven, and she had just finished basting it. *Hopefully, things will go peacefully enough when my sons and their families arrive for the noon meal.* Steamed broccoli, mashed potatoes, baby carrots, green salad, homemade whole wheat rolls, homemade butter, green and black olives, pickles, celery stuffed with cheese spread and peanut butter, cornmeal stuffing, cranberry sauce, marinated artichoke hearts, and corn on the cobb, were just a few of the tantalizing items in various stages of preparation. Homemade apple pie and pumpkin pie were also in the oven, and would be served for dessert, along with homemade blackberry ice cream that Frank was out back preparing. It was a veritable feast.

Gifts for each of her new grandchildren included several baby outfits Bell had made herself. Loaves of her famous fruit-nut bread were gifts for each of the parents.

Bell's secluded dining room was accessed through an arched opening that led to the kitchen. The only other exit from the dining room was an arched opening that led to the living room. Two ceramic pheasant plaques hung on the beige wall of the isolated dining room. Its red linoleum floor with yellow swirls matched that of the flooring in Bell's kitchen. Nothing but her green dining table and matching chairs occupied the space; its only window looked out at the back patio but was covered with thick beige drapes that were kept closed at all times; yellow and red floral designs on them matched the linoleum floor. Today Bell had the extension leaf inserted into the table, barely making it possible to comfortably seat six adults in the small room. The two babies would need to sit in highchairs in the corners of the room, or on their mothers' laps.

Bell's very best lace tablecloth, ivy leaf china, and polished silverware were already carefully placed on the table in her dining room. Lead-glass drinkware waited only to be filled with water from the matching water pitcher beside them. Her sterling silver salt and pepper set was there, as well.

Surprised by a knock on her front door, Bell hurried to open it. "Walter, you're early."

"I know you were looking forward to having us here for dinner today," began Walter, "but our baby is in the hospital with pneumonia and I can't stay."

"I see," frowned Bell. "What about Charlotte? You both still need to eat something."

"I'm truly sorry," apologized Walter. "Charlotte is there at the hospital now with Carolyn, and won't leave her side."

"Surely the nurses can watch her just long enough for the two of you to get away and eat something," argued Bell. "It's just that I've gone to so much trouble to get everything ready."

"I know and I'm sorry," Walter apologized again, "but Carolyn is in an oxygen tent right now. We both need to be there."

"What's this?" questioned Bell when she suddenly noticed several neatly wrapped packages stacked on her porch.

"They're all labeled," pointed out Walter as he picked one of them up and started to hand it to her. "This one is for you and dad; the rest are for Willard and his family. Can you make sure they get them?"

"One moment," responded Bell while she grabbed the package for her and Frank and hurried inside to get a loaf of her delicious fruit-nut bread and a large wrapped package with homemade baby clothes inside for Carolyn. "These are for you."

"Thank you," Walter tried to appear enthused when he accepted them from her, but was too worried about his wife and sick baby to be convincing. "Merry Christmas," added Walter as he turned to walk away from Bell with the gifts.

"You, too," Bell bid him while she watched Walter walk back to his car with the gifts. *He must be doing well enough to be able to afford a vehicle like that,* she thought.

"Hey," called Frank as he came around from the side of the house. "The ice cream is ready. Shall I go ahead and put it in the freezer for later?"

"That works," mumbled Bell while she watched Walter's car pull away and drive off.

"Was that Walter?" asked Frank. "What are all these gifts on the porch?"

"They couldn't make it," pouted Bell.

"I hope they have a pretty good excuse," said Frank as he put his arm around Bell to comfort her.

"Carolyn's in the hospital with pneumonia," revealed Bell.

"Oh, no! I hope she'll be alright!" exclaimed Frank, suddenly concerned. "I was really looking forward to meeting her."

Just then, the phone rang.

"Want me to get it?" offered Frank.

"That's okay," declined Bell. She hurried back inside to answer it. "Hello?"

"Bell, this is Ruth," came the voice at the other end. It was obvious she'd been crying.

"I suppose you're cancelling out on us, too?" questioned Bell.

"I'm afraid so," apologized Ruth. "Willard has just gone to start up the car and we're taking baby Luke to the hospital. We're not sure what's wrong with him, but he needs to be seen right away."

"Hopefully he'll be alright," responded Ruth. "Are you sure the two of you can't just come over after leaving him there? I'm sure they'll take good care of him. Besides, you still need to eat something."

"I really wish we could," assured Ruth, "but we'll need to make it another time. There is one thing you can do for us, if you would."

"And what's that?" questioned Bell.

"I have some gifts for you and some for Walter and Charlotte," described Ruth. "If I were to leave them on our porch, would there be any way you could pick them up and deliver them for us?"

"Come on!" hollered Willard from the car as he began honking the horn. "Let's go!"

"I have to go right now," indicated Ruth. "Can you do that, please?"

"Sure," Bell finally agreed. "You have a Merry Christmas, and I hope Luke gets better soon."

"You, too," replied Ruth before quickly hanging up the phone.

Bell went to the kitchen and began turning off the oven and each of the burners on her stove before removing her full-body bib apron.

"What are you doing?" demanded Frank.

"I need to go run an errand," described Bell. She went to get her black silk gloves and matching purse.

"I'm coming with you," insisted Frank. "Then we can finish cooking dinner together when we get back home."

"Guess we better load those gifts into the pickup," directed Bell as she went to retrieve the other loaf of her delicious fruit-nut bread and a large wrapped package with homemade baby clothes inside for Luke.

Just when she was getting into the red and black Ford pickup truck, Bell hesitated. "You know, it really makes no sense to stop baking the turkey now. Otherwise, it won't be done until tonight. Plus, the pies need to come out in 20 minutes. Maybe one of us should just stay here. Would you mind?"

"You want *me* to stay here with the turkey?" asked Frank. "And you're trusting *me* to get the pies out on time?"

"I'm already dressed, anyway," pointed out Bell. "That way you won't miss any of the game when it comes on. The only thing you need to worry about are the pies."

"The Super Bowl ain't until December 30th," responded Frank as he lit up a cigarette and inhaled deeply.

"What about that hockey game you wanted to watch?" Bell reminded him. "Didn't you say the Red Wings were playing against the New York Rangers today?"

"That would be nice to see," admitted Frank.

"Then it's settled," informed Bell while she put her apron back on, relit the oven, and basted the turkey again. "There should be nothing else to do but be here and keep an eye on the pies. The stovetop stuff will keep until I get back."

"You sure you feel comfortable driving?" Frank asked her again.

"I'll be fine," promised Bell as she removed the apron again and smiled seductively at Frank before reaching into his front pants pocket to remove his keys.

"Okay, I'll stay here then," flirted Frank from the front porch while he watched Bell get into his pickup, start it up, shift it into gear, and slowly drive away with the many packages in its truck bed.

Bell glanced at herself in the rearview mirror as she approached the first intersection and came to a stop at the light. Forgetting at first to push in the clutch before shifting to neutral, Bell became flustered when the engine died. "I got this," said Bell out loud while she restarted the engine, pushed in the clutch with her left foot, applied the gas and started to roll forward again. "Nothin' to it," grinned Bell as she finally pulled up in front of Willard and Ruth's rental home.

Bell pushed in the clutch with determination, shifted into neutral, and put on the emergency brake so she could leave the pickup running. Bell began carrying the gifts from her and Frank to the porch and neatly placed them near the door. Upon seeing the other packages already there, Bell quickly checked to be sure no one was watching. *I'll open just one to see what it was.* Bell carefully sliced open the tape on one of them with her long pink fingernails and peeled back the wrapping paper. *Sale rack towels? Seriously?* Bell then picked up and shook each of the other packages, and they were all the same. *All cut-rate quality towels,* deduced Bell as she wrinkled up her nose. Then she saw the blackberry jam inside her old mason jars. *Frank must never see these! What should I do?* Bell glanced around again to be sure no one else was in the area. She carefully scooted the gifts from her and Frank over to the opposite end of the porch to keep them safe before focusing her attention on those left there by Ruth for Bell to deliver to Walter and Charlotte.

Oops! Looks like Walter and Charlotte were unhappy with the towels, snickered Bell. She suddenly picked up and tossed each of the packages intended for Walter and Charlotte back down again at impossible angles on Willard and Ruth's porch. Finally, she picked up each of the jars of blackberry jam and tossed them against the front door, one at a time, and watched with satisfaction while they broke and slowly oozed down onto the doormat. *That oughta do it,* smirked Bell as she brushed her gloved hands against each other with gratification before getting back into the pickup truck to continue making her *"deliveries." Willard will never speak to Walter again after seeing that mess,* sneered Bell. Not only that, she was still fuming mad at being stood up by both of them after all the work she had put into trying to make a nice meal for them!

Upon reaching Walter and Charlotte's house, Bell again pushed in the clutch, shifted into neutral, and put on the emergency brake so she could leave the pickup running. Surreptitiously glancing in both directions first before retrieving the packages from the pickup truck bed Walter had entrusted to her that morning, she deliberately tossed them onto Walter and Charlotte's porch at various angles. *Walter will assume Willard was unhappy with them and brought them back,* smirked Bell. Then, upon noticing a Christmas card stuck to one of the packages, she stealthily made her way back to the porch, looking both ways again to be sure none of the neighbors were watching. After slicing open the envelope with one of her long pink fingernails, Bell noticed a baby picture of Carolyn inside. *They sure haven't bothered to give me one of these,* fumed Bell. She suddenly ripped up the picture, put it back inside the Christmas card, stuffed it into its envelope, and tossed it onto the pile of packages. *Walter will never speak to Willard again after this,* believed Bell as she got back into the pickup truck, pressed the clutch, and shifted into gear for her journey back to Simpson Street. *True, what I just did was a little extreme, but the least those boys could have done was to call me last night!* Bell rationalized. *Besides, there's no love lost between them, anyway. Best of all, this will reduce the chance of them figuring out what really happened to the money they paid me for the 1939 Ford 4-door sedan they previously purchased from me.*

It was well after midnight before baby Carolyn was stable enough to breathe on her own, but would need to remain in the oxygen tent for at least another day.

"Perhaps I should go home and take a quick shower," suggested Walter. "I could use a change of clothes, and should make sure the porch light is on. Then when I get back, you can run home for a bit."

Charlotte merely sniffed while she nodded and looked up at him. Tears were still oozing down her cheeks.

"Hey, don't worry," Walter comforted her. "Carolyn will be just fine. They have her on antibiotics; it's just a matter of time."

"Oh, my baby," wailed Charlotte as she began to cry again. "Please, God, don't let her die!"

Walter pulled Charlotte close and gave her a long, tender hug.

"I hope your mother wasn't too upset we couldn't be there for dinner today," mentioned Charlotte when she finally looked up at him before wiping and blowing her nose on a handkerchief. "Are you sure she didn't mind you leaving Willard's and Ruth's gifts there with her?"

"Actually, I called my mother just a little while ago and she said she already put them on their porch," revealed Walter.

"Why wouldn't Bell just give them the gifts at her house?" asked Charlotte as she furrowed her eyebrows.

"It seems they had to cancel out on her, too," revealed Walter. "Luke got into some sleeping pills and had to have his stomach pumped at emergency."

"They were *here* at the hospital?" Charlotte questioned him with a dubious look on her face.

"For a while," confirmed Walter, "but I'm sure they're probably back home by now. I did get a glimpse of them walking down the hall, but I don't think they saw me."

"Do you think they'll like the new baby things we got for Luke?" queried Charlotte. "You wouldn't believe how hard it was to find a handmade baby quilt to match that little jumpsuit."

"I'm sure they'll love the matching sweaters you got for them, as well," presumed Walter when he turned to leave. "You go ahead and stay here. I'll be back before you know it."

"I love you," smiled Charlotte while she watched her husband leave. *How nice it will be to have Walter and Willard speaking again.*

Already angry with Ruth for having left her sleeping pills out where Luke had been able to get to them, Willard was in no mood to have anything else go wrong. It was well after midnight, and he was exhausted. Worst of all, he was slated to return to work later that day.

"So much for Christmas," muttered Willard while he pulled into the driveway of their rental home before noticing someone had thrown something at their front door.

"What in the world is that?" questioned Ruth as she adjusted the blanket around baby Luke and squinted her eyes to get a better look.

"Stay here," Willard commanded her as he turned off the engine, yanked the emergency brake into place, and got out of the car.

Flabbergasted at seeing the sticky jam and broken glass on his front porch, Willard became angrier still when he noticed the very gifts his mother had delivered to Walter and Ruth for them were now brought back and viciously tossed onto their porch.

"That son of a bitch!" cursed Willard as he kicked the front door so hard the doorjamb splintered on the doorknob side. "How dare he do such a thing!" The strike plate was torn out; the door's hinges had become dislodged from the force of impact. It was clear from Willard's new limp that he'd also managed to injure his leg in the process.

Terrified though she was, Ruth slowly got out of the car, put Luke's diaper bag over one shoulder, picked him up, and cautiously approached. "Are those the gifts we left here for Bell to deliver for us?" She, too, was stunned. *How could something like this happen?*

"Get inside!" barked Willard. "We're gonna need to use the back door until I can get this fixed. It could be a few days."

"You're hurt," argued Ruth. "Please let me help you clean up this mess."

"I'll clean it up," insisted Willard. "He's *my* brother!"

Ruth merely nodded as she scurried around the house toward the kitchen door in the back, unlocked it, and went inside. *Why were the gifts from Bell untouched?* wondered Ruth while she gently put baby Luke into his crib and tucked him in. *And more importantly, why had the jars of jam been thrown against the front door?* Ruth asked herself. *Bell is the only one who could have brought them back, and that's if she even bothered to take them in the first place! There's no way Walter or Charlotte would have brought back their gifts.* Ruth had spoken with Charlotte the previous day and learned that she was just as anxious as Ruth was for their husbands to reconcile with one another.

This must be Bell's way of getting even with me for refusing to buy any more of her poppy seed tea, concluded Ruth while she walked over to turn on the front porch light so Willard could see better. After pacing back and forth for what seemed an eternity, Ruth slowly pulled back the living room drapes to see outside.

Sitting by himself near the incinerator can in a lawnchair, Willard was drinking a bottle of beer. The glass appeared to be gone. The front door and porch had been thoroughly hosed off. The doormat had also been hosed off and was stretched out on the front lawn to dry. Even the packages containing towels that had been catawampusly thrown on the porch were gone. Only the presents from Bell remained, and they were sitting on the ground beside him.

Ruth guardedly went back outside, grabbed the other lawnchair, and set it up beside Willard. "Mind if I join you?"

Willard shrugged his shoulders and motioned for her to sit down. "Sorry, but the towels got ruined, so I burned 'em."

"What about the glass?" asked Ruth while she held her hands near the incinerator for warmth.

"I was so angry, I just tossed everything in there," admitted Willard as he gave her a sheepish grin. "And, of course, glass cannot burn because it's an amorphous solid that doesn't have a definite melting point. Instead, it softens and deforms under heat."

"Will we need to get a new incinerator?" questioned Ruth.

"Nah, it won't hurt anything," Willard assured her. "Later after it cools down, I'll just dump out the slag before we burn anything else."

"Would it hurt to just leave it there?" pressed Ruth.

"Who knows," responded Willard while he took a big sip of beer. "Most of what's left is reduced to nothing but a pile of lead and arsenic anyway. We could always just spread it out back to help with the mice."

Ruth and Willard both chuckled at that.

"Hey, I'm really sorry about the door," apologized Willard as he gave Ruth a remorseful look.

"I hope you're gonna call in sick today so you can get your leg looked at," mentioned Ruth while she scooted closer to him and gently put her hand on the knee of his injured leg.

"I may have to," admitted Willard. "Don't suppose I can go in drunk after only two hours sleep."

"Should we open the gift from your mother?" Ruth finally asked with a raised eyebrow. *Or burn it,* she thought to herself.

"Sure, you do the honors," insisted Willard as he handed the large package to Ruth.

"Oh, baby clothes for Luke!" exclaimed Ruth with surprise.

"I'm sure she made them herself," realized Willard. "I guess tomorrow we'll need to call her. We can thank her for the gift and apologize again for missing Christmas dinner."

"Hopefully, she'll want to know how Luke is doing, too," added Ruth while she neatly folded the little outfits and put them onto her lap.

"But, we can certainly burn this," chuckled Willard as he threw the wrapping paper and box into the incinerator, bringing it back to life.

"What about the fruitcake?" asked Ruth with a crooked grin.

"We may need to live on that for a few days," Willard informed her. "Especially after I spend the rest of our grocery money for the week on what I need to fix that door."

Walter had made sure their porch was cleared off and neatly swept before bringing Carolyn back home from the hospital three days later. Charlotte had remained at the hospital with Carolyn the entire time. She had no idea about what had happened with the packages his brother Willard had callously tossed back onto their porch. *I'll never understand how Willard could do such a thing, but I certainly won't be speaking to him again!*

Walter decided to wait until after Charlotte had showered and slept before telling her about the presents; he was still undecided on whether to tell her about Carolyn's torn-up baby picture. That would absolutely break her heart.

It was not until February of 1957 that baby Carolyn was well enough to meet her grandparents.

Apprehensive about whether or not Willard might be there, Walter decided to call ahead to make sure he wouldn't be.

"I just can't understand why your brother would have done such a thing," Bell consoled Walter during their phone conversation.

"That makes two of us," replied Walter, who had been deeply hurt when the Christmas presents Charlotte had so lovingly selected for his brother's new baby were brought back and tossed onto their porch in such a manner.

"Well, no need to worry," Bell assured him. "I doubt he plans to come here again anytime soon."

"Really? Why is that?" Walter asked suspiciously.

"I'm sure I have no idea," responded Bell in her most innocent and convincing voice.

"There is something else," added Walter, hesitant to mention it.

"What would that be?" questioned Bell.

"Well," Walter cleared his throat, "we had put one of Carolyn's baby pictures inside the Christmas card they didn't seem to want."

"What a shame. Perhaps you can just send it to them in the mail," suggested Bell. *This is getting too close for comfort.*

"The thing is," continued Walter, "it was ripped up into pieces and put back inside the card before being tossed on top of the other presents that he brought back."

"Oh, no!" exclaimed Bell. "That's horrible!"

"And of course, Charlotte was devastated," revealed Walter. "She cried for hours."

Bell was silent for several moments. *Should I ask whether they intend on giving me one of Carolyn's baby pictures?*

"Are you there?" asked Walter.

"Oh, of course," responded Bell. "I was just thinking how horrible it was for Willard to do such a thing. It must have been a beautiful picture, I'm sure."

"Well, you're in luck," Walter informed her, "as you'll be getting your copy when we bring her by for a visit today."

"Oh, how wonderful," grinned Bell. *He doesn't suspect a thing.* "I can't wait to meet her."

"There is one other thing, though," stipulated Walter.

"Yes?" questioned Bell.

"Charlotte and I are both concerned about Carolyn's asthma," explained Walter. "She's not contagious or anything like that, but until her breathing improves, we need to make sure she's not around any cigarette smoke."

"I'm sure Frank can be persuaded to go outside if he needs to have a smoke while you're here," responded Bell.

"Excellent," answered Walter. "We'll see you shortly."

* * *

It was Saturday evening on September 9, 2023. Jim, Carolyn, Janette and Leticia were each deep in their own thoughts as they rode toward Rosewood Memorial Hospital in the sleek black Lamborghini.

"We're here," announced Jim as he opened the doors and waited for his passengers to get out.

"Thank you, Jim," mentioned Carolyn while she gave him a weak smile. "I truly appreciate all you're doing for us."

"My pleasure," Jim assured Carolyn. His piercing blue eyes seemed to bore right through her, making her uncomfortable enough to look away.

The exterior lights of the hospital were just coming on, including the many outdoor path lights mounted alongside the low-lying brick wall beside the flagstone walkway leading up to its front entrance.

"I'm scared," Leticia admitted to Carolyn when they entered the building and made their way toward the elevator.

"Me, too," replied Carolyn as she put a comforting hand on Leticia's shoulder while they waited for the elevator doors to open.

"What if he really doesn't want to see me?" asked Leticia. She suddenly felt a sense of dread.

"He seemed happy to see us earlier," Carolyn reminded her when the elevator doors opened.

"We should be more worried about whether or not his fourth wife is there," opined Janette. "What was it, Trixie?"

Leticia merely nodded as the four of them climbed into the elevator. Carolyn pressed the button for the sixth floor.

"We can cross that bridge if we come to it," Jim cautioned her.

"Wonder if *Nurse Ratched* will be there," snorted Janette.

"Even Natalie must take off sometime," grinned Jim.

"*Touché*," smiled Janette when they reached their destination and the elevator doors opened for them to get out.

"Janette and I'll just be out here in the hall," Jim mentioned to Carolyn and Leticia as he headed for the coffee machine.

"I'll have some, too," decided Janette. "It could be a long night."

Carolyn and Leticia approached the nurse's station and waited for Cole to get off the phone.

"Ladies, you're here," beamed Cole. "Perfect timing. His wife just left five minutes ago."

"Thank goodness," agreed Leticia with a look of relief.

"Indeed," smiled Carolyn when she and Leticia headed for Willard's room.

"Oh, he's not in ICU anymore," Cole informed them. "He's been moved to a private room at the end of the hall. It's the last door on your right."

Carolyn nodded in response while she and Leticia made their way down the long hallway.

"Please come in with me," Leticia requested of Carolyn when they got there. "I don't want to go in alone."

"Are you sure you don't want some individual time with him first?" asked Carolyn.

Leticia put her arm through Carolyn's. "I'm not ready for that yet. I still don't know whether he's forgiven me."

"For what?" Carolyn furrowed her brows. "What could you possibly need forgiveness for?"

"For doing the newspaper interview after my mother's remains were found," elaborated Leticia. "In Willard's mind, I sullied the family name by giving them all the information I did."

"His name wasn't even in the article," Carolyn reminded her. "Besides, he may not even remember it by now, depending upon how bad his dementia has gotten."

"What if he doesn't even know who *we* are?" Leticia suddenly asked. "That would be even worse!"

"Come on, let's go in," Carolyn urged her as they walked into his room and approached his bed.

"Uncle Willard," said Carolyn. She came over and took one of his hands in hers. "I'm your niece, Carolyn. And this is your daughter, Leticia. We're both so happy to see you!"

"Carolyn," repeated Willard with slurred speech. "How nice of you to come." He gently squeezed her hand and pulled her towards him for a brief hug and then kissed her on the cheek. She kissed him back before pulling up a chair and sitting down.

"Hi Dad," muttered Leticia while she reached for his other hand with trembling hands. "Do you know who I am?"

"Leticia," mumbled Willard as he pulled her close, too, and gave her a hug and a kiss on the forehead. She quickly hugged him back and gave him a kiss on the lips. "Thank you for coming," he added.

"We're so glad you're going to be alright," said Leticia when she sat down in the other chair beside Carolyn. "There are some things we would like to ask you."

"Sure," nodded Willard as he tried to smile. "Do you think you can get rid of all this first?" He motioned towards the IV stand, heart monitor and other equipment to which he was attached.

"Only the nurse can do that," replied Leticia while she squeezed his hand again.

After an uncomfortable pause, Carolyn decided to break the silence. *It's important to get every possible bit of information from Willard while we still can.*

"Uncle Willard," urged Carolyn, "can you tell us about why you and my dad were not speaking for all those years? What happened between you?"

Willard hesitated before responding in his slurred voice. "It was our mother. Bell was behind all of it."

Carolyn and Leticia gave each other a surprised look.

"She was an evil woman," added Willard. "Always turning everyone against each other, but she was behind it all."

"What did she do?" questioned Carolyn while she gently squeezed his hand again. "Can you tell us?"

"Yes, we really would like to know," added Leticia as she gave him a pleading look.

Willard took a deep breath, let go of Carolyn's hand, and started to reach for a water bottle on the stand beside him.

"Are you thirsty?" questioned Carolyn. She picked it up and handed it to him, carefully positioning the straw so he could drink.

Willard took a few sips before handing the bottle back to Carolyn. "Thank you," he muttered with difficulty.

"Perhaps we should come back later," Leticia whispered to Carolyn. "He looks pretty tired."

"All I do is sleep around here," smiled Willard. "It all started when we were boys and had our first paper route."

"My dad told me that once," interjected Carolyn. "He said your mother kept all the money each of you earned."

"That's right," confirmed Willard. He slowly nodded his head. "We wanted to join Little League, but they said we had to have our own baseball gloves if we wanted to play."

"Was that when she bought the left-handed baseball glove for Walter?" Carolyn grilled him.

Willard nodded affirmatively and mumbled, "Bell said I could just go borrow one from somebody, since right-handed gloves were more common and easy to come by."

"That doesn't seem fair," opined Leticia.

"Bell was never fair," confirmed Willard while he slowly shook his head. "She sent us both to military school when we were in high school, just to get rid of us."

"Why would she want to do something like that?" Carolyn pressed him. "She should have been happy to have such beautiful twin boys like she did."

"We lived in a pretty bad neighborhood," mentioned Willard, "and were always getting into trouble."

"What kind of trouble?" asked Carolyn with an inquisitive look.

Willard paused and considered whether to answer but finally continued. "Bell was trying to get us away from our cousins."

"Didn't a lot of them live in the same neighborhood with you?" queried Carolyn.

"Oh yes, but not them," assured Willard. "The ones she was trying to keep us away from were the ones who came to stay with us each summer. Joanie and Verna."

"Really?" Carolyn raised her eyebrows. "Violet's daughters?"

"Wasn't she Bell's older sister?" asked Leticia.

"She was," answered Willard. "Joanie and I were in love, and our mothers didn't approve since we were cousins."

"That's understandable," responded Carolyn.

"Joanie and I were planning to elope, but our mothers put a stop to it when they sent us away to military schools."

"Even Joanie?" doubted Leticia.

"Yes, even Joanie," revealed Willard with difficulty.

"It says here," mentioned Carolyn, who had just looked it up on her cellphone, "that legislation formally allowing women into the military was first passed in 1948."

"Wow!" exclaimed Leticia. "That's incredible."

"But they kicked her out," muttered Willard. "After just a few months, she came back home and married someone else before I found out she was back or could do anything about it."

"How many months before they kicked her out?" Carolyn grilled him. "Do you have any idea?"

"Nine or ten, I think," recollected Willard.

"Nine months," repeated Leticia with disbelief. *Could I have another sibling out there in the world?*

Understanding the implications immediately, Carolyn gently shook her head in the negative at Leticia. It was clear Willard hadn't made the connection and now wasn't the time.

"Do you know what they kicked her out for?" Leticia asked.

"No idea," slurred Willard. He was getting tired quickly.

"I understand you and my dad were in the same welding courses together," mentioned Carolyn. "Is that where you each got your high school diplomas?"

"Yes," answered Willard. "It was a technical program at Ashton City College, where they offered high school diplomas."

"How awesome that you were able to do that," Carolyn encouraged him. "And then you went on to make a career out of it."

"That's right," nodded Willard. He proceeded to describe the details of his welding career to them.

"Very impressive," agreed Leticia.

"Let me ask you something else," continued Carolyn. "Wasn't there a car the two of you were buying together?"

"Oh, yes," confirmed Willard. "That was when we had our next big blowout."

"What happened?" Leticia grilled him.

"Our parents decided to let us buy their old car," mumbled Willard. It was becoming more and more difficult for him to talk.

"What kind of a car?" Carolyn asked. "Was it the 1939 Ford in this picture?" She then held up her cellphone to show him the picture.

"Yes," confirmed Willard.

"What sort of disagreement did you have over it?" Carolyn interrogated him.

"It was our mother again," revealed Willard. "Bell took all the money, and told each of us the other one hadn't paid their half, so we each gave her even more."

"How could she do something like that?" frowned Leticia.

"Bell was an evil woman," muttered Willard. "We didn't realize what she'd done until years later."

"Was that when you came to visit my dad on his deathbed back in 2004?" questioned Carolyn.

"Yes," replied Willard while he gave her a helpless look. "I'm so sorry for all the years we missed out on."

"Well, we're here now," Carolyn comforted him as she gave Willard another hug.

"Wasn't there an incident about packages being tossed on your porch at Christmas one year?" asked Leticia.

"My parents had packages tossed on their porch that year, too," added Carolyn. "And it wasn't until years later when they realized it was Bell who did it. Obviously, she was trying to turn you two against each other and keep you apart."

"That's true," agreed Willard. "She was an evil woman."

"Is there anything you can tell us about when they found Ruth?" Carolyn suddenly asked. "Do you think Luke might have done it?"

"I do," nodded Willard as his eyes became watery. "He was a very sick boy."

"Ladies, you need to leave now," Natalie informed them. "Willard is getting tired and needs his rest."

"Can we please just ask him a couple more questions first?" requested Leticia with a pleading look.

"I'm sorry, but this visit is over," insisted Natalie with finality.

"May we come back and see you tomorrow?" Carolyn asked Willard as she gave him another hug.

Willard merely nodded. "I'd like that."

"Be sure to call first," stipulated Natalie while she narrowed her eyes at them.

"We will," promised Carolyn as she returned her steel gaze.

"I love you, dad," said Leticia when she hugged him, too.

"Thank you for coming," he responded as he reached for his water bottle.

Natalie hurried over to help him and put the straw to his lips.

"We'll be back," bid Carolyn when she and Leticia turned to leave. "I love you, too, Uncle Willard." *Hopefully, Natalie didn't notice what I just said to him, especially since she believes I'm his daughter.*

As they exited Willard's room to rejoin Jim and Janette out in the hallway, Leticia became somber.

"You alright?" asked Carolyn with concern.

"I don't think my dad's ever told me once that he loves me," sniffed Leticia.

"He still could," encouraged Carolyn. "Just give him time."

"He's had an entire lifetime to tell me that," frowned Leticia.

"At least we're finding out some things we didn't know," pointed out Carolyn as they began walking towards the elevator. "And we do need to get as much information from him as we possibly can, while he's still here."

"True," realized Leticia. "Like finding out about the kissin' cousins, for example."

"What?" inquired Janette. "What in the world are you guys talking about?"

"Apparently Willard and Walter were dating their cousins Joanie and Verna," clarified Carolyn, "and even after all these years Willard's still in love with Joanie. He even mentioned they were planning to elope but their mothers had put a stop to it."

"I should hope so!" exclaimed Janette. "Especially being cousins like they were."

"That was why the boys were sent away to military school when they were 15 years old," Carolyn mentioned when they arrived at the elevator and pushed the down button.

"Oh, my goodness," Janette shook her head with disbelief.

"Now, that makes sense," nodded Jim. "It explains a lot."

"He also talked about his cousin Joanie being sent to military school at the same time," added Leticia. "For nine months before being kicked out and sent back home."

"Uh, say what?" Janette began to smile a crooked smile.

"Yeah, that's what I thought, too," grinned Carolyn.

"Willard didn't even make the connection about the nine months thing," said Leticia.

"Typical man," joked Jim to lighten the mood as the elevator doors opened.

"Not really," differed Leticia while they walked into the elevator. "Willard can be pretty thick headed sometimes. The worst part is, I could have another brother or sister out there somewhere."

"Back then, babies like that were usually given up for adoption, and the records sealed up like Fort Knox," pointed out Carolyn as she pressed the first-floor button. "But now I understand why Joanie and Verna came to my dad's funeral back in 2004 when none of the other cousins showed up."

"No way," muttered Janette while she shook her head. "Seriously?"

"Oh yes," Carolyn assured her. "And not only that, one of them came up to my mother and introduced herself as one of my father's *kissin' cousins* from *back in the day.*"

Jim began to chuckle.

"It's not funny," objected Carolyn while she playfully slapped Jim on the arm. "And at the time, we had no idea the woman was serious. We just thought she had a twisted sense of humor, especially saying something like that to the family at a funeral."

"Maybe you ought to reach out to them," suggested Janette when they reached the first floor, stepped out of the elevator, and headed for the door. "It'd be interesting to find out what else they can tell you."

"Unfortunately, both are long gone," replied Carolyn. "I know from when I was doing my genealogy not too long ago. Joanie died in 2007 and Verna died in 2012, both from lung cancer."

"Bummer," responded Janette as they stepped outside. "Just think of the stories they could have told you."

"What else did you find out just now?" Jim questioned Carolyn while they headed for the sleek black Lamborghini.

"Willard confirmed my dad's story about the paper route money, and also told us about the 1939 Ford they bought together from their parents," replied Carolyn, "but of course Bell managed to get each of them to pay double, kept all the money, and used the whole deal to turn them against each other."

"Willard knows now that Bell was behind everything," clarified Leticia, "and kept telling us what an evil woman she was."

"I was just getting ready to ask him about each of his wives," Carolyn volunteered, "but that was when Natalie showed up."

"That old battle-axe," opined Janette as they reached the car and waited while Jim opened the doors for them; they quickly climbed inside and fastened their seatbelts.

"It would be nice to know if Willard has any information besides what's in the newspaper articles or the Coroner's report about his first wife Ruth," said Jim while he shut the doors, started up the engine, and pulled out of the parking space.

"You still need to tell *us* about the Coroner's report," Leticia reminded him. She was also anxious to learn the results of the toxicology report referred to in the newspaper article.

"We can go over it while we eat," suggested Jim as he put the vehicle into drive and took off at an accelerated rate of speed, despite Carolyn's scowl of disapproval. "How does dinner at the Rosewood Hilton sound?"

9. Comfort Zone

Luke had wanted for years to attend Camp Deliverance, a special retreat offered to high school graduates planning to attend the Bible College recommended by his best friend Richard. Orientation regarding what to expect during dormitory life, career planning and team building activities were just a part of it. The entire experience was also a chance to meet new friends and become more focused on spirituality as a guide in daily life before delving into the routine grind of college life that followed.

It was Luke's goal to become a pastor someday, and to help others like himself who had come from difficult home life situations. Being a straight A student hadn't hurt, either; his application had been accepted without hesitation. Luke was slated to begin classes in the fall semester of 1974, only two short weeks away, but his immediate task was packing his suitcase for the upcoming retreat at Camp Deliverance. Luke picked up the color brochure lying on his bed and began leafing through it again. Pictures of A-frame cabins surrounded by dense forest were most appealing. *A chance to finally get away from it all,* thought Luke as he set down the brochure and resumed packing the golden-brown hard-sided Samsonite suitcase he had borrowed from his mother.

Like his father Willard, Luke had red hair and freckles, making him the constant target of bullies in school while growing up. It was his dear mother Ruth who had always been there for him, no matter what, and who had encouraged him to follow his dreams. Now, it was his turn to be there for her. *Should I still go away, in light of current circumstances?* he wondered. Poor Ruth was not in the best of health and suffered from frequent bouts of depression, especially as of late. *At least it'll be two more years before Leticia graduates from high school or leaves for college, so Ruth won't be alone just yet,* Luke reasoned.

It was during Luke's senior year of high school when his father Willard had unexpectedly filed for divorce from Ruth. Literally on the day of Luke's high school graduation in June of 1974, the divorce became final. Worse still, Willard had chosen that very same day to marry a woman named Beatrice. Luke was beside himself when learning that Willard had been secretly involved with Beatrice for several years.

A sin for which Willard will certainly burn in hell, thought Luke while he neatly folded his best red pullover sweater and added it to the items already in the suitcase. Then, as an afterthought, he added a couple of plaid flannel shirts; one was red and black, the other green and black.

"Dinner's ready," called Ruth from the next room.

"I'll be right there," answered Luke while he quickly put several pairs of men's crew socks, V-neck t-shirts and underwear briefs into the suitcase, too. Luke had already spread out a pair of black-and-white plaid flannel pajamas on his sky-blue cotton bedspread and was undecided about whether to take them. *What if the other guys make fun of me? Perhaps I should just take a pair of sweat pants instead.*

"Your food's getting cold," cautioned Ruth from behind him. She'd come to see what was keeping him.

"I'm sorry, mom," apologized Luke as he gave her a warm embrace and a kiss on the cheek. "I was just trying to decide what to take to camp."

"Don't forget a jacket," Ruth advised him. "It gets cold up in the mountains like that. You should probably take a cap and a pair of mittens with you, too."

Luke quickly grabbed his jacket and tossed it onto the bed beside the half-packed suitcase. "I'm not sure where the cap or mittens are."

"We can find 'em after dinner," suggested Ruth. "You're also gonna want to take your comb, toothbrush, and stuff like that."

"I know, I know. So, what's for dinner?" asked Luke when he put his arm through his mother's arm to escort her to the dining room.

"Your favorite," smiled Ruth as she pulled away from him and hurried to the kitchen to retrieve the dinner items she brought back to the table where the plates, napkins and silverware were already set.

"Where's Leticia?" questioned Luke upon noticing she was not there yet.

"At her friend Kari's house," revealed Ruth while she placed a serving dish of green salad on the table next to the lasagna and garlic bread that were already there. "She's having dinner with them."

"More for us," grinned Luke as he pulled out one of the four aluminum-framed chairs with seaweed-green vinyl seats and backs. The matching Formica tabletop sat on an aluminum frame with hollow legs, still quite common in many homes during the 1970s.

In contrast to the red-and-yellow swirled linoleum floor and bright yellow walls in the dining room sat a corner hutch painted white. Behind its upper glass cupboard doors were Ruth's relatively new Butterfly Gold patterned Corelle dinnerware set. Two small serving drawers with Rubbermaid cutlery trays housed her Oneida stainless steel flatware, and on the area above them sat a lead-glass bowl containing artificial green grapes. The bottom cupboards were filled with placemats, cloth napkins, hand towels, dish cloths, and board games. All of the hutch's cupboard doors and drawers opened with lead-glass knobs.

A matching white bookcase on the opposite wall was filled with several dime store romance novels, used school books, photograph albums, and a well-used encyclopedia set. On top of the bookcase sat a walnut mantle clock that chimed on the hour and two ceramic pheasant figurines. Above it hung a walnut-framed oil painting of Half Dome in Yosemite National Park.

Separating the kitchen from the dining room was a wall where the upper half had been cut out and finished off to make room for a breakfast counter, making it possible to easily see the dining room from the kitchen and vice versa.

Sliding patio doors on the final wall of the dining room led to a covered patio outside where a traditional wooden picnic table and a small round charcoal grill with three legs were kept.

"Do you mind closing the curtains?" asked Ruth as she brought a bottle of Italian salad dressing to the table. "The sun really comes in this time of day since those sliding glass doors face west."

"Absolutely," responded Luke when he got up to comply and quickly pulled the floor-to-ceiling pinch-pleat curtains closed.

Ruth hurried back to the kitchen for the salt and pepper shakers, a plate of butter, and a can of dry parmesan cheese.

"Is there anything to drink?" asked Luke while he shook open the cloth napkin and tucked one corner of it into the top of his rust-colored polo shirt.

"Oh, of course," laughed Ruth as she hurried back to the kitchen, took two aluminum tumblers out of a cupboard near the sink, and filled them with tap water. "Good thing we saved all those old cottage cheese containers."

"Cottage cheese really came in these?" questioned Luke when she brought the tumblers to the dining room and set them on the table by their plates.

"They sure did," confirmed Ruth. "My mom had a set of these colorful aluminum tumblers, a pitcher, and even bowls. I'm not sure where she got the pitcher, but the tumblers and bowls came filled with cottage cheese. When you had accumulated enough cottage cheese-filled tumblers, the dairy would give you the wire carrier. You could buy them at the store, too. We had a blue juice-sized aluminum tumbler in the bathroom that came from Woolworth."

"Huh," nodded Luke as he started piling salad, lasagna and garlic bread onto his plate.

"Let's pray first," stipulated Ruth.

Luke closed his eyes and bowed his head while Ruth said grace. The moment she was done, he began shoveling food into his mouth. "This is so good!" exclaimed Luke with his mouth full.

"Glad you like it," beamed Ruth. *Which is more than I can say for Willard. He never appreciated anything!*

"I was thinking," mentioned Luke, "perhaps I should just go to Ashton City College this fall. It might be cheaper."

"Nonsense," objected Ruth while she squeezed some of the Italian dressing onto her salad. "Bible College is much better than public school, anyway, don't you think?"

"I suppose so," Luke shrugged his shoulders.

"Especially if you plan to become a pastor," Ruth reminded him as she picked up her fork and gently stabbed a piece of lettuce before putting it into her mouth.

"I do have that scholarship from the State," recalled Luke. "Still, the only money you'll have coming in now that Willard's gone is what you make at the Social Security office."

"They have good benefits," countered Ruth before taking a bite of bread and slowly chewing it.

"At least Leticia will be here," mentioned Luke as he took a drink of water before wiping his mouth on the napkin. "I really don't like the idea of you being here alone, if she should decide to leave."

"She still has two years of high school left," pointed out Ruth as she took a sip of water. "I'll be fine."

The refurbished school bus used by Camp Deliverance to transport its guests from Ashton up to its campus slowly wound its way along the winding, two-lane road. A mountain on one side was offset by the frightening drop-off on the other.

Luke's suitcase, along with those of the other guests on their way to Camp Deliverance, was stowed in a compartment beneath the bus. They could all be heard sliding back and forth while the bus made its way around some of the hairpin turns. Wearing a pair of blue jeans, his rust-colored polo shirt, and a new pair of waffle stompers that had not yet been broken in, Luke stared nervously out the window on his side of the bus where the drop-off loomed. *Hopefully, the bus driver remembered to drink his coffee this morning,* thought Luke as he tightened his grip on the seat beneath him. Although many automobiles began including seatbelts as early as 1968, buses just did not have them in the 1970s, if at all.

"I wouldn't go back there if I were you," Richard advised Luke after returning from the solitary restroom stall at the rear of the bus. Richard smiled and pinched his nose to get the point across.

"I'll be sure to keep that in mind," nodded Luke. He would need to use the restroom soon. "Do you know when we'll get there?"

"Probably another hour," volunteered a young man from the seat across the aisle.

"Gee, thanks," sighed Luke. He would try to wait until the odor dissipated before making his way back there.

Richard and Luke had been best friends since grade school, though Richard's constant tendency to make light of things often grated on Luke's nerves. In fact, Richard's goal in life was to become a stand-up comedian. His dark brown hair and blue eyes were something Luke had always been envious of, not to mention the fact that girls seemed to find Richard irresistible.

"Hi, my name's Denise," came a female voice from behind him.

Assuming at first that she was speaking to Richard, Luke abstained from turning around until feeling a gentle hand resting on his shoulder. Irritated, startled and surprised, Luke cautiously turned to face its owner. *She's beautiful,* recognized Luke when he saw Denise for the first time. Her deep green eyes were kind but alluring, framed by long dark lashes; her dark red hair hung in luxuriously smooth curls around her shoulders. Despite being red-headed, Denise did not have any freckles whatsoever; her clear alabaster skin was enchanting. Luke became speechless and simply stared at her with disbelief. *Could she really be wanting to talk to me?*

"You do have a name, don't you?" asked Denise with a slightly flirtatious smile while she removed her hand from his shoulder and held out her hand for him to shake.

"Oh, yes, I'm Luke," he finally managed to say. Despite being flustered, he warmly shook her hand.

"Nice to meet you," responded Denise with a warm, sincere smile. She allowed her hand to linger in his for a moment longer than necessary, a fact that did not go unnoticed by Luke.

"And I'm chopped liver," joked Richard upon noticing their interaction with each other.

"Does that mean they plan to feed you to the hogs?" questioned Denise with a crooked grin.

Luke suddenly felt a pang of jealousy because Richard had interrupted his first ever positive encounter with a beautiful young woman that seemed truly interested in him.

"Actually, my name's Richard," he smiled while he shook Denise's hand, too. "Luke and I are best buds."

"Hopefully, then, I'll be seeing more of both of you," responded Denise as she removed her hand from Richard's lingering grasp and refocused her attention on Luke.

"It's so nice to finally meet another redhead," mentioned Denise while she winked at Luke. "Hopefully, we'll be seeing more of each other this next week."

"I hope so, too," stammered Luke, who was clearly under her spell. *Who knew someone with red hair could be so beautiful!*

"I take it you're planning to attend Bible College afterwards," presumed Denise while she readjusted herself in her seat.

"Luke and I plan to be roommates," interrupted Richard again. He shamelessly flirted with Denise, seemingly unaware of how his behavior was upsetting his friend Luke.

Plans can always change, Luke silently fumed.

"What do each of you plan to major in?" Denise suddenly asked.

"Apparently, Richard intends to make a career at being a stand-up comedian," sniggered Luke, a little more sarcastically than intended.

"Guilty as charged," laughed Richard as he raised his eyebrows in a comical way and shrugged his shoulders.

"What about you, Luke?" Denise asked him.

"I'd kind of like to become a pastor," revealed Luke when he returned her steady gaze. "To help people."

"That's very admirable," Denise responded. "I'm sure you'll make a good one."

"What about you?" Luke grilled her.

"Undecided," revealed Denise with a sheepish grin. "I was hoping the week up here could help me gain some clarity on that."

"Young people," came the booming voice of an athletic-looking blonde man in his late thirties who had been seated near the front. He was now standing in the aisle beside the bus driver. "My name is Bob Locke, and I will be the Team Leader for all you Ashtonians while you're at Camp Deliverance this week."

"He means everyone from Ashton," whispered Richard.

"I get it," snapped Luke, who was still irritated with his friend for trying to horn in on Denise.

"In real life, I'm an electrician with a wife and five kids," added Bob as he spread his arms wide as if to embrace the crowd, "but this week I'm all yours."

Everyone but Luke chuckled at that. *Great, another comedian,* thought Luke while he shook his head.

"We should be arriving there in about five minutes," continued Bob, "so everyone needs to gather up their things and be ready to disembark when we get there. Any quick questions?"

"How many other teams will there be?" asked one young woman who was seated near the front.

"There are nine teams altogether," Bob informed them, "with 10 girls and 10 boys on each team."

"Looks like we've only got 19 on our team," piped up a young man near the back. "My sister Katie couldn't make it. Is that going to matter?"

"Not at all," Bob assured him. "Adaptation's the name of the game, and the Camp Director will answer any other questions you might have once we get there. People, we're going to have a **g-r-e-a-t** week!" exclaimed Bob as he pushed his fisted right hand into the air above his head. "Everyone, say it with me: Go Ashton!"

Everyone on the bus except Luke shouted "Go Ashton!" while they raised their right fists into the air.

"Yeah!" exclaimed Bob as he raised his right fist one more time before sitting back down.

Bob Locke's gray pullover sweatshirt was embossed with bold white letters that said *Camp Deliverance;* his well-worn waffle stompers and blue jeans had seen many adventures.

"Sounds like we're gonna have a great time," Denise whispered to Luke from behind. "I'm glad we're on the same team."

"Me, too," agreed Luke as he turned to give her a smile. *Perhaps if I play my cards right, she might just turn out to be the one.*

Richard noticed the interaction between them and elbowed Luke in the side, giving him a sly smile.

"People, we're here," announced Bob Locke when he stood again and held onto the pole by the door while the bus turned into the narrow entrance. A huge wooden sign beside it read *Camp Deliverance* in large bold letters that had been burned into its surface.

After winding for several hundred feet through the dense forest, the bus emerged into a large meadow where the Camp Deliverance complex was built. Towering granite mountains with snow-covered caps could be seen behind the giant sequoias, incense cedar, white fir, hazelnut, and other members of the surrounding forest. Dogwood, columbine bushes, ferns, salmonberries, and even some poison oak grew beneath them, spread out amongst the lush foliage. At the uppermost end of the meadow grew a towering redwood tree, beside which stood a large central A-framed lodge big enough to hold all members of the camp simultaneously. Its stone chimney prominently jutted upward from the side of the building, but far enough from any nearby trees to allow for safety. The same stonework was used to build out its wide front A-shaped entrance. Long benches, made from logs which had been cut in half, sat on either side of the entrance door. An overhanging ledge above the front area was intended to provide shelter from the weather when necessary.

Slightly downhill from the lodge was a blacktop area containing a small basketball court and a flagpole displaying the American flag alongside the Camp Deliverance flag. Immediately downhill from the blacktop area was a large firepit area surrounded by four sets of five-rowed aluminum bleachers. A wide flagstone walkway led from the blacktop area to the firepit area. Additional flagstone walkways led separately to five small A-framed cabins on one side of the firepit area, and to five more on the other side. Farthest downhill from everything else was the cafeteria, a long narrow structure with a food delivery truck, and several other camp buses that had already arrived, parked beside it in an oblong blacktop parking lot. A wide cement staircase leading to the cafeteria was flanked with wrought-iron hand railings for safety.

"Wow!" exclaimed Richard while he and Luke got up to get off the bus once it had parked in the cafeteria parking lot where two workers were busy unloading boxes from the food delivery truck and carrying them inside. Upon seeing Denise, Richard hung back to allow her to go ahead of them in line to get off the bus.

"Thanks," nodded Denise as she walked past them. Her firm young hourglass figure was perfectly proportioned; the tight pink pullover sweater she wore was lowcut in front and revealed just enough cleavage to be noticeable but within acceptable limits; her blue jeans, however, were so tight they almost appeared to be painted onto her body. Still, she walked with the grace of a ballerina dancer, even in the well-worn waffle stompers she wore.

Being closest to the window, Luke purposely shoved Richard into the aisle behind Denise, the moment she had passed their seat. *I'll stay behind Richard to keep from losing track of Denise in the crowd.*

It was early Saturday afternoon on August 16, 1974, and the young people in attendance at Camp Deliverance for the upcoming week-long adventure were seated by team on the aluminum bleachers surrounding its large welcoming firepit.

Bob Locke and the other eight Team Leaders had just finished stacking logs in the middle of the firepit which would be lit later that evening, and had returned to sit with their respective teams. An imposing man in his late fifties who appeared to be a weight lifter, stood at a microphone mounted on a freestanding pole attached to a power cord leading to an undisclosed location nearby. The man was short and stocky but intimidating nonetheless.

"Can you all hear me?" he asked as he tapped on the mic, causing it to make loud squealing noises.

"Yes!" responded the crowd in unison.

"Excellent," smiled the man. "I'm Dr. Michael John, Camp Doctor and Director. I also happen to do trapping in my spare time, so y'all can just call me Trapper John."

Everyone except Luke broke out into raucous laughter.

Richard leaned over and whispered to Luke, "*Trapper John, M.D.* is a popular medical drama on TV."

Luke merely nodded. *How had I not gotten it?*

"And before we go any farther," added Dr. John, I'd like you to meet our staff. "Each of you is already familiar with your Team Leader, of course, so no introductions are necessary."

Voices began whispering for several moments.

"Very important to all of us," boomed Dr. John, "is my lovely wife Rachel, who is also Camp Chef."

The crowd clapped in unison as she stood and nodded at them.

"Next, is our Maintenance Coordinator," introduced Dr. John. An elderly Filipino man in excellent health slowly stood and bowed to the crowd with the palms of his hands pressed together.

"Mr. Kim is the one you can thank for everything you see around you," described Dr. John.

The crowd clapped again.

"Finally," added Dr. John, "This is Norma, who is our Summer Camp Ministries Director, and her Administrative Assistant, Sandra."

Both women were tall and thin with blonde hair and in their mid-thirties. The group whistled and clapped while they applauded them.

"Most of you intend to go on from here to attend Bible College," continued Dr. John, "so this will hopefully give you a better idea of what to expect during dormitory life. Having a roommate will undoubtedly be different than your current living situation at home."

The voices and whispers started up until noticing Trapper John holding up his hands and patiently waiting for them to be silent.

"Unlike school, however, this week is intended to be fun," grinned Dr. John. "The various team building activities you will be participating in this week are designed to give you a better idea of whether or not the career you've chosen is suitable for you. And best of all, this will be a chance to meet new friends and learn how being more focused on spirituality can help guide you to make better choices in your daily lives. Is everyone ready to have a good time this week?"

"Yes!" came the enthusiastic response from the crowd.

"Good," beamed Dr. John. "Each of you has been assigned to a specific A-frame cabin where your luggage has already or soon will be placed. Your Team Leader can take you there now. I look forward to seeing everyone in the cafeteria for dinner at 6:00 p.m. That's the long, skinny building down there where the buses are parked, though it's probably not on a diet."

Again, everyone but Luke erupted into laughter while they stood and gathered into groups beside their respective Team Leaders.

Is Trapper John really trying to say the cafeteria's not on a diet? wondered Luke. He seriously did not see the humor in it.

"Team Ashton, we're in Buildings A and B," called Bob Locke. "Girls, you will be in Building A. My lovely wife Sarah will be your counselor."

"Hi girls, follow me," directed Sarah as she motioned toward the A-frame where they would be staying.

"Here I thought she was at home with all those kids of yours," Richard teased Bob Locke while they watched Sarah and the Ashton girls head towards Building A.

"At least two of my kids are older than you," chuckled Bob. "Ashton guys, we'll be staying in Building B."

Luke followed Bob Locke, Richard, and the other eight young men from Ashton toward Building B.

"Only half of you get to sleep on top," Bob informed them while he motioned toward the six sets of bunk beds. "Mine, of course, is the one on the bottom closest to the bathroom. The other beds are all fair game; first come, first serve."

Luke frowned as he watched everyone else bolt for the various beds they were interested in, almost immediately leaving only two top bunks available; one above Bob Locke.

"Hey, can we switch?" Luke asked the guy who had claimed the top bunk above his friend Richard. "Richard and I were hoping to share the same bunkbed."

"Oooh," sniggered the guy while he gave Luke a crooked grin. "We certainly wouldn't want to keep you two love birds apart."

"It's not like that at all," frowned Luke. He watched the guy grab his sleeping bag and toss it onto one of the other two available top bunks before raising his eyebrows at them in an exaggerated fashion.

"Damn right, it's not," growled Richard when he turned toward the guy in a combative manner.

"Enough!" hollered Bob Locke. "That's no way to get the week started. We all have to learn to get along and live together as a team. That's not the way to do it."

"Sorry," Richard apologized to the group.

"I think introductions are in order," continued Bob. He turned to Richard first. "I guess we already know your name is Richard. How about you?"

"My name is Luke."

"What about you?" Bob turned to the young man who had vacated the bunk above Richard.

"John."

"I know," decided Bob. "In addition to your name, I'd like each of you to tell us what you plan to major in when you get to Bible College, and in a sentence or two tell us why you decided to come to Camp Deliverance this week." He then turned to Richard.

"Okay," Richard shrugged his shoulders. "As you know, my name's Richard, and it's my goal to become a stand-up comedian someday. I just needed a chance to unwind for a week before delving into the routine grind of college life."

"Same here," said Luke, "except my goal is to become a pastor to try and help people."

"Excellent," approved Bob. "And how about you, John?"

"I plan to become a professional football player," John indicated while he folded his arms to appear more intimidating.

"Just don't be tackling anyone here," Bob reminded him with a raised eyebrow, causing everyone to chuckle.

"I wouldn't dream of it," John assured him while he gave Luke a sideways glance.

"My name is Mark," volunteered the young man who would be sharing a bunk with John. "Anytime he wants to trade bunks, that's fine with me."

"I'm not that heavy," snickered John while he flexed the muscles in his arms to show off his well-developed biceps.

"Nevertheless, the offer's open," insisted Mark. "And my goal is to become a negotiator."

Everyone chuckled at that.

Bob Locke nodded with approval before turning to the next young man.

"I'm Matthew and this is my brother Douglas." Both of them smiled at the group. "We come from a family of ranchers and plan to continue our father's business."

"You do rodeo?" questioned John.

"Just cattle drives, that kind of thing," revealed Douglas. He was clearly a man of few words but also quite muscular and completely unafraid of John.

"We will be doing some horseback riding this week," mentioned Bob Locke with a sly smile.

Luke became pale upon hearing the news but refrained from commenting. He had never ridden a horse before in his life.

"I'm David," indicated the next young man, "and my goal is to become a computer programmer someday. Being here will be a nice change of pace."

"Same here," said the next guy. "My name is Bruce, I'm his brother, and both of us work for my father's software company. Hopefully our week here will give us some ideas we can incorporate into a computer game we're developing."

"Guess the cat's out of the bag," grinned David as he shrugged his shoulders.

"Hold it," interrupted Luke. "How can your father have a software company already when the first BIOS and 8-bit operating system CP/M didn't even come out until this year? I was reading about how it was just created by a guy named Gary Kildall."

"BIOS?" questioned Mark with a puzzled look.

"BIOS stands for basic input/output system," clarified Bruce, "and Kildall wasn't the only one. IBM developed SEQUEL earlier this year, too. It's a structured query language program that I predict will go hand-in-hand with the SNA they created with it. Our father's company is just one of many that have sprung to life this year."

"Well, bully for him," snickered John while he rolled his eyes, put his left hand on his hip, slid the fingers of his right hand into one of his jean pockets, and began tapping his right boot against the floor.

"SNA stands for Systems Network Architecture," added David with a smug look at look at John. "Someday they may even make it easy enough for someone like you to use."

"Nah," disagreed Bruce. "Guys like him are more the gaming type. And, of course, the first computer game was developed in 1962. That's nothing new."

"He's right," agreed Luke. "Spacewar was developed in 1962 at MIT by a guy named Stephen Russell. In fact, Spacewar originally ran on a PDP-1 computer the size of a large car."

"Okay, that's absolutely enough!" interrupted Bob Locke while he waved his hands back and forth in front of him with frustration. "Let's finish with our introductions first." Bob then turned to the next young man. "How about you?"

"My name's Ken. I just started my own landscaping business," revealed Ken. "Being here gives me a chance to get out into the great outdoors."

"And I'm Rodney," said the final young man. "I've spent my summer so far as a retail clerk at a grocery store, but am hoping this week to consider other possibilities or at least get some ideas."

"Marvelous," approved Bob Locke as he looked over his young charges. "This should be an exciting week to say the least."

"Why do we need hiking boots?" Luke suddenly asked.

"That's a very good question," smiled Bob. "Because we will be doing quite a bit of it. I hope your boots aren't as new as they look, Luke. Perhaps our brochure should have specified to wear boots that are broken in, but no worries, they soon will be."

The others snickered and laughed at his comment, especially John.

"What will we be doing between now and dinner?" questioned Luke. He had hoped to write a postcard to his mother, letting her know of his safe arrival.

"Well, since we've all been riding on a bus for the past two hours," answered Bob, "I think we should go for our first informal hike together, right now. Then I can show you the rest of our campus."

"It's pretty obvious what's here," argued Luke, who was anxious to take off his waffle stompers.

"Actually, no," differed Bob. "I'm sure you must have read about our Olympic-sized swimming pool. In fact, it's nestled in the forest, only a quarter of a mile away, where you will be taking a basic lifesaving course while you're here."

"What if we can't swim?" asked Rodney, who was terrified of water after watching a younger sibling drown during a family picnic five years go.

"Just learning how to swim could save your life someday," predicted Bob Locke. "No worries, there will be basic swimming instruction available, too, but everyone who can will be expected to participate in the lifesaving course."

"What if we didn't bring a swimsuit?" queried Rodney.

"No problem," Bob assured him. "We have swimsuits of every size imaginable in our campus supply store, just in case anyone forgot to bring one."

"They must be expensive," argued Rodney.

"On the house," promised Bob with a crooked grin. "Then, after we get a look at the pool, we'll be taking a quick hike over to our new barn and corral to get a look at the horses."

"Awesome!" exclaimed Matthew. "I was wondering where the horses were kept. That's one of the main reasons we wanted to come, after reading about them in your brochure."

"Indeed," agreed Douglas. *This will be our big chance to show the others what me and my brother Matthew can really do.*

"How much farther is it from the pool to the corral?" inquired Luke, who was apprehensive about hiking too much in his new boots.

"You'll see," smirked Bob without giving him an answer. "And if we have enough time afterwards, we can go get a look at the chapel."

"The chapel?" questioned Luke.

"It's an outdoor church in the forest, with pews made of giant logs cut in half, and behind the pulpit are views of the snow-capped mountains behind it," described Bob.

"Sounds breathtaking," responded Luke. *In more ways than one,* he thought.

"So, the sooner we get going, the better chance we have of being on time for dinner," answered Bob. "Trapper John will not allow anyone to begin eating until everyone is there, and we don't want the other teams upset with us on our very first day, now do we?"

"No," responded the group.

"Excellent, grab your jackets," Bob instructed them. "And above all else, do **not** touch *anything* in the forest. We must stay on the trail. The last thing we need is for one of us to get poison oak."

Last in line on the heavily forested trail they were traversing, Luke did his best to try and keep up with the rest of the guys from

Team Ashton, but the blisters forming on his feet were painful. He was winded and not used to such strenuous exercise. *Why in the world did I bother to come?*

After visiting the Olympic-sized swimming pool, the group headed for the barn where several dozen horses were kept. Matthew and Douglas were particularly interested in the corral area. Lastly, the group made its way to the outdoor chapel. There was at least a quarter of a mile in between each location, though it was as beautiful as Bob Locke had described. Luke reverently sat down on one of the outdoor chapel pews and gazed up at the snow-capped mountains in the distance behind the pulpit. He could visualize himself standing at such a pulpit, preaching to his own congregation someday. For now, he needed to take off his boots; he could not stand to keep them on another moment.

"What are you doing?" questioned Bob Locke when he noticed Luke starting to unlace his waffle stompers. "I'd leave those on if I were you. You certainly can't walk around barefooted, not out here."

"I'll manage," Luke assured him. He continued unlacing his boots. "My feet are killing me!"

"You will leave them on," insisted Bob with finality. "Once you take those boots off, you'll need to disinfect any places that are raw and put some moleskin on 'em. Otherwise, they could get infected."

John shook his head with frustration. *Why in the world would Luke come to camp with new boots that hadn't been broken in?*

"Luke, trust me on this," added Bob when he sat down beside him. "I'm sorry your feet are sore, but we need to wait until we get back to take a look at them."

"Don't you have your first aid kit with you?" asked Luke. He frowned at Bob.

"My apologies, but it's back in our A-frame," explained Bob. "I didn't realize we'd need it for such a short excursion. Sorry, but I don't happen to have any moleskin or other first aid supplies with me."

And you're a Team Leader? Luke shook his head with dismay, but finally relented and began retying his boots.

Back at Building B, the other members of Team Ashton waited with impatience while Bob Locke treated Luke's feet by putting moleskin on his blisters. "You will need to keep those blisters covered," instructed Bob as he handed Luke an extra sheet of moleskin.

"It's 6:05 p.m. already," complained John while he watched Luke pull on a clean pair of crew socks before donning his slippers. "Are you really wearing *those* to the cafeteria?"

"Yep," answered Luke, "if you want me walking there tonight."

"What about tomorrow and then the next day," pressed John as he turned to Bob. "Is our whole team going to be held up all week long if Luke can't wear his boots again?"

"I have an extra pair of boots his size that are broken in," revealed Bob when he picked up Luke's boots to take with him. "We'll consider it a trade."

"Uh, my mom paid $85 for those," objected Luke as he reached out to try and grab them back.

"Just for the week," promised Bob. "There's no way I can allow you to continue wearing these new boots for all the hiking we're going to be doing while you're here. I'll bring you the other pair later tonight."

"I'm wearing these," differed Luke.

"I'm afraid not," countered Bob. "Especially when we do the five-mile hike to where the canoes are kept later in the week."

"Great," muttered Rodney, who was terrified at the prospect of going anywhere near a lake or a canoe. *Learning to swim in the Olympic-sized swimming pool will be bad enough!*

"I'll tell you what," decided Bob. "Since everything each of us does affects everyone else on our team, let's put it to a vote. Agreed?"

Luke finally nodded.

"Everyone in favor of Luke wearing his new waffle stompers for the rest of the week raise your hand," proposed Bob.

No one raised their hand.

"Everyone in favor of Luke wearing my extra pair of boots for the rest of the week, raise your hands," offered Bob.

All hands went up, including Luke's.

"Now, if we hurry, we can get to the cafeteria by 6:10 p.m.," urged Bob. The young men from Team Ashton stood to follow him there.

Embarrassed by the bedroom slippers he needed to wear when they entered the cafeteria, Luke immediately noticed Denise sitting at the table reserved for Team Ashton. *We'll be sitting with the girls!*

"Now that everyone is here," announced Trapper John from a microphone at one end of the cafeteria, "we can have grace and get started. I believe a member of Team Ashton may wish to volunteer?"

"I'll do it," offered Richard as he stood and raised his hand.

Dr. John nodded with approval while Richard made his way toward the microphone and then offered prayer to bless the food.

Once Richard made his way back to the Team Ashton table, Dr. John continued. "A roster of duties is posted by the door, showing which team will be serving everyone at each meal, and which team will be doing the dishes afterwards."

Whispers erupted from among the crowd.

"Team Rosewood will be serving tonight," announced Trapper John, "but due to the lateness of their arrival, Team Ashton will be doing the dishes for them after everyone has finished eating."

"What does that mean?" asked Luke as he turned to Bob Locke. "I need to go put my feet up after this."

"Apparently, we'll be doing all the dishes first before being excused," interjected John. He was clearly not happy about being one of Luke's cabinmates. "Thanks to **you**!"

"It shouldn't be too bad," intervened Denise. "Not with all of us working together as a team."

"She's right," agreed Bob's wife Sarah.

Just then, a young man from Team Rosewood began plopping plates down in front of them.

"Gee, thanks for being on time, guys," muttered John, who was being sarcastic. "Who knows, with Luke on our team, we could end up washing dishes after every meal!"

"Guess there's no hurry about eating it, then," countered Luke. He made a face of disgust upon seeing his plate contained meatloaf, mashed potatoes and mixed vegetables from a can. Worse still, the mixture contained peas!

"At least it's better than freeze-dried backpacking food," Denise whispered to Luke, who was seated beside her.

One-half hour later, Trapper John's voice could be heard coming from the microphone again. "Once everyone in your team has finished eating, your table is free to go, but absolutely everyone at your table must be finished first."

The sudden clamor of benches by the teams who had finished eating was interrupted by another announcement from Trapper John. "You will all bus your own dishes to the receiving window at the back. Paper napkins in the trash can, food in the compost can, and dishes left on the counter for Team Ashton to wash tonight. You will then push in your benches and wash off your tables before leaving. Any questions?"

Within minutes, the entire cafeteria was deserted, except for Team Ashton. Luke had not eaten his peas and was scowling as he continued to pick at them.

"Are you going to finish your food or not?" John grilled him. He was sick and tired of Luke ruining things for them.

"I ain't eating the peas," announced Luke when he set down his fork. "Even if it means sitting here all night."

"You're done eating, then?" questioned Bob Locke.

"Yes, I'm done," confirmed Luke.

"Yeah!" came the unanimous cheers from the other members of Team Ashton.

"Okay, folks. Please be sure to put any uneaten food in the compost can," Bob reminded them while everyone at the Ashton table began getting up to bus their dishes, clean off their table, and shove in their benches.

"Nice job," muttered Richard in a sarcastic voice while he passed by his friend Luke and deliberately gave him a hard nudge with his shoulder.

"May I please go put my feet up?" Luke asked Bob Locke.

"No, you may not," responded Bob. "We are a team, and it's everyone's responsibility to wash the dishes when we're assigned to do so. The only way of getting out of it is when you're too sick to be here and intend to go home without finishing up your week here at Camp Deliverance. Would you like me to have a call placed to your mother?"

"Fine, I'll help wash the dishes!" snapped Luke, clearly unhappy about it. "There's no need to bother my mother, she has enough to worry about."

"Hey, it shouldn't be all that bad," whispered Denise. "Not if we all work together."

Luke slowly nodded. Perhaps having Denise by his side would help make the job less daunting.

"I think we should draw straws to see who washes the pots and pans, and who washes the dishes," suggested Sarah while she held up a handful of straws she had located inside the kitchen.

"That's an excellent idea," grinned Bob as he took half of them from his wife and broke off the ends. He then gave them back to her to tap into alignment with the other straws. "Everyone, draw a straw."

Each member of Team Ashton complied, though none of them realized just yet what the implications of drawing short or long straws wound entail.

"All short straws to the kitchen," Sarah directed them. "You'll be washing the pots and pans."

"Everyone else to the serving area," Bob instructed the Ashton team members. "We'll be washing, drying, and putting away all the plates, cups and silverware."

"How will we be able to wash the pots and pans if *they're* using the sinks?" questioned Luke. The last thing he needed was to continue standing longer than necessary on his sore feet while waiting in line to perform the unpleasant task.

"Oh, you won't be using the sinks for *these*," smirked Sarah as she motioned toward the largest pots and pans Luke had ever seen in his life. "They're too big to fit."

"Then how in the world are we supposed to wash them?" asked Luke while he gawked at the gargantuan cooking vessels with disbelief. *A person could easily climb inside one of those pots,* he thought.

"Well," laughed Sarah, "after scooping all leftovers into these square white storage containers, you'll need to put them inside the walk-in refrigerator. Next, the pots and pans will need to be taken out back to be cleaned. You should work in pairs. For example, one of you can squirt the soap while the other one scrubs. Other team members can hose and dry them off. Finally, the sparkling clean pots and pans will need to be hauled back inside, ready for the chef to use when preparing breakfast tomorrow morning at 4:00 a.m."

Groans and murmurs of complaint could be heard.

"And," warned Sarah, "if the chef discovers any pot or pan isn't cleaned to her satisfaction, the entire team assigned to wash them will be gotten up out of bed and brought here to finish the job."

"At 4:00 a.m.," added Bob with a mischievous grin.

"With the expectation you'll be completely finished before reveille at 6:00 a.m. when everyone else gets up for the day," grinned Sarah. "Otherwise, Team Ashton could be penalized."

"In what way?" asked Matthew.

"That's a good question," smiled Bob. "Throughout the week we will accumulate or be docked points for how we perform as a team. Then at the final campfire, the winning team will receive an award. The losing team will be assigned an unpleasant cleanup task that involves all of the A-frame cabins."

"We do *not* want to be that team," added Sarah.

"Man, this sucks," grumbled Luke. *I'll undoubtedly get my new bedroom slippers all wet, too.*

"Let's take this one, it's empty," Denise suggested to Luke. "I can scrub, Richard can squirt on the soap, and you can hose it off."

At least I'll be in control of the water, realized Luke while he nodded in agreement.

Nevertheless, it was not long until all members of Team Ashton were fully engaged in a water fight, squirting each other with dish soap and water. Even Luke began to laugh and have a good time as he got into the spirit of things. *Squirting John with the hose was most satisfying.*

"People," shouted Bob Locke. "Once you are finished, you will need to get changed into dry clothes so we can report to the campfire as a team. They will be lighting the fire at precisely 7:00 p.m."

The soaking wet members of Team Ashton suddenly became somber while they hurried to finish their task in silence.

"You'll need to hose all the soap and any food particles from the cement pad back here, too," directed Sarah, before they could manage to make their escape. "We don't want anyone slipping or falling later on, especially our chef."

"Wait a minute," said Denise. "Didn't they introduce *you* as the chef earlier?"

"No, that would be Trapper John's wife, Rachel," Sarah reminded her. "Nice try."

"Oh yeah, that's right," nodded Denise before hosing off the cement pad in earnest.

It was 7:00 p.m. on August 16, 1974, and it had been a long first day of camp. Trapper John stood at the microphone by the large firepit. All the other teams were already seated on the aluminum bleachers when Team Ashton arrived. "Good of you to join us," he mentioned in his booming voice. "I see you've all managed to finally change into something dry."

Laughter from the entire camp erupted.

Team Ashton quickly seated themselves. Denise had chosen to sit by Luke and waited to see if he would scoot closer.

"Norma, our Summer Camp Ministries Director, will start out our evening campfire by offering a word of prayer," announced Dr. John. "After that, her assistant, Sandra, will lead us in song."

When everyone's eyes were closed for prayer, Denise gently reached over and slipped her hand into Luke's. When prayer was over, Luke tenderly squeezed her hand and continued to hold it. *Is she the one?* He truly hoped so.

"I hope everyone knows the words to *Kum Ba Yah*," mentioned Sandra. She raised her right arm to begin leading them in song while Trapper John lit the campfire.

After several more songs and a moving spiritual talk by Norma, Dr. John gave the closing prayer.

"People," he added, "You will hear reveille at 6:00 a.m. and you need to be showered, dressed, and report to the blacktop area by the flagpole at 6:30 a.m. where we will raise the flag and then march together to the cafeteria for breakfast. You'll find out when we get there what our activities will be for the day. Goodnight, everyone."

"Goodnight," echoed the group as the various teams vacated the bleachers and headed toward their assigned cabins.

Luke turned to Denise, wondering if he should kiss her goodnight, but hesitated. *Perhaps it's too soon. I don't want to do anything to turn her off.*

"I look forward to seeing you tomorrow," smiled Denise while she tenderly kissed Luke on the cheek. "Sweet dreams."

Luke stood in the moonlight watching while she followed the other girls from Team Ashton to Building A.

"I thought you wanted to get off your feet," Bob reminded him with an elbow jab in the ribs when he appeared beside him and waited for Luke to start walking again.

"Just how in the world are we supposed to be dressed and ready in only 30 minutes in the morning while sharing a single bathroom with everyone else in our cabin?" Luke asked Bob while they made their way toward Building B.

"Sleep lightly," grinned Bob.

It was Friday morning, August 23rd. The week had passed quickly, with Luke and Denise becoming quite close. Breakfast was over; each suitcase was in the process of being stowed beneath the bus on which its owner would be riding. Everyone had been given one hour to say their final goodbyes to everyone before reporting to their assigned bus for the trip back home. The entire camp would need to be vacated of guests before the new group arrived the following day.

Surprised at how much he enjoyed the activities when Denise was involved, Luke was sorry to see his stay at Camp Deliverance end so quickly. *Thank goodness for Bob Locke's broken-in boots,* he thought. *Too bad I have to give them back.*

Should I tell Denise yet I'm in love with her? Luke asked himself. *Or should I wait until we're at Bible College?*

"What ya thinkin'?" questioned Denise as she put her chin on Luke's shoulder and nestled beside him.

"Oh, I was just thinking how nice it will be that we are both going to Bible College together," responded Luke while he squeezed her hand. "I hope you know how much you've come to mean to me this past week."

They were seated on one of the half-log benches outside the lodge, a place where basket weaving, beading, oil painting, and various other craft activities had taken place throughout the week. It was also where firesides were held during the winter or when the weather outside became inhospitable.

"You've come to mean a lot to me, as well," replied Denise as she scooted closer to him and put one hand on his leg.

Luke's breath became shallow and he readjusted himself on the bench to try and hide his physical response to her closeness. *Does she realize the effect she has on me?*

"What will you be doing this next week?" Denise suddenly asked. "Are you all packed for Bible College yet?"

Luke shook his head in the negative. "I actually was waiting until after our week here before making my final decision on whether to go there, or not."

"And have you decided?" asked Denise with a raised eyebrow.

"Yes, I've made up my mind," answered Luke. "I'm going."

Denise smiled a sensuous smile and put one of her hands on his cheek. "I've been wanting to touch your beard all week long."

Luke became nervous. *What is she trying to say?*

"Your whiskers are as soft as I imagined," grinned Denise. She then moved her hand down to his chest hairs, where they protruded from the top of his V-necked polo shirt. "I've also been wanting to touch these, ever since seeing you in swimming class."

"Denise," Luke cleared his throat while he reached for her hand, removed it from his chest, and put both of his hands around it. "Will you go steady with me?"

Denise beamed as she nodded her head. "Yes! Of course, I will. I thought you'd never ask."

"May I kiss you?" inquired Luke, rather cautiously.

Without hesitation, Denise moved in and began kissing him softly on the lips. It was a long, lingering kiss. She then pulled back and looked him in the eyes. "Please do."

Luke stood, pulled Denise up, and took her passionately in his arms. Surprised by his own reaction, Luke decided to go with it and began to kiss her with fervor. He had never done anything like this before and hoped he was doing it right.

Suddenly, realizing the bulge in his pants was pressed tightly against her, Luke turned red with embarrassment. "I'm sorry," he apologized. "I hope you don't think I have bad intentions."

"It never crossed my mind," flirted Denise while she yanked him close again and kissed him back, deliberately pushing her breasts against his chest in a sensuous manner.

"Way to go," came Richard's voice from beside them.

Luke immediately stopped kissing Denise and cleared his throat again. "My apologies, I thought we were alone."

"Luke and I are going steady now," beamed Denise when she announced it to Richard.

Just then Bob Locke walked up, carrying Luke's new waffle stompers. He set them down on the half-log bench. "Time to try and put 'em back on."

Luke quickly sat down and began unlacing the comfortable boots Bob had allowed him to wear for the week. After pulling them off and tucking in the shoelaces, he handed them to Bob. "Thank you!"

"Maybe by next year, you'll have these ones broken in," grinned Bob when he turned to leave with his shoes. "And good luck to both of you at Bible College."

"Thanks," called Denise while they watched Bob walk away.

Once Luke had donned and laced up his waffle stompers, they began walking hand-in-hand across the Camp Deliverance campus, down to where the buses were parked.

"I'm really gonna miss this place," acknowledged Luke as they climbed onto the bus to head back to Ashton.

"Me, too," admitted Denise when they sat down together near the back of the bus.

"I'd like for you to meet my mother," mentioned Luke as he put his arm around Denise and pulled her close.

"That would be nice," agreed Denise while she gave him one of her sweet smiles.

She's definitely the woman I'm going to marry someday, decided Luke as the bus started up and headed for home.

Move-in day on Saturday, September 7, 1974, was a flurry of activity while 900 students simultaneously scurried this way and that to try and get moved into their respective dormitories at Bible College; classes were slated to begin on Monday.

Built in 1926, the Mediterranean-style architecture of its buildings, landscaping, and overall ambience of the campus made Bible College feel more like a resort than an academic institution. The smells of monarda, buddleia, salvia and other fall bloomers on the breeze combined with the sounds of bubbling tiled fountains flanked by inviting stone benches. Large square-brick planting stations in an open courtyard housed mature maple trees that reached towards the heavens. Arched dormitory balconies on either side of the courtyard enjoyed views of mountains in the distance and overlooked the lovely, pretty oasis, removed and protected from the outside world.

Characterized by white stucco walls, red terracotta roofs, painted tiles, curves and arches, the connecting trellis-covered walkways were loaded with mature grapevines. Intended to engender an intimately spiritual atmosphere inside the wrought-iron gates that encircled the Bible College perimeter, its grounds felt like a large courtyard within itself. The 32-acre campus of winding stairways and hidden meditation gardens was truly like nowhere else on earth.

Where is Denise? Luke asked himself as he glanced at the various cars parked in the alley behind the two dormitories.

Dozens of people were scurrying in various directions carrying boxes and armloads of clothing on hangers.

"May I help you carry some of your things up to your room?" asked Ruth. She had come with Luke and was sitting beside him in the blue Toyota Corolla she planned to leave with him to use while he was at Bible College. Her new green Pinto was parallel parked behind them next to the curb. "I'd kind of like to see where you'll be."

Will allowing mother to help me be a mistake? What if some of the other students notice and brand me as a mama's boy? worried Luke while he nervously watched the other students; very few of their parents were helping them, except with furniture. *Perhaps I should have brought my stereo,* realized Luke.

"Unless you don't want me to," stipulated Ruth.

"Oh, of course you can," agreed Luke. "I was just hoping to see Denise first, so I could introduce you, but she's not here yet."

"Maybe she arrived early and is already inside the girls' dorm," speculated Ruth. "Either way, I can always meet her later. Perhaps you can just bring her home for a visit next weekend?"

"If I can," replied Luke while he opened the car door to get out. "Things might get very busy, especially during the first week of school. There's no telling how much homework there'll be, either," he added as he began undoing the bungy cords holding his luggage to the top of the car that was now his.

Luke had always gotten straight As in all his classes, except for physical education, of course. Applying himself scholastically would be crucial if he were to maintain his GPA. There might not be time for extra trips home, especially after only one week.

"Is there any reason why you need to have two majors?" queried Ruth when she opened the other door and got out.

"My Psychology Degree will go hand-in-hand with my Theology Degree," explained Luke. "Any good pastor must be able to counsel the members of his congregation on an individual level."

Ruth put a gentle hand on top of Luke's to stop him from untying the bungy cords. "Perhaps it would be a good idea to see the room first before we start carrying things in."

Luke nodded in agreement and motioned toward the back door of the dormitory, which was currently propped open. "Let's go."

Once inside, the young college student stationed at the front desk of the boys' dormitory smiled in acknowledgement. He appeared to be a little older than Luke. *Definitely a return student,* realized Luke as he approached.

"Hello, my name's Mike. Welcome to Bible College. How can I help you?"

"I'm Luke Bennett and this is my mother Ruth," he explained. "She'll be helping me carry in my things."

"I suppose you would like to know where your room is?" grinned Mike while he pulled open a file drawer and began leafing through it until finding a folder on Luke. "Ah, here it is," declared Mike when he opened the file, pulled out a form, and slapped it down onto the counter. "I just need you to sign here for your key."

After carefully perusing the form to be sure the information already filled out on it was correct, Luke grabbed a pen from the cupholder of pens on the counter and neatly signed it.

"Oh, look," noticed Ruth. She took out one of the pens to examine it more closely. "The name and phone number of Bible College is embossed on them. Can I have one?"

"All yours, ma'am," grinned Mike as he checked Luke's name off on his list before dropping the signed form into Luke's file. Mike then pulled out a room key, placed on the counter, and shoved it towards Luke. "And this is yours. Once you get to the second floor, take the first hall on your left; your room's about half way down on the right."

"Thanks," replied Luke with a cordial nod. He and Ruth quickly headed for the large spiral wooden staircase with wrought-iron handrails that led to the second floor. Its terracotta and white colored runner rug blended seamlessly with the Mediterranean-style carpet that spanned the lobby beneath it.

Across from the staircase was a large Mission-style oven being used as a fireplace in the lobby; terracotta tiles trimmed the edges of its opening and its mantle. Various large sports trophies sat on top. Brown leather couches sat on each side of the room; a large square mahogany coffee table stood in the middle. On it was a large black Etruscan style vase decorated with golden warriors and leaflet designs; it looked as if it belonged in a museum. Large terracotta-colored pots with fern palms growing in them sat in each corner of the room. From the ceiling was suspended a black wrought-iron chandelier with six arms, each bearing an electrically-powered candle.

"I feel like I've just stepped into a Harlequin romance novel," whispered Ruth.

"Mother!" objected Luke in hushed tones.

"Don't they have an elevator?" asked Ruth while she continued to glance around the common room in awe.

"You're not all that old," teased Luke. "I'm sure the stairs will be just fine."

"I wasn't asking for myself," laughed Ruth as they began ascending the staircase together. "I was thinking of when someone might have furniture to move."

"There's got to be one somewhere," guessed Luke once they reached the second-floor landing and turned left.

"This really is a beautiful rug," admired Ruth while she squatted down to feel it with her hand. "Just like in the foyer and on the stairs."

Luke merely nodded.

"My grandmother used to have a Moroccan runner rug similar to this, but certainly not as long," added Ruth as another student carrying an armload of clothes on hangers passed by them and continued down the long hallway.

"The terracotta and white colors do go well with the whole Mediterranean theme they have going," agreed Luke while he checked each of the room numbers on the right until finally finding Room 243.

The hallway walls were white stucco; each door was framed with a single layer of terracotta bricks. The deep red mahogany wooden doors were labeled with brass-plated numbers designed to look like pure gold. Black wrought-iron Mediterranean-style wall lanterns hung at 30-foot intervals near the ceiling on the southern wall of the hallway.

At the far end of each hallway in the dormitory were the common restrooms, showers and laundry area for that hall.

Luke wasted no time inserting his new key into the lock on the doorknob of Room 243. "Doesn't look like Richard's here yet."

Ruth followed Luke into the room and looked around. "Where is the restroom?" She desperately needed to use it.

"The handbook indicated they have a common facility at the end of each hall."

"Oh, no!" exclaimed Ruth. "I'll be right back, then."

After his mother had scurried from the room to go find the facilities, Luke walked over to the sliding glass door; it led to a patio overlooking the courtyard below. Its rounded white stucco arches were trimmed with terracotta tiles consistent with the whole Mediterranean theme. *I will need patio chairs,* decided Luke when he leaned against the railing and glanced at the bustling crowd of new students below in the hope of seeing Denise, but alas, she was nowhere to be seen. *Where in the world can she be? I'll have to go downstairs to the payphones in the lobby to try and call her later.*

Hesitant at first to enter a common restroom area in the boys' dormitory, but urgently needing to pee, Ruth cautiously walked through the open rounded arch leading inside. *Thank goodness no one else is here right now,* she thought while she dashed for the nearest toilet stall, went inside, and secured the door latch. Not seeing any toilet seat covers, Ruth painstakingly placed the little squares of toilet paper onto its seat until all of it was adequately covered before sitting down. *Will Luke really be safe from germs here?* she wondered as she finished up and flushed the pull-chain toilet.

After exiting the stall, Ruth glanced around again before hurrying over to the row of sinks. She put a generous amount of liquid soap from a dispenser onto her hands, but then realized she wasn't sure how to turn on the water faucet.

"It's one of those new single-hole faucets," came the voice of a tall handsome young man behind her. "Just push it up to turn it on; then to the left or right for hot or cold. When you're done, just pull it towards you and it will shut off again."

"Thanks," blushed Ruth while she pushed it on and rinsed off her hands. "We have the old-fashioned kind at home with a handle on each side. I don't think I've ever seen one of these."

"I'm told they just installed them all over the summer," grinned the muscular young man; he was clearly amused by Ruth's predicament. "I'm guessing your son must be a student here?"

"Uh, yes," stammered Ruth. "I waited until we got to his room to use the restroom and then realized there wasn't one."

"That's dorm life," chuckled the young man as he washed and dried off his hands. "Say, what's his name, maybe I know him?"

"Luke," revealed Ruth while she dried off her hands on a paper towel. *Thank goodness the paper towel dispensers are standard.*

"Was he at Camp Deliverance a couple of weeks ago?"

"Yes, he was," answered Ruth rather nervously.

"I remember Luke," grinned the young man. "Red hair and brand-new boots. We were in the same cabin. My name is John."

"Nice to meet you, John," acknowledged Ruth with a pleasant nod. She was clearly uncomfortable.

"And of course, there's the shower area," pointed out John while they passed by it on their way to the arched doorway leading back into the hall. "Good thing nobody decided to take a shower just now."

Ruth turned to see the huge, Roman-style shower with a single pole that had six showerheads mounted to it at eye level. "Oh, my goodness! They don't have individual stalls?" *How had I not noticed it on my way in?*

"Nope," sniggered John while he tried not to laugh.

"Will they be putting up shower curtains?" asked Ruth with concern. *Does Luke know about this?*

John could hold back no longer. He began laughing heartily before finally responding. "That's doubtful, ma'am. And, over there are the washers and dryers. They're coin operated. Hope Luke remembered to bring his own laundry soap."

"I'll have to make sure he has some," nodded Ruth. She was clearly apprehensive about the entire setup.

"Well, be sure and tell Luke I said hello," chuckled John when he started down the hallway. "I'm sure he'll remember me."

"I sure will," mumbled Ruth before scurrying towards Room 243 and knocking on the door.

"Who is it?" came the voice of her son.

"It's your mother," she replied.

Luke opened the door and stepped into the hall. "Let's go get my stuff."

"Are you sure you really want to do this?" Ruth suddenly asked.

"What brought that on?" questioned Luke as they headed toward the landing.

"Have you seen the shower area?" Ruth grilled him.

"Not yet," frowned Luke. "I just got here. Why?"

"It's one big open stall with no shower curtains separating the individual spaces," described Ruth. "Just a bunch of shower heads on a single pole squirting out in various directions. Absolutely NO privacy whatsoever!"

"The locker rooms in the gymnasium at Ashton High were like that, too," revealed Luke. "That's pretty much the way they do it now."

"Well, I don't like it," decided Ruth. "Did you know that you have to have your own laundry soap? And a supply of quarters on hand in order to use the washers and dryers?"

"Hmm," muttered Luke. "Guess I can work that out, it shouldn't be a problem."

"It makes you wonder what else is not in the brochure," retorted Ruth when they reached the landing and began descending the spiral staircase leading to the lobby.

"Mom, please don't worry," said Luke as he stopped on the stairs where they were, put his hands on her shoulders, and pulled her close for a hug. "I'll be just fine."

"Hello again," came the voice of John, who was descending the stairs behind them. "Long time, no see."

"John," recognized Luke while he let out a deep sigh and let go of Ruth. "This is my mother."

"We've met," grinned John as he gave Ruth a flirtatious smile.

"Where do you two know each other from?" questioned Luke with a puzzled look on his face.

"We *just* met," clarified Ruth. "In the restroom."

"Like I said, long time, no see," chuckled John when he passed by them to continue down the stairs.

"Oh, Mother, I'm sorry," apologized Luke.

"At least now I know how to use one of those new single-hole faucets," replied Ruth rather sheepishly. "I probably wouldn't have been able to rinse the soap off my hands without John's help."

"I guess he told you he knows me from Camp Deliverance?" Luke grilled her.

Ruth merely nodded her head as they passed through the lobby before going back outside where other students, including John, were retrieving boxes and suitcases of things from their vehicles.

Nearly a week passed since the first day of classes, and Luke had managed only once to get a glimpse of Denise at the back of the auditorium during general assembly. *Is she avoiding me?*

"Hey, Luke, wanna go to the cafeteria for lunch a little early today?" asked Richard, who was walking beside him.

Their English literature class had been cancelled due to the teacher's unexpected absence that day.

"Works for me," agreed Luke while they headed down a trellis-covered walkway from which most of the ripened grapes had already been picked for the season.

"You've been eating most of your meals in our room," Richard reminded him. "It should do you some good to get out. Especially if you want to run into Denise again. There's more to life than studying."

"Do you think she's avoiding me?" Luke suddenly asked. "Last I knew, we were supposed to be going steady, and now I'm doing good to get a glimpse of her at the back of a crowded room. Then, by the time I made my way over there, she was gone!"

"Have you tried calling her room?" Richard questioned him as they passed by a meditation area where a Mediterranean water feature was surrounded by black wrought-iron benches and olive trees.

"A couple of times," confessed Luke. "The gal at the reception desk there keeps saying she'll leave her a message I called. It's not like we're allowed to go inside the girls' dorm, you know."

"Hey, look," Richard nudged him. "There she is, and she's headed toward the cafeteria."

"Who's with her?" inquired Luke while he furrowed his eyebrows and began to frown.

"It looks like that John guy. The one who was in our cabin at Camp Deliverance," recognized Richard. "Still wanna eat now?"

"Oh, you bet I do," fumed Luke as he began walking faster in the hope of intercepting them before they could reach the cafeteria.

"Wait for me," said Richard while he half-ran to keep up. "I wouldn't miss this for all the tea in China!"

"Hey, Denise!" shouted Luke when he began running towards them.

Oblivious to the impending encounter, John reached out and pulled open the door to the cafeteria. In true gentlemanly fashion, he continued to hold it open for Denise.

"Why, thank you," flirted Denise while she adjusted her books and the shoulder strap on her purse before starting to walk inside.

"Wait!" hollered Luke as he got closer. "Denise!"

Upon hearing her name, Denise paused to glance back and was just in time to see Luke punch John in the face.

"How dare you try and steal my girl," yelled Luke while he knocked a surprised John to the ground and continued to hit him repeatedly with all his might.

Even with his sturdy frame and muscular build, John was having difficulty fending off the blows. Luke was enraged and out of control. Blood was flowing from John's nose; a shiner on his left eye would undoubtedly turn black and blue.

"Luke, stop!" commanded Richard as he threw down his books, grabbed Luke, and tried to pull him off of John.

Two other young men noticed the situation and came to assist.

Once Luke was being held in place by the two strangers, Richard demanded to know, "What in the world are you trying to do, Luke?"

"Where am I?" Luke asked in a confused tone when he saw John slowly getting up, pull a handkerchief from his pocket, and pinch his nose with it to stay the flow of blood.

"Are you alright?" Denise asked John with concern. She had been standing in a shocked daze, not believing what she was seeing.

Luke seemed just as surprised as Denise when he turned toward John. "John? What happened here? Who did this?"

"As if you don't know," growled John while he glared at Luke with unconcealed hatred. "You'll definitely be hearing from my father's lawyer. Count on it!"

Denise began picking up John's books. "Can I help carry them back to your dorm for you?"

John let go of the handkerchief on his nose just long enough to grab the books away from her. "You and your *mama's boy* can just stay the hell away from me!"

Luke shook his head and stared with disbelief while he watched John angrily stomp toward the boys' dormitory.

The two strangers finally loosened their hold on Luke. One of them asked Richard, "You got this handled?"

Richard nodded affirmatively when they let go of Luke and quickly left; neither was anxious to become involved in a potential legal matter.

"Why did you do that?" Denise suddenly asked Luke.

"Do *what*?" questioned Luke.

"Beat the holy heck out of Bible College's star football player," interjected Richard. "That was totally uncool, dude."

Luke shook his head in denial. "The last thing I remember was walking through one of the meditation gardens with you, Richard. Our English class had been cancelled, and you asked me if I wanted to go to the cafeteria for an early lunch. Honest to God, I don't remember anything after that until now."

"You seriously don't remember?" Denise questioned him with a doubtful look on her face. "How in the world could you possibly have done something like this and claim to have no memory of it?"

"I don't know," muttered Luke. He was sincere.

"Let's get you to the medical building," suggested Denise upon noticing the blood on Luke's swollen knuckles; not all of it was John's. "Maybe they'll buy some story about you punching out a wall or something, especially since someone like John isn't likely to want his friends knowing he was beaten up so easily."

"We can only hope," agreed Richard while he picked up Luke's books and added them to his own stack.

"Not only that, John's only potential witnesses didn't seem very anxious to hang around," pointed out Denise. "Most likely, becoming involved in a fight could get John tossed off the football team, regardless of who started it."

Luke merely nodded. *Could I really have beaten up someone like John without even knowing it? What's going on?*

"After we get your knuckles looked at, you and I are going to have a serious talk," Denise advised Luke as she tenderly put one of her hands on his right cheek and studied him more closely. "I need to know something like this will never happen again."

"Me, too," agreed Luke.

"I'll come with you guys, just in case," offered Richard. He glanced at Denise with a troubled look.

"We'll be fine," Denise assured him.

"I insist," replied Richard while he studied his new roommate more closely. *Had agreeing to room with Luke been a mistake?* he wondered as he straightened the pile of books.

Luke's second year at Bible College was nearly over; it was June of 1976. As far as Luke was concerned, everything was going smoothly with Denise, who had continued to be his girlfriend despite the incident with John during the fall of 1974 two years prior.

John had come to realize rather quickly he did not want the general public to find out he'd been beaten up by the likes of a red-headed punk like Luke, especially since something like that could get him kicked off the football team at Bible College, not to mention how it would affect his eligibility to become a professional football player down the road.

Richard and Denise were walking towards the cafeteria together.

"Are you *sure* Luke's gone home to visit his mother for the weekend?" Denise asked Richard while she glanced around.

"Absolutely," Richard assured her as they reached its doors.

"We sure don't want a repeat of two years ago," Denise reminded Richard when she again checked their surroundings before going inside. "Especially with the school year ending next week."

"Do you plan to stay for another two years?" Richard asked her while they each picked up a brown plastic food tray and began going through the food line.

"I'll have the tacos," Denise directed the food server on the other side of the glass counter.

"Rice and beans?" asked the food server.

Denise glanced at them through the glass window before making up her mind. "Just some rice."

"I'll have the same, but with beans," indicated Richard as the food server handed Denise's plate to her.

"Any hot sauce for either of you?" questioned the server while he prepared and handed Richard his plate.

"Sure," they both replied at once.

"Here you are, enjoy," smiled the food server as he grabbed two of the sealed packets of hot sauce and handed one to each of them.

"We definitely should get some ice cream," recommended Denise when they arrived at the self-serving condiment table that included an ice cream dispenser.

"I wonder what flavor they have today," grinned Richard. It was always a surprise, and one never knew for certain. *At least all the food's included in our tuition.*

"Oooh, it's strawberry," beamed Denise as she filled up one of the bowls with the delicious-looking substance.

"Nice," approved Richard when he got some for himself.

"No cafeteria meal is complete without water to wash it down afterwards," added Denise with a smile while she moved down to the water machine, picked up a glass, and held it to the nozzle for ice before filling it up with water.

"Thanks," nodded Richard when she handed it to him and then got another one for herself.

"Where do you wanna sit?" asked Denise, who was still slightly nervous to be seen with anyone but Luke in public, especially his best friend Richard.

"How about over there in the corner," suggested Richard as he nodded toward a secluded table by a plate glass window overlooking a flower garden featuring a marble statue of a woman pouring water from a pitcher into a bucket.

"Perfect," approved Denise when they both sat down.

"Silverware," realized Richard as he got back up. "I'll get some for both of us. Be right back."

Denise seemed slightly sad while she watched Richard make his way back to the condiment table. *Why couldn't I have become involved with Richard, instead of with Luke? Richard is so handsome, so thoughtful, and so considerate.* With Richard, there was no need to be constantly on guard lest she say the wrong thing.

"Here you are," smiled Richard when he returned and set down the two silverware packets wrapped in cloth napkins.

"Thank you," said Denise as she gave Richard a longing glance when he sat back down across from her.

"You never answered my question," Richard reminded her when he took out his spoon and took a bite of rice.

Denise gave him a puzzled look.

"Do you plan to stay here for another two years?" Richard asked again while he studied her more closely. *How in the world did she end up with Luke instead of me?*

"Funny you should ask," replied Denise before taking a bite of her strawberry ice cream.

"Dessert's for last," teased Richard.

"I just don't want it to melt," mentioned Denise as she sensuously licked her spoon in a manner that did not go unnoticed by Richard.

"Seriously, do you plan to finish out here, or at Ashton City College?" Richard questioned her.

"Why?" Denise narrowed her eyes at him.

"Maybe to save your parents some money," described Richard. "And other reasons."

Denise became serious. "You must promise not to tell Luke we had lunch together today."

"I swear," agreed Richard while he held up his right hand. "Scout's honor. And seriously, do you really think I would risk upsetting him?"

Satisfied Richard could be trusted, Denise decided to tell him her plans. "Honestly, I just don't think I can take anymore, but have no idea how to tell him."

"You're breaking up with Luke?" Richard looked worried.

"Not until after the school year is over," Denise assured him. "That way, he'll have the summer to cool off."

"Luke's obsessed with you," Richard reminded her. "I probably shouldn't tell you this, but the incident with John is not the only thing I've noticed about his behavior."

"What do you mean?" Denise grilled him.

"Well, Luke and I have been friends since grammar school; we've known each other for a long time," elaborated Richard. "There have been other times when Luke's personality seemed to suddenly change like that."

Denise looked horrified but remained silent while she considered the information.

"I believe the incident where he beat up John was the third time I know of when something traumatic happened to Luke where he had no memory of how he reacted to it afterwards," described Richard. "One of those times was when his parents split up."

"I knew they were divorced," mentioned Denise.

"Did he also tell you his father had been cheating on his mother for quite some time before that?" asked Richard.

"Oh, my goodness!" exclaimed Denise. "That's horrible! Especially with how close Luke is to his mother. I can imagine he probably took it pretty hard."

"That's an understatement," replied Richard, "and if you ask me, Luke's just a little bit too attached to his mother."

"I know, I've noticed that, too," admitted Denise.

"In fact," continued Richard, "his father Willard ended up marrying the *other woman* the exact same day the divorce from Luke's mother Ruth was final. It also happened to be the very same day Luke graduated from high school."

"Having his father bail out on his graduation ceremony would be traumatic enough, not to mention a situation like that," recognized Denise. "I'm assuming Luke's father didn't manage to squeeze in the graduation ceremony?"

"No, not on his wedding day," confirmed Richard. "And I'm afraid to even say it, but after taking Psychology class these past two years, it almost seems to me like Luke may not only have schizophrenia, but multiple personality disorder, as well."

"Oh, my God! Isn't he in that class with you?" queried Denise.

"Yes," answered Richard as he pursed his lips. "Oddly, Luke actually asked me once whether that might be why he didn't remember what happened the day he beat the tar out of John."

"And you waited until *now* to tell me this?" Denise was clearly upset. "Do you think Luke could be dangerous?"

"Yes, I do," replied Richard. "I'm sorry I didn't say anything before, but I know how crazy you are about him."

"Not really," confessed Denise. "Even without knowing about the possibility of him having schizophrenia and multiple personality disorder, his temperament alone is why I need to get away from him. I just don't feel safe when I'm around him. Does that make any sense?"

"I'm so sorry," consoled Richard while he reached over to put both of his hands on hers and gazed deeply into her blue eyes.

"We should go for a walk after we finish eating," suggested Denise as she smiled at Richard.

"I'd like that," smiled Richard when he reached out to touch her deep red hair. "Did anyone ever tell you how beautiful you are?"

"I don't know," blushed Denise as she smiled coyly at him and shrugged her shoulders.

No wonder Luke is in love with her, realized Richard while he gently stroked her perfect alabaster skin. *Nevertheless, it should be up to Denise to choose who she wants to be with.*

"And you're absolutely positive Luke won't be back until Monday?" Denise quizzed Richard again.

"I doubt he'd give up an opportunity to spend more time with his mother," assumed Richard.

"I know," sighed Denise. "It's almost unnatural how close those two are, if you know what I mean."

After eating and walking hand-in-hand through several of the romantic meditation areas on campus, Richard suddenly pulled Denise close and began to kiss her. Without hesitation, Denise kissed him back.

"You should come to my room tonight," Richard unexpectedly suggested. "No one else will be there."

"How in the world would I get inside?" questioned Denise. "Especially since no girls are allowed in the boys' dorm."

"If you come up the fire escape steps in the back, I can let you in after everyone else is asleep for the night," described Richard with a mischievous grin. "What time does your watch say?"

"Right now?" Denise looked at her watch. "I have 7:30 p.m."

Richard adjusted his watch, which was normally five minutes fast, to exactly 7:30 p.m. "There, now I can be there at midnight to let you in. It's perfect; no one else will be up at that time, and you can wear that dark hooded sweatshirt you have, just in case. No one will suspect a thing."

"Won't an alarm go off if you try to open it?" Denise grilled him.

"I thought the same thing," replied Richard, "until accidentally opening it one night when one of the other guys and I were tossing a football back and forth in the hallway. Once it hit the door, we quickly learned there's no alarm on it. The only thing is, it's self-locking and can only be opened from the inside."

Denise hesitated. "What if Luke does decide to come back early? He would be devastated, to say the least."

"We might not get another chance like this until who knows when," pointed out Richard while he ran his hands along the sides of her hourglass figure. "Luke may be a virgin, but I suspect he's the only one of us that is."

Denise blushed deeply but then nodded her head.

"I think we could be happy together," proposed Richard.

"It would break Luke's heart if he ever found out," objected Denise when she considered how he might react.

"Okay, it'll be like in *An Affair to Remember*," described Richard. "Did you ever see that movie?"

"That's an old one," acknowledged Denise. "Didn't it come out about the time we were born?"

"Actually, it came out one year later in 1957," clarified Richard. "It's about a man and a woman who had a shipboard romance while on a cruise. Despite being engaged to other people, they finally agreed to meet each other at the top of the Empire State Building in six months to see if they still felt the same way about each other."

"I remember that," grinned Denise. "And one of them is in an accident that keeps them from meeting there. Still, in spite of everything, they somehow managed to get together in the end anyway."

"Except, instead of six months, let's make it 4½ hours," grinned Richard.

"And instead of the Empire State Building, you want me to meet you at the top of the fire escape on the back of the boys' dormitory," guessed Denise with a naughty smile.

"Something like that," replied Richard as he pulled her close and kissed her again. "And if you don't show up, then I'll know you aren't interested."

"I may surprise you," flirted Denise when they arrived at the steps to the girls' dormitory and parted ways.

Precisely at the stroke of midnight on Saturday, June 8, 1976, Denise found herself at the top of the fire escape behind the boys' dormitory. *I can't believe I'm actually doing this,* she thought with apprehension while she glanced around to be sure she was alone. *It would be a shame to be kicked out of school so close to the end of the semester.*

Denise pulled the black hood close around her face while she waited. The baggy black sweatpants she had chosen to wear would hopefully disguise her appearance just enough to conceal her identity.

A sliver of light suddenly appeared around the crack of the door when it opened. The outline of Richard standing in the shadows just inside caused her to let out a deep sigh of relief.

"Shhh!" warned Richard as he put his right finger to his lips. He gallantly offered her his other hand while he held the door open with his hip.

There will be no going back from this, realized Denise when she took his hand and came inside.

Richard stealthily closed the door and then led her down the hall to Room 243. Hurrying in case one of the other residents should get up in the night to use the restroom and see them, Richard pulled out a lanyard from beneath his T-shirt on which the room key hung before opening the door as quietly as possible.

Once inside, Richard pulled her close and began kissing her. "I'm so glad you decided to come."

"Me, too," responded Denise while she kissed him back with unbridled passion.

Meanwhile, Luke had decided to return to Bible College early. It was 5:00 a.m. on Sunday morning, June 9, 1976. Obsessed with maintaining his straight A status and having left one of his school books in his room, it was a no-brainer he needed to come back a day early. He wanted to get in all the studying he could for finals.

"Are you sure you don't want to have breakfast here?" asked Ruth as she gave Luke a hug and a kiss on the cheek. "I can make you anything you like."

"The cafeteria opens at 6:00 a.m.," described Luke. "I'm sure it will be open when I get there. Besides, the food's included."

"It is a two-hour drive," Ruth reminded him with concern. "Can I at least make you a cup of coffee first?"

"Sure," agreed Luke before going to his bedroom, closing his suitcase. and taking it to the car. *That way it'll be ready to go.*

"Have you considered going to Ashton City College next year?" questioned Ruth. "I'm not sure whether or not we will have enough for another year of tuition at Bible College. It's pretty expensive."

Luke hesitated. *What about Denise? I don't want to be so far away from her for that long.*

"Most households make an average of $4,800 per month," described Ruth, "but those of us who work at the Social Security office barely get $3,500 per month, and that's before taxes."

"Aren't you still getting alimony payments from Willard?" Luke grilled her. "He is supposed to help with my education, isn't he?"

"Not now that you're an adult," countered Ruth. "The only alimony I get is for Leticia, and that will stop as soon as she turns 18. I don't know what I'll do after that. Especially, since the tuition at Bible College is $12,000 per year. I've already taken out a second mortgage on the house." Ruth then began to sob.

"I had no idea it was so bad," responded Luke while he tenderly put his arms around his mother and pulled her close. "I'll just have to tell Denise I'm going to Ashton City College next year, and that's that. Hopefully, she'll be able to do the same."

"If she loves you as much as you say she does, I'm sure she will," sniffed Ruth while she hugged him back. "Plus, it would be so nice to have you back home again. I hate having you gone so much!"

"Then it's settled," agreed Luke. "I'll go to the registrar's office first thing Monday morning and let them know."

Deep in thought while his blue Toyota Corolla meandered up the winding mountain road leading to Bible College, Luke decided to pull over in the first turnout he could find to get out and pee. *They really should have a rest stop along this stretch,* thought Luke as he parked his car, got out, walked over to a large tree, unzipped his pants, and proceeded to urinate.

Just when he was nearly finished, the sound of an approaching vehicle could be heard in the distance. Luke rapidly completed what he was doing, zipped his pants back up, returned to the car, and got inside.

The Highway Patrolman passing by just then slowed to study the situation before continuing without stopping.

That was close, sighed Luke while he started the engine back up, put the vehicle into drive, and continued on his way.

I'm very fortunate to have a nice girl like Denise, thought Luke. He quickly double checked to be sure the engagement ring he had recently purchased was still in his pocket. *Very few girls are virgins anymore,* considered Luke as he smiled to himself. He would wait until the last day of school to present her with it. *Who knows,* grinned Luke, p*erhaps by this time next year, we'll be man and wife.*

When reaching the large wrought-iron entrance gates to Bible College, Luke pulled up beside the gate's call box, came to a stop, rolled down his window, and pressed the intercom button.

After a brief pause, a voice responded, "May I help you?"

"It's Luke Bennett from Room 243, and I'm back a day early from my weekend home leave," he announced.

The surveillance camera mounted at the top of the gate by a wrought-iron security lantern slowly moved back and forth. After several moments, there was a loud buzzing sound; the gates slowly swung open.

"Welcome back, Luke," came the voice on the speaker.

"Thanks," responded Luke while he rolled his window back up, put his car into drive, and pulled forward to continue his journey through the scenic Bible College campus.

Too bad there isn't a system yet where all you have to do is enter in a security code, like on a padlock, contemplated Luke as he admired the beautiful landscaping. True, he had recently read about an interactive kiosk system currently being developed by Murray Lappe, a pre-med student at the University of Illinois at Urbana-Champaign, but the prototype still required testing and would not be slated for use by the general public until 1977.

Luke slowed when he passed by the meditation garden where he and Denise had talked about their future together following the unfortunate incident with John back in 1974. *Thank God she forgave me,* thought Luke. He felt a pang of regret over his behavior that day. Now, he would do everything in his power to convince her to attend Ashton City College next year. He could not allow them to drift apart like they had during the first week of school two years ago. He'd done everything in his power to keep the bond strong between them ever since.

Denise slowly opened her eyes, startled at first to find herself in unfamiliar surroundings.

"Good morning, sleepyhead," flirted Richard as he pulled her close and gave her a passionate kiss.

"I need to brush my teeth," objected Denise while she pulled away. "Oh no, it's light outside already."

"You looked like you could use your rest," smiled Richard.

"And I need to use the restroom, too," added Denise with trepidation. "What if someone sees me go down the hall like this?"

"Well, we do have a sink," pointed out Richard. "You can always brush your teeth here. And, beneath it is an empty coffee can, for emergencies like when you need to pee and just don't want to make the trip down the hall. You're welcome to use it, and then I'll be happy to go empty it for you."

"I'm basically stuck here until tonight, then," realized Denise with a deep sigh.

"It is Sunday," grinned Richard. "We can still have one more day together until Luke returns."

"I suppose I could just take an Army bath here," Denise finally agreed. "Sure, why not. I suppose that means you'll be bringing me breakfast, too?"

"We've got quite the selection," Richard informed her when he opened the cupboard above the sink to reveal a small pantry of quick-prep food items in boxes and cans.

"Nice," approved Denise, "but I would like some privacy while I use the can."

"I'll tell you what," proposed Richard while he pulled on a forest green polo shirt. "I can run over to the cafeteria and bring back a tray of anything you like."

"Deal," laughed Denise as she gave him a hug. "How about bacon and eggs, hash-brown potatoes and strawberries on the side?"

"I'll even try to grab some things we can save to eat for lunch while I'm there," described Richard when he put on his blue jeans, zipped them up and winked at her.

"As long as I can sneak out of here tonight, we should have nothing to worry about," predicted Denise.

"No problem," Richard assured her while he quickly combed his hair, put on his shoes, grabbed his sweat jacket, and left.

Once alone, Denise carefully squatted to use the empty coffee can, careful to put its plastic reusable lid tightly back into place when finished. *Okay, this could be worse,* she thought when she examined herself in the mirror above the sink. She did not have her toothbrush with her, but was able to put some of Richard's toothpaste onto her finger and swish it around in her mouth before spitting into the sink. Unfortunately, she would not be able to sit on the side of the freestanding sink to clean her privates, as the weight of her body might be too much for it, but she was able to use a wet wash cloth to clean the various parts of her body until satisfied with the result.

Should I put my clothes on, or climb back into bed? wondered Denise with a devious grin. *I'll decide after Richard returns with our food*, nodded Denise. She paused to straighten her dark red hair with her fingers before returning to the warmth of Richard's bed and pulling up the covers over her naked body.

Just when Denise began to drift back off to sleep again, she heard the door to the room open and slowly stretched and yawned. "It's about time you got back," she said as she opened her eyes. *It's Luke!*

Luke stood there gawking at her with complete disbelief at first. It was like he was frozen in time.

"Luke, I can explain," said Denise while she pulled the covers more tightly around her. She could feel her heart pounding in her chest and was terrified of what might happen next.

"You filthy whore!" shouted Luke as he suddenly dropped his luggage, lunged toward her and ripped away the covers. Momentarily startled by her naked body, Luke froze again, just long enough for Denise to scramble over to where her black sweatpants and hooded sweatshirt were draped over the chair at Richard's study desk.

"I don't expect you to understand," Denise tried to explain while she struggled to put on her clothes as fast as she could.

"How could you do such a thing?" Luke grilled her while he glared at her with loathing. "I thought we meant something to each other," hollered Luke. He unexpectedly removed the small black velvet box containing the engagement ring from his pocket and threw it at her.

Denise carefully bent down to pick it up from the floor where it landed after bouncing off her stomach and then opened it, flabbergasted to see that it was a diamond engagement ring.

"*That* was why I came back early," snarled Luke as his nostrils flared. "I was going to ask you to marry me!"

"Luke, I'm so sorry," apologized Denise while tears began to flow from her eyes. "It would never have worked between us," she added as she closed the lid to the ring box and cautiously held it out to him with trembling hands.

Luke snatched back the ring box, put it into his pocket and demanded, "Where is he? Where is Richard?"

Just then the door to the room opened again. This time it was Richard, carrying a food tray heavily laden with delicious-smelling breakfast items.

"Sorry it took me so long," apologized Richard when he came inside and started toward his study desk where he intended to set the tray.

"You traitor!" bellowed Luke as he slapped the food tray out of Richard's hands, causing everything on it to fly across the room and crash against the opposite wall. The china plates and bowls shattered into pieces and fell onto the floor beside the food items that were still dripping down on top of them.

"Go get help," Richard anxiously directed Denise before turning to face Luke. "Hurry!"

"It's daylight already. If I go out there now, someone will see me," panicked Denise.

"Give me one good reason why I shouldn't kill you where you stand," Luke said to Richard when he grabbed him by the front of his shirt and pulled him close.

"Because you're my best friend," answered Richard as he put his hands onto Luke's to try and extricate them from his shirt.

"You don't even know who I am," sniggered Luke when he head-butted Richard with his head as hard as he could and then punched him in the jaw while bouncing in place like a professional boxer.

Richard regained his balance and put a hand on his sore jaw before wiping away the trickle of blood coming from his mouth.

"Luke, what are you doing?" questioned Denise in an attempt to try and reason with him.

"I'm not Luke," he responded with an evil laugh as he began shadowboxing at imaginary specters in the room, "but if Luke were here, I have no doubt he would have killed you both by now."

Denise fumbled to put on and tie her tennis shoes. *No matter what, I'll need to make a run for it, but not without Richard.* "Come on," she urged Richard while she held out her hand to him. "We need to leave. Now!"

"Defend yourself, you coward," challenged Luke as he began taking air swipes toward Richard.

At that moment, Richard and Denise grabbed hands and made a beeline for the door, exited, and ran down the hallway as fast as they could without looking back. Both were somewhat frightened by Luke's schizophrenia, but their main concern at the moment was his multiple personality disorder. *How dangerous is he?* they worried.

"That's right, run!" hollered Luke from behind them while he continued to bounce in place and shadowbox. "And don't even think about coming back!"

10. Leverage

Bell finished putting on her lipstick and making sure her hair was perfectly in place before putting on her black silk gloves and hat. *Strange that Luke would call me instead of Ruth at a time like this,* she thought while she put on her royal blue wool coat and headed for the door.

Thankfully, Frank is away fishing for the weekend with his friends, considered Bell as she walked toward the new tan Buick. *It's about time we finally had two vehicles.*

Bell started up the engine, shifted into reverse, and backed out of her driveway. *This house on Simpson Street is where I intend to live for the rest of my life*, decided Bell while she put her car into drive and began her journey. It would take her at least two hours to get to the small town of Hope near Bible College where her grandson Luke was being held on charges of assault against his roommate.

Ruth wouldn't have had the money to bail him out anyway, realized Bell with a smug grin. *Helping Luke out of this predicament will certainly give me leverage in the future. Undoubtedly, Luke will not want Willard to know about it, either.*

"Such a shame about Willard and Ruth," mumbled Bell out loud, to no one in particular while she momentarily glanced at herself in the rearview mirror to see how her makeup looked in the light. Despite everything she'd taught her sons about the responsibilities of marriage, it was unthinkable that Willard had stepped out on poor Ruth. Even worse, Willard had married Beatrice the exact same day the divorce from Ruth had been final. "No wonder Ruth is so depressed all the time."

After two hours of driving through the scenic countryside, Bell finally spotted a green road sign with bold white letters that read "Welcome to Hope." Noticing a gas station just up ahead on the right, Bell pulled into it, and came to a stop next to one of the pumps before rolling down her window.

"Fill her up?" questioned the solitary gas station attendant.

"I'm good on gas," replied Bell, "but I could use some directions. Do you happen to have any maps for sale?"

"A map of Hope?" asked the attendant while he scratched his scraggly blonde hair and pulled up one of the straps on his worn out, grease-stained overalls.

"Yes," Bell let out a frustrated sigh. *What does he think I want anyway, a map of Canada?*

"That'll be $2.29, ma'am," the attendant informed her as he turned to go retrieve one.

"Wait! Don't you just have one I can look at tacked up in your office or something?" Bell grilled him.

"Where are you trying to go, ma'am? Perhaps I can just give you directions," offered the attendant as he smiled, revealing a missing front tooth. The man's other teeth were badly stained, most in various stages of decay; his cheek was stuffed with chewing tobacco that he suddenly spit out into a trash can by the pumps.

"The courthouse," snapped Bell while she made a face of disgust. "And I need to be there by 9:00 a.m. for a hearing."

"It's 8:45 a.m. now," the attendant advised her after looking at the big clock mounted by the empty service bay next to his office. "It's three blocks down on the right, the big brick building on the corner of Water and Division. Can't miss it."

"Okay, thanks," nodded Bell. She cranked the tan Buick into drive and took off so fast she made the tires squeal.

"You're welcome," muttered the attendant with a frown while he watched her drive away.

He looks just like one of the characters on Hee Haw, thought Bell as she suddenly began to laugh. She could never understand why Frank insisted on watching such a show.

"All rise," came the voice of the Courtroom Deputy. "Today is June 10, 1976, at the Hope City Municipal Courthouse. The Honorable Judge Henry Deringer presiding."

The few people present in the small courtroom stood while an elderly gentleman in a black robe emerged from a side door and made his way to the bench.

Just then, the lobby doors opened and Bell slipped inside the courtroom, nodding politely at the other people present as she made her way towards the front of the courtroom to stand by an empty seat.

Judge Deringer gave her a sharp look for being late when he took the stand. "Good morning folks, please be seated. Court is now in session. We are here today in the criminal matter of *State v. Bennett,* Case Number 06101932-74. Bailiff, please bring in the defendant."

Bell gasped when she saw her grandson Luke being escorted into the courtroom with his hands handcuffed behind his back.

"Mr. Bennett, please take your place beside Mr. Persing, the court-appointed counsel here to represent you," the Judge instructed him.

Bell suddenly stood and raised her hand. "Your Honor?"

Judge Deringer frowned with displeasure at the interruption. "What is the meaning of this?"

"The defendant is my grandson," revealed Bell while she maintained eye contact with the Judge. "My name is Bell Bennett. I will be representing Luke here in court today."

Judge Deringer suddenly began to laugh quite heartily while he studied the nicely dressed 66 year old woman before him. *She looks as if she's dressed for some 1940 speak-easy club in a bad gangster movie,* thought the Judge while he looked her over with amusement.

"I'm also here to pay his bail, if any," added Bell as she winked at the Judge and gave him a coy smile.

"I'm sorry, Mrs. Bennett, but you will need to sit down now," replied Judge Deringer. He then turned his attention toward Luke. "Luke Bennett, I am advising you at this time that if you do not wish to be represented by Mr. Persing, you do have the option of representing yourself. You may not, however, be represented by your grandmother or by any non-lawyer individual in this courtroom. How do you wish to proceed?"

Luke turned toward Bell with a perplexed look on his face.

"Tell him you wish to represent yourself," Bell spoke up, causing the Judge to frown with irritation.

Luke finally nodded his head affirmatively.

"The defendant will address any responses he might have directly to the Court," the Judge admonished Luke, "and all responses must be out loud so our Court Reporter can record them."

Luke refocused his attention on the Judge. "Yes, Your Honor, that would be fine. I would like to represent myself."

"Very well," agreed the Judge. "Mr. Persing, you are dismissed, for now. And Grandma, please refrain from any further outbursts in this courtroom. Do we understand one another?"

"It's Bell, Your Honor. Bell Bennett. And yes, I understand," she informed the Judge before seating herself immediately behind the defense table.

"Okay," began the Judge while he opened the file in front of him. "It says here, Mr. Bennett, that you physically assaulted your roommate Richard Springfield by punching him in the jaw yesterday morning at Bible College. I've read the sworn statements by Mr. Springfield and his friend Denise Jones, who witnessed the attack, and it says here that you also made verbal death threats toward each of them. Is that correct?"

Luke froze and seemed for a moment as if he were going into a trance before responding. "Yes, Sir, that is correct."

"Then where are they?" Bell suddenly asked while she motioned toward the plaintiff table, occupied only by the Deputy District Attorney assigned to prosecute the matter.

"Grandma Bennett, this is your last warning! You will not interrupt this proceeding again," cautioned Judge Deringer. "Is that understood?"

"Yes, Your Honor," answered Bell as she returned his steady, even gaze without flinching.

"Let the record show that Mr. Springfield and Ms. Jones are not present today," announced the Judge while he maintained eye contact with Bell.

"That's correct, Your Honor," informed the Deputy District Attorney. "But in spite of everything, both victims have informed me they are not willing to press any charges against the defendant. In fact, both have agreed that this case can be summarily dismissed, if that's the decision of this court."

"I see," nodded the Judge. He then turned to Luke. "Mr. Bennett, is there anything you wish to say for yourself at this time?"

Luke looked at Bell with a pleading look. "What should I do?" he whispered.

"Mr. Bennett, the patience of this court has reached its limit. Your grandmother is *not* representing you. You have chosen to represent yourself in this proceeding," pointed out the Judge.

"No, Your Honor," Luke finally responded. I have nothing else to say."

Bell then raised her hand.

Astonished by Bell Bennett's brazen disregard for decorum in his courtroom but overcome by curiosity at what she might have to say, he recognized her. "Yes, Mrs. Bennett?"

"It's my understanding Luke has the right to a speedy trial," Bell reminded Judge Deringer while she adjusted her sleeve.

"That's correct, ma'am, and that's what's happening now," the Judge informed her. He narrowed his eyes at Luke before continuing. "Since this is your first offense, Mr. Bennett, and because the victims have agreed not to press any charges against you, it is hereby the decision of the Court that this case be dismissed without prejudice and without costs to any party herein."

"Thank you, Judge," responded Luke.

"Don't thank me yet," continued Judge Deringer. "Luke Bennett, before you leave this courthouse today, a fine of $250 is due immediately, payable to the Court Clerk in the lobby on your way out of the building. Next case." He then pounded his gavel on the podium while handing Luke Bennett's file to the Bailiff.

Bell shook her head as she pursed her lips. *Great, now I'm going to have to pay his fine, too!*

"That way to the lobby," pointed out the Bailiff. He gingerly removed Luke's handcuffs.

"Thank you, Sir," added Luke while he rubbed his wrists and gave Bell a look of gratitude.

"Come on, let's get out of here," Bell instructed Luke as they got up to leave the courtroom.

"I'll go with you," the Bailiff advised them while they made their way toward the lobby.

"We'll be fine," Bell assured the Bailiff.

"I'm sure you will be," replied the Bailiff with an even look at Bell. It was clear he would be waiting with them at the counter for the Court Clerk to help them.

"May I help you?" the Court Clerk finally asked as she gave Luke and Bell a questioning look.

The Bailiff silently handed Luke's file to the Court Clerk and then stepped back to wait for the transaction to take place.

"That'll be $250," the Court Clerk advised Luke after checking the Judge's notes in the file.

Bell opened her black clutch purse and took out a roll of hundreds, counting off three of them and putting them down onto the counter. The rest she rapidly put back into her purse.

"What'd you do, rob a bank?" teased the Court Clerk while she made change and handed Bell a $50 bill.

"Not yet," responded Bell with an amused grin.

"Be sure to hang onto this receipt," cautioned the Court Clerk when she finished making it out and handed it to Bell.

"You can count on it," Bell assured her as she glanced at Luke. "Let's go."

Once inside the tan Buick, Bell shook her head when she turned to Luke. "Before we get going, you will tell me everything that happened."

Luke began to pout like a little boy and remained silent.

"You can either tell me now, or tell Willard after I drop you off at his house," Bell gave Luke a choice.

"Willard can never know!" exclaimed Luke.

"Then I guess I'll be taking you home where you can explain yourself to Ruth," countered Bell when she slid the car key into the ignition.

"Wait," requested Luke as he put his hand on Bell's wrist to stop her from starting the car. "I'll tell you anything you need to know, but neither one of my parents must ever find out what happened, especially my mother. Ruth's been so depressed lately; this might just push her over the edge."

"I'm listening," Bell prompted him while she took her black gloved hand off the key and put it in her lap with the other one.

"It all started when I decided to go back to Bible College a day early," began Luke. "Especially with finals next week, I needed more time to study."

"I guess you won't be taking finals now," assumed Bell as she shook her head with disappointment.

"No," confirmed Luke while he bowed his head with shame.

"Go on," Bell urged him.

"Well, when I got back to my room," described Luke, "that's when I blacked out."

"What do you mean, you blacked out?" Bell grilled him.

"Just that," revealed Luke. "I remember seeing Denise laying there naked in Richard's bed one minute, and then the next thing I knew I was in the Dean's office waiting for the police to come take me away."

"Perhaps you could have plead temporary insanity," considered Bell as she studied her grandson more closely. "You seriously have no memory of anything that happened?"

"No," Luke assured her. "I wish I did."

"There must be a reason why Richard and Denise decided to drop the charges against you," decided Bell while she considered what it might be.

"I was going to ask her to marry me," revealed Luke.

"You were going to propose to Denise?" Bell interrogated him. "Without a ring?"

Luke slowly took out the small black velvet box he had in his pocket and showed it to Bell.

"Huh," nodded Bell when she took the box from him to get a better look at the diamond ring inside. "This will do nicely," she said as she snapped the box shut and quickly put it inside her black clutch purse.

"Hold it," objected Luke while he tried to grab her purse. "I'm still making payments on it."

"I'm sure you are," replied Bell as she suddenly dropped her purse into the small space between her seat and the driver's side door, completely beyond Luke's reach. "And once you pay me the $250 you owe me for getting you out of there, then you can have your ring back. I'll be hanging onto it for collateral."

Luke took a deep breath and then let it out before folding his arms in front of him. "Okay, fine."

"I suppose our next stop will be Bible College, to pick up your things," assumed Bell as she gave Luke a questioning look. "Or, did you want one of your parents to take you there?"

"Bible College," muttered Luke. He was not anxious to show his face there again, but did need to pick up his things and his car.

Bell started up the tan Buick, put it into reverse and looked both ways before backing out of the parking space. She then put the vehicle into drive and headed for the nearest gas station, where she pulled up to the pump and came to a stop. "I'll just add this to your tab," she mentioned to Luke with a decisive nod of her head.

"Fill her up?" asked the attendant while Bell rolled down her window and shut off the engine.

'Yes, please," responded Bell.

"I'm in your debt," muttered Luke.

"You certainly are," responded Bell while they waited for the tank to fill with gas.

The gas prices displayed on the Texaco sign advertised 53¢ a gallon for regular, which was slightly less than the competitor gas station across the street.

"Can you believe they want 55¢ over there?" questioned Bell.

"I really do appreciate your help," mentioned Luke.

"We'll see," replied Bell. "You'd think this guy would do more than just wash the windows. I remember when a whole crew of guys would come out. They'd check the oil, the radiator fluid, the brake fluid, and even checked the air in your tires. They used to wear white shirts and bowties, too!"

"They quit checking oil last year," Luke informed her.

"Well, they sure don't have very good customer service anymore," complained Bell. She watched the attendant from her rearview mirror while he removed the gas pump nozzle from the Buick before hanging it back up on the side of the pump.

Once the gas station attendant finished putting the gas cap back on her car's tank, he came to the driver's side window. "You were still half full already, so that'll only be $4.95."

Bell handed him a $5 bill. She was clearly displeased.

"Did you need the change, ma'am?" he asked.

"Yes, I want the change!" she exclaimed. *Do you really think I'd give you a tip after such lousy service?*

"No problem," responded the attendant. He hurried into the building to retrieve Bell's change.

Once they started up the windy mountain road leading to the campus entrance, Bell asked, "How will you explain to your mother why you're home early when I take you home after this?"

"I don't know," admitted Luke. He folded his arms and began to glare out the window.

They drove along in silence until finally reaching the large wrought-iron entrance gates to Bible College.

"I probably will need somewhere else to stay for a week," realized Luke while he watched Bell roll down her window and press the intercom button on the gate's call box.

"Well, I certainly can't have you staying at my place," decided Bell. "Frank would flip his lid if he found out I helped you like this."

"Yes?" came a voice on the intercom.

"I'm Luke Bennett's grandmother, and we're here to see the Dean," Bell responded. "We're also here to pick up his things."

"Please wait," instructed the voice as the surveillance camera scanned them. "Campus security will be there shortly to escort you to your destination."

"I know of a rooming house where you can stay for the week," Bell revealed to Luke while they waited. "A customer owns it."

"One of the people you sew for?" asked Luke.

"Madame Claudia," smirked Bell as she thought of her client. "She still owes me for some of the dresses that I made for her girls."

"You want *me* to stay in a house of ill repute?" queried Luke with a look of indignation.

"Maybe you'll learn something," chuckled Bell.

"How can you do sewing for such people?" questioned Luke.

"Do you want my help, or not?" Bell raised her eyebrows and gave Luke a probing glance.

"Yes, of course I do," Luke assured her with a sigh of resignation.

All at once, there was a loud buzzing sound; the gates slowly swung open. The campus security officer on duty emerged from the gate shack and approached their vehicle.

"You must be Luke's grandmother," assumed the officer when he glanced inside the vehicle. "And Luke."

It's John, realized Luke as he folded his arms again. *This is beyond humiliating!*

"I'm going to get into my vehicle now. You will then follow me to the boys' dormitory," described John with a poker face. "Once we get there, you'll park your vehicle and wait inside of it until I come get you. At that time, we'll go to the Dean's office together. Understood?"

"Understood," answered Bell with an even nod.

Once Bell and Luke were seated in the Dean's office and waiting for him to come into the room, Bell turned to Luke. "Let *me* do the talking, okay?"

"Absolutely," agreed Luke, who was clearly nervous.

The Dean nodded cordially at both of them when he entered the room and sat down at his desk. "Luke, I will need your car keys."

Luke turned to Bell for her input.

"So that your things can be put inside your car while we talk," explained the Dean as he held out his hand for the keys. "You will *not* be returning to room 243, not under any circumstances."

Luke took out his keys and plopped them into the Dean's hand.

"John?" questioned the Dean while he glanced at the security guard and tossed him the keys. "Can you please take care of it?"

"Will you be alright, Sir?" hesitated John as he gave Luke a look of disapproval.

"I think so," replied the Dean while he turned to study Bell more closely.

Without further comment, John left the room.

"So, you're Luke's grandmother?" inquired the Dean.

"Yes, I am," confirmed Bell when she met the Dean's even gaze. "And, as you may or may not know, Luke's mother has been severely depressed for two years, ever since being abandoned by his father. I'm afraid the emotional trauma of finding out about all of this would be too much for her."

"Which is why you are here," nodded the Dean.

"Precisely," answered Bell. "And Luke will be staying with me until the school year is over," she lied convincingly.

The Dean inhaled deeply and then let it out. "Have you considered that at some point his mother is likely to realize Luke didn't take his finals?"

"Let me put this another way," bargained Bell with a slight smile on her face. "Are you in the habit of allowing girls into the dormitory?"

"Absolutely not," assured the Dean indignantly.

"Are you aware of the fact neither Richard nor Denise bothered to show up for Luke's arraignment today?" Bell grilled him.

"I figured as much," admitted the Dean.

"In fact, the Deputy District Attorney indicated to the Judge in open court that neither of them was willing to press any charges against Luke, pending the decision of the Court," concluded Bell with a triumphant look on her face.

"I take it the case was dismissed?" asked the Dean with a troubled look on his face.

"Indeed, it was," confirmed Bell. "Undoubtedly, because neither of them wanted you to find out how Denise was discovered lying naked in Richard's bed the morning Luke returned early and saw her there! Can you imagine how traumatic that must have been for him?" Bell then put a comforting arm around her grandson, who continued to remain silent.

"I'm not sure what you want me to do," admitted the Dean.

"Perhaps some bad publicity about your institution allowing such things to happen should be leaked to the press," threatened Bell.

"Look, we don't want any trouble," replied the Dean.

"Then this is what's going to happen," stipulated Bell. "You will allow Luke to take his final examinations as planned."

"We can't possibly allow him around the other students at this point," objected the Dean.

"Then he can come here and take them in your office," proposed Bell. "I will bring him here myself."

"I don't know," the Dean shook his head with dismay.

"That way, Luke can transfer to Ashton City College as planned, and you will never have to see him again," elaborated Bell. "It would be a shame to see this school's reputation tarnished, when it could have been so easily avoided."

The Dean glared at Luke for several moments and then thumbed through the file on his desk before responding to Bell's proposal. "I see from your transcript you've managed to get straight As in all of your classes so far, Luke, and that's impressive."

"Thank you, Sir," responded Luke.

"In view of that fact, I see no reason why any of your professors would object to you taking your tests early, provided they have them ready," stipulated the Dean. "Let me make some phone calls."

Luke took a deep breath.

"You are ready to take your exams, I take it?" asked Bell as she turned to her grandson.

Luke merely nodded.

"I'll be right back," the Dean advised them when he got up to leave.

After spending a week at Madame Claudia's boarding house, Luke was more than ready to return home.

It was late afternoon on Saturday, June 15, 1976, when the blue Toyota Corolla pulled up in front of the house Ruth shared with her children. Noticing his arrival through the front curtains where she had been watching for Luke, Ruth hurried to the front door and opened it.

"Luke," she greeted him with open arms. "So good to have you home! How did finals go?"

"Straight As," revealed Luke when he hugged her back and gave his mother a kiss on the cheek.

"I'm so proud of you, Luke," beamed Ruth as she took his suitcase from him and started to carry it to his bedroom.

"I got that," Luke advised her. "Plus, I got all the rest of my stuff in the car."

"Luke, I'm so glad you've decided to go to Ashton City College this fall," Ruth reminded him while she set down the suitcase and hugged him again. "It's so wonderful to have you back!"

"Hey, where's Leticia?" he suddenly asked. "Does she know I'm moving back home?"

"I mentioned it to her last weekend," responded Ruth, "but tonight she's spending the night with Melody and Colette at their parents' house."

"Aren't those the two blonde girls from church that always sit up in the second row on the right?" questioned Luke as he opened the pantry cupboard to look for a bag of chips.

"Yes, and they're very nice girls," described Ruth. "Hey, are you hungry?"

"Something good to eat would be nice," suggested Luke. "I can unload the car while you get it ready."

"You got it," smiled Ruth as she glanced at the refrigerator. "What would you like?"

"How about spaghetti?" suggested Luke. *Thank goodness Bell didn't tell my parents about going to court!*

Ruth hurried to fix her son some spaghetti, salad and garlic bread while he brought in the few boxes containing his things. When finished, he returned to the kitchen.

"Do we have any parmesan cheese?" asked Luke as he checked the refrigerator door.

"No, we're out of it," apologized Ruth while she stirred the spaghetti sauce on the stove.

Luke came up behind Ruth, put his arms around her and gave her another kiss on the cheek. "How about I run to the store and get some? While I'm there, I can pick up anything else you might need."

"It should be another 15 or 20 minutes before everything's ready," described Ruth. "Sure, why not? And we probably could use another bottle of Italian dressing, too."

"Your wish is my command," grinned Luke while he headed for the door. "I'll be right back."

Luke had initially lapsed into a state of depression while staying at Madame Claudia's during the past week, but he had quickly bounced back after succumbing to the few amenities available there. A young seductress named Cindy had introduced Luke to the use of recreational drugs to help him forget the traumatic events he had recently experienced. Quickly becoming addicted to the use of marijuana and alcohol as a means to relieve the deep sadness he felt over his breakup with Denise, Luke's life would never be the same again.

In addition to the parmesan cheese and Italian dressing, Luke had picked up a bottle of red wine and a six-pack of beer. *That should last a day or two,* he calculated as he pulled the top on one of the cans and guzzled it down while driving back home.

"Everything's ready," called Ruth when she heard him open the door to come inside.

"It smells great," grinned Luke while he inhaled the aroma.

Ruth frowned when she turned to see Luke taking the bottle of red wine and the five remaining cans of beer from the paper bag. "Alcohol? Since when did you start drinking?"

"And here's the Italian dressing and the parmesan cheese," mentioned Luke as he placed them on the table.

"You didn't answer my question, young man," said Ruth while she put her hands on her hips. She was not pleased.

"Denise and I broke up," blurted Luke as he brought the bottle of wine to the table. "Do you have a corkscrew?"

"Certainly not!" Ruth was indignant.

"I'm sure I can pick one up tomorrow, then," muttered Luke while he retrieved a can of beer, pulled the top, and took a sip before sitting back down.

Ruth sat down across from him. "I'll bless the food."

Luke merely nodded as he wiped the beer foam from his mouth with his sleeve.

"Dear God," began Ruth. "Thank you for helping Luke to make it safely home, and for this food we are about to eat. Please help me to understand why he has decided to use alcohol and to be patient as I listen to his explanation. Amen."

Ruth and Luke exchanged a long look afterwards before either of them spoke.

"Denise and Richard were seeing each other behind my back," began Luke while he piled some spaghetti onto his plate and slathered it with parmesan cheese.

"Oh, no," lamented Ruth. "I'm so sorry."

"I was planning to marry her," added Luke as his lower lip began to quiver. "Until seeing her naked in Richard's bed!" Luke then took another sip of beer.

"Alcohol isn't the answer, son," mentioned Ruth while she sadly shook her head. "Believe me, you wouldn't want to be married to someone who steps out on you, anyway. I should know." Silent tears then began to escape the corners of her eyes.

"Oh, Mother, forgive me," said Luke. "I didn't mean to remind you of what happened with Willard."

"Water under the bridge," replied Ruth while she put some salad on her plate before opening the new bottle of Italian dressing.

"There's no way to forget something like that, is there?" asked Luke as he broke off a piece of garlic bread and put it on his plate.

"No, I'm afraid there isn't," admitted Ruth when she shook the bottle of dressing before trying to open it. "How in the world do they expect people to get the lids off these things?"

"Allow me," offered Luke as he took the bottle from her and finally managed to loosen up the lid.

"Thanks," said Ruth when she took off the lid and poured a generous helping of it onto her salad.

"It's not like I'm an alcoholic, or anything like that," Luke suddenly assured her. "I'm just having a rough patch, and needed something to help me through it." He definitely would not be telling her about the marijuana!

"I hope that's true," responded Ruth while she put some spaghetti onto her plate and grabbed a piece of garlic bread.

"Parmesan cheese?" offered Luke as he held out the can.

"No, thanks," declined Ruth. "The doctor told me I can't eat any more cheese. He said my cholesterol's too high."

"Bummer," replied Luke while he took a big bite of spaghetti.

"Have you decided what classes you're going to be taking this fall?" Ruth suddenly asked.

"I was planning on picking up one of their catalogs next week, so I have a chance to look it over," described Luke as he took another sip of beer.

"Willard is teaching an entry level welding technician course there now," Ruth informed him as she took a sip of water.

"So?" Luke shrugged his shoulders while he wiped off his mouth on his sleeve.

"You really should use a napkin," recommended Ruth when she handed him one from the napkin dispenser she kept on the table.

"And you really should be drinking bottled water," rebutted Luke with an impish grin. "They say tap water can kill you."

"*Touché*," responded Ruth as she took another sip of the tap water in her glass.

"I thought Willard was supposed to be the head welding professor at Ashton City College," mentioned Luke in a sarcastic tone.

"He is," confirmed Ruth. "Willard also teaches classes in production, repair and fabrication welding, using both shielded arc and oxyacetylene gas techniques."

"You're still proud of him, aren't you?" asked Luke. "Even after everything he did to you?"

"He's still your father," Ruth reminded him. "I think you should sign up for one of his classes. Show him what you can do."

"Why? So Willard can ruin my perfect GPA for me?" Luke shook his head in the negative and rolled his eyes. "There's no way he'd give me an A, no matter how well I do in his class."

"Willard may be a lot of things," stipulated Ruth, "but as a teacher he's fair. He cares very much about his students and he would never give anyone a grade they didn't deserve."

"Perhaps during registration, I'll stop by his welding shop and ask him if that's true," decided Luke as he finished off the can of beer. "If Willard can guarantee me an A, provided I deserve it of course, I'll sign up for one of his classes, but only to make *you* happy. How's that?"

"That would be nice," responded Ruth, "but what'd really make me happy is knowing you won't be drinking any more after this. Alcohol can ruin your life, son."

11. Heavy Metal

Beatrice was a short, attractive and vivacious woman, well-liked by her students in the nursing course she taught at Ashton City College. Her short silver hair was parted in the middle, feathered on the sides, and neatly combed away from her face. It had never been her plan to fall in love with a married man, especially one 20 years younger than her, but seeing Willard each day in the cafeteria and spending time with him soon found them inseparable. They had been married in June of 1974, the very same day his divorce had been final, so many of the students would be surprised to find out about the two professors being married during the summer.

"Perhaps we should keep it a secret," recommended Willard as he finished off his sandwich and began eating the potato salad that had come with it. "The cafeteria at school has better food than this."

"But not the ambiance," flirted Beatrice while she nuzzled Willard's leg with hers beneath the table. "There's nothing like a sidewalk cafe on a beautiful fall day; the sun is out, the birds are singing, the company's great."

"Seriously," persisted Willard, "I'm not sure we should let our students know about our marriage."

"You know how kids are," grinned Beatrice. "They're bound to find out one way or another, and I'd rather they hear it from us than some other way, as if we're trying to hide something. Plus, we need to let administration know about it, too. Full disclosure."

"I suppose you're right," agreed Willard before taking a sip from the can of Coke.

"Maybe I'll sign up for one of your classes," teased Beatrice.

"Ha, that'll be the day," chuckled Willard.

"Why not?" questioned Beatrice. "It might be fun."

"Well, if the school has no problem with two of its professors being married," reasoned Willard, "why not let them take each other's classes, right?"

"Were you planning on signing up for a nursing course?" asked Beatrice as she licked her lips in a sensuous manner.

"Hardly," Willard assured her, "but if you wanna knock yourself out in the beginning level welding course, be my guest. Remember, I don't play favorites when it comes to grades."

"I'll keep that in mind," trifled Beatrice while she picked up a napkin, dipped it into her water glass, and gently dabbed a piece of potato salad from Willard's chin.

"Thanks," blushed Willard as he picked up a napkin and wiped his entire mouth off.

It was Monday morning on September 9, 1976, the first day of classes at Ashton City College.

Luke was mildly apprehensive about taking a class from Willard, but at least it was first thing in the day and he could get it over with. *He certainly had better not ruin my perfect GPA,* thought Luke.

Unfortunately for Luke, he had not been able to stop drinking or using marijuana, but had become secretive about his habits and, so far, had managed to hide them from his mother Ruth. *Keeping it from Willard should be a cinch.*

"Thank goodness the welders, rods and wire are all provided," thought Luke while he tightened his grip on the heavy-duty tote bag containing his helmet, gloves, safety glasses and fire-resistant clothing. *I wonder if these things are tax deductible?*

"Luke," came a voice from behind him. It was Ken, who had been in his cabin at Camp Deliverance. "How in the heck are you?"

"Okay," responded Luke in a guarded manner.

"Did you ever make it to Bible College?" asked Ken.

"For just the first two years," clarified Luke. He relaxed a little while they continued walking together toward the machine shop.

"Sure wish I could have gone, but my landscaping business was at a critical point, so I had to wait until now to go back to school," elaborated Ken, who was also carrying a heavy-duty tote bag. "Hey, are you in welding class?"

"Yep," answered Luke. *Thankfully, Ken doesn't know what happened to me at Bible College.*

"That's great," beamed Ken. "I was hoping someone I know would be here."

"Uh, there's something I should tell you," mentioned Luke as they entered the machine shop and sat on stools beside one another.

"You decided not to become a pastor?" guessed Ken.

"My dad's the professor teaching this class," blurted Luke.

"Nice to have a shoe in," assumed Ken.

"Just the opposite," Luke assured him. "Willard does not play favorites, and I'll probably be doing good just to pass this one."

"Luke, how are you?" asked Beatrice as she approached from behind him.

Luke's nostrils flared when he turned and saw the woman Willard had abandoned his mother for. "What are you doing here?"

"I've decided to take your father's beginning welding course," Beatrice informed him with a slight smile. "It should be fun, and will give me a better idea of what it's all about."

"I see," muttered Luke, who was clearly displeased.

"I'm Luke's step-mother, Beatrice Bennett," she introduced herself to Ken. "Looks like you two know one another?"

"We went to Camp Deliverance together a couple of years ago," replied Ken.

"Nice to meet you," nodded Beatrice. "I think I'll go sit up near the front, so I can get a better look at the blackboard."

You do that, fumed Luke. *How dare she sign up for this class!*

"I take it you and your step-mother don't get along," whispered Ken while he scooted his heavy-duty tote bag under his stool.

"It's not that," answered Luke. "It's just that I wasn't expecting her to be here."

"It'll be fine," Ken promised him. "We'll be too busy welding to even notice she's here."

"I hope you're right," muttered Luke.

Most of the students were loudly visiting with one another.

"Greetings, class," came the voice of Willard from the front of the room. The noise and commotion ceased immediately, causing the classroom to become so quite you could have heard a pin drop.

"I'm Professor Willard Bennett, and you are in the entry level welding technician course. Please sign your name on the roll sheet as it goes around."

"Professor?" asked a student in the front row.

"There will be time for questions after I've finished my opening remarks," Willard informed the student, who merely nodded.

"There are several welding stations available, but only enough for half of you," grinned Willard. "In other words, you will be assigned a partner while you're in this class, and the two of you will not only share your unit, but will be responsible for its maintenance and upkeep. So, if you notice anything whatsoever is wrong with it, you need to let me know right away."

Several moans and groans from various students could be heard throughout the room.

"Rods and wire are also provided," added Willard in a loud voice in order to silence them, "but you are expected to have your own helmet, gloves, safety glasses and fire-resistant clothing. I expect most of you have those things in the tote bags I see around the room."

Many heads nodded.

"In addition to that," continued Willard with a twinkle in his eyes, "you will need to have your own chipping hammer, wire brush, 9-12-inch adjustable-end crescent wrench, a pair of diagonal cutting pliers, 2-4-inch C-clamps, a rat tail file, and a torch tip cleaner."

"Where would one acquire those things?" questioned Beatrice when she raised her hand.

Several surprised students suddenly realized she was in the class.

"Before we go any further, class, this is my wife, Beatrice Bennett," introduced Willard. "Those who are returning from last semester may already know she is the head nursing professor here at Ashton City College, and knew her as Beatrice Nightengale."

"Congratulations!" exclaimed several of the students.

"Thank you," responded Willard. "And, in answer to her question, I would recommend you make a trip to your local hardware store with the list you just wrote down and I'm sure they can help you."

Several of the students suddenly began making notes after seeing the list Willard had written on the chalkboard before class.

"That's a lot of stuff to be lugging to class each day," complained Luke from the back row where he was sitting beside Ken.

"See that row of lockers on the far wall?" questioned Willard, without bothering to tell the class who Luke was.

Everyone turned to look.

"You will each be assigned a locker where you can keep those things, as well as the things in your tote bags that you have with you now," elaborated Willard. "You have probably heard I do not play favorites, and you will find it to be absolutely true. If you do get an A in this class, it will be because you earned it." Willard chose that moment to lock eyes with his son Luke.

It was Friday, June 6, 1977, and the school year had passed uneventfully, though maintaining his GPA had become more challenging now that Luke was secretly drinking and smoking pot. His increasingly frequent visits to the boarding house run by Madame Claudia included late-night sessions with several of her girls, Cindy being his favorite. In fact, Luke was looking forward to a special session with her that night, but needed to figure out a way to get more cash first. Sessions like that were adding up fast and rapidly depleting what little money he had left. Luke was considering a road trip to Vegas to try and strike it big at the poker table. With what Cindy had taught him about gambling already, winning should be a cinch. In fact, if he was successful enough, perhaps he could become a professional gambler.

"You're kind of late," complained Willard when Luke entered the machine shop to pick up his things.

"How's that?" asked Luke as he headed for his locker to retrieve his belongings. "Last I heard, school's over for the year, anyway."

"You were instructed to pick up your things by 3:00 p.m. today," Willard reminded him as he straightened a stack of papers on his desk. "It's 2:45 p.m. now."

"Then I'm not late, am I?" asked Luke in a flippant tone while he unlocked the padlock on his locker and opened its door.

"All the other students have already been here and gone," described Willard.

"Well, bully for them," retorted Luke.

"Look, son," mentioned Willard as he approached. "I'm sure you did the best you could in my class this year, but I think you should hear this from me first."

"Hear what?" frowned Luke while he starting shoving things into his heavy-duty tool tote bag.

"You'll be getting a C minus," Willard informed him.

Luke stopped and turned to glare at Willard. "What do you mean, a C minus? I've never gotten anything but an A in my life!"

"Actually, you received an A minus from me last semester," Willard mentioned unemotionally. "I'm sorry, Luke, but your studies have declined quite a bit this semester. You may find that the grades in your other classes are not what you expected, either, but that's what happens when you don't apply yourself."

Luke's nostrils flared with rage. He suddenly began hopping in place and shadowboxing, punching air strikes toward Willard in a menacing manner. "Come on, old man, let's see what you've got."

"I'm not fighting you," Willard informed him rather coldly as he turned and started to walk away.

All at once, Luke punched Willard in the shoulder, causing him to turn and face him again. Without hesitation, Willard grabbed the chipping hammer from Luke's open tool tote and held it up to defend himself. "You don't want to do this."

"As if you care," hollered Luke as he tried again to hit Willard but found his punch blocked by the chipping hammer his father was using to defend himself.

"I made a phone call to Bible College last night after grading the general knowledge written exam you took in my welding class," revealed Willard, who was not about to back down.

"You *what*?" Luke stopped hopping up and down and lowered his arms. "Whatever for?"

"They allowed me to review your transcripts. I wanted to see why your grades are not what they should be. That's when I discovered your final examinations at Bible College were taken an entire week before the end of the school year there," elaborated Willard, who was still holding the chipping hammer.

"You really called them?" guessed Luke.

"I did," confirmed Willard as he shook his head and glared at Luke with disappointment in his eyes. "And, as you can guess, my next call was to your grandmother."

Luke swallowed hard. *This can't be happening!*

"What did Bell tell you?" Luke demanded to know.

"Let's just suffice it to say that you're lucky I don't have you expelled from school for withholding information like that on your application," Willard replied with an unsympathetic gaze.

"Well, I don't plan to come back next semester, anyway," snapped Luke as he grabbed the chipping hammer from Willard, pushed him in the chest with the palm of his hand, and shoved the unwanted tool into his tool tote before zipping it up.

"Make sure you don't even try, or I will be obligated to inform them of your situation," threatened Willard.

"I suppose Ruth knows about it too," probed Luke.

"Actually, she does not," revealed Willard. "Your mother's been through too much already. Finding out what a disappointment of a son she has would be too much for her."

Overcome with rage, Luke flung his tote bag at Willard as hard as he could, hitting him in the gut with it. Luke then stormed out of the machine shop.

* * *

It was Sunday morning on September 10, 2023. Jim, Carolyn, Janette and Leticia had met in the lobby of the Rosewood Hilton for breakfast, though none of them felt very talkative.

"You were going to tell us what was in the autopsy report last night, but we were interrupted," Carolyn reminded Jim as she took a bite of oatmeal.

"I know, I'm sorry," apologized Jim before taking a sip of coffee. "Sometimes things come up at the home office that I have to deal with."

"How many offices do you have, anyway?" questioned Janette. "Isn't running a museum and a detective agency enough?"

"Actually, I've got a consulting firm that deals with most of my other companies, like this one here," revealed Jim as he motioned at their surroundings.

"Interesting," nodded Janette.

"Also," Jim reminded her, "my wife Sheree and I own and operate The Killingham Lighthouse Bed and Breakfast."

"Oh, of course," nodded Janette. "Didn't you say it's a two-hour drive down the coastline from your detective agency? That seems like quite a distance to commute."

"Not in my Learjet," grinned Jim. "Trips to my mortgage brokerage firm, or to the Priest and Krain Detective Agency in Ocean Bay are rather enjoyable in my aircraft of choice. Best of all, The Ocean Bay International Institute of Science and Anthropology is located within walking distance of my office."

"A man of convenience," smiled Janette. "I like it!"

"Not to change the subject, but as soon as we're finished eating, we need to head over to the hospital," Carolyn pointed out to Jim.

Suddenly shoving his plate aside, Jim opened his laptop and put it on the table in front of him.

"Let the man eat," objected Janette. *Especially after all he's done to help us.*

"It's okay," Jim assured her while he took another sip of coffee. "I could stand to lose a few pounds, anyway."

"Couldn't we all," sniggered Janette as she put a slice of bacon into her mouth and devoured it.

"I believe we finished reviewing the newspaper articles," muttered Jim while scanning through the pages on his laptop.

"That's correct," confirmed Carolyn as she took as sip of orange juice. "We also talked about how it would be nice to know if Willard has any information besides what's in the newspaper articles."

"Or the Coroner's report," added Jim as found the page he was looking for. "Here it is, and most of the information is duplicative of what was in the newspaper articles, including the fact that neighbors had not seen the decedent for at least a year. Then it goes on to say that her son, Luke, would not allow them in, so the police officers forced entry through the back door."

"Did it mention them having to use flashlights when they went into the house because of the electricity being turned off?" asked Carolyn. "It said that in one of the newspaper articles."

"No, it doesn't mention that part in the Coroner's report," replied Jim, "but it does mention the decedent's son was combative and mentally confused when they took him away to the Psych Unit at Ashton Medical Center."

"Maybe they have some records we can get," suggested Carolyn.

"That's not a bad idea," agreed Jim. "Perhaps we can find out more about how many personalities Luke actually had, and whether or not any of them were considered dangerous."

"I'm sure it mentions they interviewed me, as well," mumbled Leticia, who seemed ready to cry again.

"What it says," responded Jim, "is that you had not spoken to your mother in two years, and that when you did, Ruth had been very depressed and was refusing to take her medication. It also indicates you hadn't contacted her since that time."

"That's not true, I wrote to her all the time!" Leticia suddenly burst into tears, and Carolyn put a comforting arm around her.

"You didn't think it peculiar she never wrote back?" asked Jim as sympathetically as he could.

Leticia sniffed and blew her nose before answering. "I knew my mother was severely depressed, but she and Luke were both sick. That's why I kept asking them to start taking their medications, but neither of them would. In fact, both of them were quite upset with me for continuously bugging them about it. I just figured they didn't want me around, especially after that last visit."

"Leticia was also concerned with the safety of her family," interjected Carolyn. "Especially with Luke being like he was."

"Did you feel Luke was dangerous?" Jim gently asked her.

Leticia merely nodded her head.

"But you kept writing to Ruth, hoping she might respond," Jim reminded her while he studied the report on his laptop.

"None of my letters to her were ever answered after that," sobbed Leticia. "It became clear she wanted nothing more to do with me."

"But in actuality," assessed Jim, "your letters were laying unopened on the kitchen counter there at her house since 1995."

"Yes," mumbled Leticia as she blew her nose on her napkin and began weeping again. "If only I'd gone there to find out why."

"The Coroner's report indicates only two medication bottles were found at the residence," continued Jim. "One contained Thiothixene, 2 mg, and the bottle was new, yet the prescription had not been filled since 1994. In other words, none of the pills had been taken."

"That's odd," commented Janette.

"The other was for Benztropine, 1 mg, same story with it being a new bottle where none of the pills had been taken, and the prescription not filled since 1994," added Jim with a concerned look on his face.

"What are they for?" asked Janette.

"Both are for schizophrenia, and both were prescribed to Luke," answered Jim. "It says nothing about any other medication being found at the residence, for depression or otherwise."

"But, I know my mother was supposed to be taking something for it," countered Leticia. "She was severely depressed."

"It could be that Ruth had never bothered to fill the prescription, even if there was something she should have been taking," assumed Jim.

"Unbelievable," muttered Leticia as she shook her head.

"The Thiothixene prescribed to Luke comes from a group of medications called conventional antipsychotics," described Jim. "It works by decreasing abnormal excitement in the brain, and is normally taken in the form of a capsule by mouth three times daily."

"What about the other one?" questioned Carolyn.

"Benztropine is an anticholingergic class of medication," continued Jim. "It contains substances that block the action of the neurotransmitter called acetylcholine at synapses in the central and peripheral nervous system. These agents inhibit the parasympathetic nervous system by selectively blocking the binding of ACh to its receptor in nerve cells."

"Try speaking in layman's terms," suggested Janette. "So the rest of us can understand."

"Well," replied Jim, "it is a medication that's often used for schizophrenia, but also to treat Parkinson's Disease and a host of other symptoms, including tardive dyskinesia."

Janette gave Jim a frustrated look.

"It involves abnormal or involuntary muscle contractions that cause unintended movements of the body," explained Jim.

"I've seen commercials on television about how many mental health medications can cause tardive dyskinesia," mentioned Carolyn.

"Okay, yeah," nodded Janette. "I know what you're talking about now. So, does that mean the Thiothixene would have caused Luke to have tardive dyskinesia?"

"Probably so, if he'd bothered to take it, yes," confirmed Jim. "Not only can Thiothixene cause tardive dyskinesia, but in some cases, it can become permanent. Patients are advised to tell their doctor right away if they develop any involuntary or repetitive muscle movements such as lip smacking or puckering, tongue thrusting, chewing, or finger and toe movements."

"Oh, my God!" exclaimed Janette. "No wonder he didn't want to take it."

"Which, in turn, left his schizophrenia untreated," said Jim. "Not to mention his multiple personality disorder, for which little can be done. Sometimes, anti-psychotic medications can be prescribed to lessen its symptoms."

"Perhaps Luke had some other prescription that we don't know about," hypothesized Carolyn.

"It's doubtful he'd have taken it if he did," speculated Jim.

"How is a multiple personality disorder different than schizophrenia?" questioned Janette. "Aren't they the same thing?"

"MPD and schizophrenia have some overlapping symptoms, but are separate conditions," elaborated Jim. "People with either condition may experience delusions, depression, and suicidal thoughts, but those with MPD experience multiple identities or personalities; those with schizophrenia do not."

"Unbelievable," responded Carolyn.

"What causes schizophrenia?" asked Janette as she ate another slice of bacon. "

"Well," replied Jim while he grabbed a slice from her plate and stuffed it into his mouth, "the exact causes of schizophrenia are unknown. Research suggests a combination of physical, genetic, psychological and environmental factors can make a person more likely to develop the condition. Some people may be prone to schizophrenia, and a stressful or emotional life event might trigger a psychotic episode. Drug and alcohol use can make it worse."

"Luke certainly had a stressful life," acknowledged Leticia. "He also used drugs and alcohol."

"Do we know what type of drugs?" questioned Jim.

"The only one I know of for sure is marijuana," answered Leticia, "but Luke hinted one time he had used some LSD and I wasn't sure whether to take him seriously or not at the time."

"Something like that could certainly push someone like him over the edge," remarked Jim.

"What about the toxicology report on Ruth?" queried Carolyn.

"Well, they tested the gray matter they found with her skeleton," read Jim, "and found absolutely no sign of drugs or alcohol. However, the heavy metal test did come back with something."

Everyone stopped eating and turned to Jim, anxiously waiting to hear what he said next.

"No sign of arsenic was detected, but they did find lead," continued Jim.

"Is that significant?" questioned Leticia.

"It could mean Ruth chewed on a lead pencil when she was in grade school," began Jim.

"I don't follow you," frowned Leticia.

"Lead can accumulate in the human body over time," elaborated Jim. "It can be caused by exposure to lead paint on the walls, or even eating from Corelle dishes made prior to 2005 that were etched with patterns such as Butterfly Gold, Snowflake Blue, Spring Blossom Green, Woodland Brown, Old Town Blue, or Meadow."

"My mother had a set of Butterfly Gold Corelle dishes," realized Leticia with astonishment.

"That particular pattern contained the highest level of lead of any of them," Jim informed her. "Butterfly Gold is listed as 14,000 ppm, but the level of toxicants in the decorative elements in these dishes tended to vary from batch to batch."

"My mom had a set of the Snowflake Blue Corelle dishes," recalled Janette as she shook her head with disbelief.

"Another cause of exposure to lead, and probably the most significant one of all, is using or drinking water from lead pipes," revealed Jim. "And all homes built prior to 1978 are presumed to contain lead piping."

"We're as good as dead," muttered Janette.

"Lead is well documented to be a contributing cause to altered mental states, including depression and schizophrenia, but can also lead to possible heart, kidney, liver or other major organ failure, as the human body has no way of naturally expelling it."

"Is there no way of expelling it?" questioned Janette.

"Chelation therapy is probably the only way," answered Jim. "It's a treatment where the chelating agents are either given by mouth or infused. The medication then binds itself with any lead in the person's system before being excreted in their urine. It can be dangerous, harmful to the liver, and should not be used except in serious cases of lead poisoning."

"How would someone know if they had it?" asked Janette.

"Chelation therapy might be recommended for children with a blood level of 45 mcg/dL or greater and adults with high blood levels of lead or symptoms of lead poisoning," elaborated Jim.

"We need to get to the hospital, it's nearly 10:00 a.m. already," interrupted Carolyn when she finished eating the rest of her oatmeal.

"Agreed," nodded Jim. He closed his laptop and grabbed another slice of bacon from Janette's plate.

"Hey," objected Janette while she grinned at him. "Get your own!"

"I want your bacon, I'll get your bacon," teased Jim as he winked at Janette.

Once inside the sleek black Lamborghini, Jim and his passengers began their journey to the Rosewood Memorial Hospital.

"In other words," Jim suddenly spoke up, "there's no safe level of lead; any amount that any of us has been exposed to during our lives will continue to remain with us indefinitely."

"You're quite the ray of sunshine," commented Carolyn as she frowned at him. "I happen to have Butterfly Gold Corelle dishes, too."

"You can always just stick 'em in your china cabinet," suggested Janette. "They're still pretty to look at."

"I believe the lead found in Ruth's body may explain a lot," opined Jim when they pulled into the parking lot at the hospital.

"Such as?" questioned Carolyn while they all got out of the vehicle and began walking toward the hospital entrance.

"For example," described Jim, "high levels of lead in a person's system can significantly increase their risk of congestive heart failure."

"And, we were talking earlier about why we thought Ruth might have had congestive heart failure because of how her body was positioned," recognized Carolyn while she nodded her head.

"That still may or may not be what she died from," Jim reminded her. "You ladies need to get in there and find out what else Willard knows about it."

Jim and Janette stopped to get cups of coffee from the vending machine while Carolyn and Leticia headed for Willard's room.

"He's not here," announced Cole from behind them.

"What do you mean, he's not here?" questioned Leticia as Cole circled around them.

"His wife Trixie came in this morning and had him moved to a private facility," replied Cole, who was not unsympathetic.

"Where?" demanded Leticia.

"Technically, I'm not allowed to tell you without her permission," explained Cole in hushed tones. "She specifically said that if you two came back, we were not to tell you where they'd taken him."

"You're kidding," gasped Carolyn while she shook her head.

"Is there a problem here?" asked Jim, who had observed the conversation taking place and come over to see what was going on.

"That witch has taken him where we'll never find him again!" exclaimed Leticia. "My own father, and I'm not allowed to see him!"

"Is there no way you can tell us where they've taken him?" Carolyn asked Cole with pleading eyes.

"It would mean a lot to us," added Jim while he pulled out his roll of hundred-dollar bills, peeled off two of them, and then offered them to Cole.

"I can't take your money," objected Cole. "I could lose my job. But I can tell you the name of the ambulance service who took him. Maybe they can help you."

"Which is?" prompted Jim.

"There's only one ambulance service in Rosewood," revealed Cole. "It's called the Rosewood Ambulance Service."

"Thank you," muttered Jim. He stuffed the bills into Cole's pocket anyway. "We appreciate your help."

Cole merely nodded while he tucked them more deeply into his pocket, to be sure Natalie wouldn't see them.

Outside the hospital entrance, Jim pressed the button on his smartwatch and said, "Call Rosewood Ambulance Service."

The others stood by silently waiting.

"Rosewood Ambulance Service, what is the nature of your emergency?" came a voice on the other end of the call that only Jim could hear on his Bluetooth.

"Hello, Sir, my name is Jim Otterman, and I am on the Board of Directors for your organization. May I speak with your supervisor?"

"One moment," came the response.

Janette and Leticia exchanged a surprised look with Carolyn.

"Yes, Mr. Otterman, this is Steve Large. How may I help you?"

"I'm going to need a list of the ambulance runs made from Rosewood Memorial Hospital today," described Jim. "We have reason to believe there may have been a problem with the insurance on one of them, and the ride will not be covered."

Janette began to grin. *Not bad.*

"There has been only one ambulance run from Rosewood Memorial Hospital today," revealed Steve Large, "and it was to the Las Flores Memory Care Center over on First Street. Personally, I see no problem with the insurance. In fact, the ride was paid for in cash."

"Oh, okay, I see," responded Jim. "That explains it. There should be no problem then, unless of course the bills are counterfeit."

Both Jim and Steve chuckled at his witticism.

"Is there anything else?" asked Steve.

"Nope, that should do it," replied Jim. "Have a nice day."

"You, too," bid Steve before hanging up.

"Ladies, Willard has been taken to the Las Flores Memory Care Center over on First Street," revealed Jim as he resumed his trek to the car.

"What if they won't let us in?" questioned Leticia.

"Well, I may not own that one," admitted Jim, "but they will let us in. Trust me."

"Perhaps Leticia should try and call Trixie on her cellphone for permission," recommended Carolyn.

"I'm not talking to that woman," declined Leticia. "Not after how she treated me last time we spoke. Why don't *you* call her?"

"Do you have her number handy?" asked Carolyn.

Leticia dialed it and quickly handed her cellphone to Carolyn. After only two rings, Trixie answered. "Hello?"

"Hi Aunt Trixie, this is your niece, Carolyn."

"I don't have a niece," snapped Trixie.

"My father Walter was Willard's identical twin brother," explained Carolyn.

"I know who you are," growled Trixie in a menacing tone. "And you have one hell of a nerve reaching out to him like this when you haven't bothered to come see him before now! I'm sorry, but it's just too late!" Trixie then hung up the phone in Carolyn's ear.

Stunned, Carolyn slowly handed Leticia's cellphone back to her while she related to the others what had just transpired.

"That's awful!" exclaimed Janette. "Someday that woman's gonna find out what karma is, that's for sure!"

"One can only hope," muttered Carolyn.

"That was disappointing," responded Leticia.

"You guys were right," added Janette, "all that woman wants is Willard's money and she's just waiting for him to die. She probably figures if she keeps you guys away, then she's got it all to herself."

"But, I don't want his money," Leticia reminded her.

"Me, neither," agreed Carolyn. "All we want is to see Willard and to talk to him. He's our family, but obviously Trixie couldn't care less about that!"

"She probably thinks he might change his will," guessed Jim.

"It would serve her right if he did," opined Janette.

"Well, all we can do now is go there and hope she's gone home for the day," recommended Jim.

"Nothing ventured, nothing gained," agreed Janette with a determined nod of her head.

"Let's go," urged Jim as he opened the doors to his vehicle and waited for them to climb inside.

Located in a quiet residential area of well-maintained homes built in the 1990s, Las Flores Memory Care Center was housed in a private residence. City-owned light poles that would come on at dusk were located every 200 feet along the roadway. Above-ground utility poles were mounted in the cement sidewalks every 100 feet.

After locating the address using SIRI, Jim parallel parked the Lamborghini on the narrow neighborhood street where parking was only allowed on one side.

"I hope a school bus doesn't decide to come through here," cautioned Janette. "There's barely room for a car to get by."

"You and me both," grinned Jim while he studied the surrounding homes by the well-maintained road-verge located between the sidewalks and the road on each side of the street. Mature oak trees were surrounded by round river rock inside each of the road-verges to cut down on weeds, but those were the responsibility of each individual homeowner along First Street. Most of the homes had green grass lawns and flowerbeds filled with shrubs and bushes. A set of locking community mailboxes stood near where Jim had parked his vehicle.

An elderly woman from one of the homes had come out to retrieve her mail for the day and seemed friendly enough as she nodded and smiled at them.

"Are you sure this is it?" questioned Carolyn while she studied the pink house with white trim and its well-maintained yard.

"This is someone's house," presumed Janette. "There's not even a sign posted."

"This is the address," Jim assured her as he started toward the door.

"Wait," called Leticia. "What if Trixie is there?"

"Then I guess we'll find out," responded Jim when he stepped onto the front porch and briskly knocked on its door.

After several moments, a Hispanic woman in her late forties wearing turquoise scrubs opened the door. "May I help you?"

"We're here to see Willard," Jim advised her in a friendly tone while he smiled and winked at the woman.

"Who are you people?" she asked suspiciously.

"My name is Jim Otterman," answered Jim. "This is Janette, Carolyn and Leticia."

"I'm Willard's daughter," Leticia explained.

"I'm his niece," added Carolyn as she smiled pleasantly at the woman.

"His wife has gone home for the day," revealed the woman. "Let me ask Willard if he'll see you. Wait here."

"Thanks," nodded Jim, surprised when the woman unexpectedly closed the door in his face.

"Nothing like a nice warm welcome," remarked Janette.

"At least Trixie's not here," stated Carolyn with a sigh of relief.

"Amen to that," agreed Leticia.

"What time is it?" Janette suddenly asked. "I forgot to charge up my phone again."

"My watch indicates it's 11:30 a.m. on Sunday, September 10, 2023," Jim informed her. "In other words, they could be serving him lunch pretty soon."

"Let's hope they haven't yet," said Carolyn, "as they'll probably ask us to leave when it's time for him to eat."

"If they even let us in," Leticia reminded her while pacing back and forth on the front walkway.

The front door suddenly opened again. "Sorry about that," apologized the woman. "My name is Sue Ellen, by the way, and Willard would be delighted to see you."

"Thank you!" exclaimed Leticia as her eyes became watery.

"We will be serving him lunch at noon," added Sue Ellen while she stood aside and motioned for them to enter. "You'll need to keep your visit brief."

"No problem," Jim assured her as he followed Leticia, Carolyn and Janette inside."

"Willard's room isn't very big," continued Sue Ellen when she began leading them down a long narrow hallway, "but I think you'll all manage to fit if two of you stand."

Jim and Janette both seemed surprised but also were relieved not to be stuck waiting in the small living room where two other residents were busy watching a game show on television. The small Yorkshire terrier with them began fiercely barking at the visitors.

"Nice boy," greeted Jim in a soothing voice when he bent down and cautiously held out the back of his hand to try and calm the animal.

"I wouldn't do that," cautioned Sue Ellen with a smile. "Goliath is not fond of visitors."

"Good to know," replied Jim as he withdrew.

The entire home was finished with highly-waxed hardwood oak floors. Absolutely no carpeting was present, not even an area rug in the living room, lest anyone should trip on it. A dingy beige sectional sofa with Herculon fabric bearing food stains sat on one side of the room, though there was still adequate room on either side of it for walkers or wheelchairs, such as the one there now that was occupied by an elderly resident. For safety reasons, there was not a coffee table, and the big screen television mounted on its opposite wall was normally kept tuned to nature or game show channels; only staff were allowed access to the television remote. All walls throughout the home were plain white; decor was simplistic and sparse. An amateurish oil painting of a bowl of fruit hung in the living room. The hallway walls were bare, save for a first aid kit and a fire extinguisher at the far end.

Besides the kitchen and living room, there were a total of eight bedrooms in all, each occupied by a different resident. Most had their own bathroom.

Janette made a face at the smell of unchanged briefs and soiled bedding in some of the rooms.

"I know," whispered Carolyn while she shook her head.

"I'm so glad we're getting to see him," said Leticia when they arrived at the room farthest down the hallway.

"Right in there," directed Sue Ellen as she nodded toward the room. "I'll be in the kitchen if you need me for anything."

"Thank you so much," replied Carolyn. "We truly appreciate getting to see him."

"I know," she smiled. "Willard said he's especially excited about getting to see his little niece; I guess that would be you."

"Yes, ma'am," confirmed Carolyn before entering the room.

"Thanks again," mentioned Leticia as she followed Carolyn into Willard's room. Jim and Janette were right behind her.

"Hi Uncle Willard," greeted Carolyn as she came into the room, sat on the bed beside him, and gave him a hug and a kiss.

"Carolyn," muttered Willard. He still spoke with slurred speech, and it was difficult for him to form his words.

"Willard, how are you?" greeted Leticia. "I'm your daughter."

"Thank you for coming," smiled Willard while he gave her a hug and a kiss, too. "Please, sit down."

Carolyn and Leticia sat in the two chairs while Jim and Janette stood by the foot of the bed.

"Who are they?" Willard asked while he studied them.

"This is our friend Janette and that is Jim Otterman," revealed Carolyn while she squeezed Willard's hand. "They made it possible for us to be here with you today."

"Thank you," mentioned Willard as he nodded at them.

"Last time when we saw you at the hospital, we were talking about Luke," Carolyn reminded him.

Willard sadly shook his head. "Luke was just not right; he was a very sick boy."

"In what way?" asked Carolyn. "Is there anything you can tell us about what was wrong with him?"

Willard reached for his water bottle and took a sip before handing it to Leticia, who carefully put it back down on his night stand.

"You mentioned Luke might have been responsible for what happened to Ruth," added Carolyn.

"Luke should have been put away somewhere, long before he was," elaborated Willard.

Carolyn gave Leticia a pleading look and mouthed the words *say something*.

"I think we should go wait in the living room," Janette suddenly suggested to Jim. "To give them some privacy."

"Agreed," nodded Jim as he came closer and held out his hand for Willard to shake it. "It was very nice meeting you, Willard."

Willard studied Jim for a moment before shaking his hand and nodding. "Nice to meet you, too," came the slurred response.

"Hope you feel better soon," added Janette when she, too, came over to shake Willard's hand. "Jim and I will wait in the living room, to give you guys some privacy."

"Thank you," smiled Willard as he warmly shook Janette's hand with both of his. "Please come back."

"We'll sure try," promised Janette while she and Jim hastily made their retreat to the small Yorkshire terrier's territory, as evidenced by its loud fierce barking in the background.

"I sure miss Bella," said Willard as his eyes became watery.

"Who's Bella?" asked Carolyn.

"My little chihuahua," answered Willard. "She died just before Trixie had me put in the other place."

"I'm so sorry," empathized Carolyn while she squeezed his hand. "It's never easy to lose a pet."

After an awkward pause, Willard suggested, "You should call the people at the Psych Unit at Ashton Medical Center if you want to know more about Luke." It had been difficult for him to say the name, and Willard's speech was becoming more slurred.

"We will do that," Leticia assured him. "I'd like to know more about what was wrong with him, too."

"Can you get me out of here?" Willard suddenly asked as he turned to Carolyn with a pleading look on his face.

"I'm just your niece," Carolyn reminded him with a sympathetic look while she gently stroked his cheek with her hand, "but perhaps your daughter Leticia can talk to them."

Willard turned to Leticia. "All I wanna do is go home; money's no object. I'll pay whatever it costs. Please take me home."

"That will probably be up to Trixie," responded Leticia. "I don't think anyone will listen to me."

"I should never have married her," lamented Willard while he shook his head. "It's just not fair! Why should Trixie get to live in my house when I can't? I shoulda divorced her a long time ago!"

"Perhaps we can talk to Sue Ellen before we leave today," interjected Carolyn.

"I hope you do," responded Willard. "This just isn't fair!"

"Does Sue Ellen know what your final wishes are?" Carolyn suddenly asked.

"I wanna be buried by Matilda," indicated Willard.

"That's your third wife?" questioned Carolyn.

"Yes, by Matilda, **not** Trixie!" exclaimed Willard as his eyes became watery.

"Do you have any arrangements made?" Carolyn grilled him.

"Yes," replied Willard while he nodded his head.

"Where?" questioned Carolyn.

"At the Hillview Cemetery in Ashton, by Matilda," muttered Willard. "Everything's already paid for."

"We'll definitely make sure Sue Ellen knows about this," Carolyn assured Willard. "When a person has arrangements with a mortuary, by law it must be honored."

"I hope so," muttered Willard.

"If we have anything to do with it, it certainly will be," Carolyn promised him. "We'll remind the people at Hillview about it, too, that your wishes are to be buried there by Matilda."

"Thank you," responded Willard as he squeezed Carolyn's hand. "I'm so glad you came here to see me."

"We're glad, too," interjected Leticia when she squeezed his other hand and gave him another hug.

"I'll be out in the living room with Jim and Janette," Carolyn informed them as she turned to leave. "I love you, Uncle Willard."

"I love you, too," he responded with difficulty when he watched her leave the room so he could have some private time with his daughter.

Upon seeing Sue Ellen putting food trays onto a serving cart in the kitchen, Carolyn approached. "I thought I'd give Leticia a few moments alone with him."

"I'm glad to know Willard has family who cares about him," mentioned Sue Ellen while she continued to load up the serving cart. "Trixie told us he didn't have any family."

Carolyn sadly shook her head. "She would say that."

"Don't worry," Sue Ellen responded when she stopped what she was doing and pulled out a notebook. "I'll be sure to keep you posted on what's going on with Willard. You're his family and have a right to know. Can I get you to write down your contact information for me?"

"Absolutely," agreed Carolyn as she took the notebook and pen from Sue Ellen before writing down her name, address, cellphone number and email address.

"Can I give you my information, too?" questioned Leticia when she overheard their conversation upon arriving at the kitchen.

"Please," encouraged Sue Ellen as Leticia took the notebook from Carolyn to write down her name, cellphone number and email address, along with her landline number, as well. She then handed the notebook back to Sue Ellen.

"It's too bad you both live so far away," commented Sue Ellen upon seeing where each of them lived. She carefully set the notebook on the counter before adding the last of the plated lunches to her cart.

"Perhaps we can come back again soon," suggested Carolyn.

"Willard would love that," smiled Sue Ellen.

"I know you're busy," added Carolyn, "but before we go, there's one other thing you need to know."

"Anna Lucia," called Sue Ellen as one of her staff entered the kitchen. "I need you to start distributing the lunches for me. I'm going to need a few more minutes with Willard's family."

"Yes, ma'am," nodded Anna Lucia as she took the food cart from Sue Ellen and wheeled it out of the kitchen. Like Sue Ellen, Anna Lucia was a middle-aged Hispanic woman wearing turquoise scrubs. Her long graying hair was neatly pulled back into a bun; the invisible-style hairnet she wore over it was barely noticeable.

"Please sit down," invited Sue Ellen while she motioned toward a set of bar stools at a breakfast counter in the kitchen.

"Thanks," acknowledged Carolyn as she and Leticia sat down.

"First of all," began Sue Ellen, "Willard is not a well man, which is why he's here."

Carolyn and Leticia merely nodded.

"He's also on hospice," added Sue Ellen, "which means he has a very limited life expectancy."

"How limited?" asked Leticia with concern.

"Let's just say you shouldn't wait too long to come back, if you intend to see him again," elaborated Sue Ellen while she opened a medical file for them to see. "This, of course, is confidential, but you are his family and have a right to know."

"What is that?" Leticia scowled at the horrifying photograph.

"It's the worst bedsore I've ever seen in my entire professional career," Sue Ellen informed them as she pointed with the eraser end of her pencil at the photograph. "As you can see here, this is right by the base of his spinal cord. This type of stage 4 bedsore usually indicates a life expectancy of 47 days or less from onset until death, depending upon the patient's prior condition."

Carolyn felt an involuntary shiver when she studied the photograph. "How horrible!"

Leticia could not bear to see it and turned away.

"What I do want you ladies to know is that we are doing everything we can to keep him clean and to try and make him comfortable, but it's actually fortunate for him he's here and not at home right now," elaborated Sue Ellen. "Especially since the hospice people only come in every other day."

"Which would have left him completely at Trixie's mercy in between their visits," realized Leticia as she nodded her head.

"Speaking of Trixie," mentioned Carolyn, "how can we make sure she won't try to interfere with Willard's final arrangements that he's already made to be buried with his previous wife Matilda?"

"If Willard has prepaid arrangements made with a mortuary, then it would be like a will and would have to be honored, regardless of what she wants," explained Sue Ellen. "In fact, it already mentions here in his file he wants to be buried beside Matilda Bennett at the Hillview Cemetery in Ashton, and as long as he's here when his time comes, I guarantee you that's what will happen."

"Thank you so much!" exclaimed Leticia while she gave Sue Ellen a hug of appreciation.

"Yes, thank you," agreed Carolyn as she hugged Sue Ellen, too. "We are so grateful to you for taking such good care of him."

"You two about ready to go have lunch?" asked Jim when he and Janette entered the kitchen. "The smell of all that delicious food is making me hungry, especially after only having two slices of bacon for breakfast this morning."

"Three," corrected Janette while she gave Jim a sly grin.

"But who's counting, right?" asked Jim as he winked at Janette.

"I promise I will keep you posted," Sue Ellen advised them when she picked up the notebook containing their contact information and tucked it into a locking kitchen drawer that she secured with a key from around her neck.

"What's our next step?" asked Carolyn while they made their way towards the Lamborghini.

"Oh, no!" exclaimed Jim as he examined the driver's side door. "I've been keyed."

All of them glanced around the neighborhood but did not see anything suspicious.

"Now I'm going to have to file a police report," complained Jim with frustration.

"Do we have to do it here?" asked Janette.

"I'll ask 'em," Jim informed her when he placed the call. "No reason why you ladies can't get in," he added as he unlocked and opened the doors.

"He's probably going to have to call his insurance company, too," guessed Leticia.

"Unless, of course, he owns it," commented Janette.

"He very well might," smiled Carolyn while she fastened her seatbelt and watched with interest as Jim circled the vehicle and began taking photos of the crime scene with the camera on his smartwatch.

"Why would someone do something like that in a nice neighborhood like this, anyway?" queried Leticia while she, too, fastened her seatbelt.

"Probably just jealous," answered Jim when he overheard her question while climbing into the car. "I guess that'll teach me to park on a narrow street like this," he added with a wink at Janette.

"Do you think it could have been done by a vehicle trying to get by?" Janette suddenly asked.

"Nope," responded Jim as he closed his door, fastened his seatbelt and started the engine. "The same damage would have been done to the vehicles behind and in front of us."

"I'm so sorry that happened," apologized Carolyn.

"It's not your fault," Jim assured her. "The guys at the rental place will just have to deal with it when I take it back."

"What's our next step with finding out more about Luke?" Carolyn quizzed him.

"Well, I think we've found out everything we're going to from Willard," assessed Jim, "but there could be something more in Luke's file from the Psych Unit at Ashton Medical Center."

"That would involve going to Ashton," realized Carolyn. "Leticia would have to file a petition with the court to release Luke's file to her."

"I'm not sure I'm comfortable with that," Leticia unexpectedly told them as tears began to stream down her cheeks. "I feel as if I'm living that whole nightmare all over again, and I just don't think I can do it."

"Let's have lunch at the Rosewood Hilton," suggested Jim. "Then, if you still want to leave us and return to Ashton to think about it, Leticia, we can try and figure out what to do next with the information we already have."

"I don't see how," frowned Carolyn.

"Perhaps we can obtain information from the neighbors, or even the investigating detective who first came to the scene," elaborated Jim. "Who knows what they can still tell us."

"If any of them are even still alive after all this time," muttered Janette as she slowly shook her head.

"Hey, I'm really sorry guys, and I hope you understand," said Leticia, "but I just need some time out from this whole thing."

"No worries," Carolyn assured her when they pulled into the parking lot at the Rosewood Hilton. "Like Jim said, we'll just do the best we can with what we have."

12. Stray Cat

Having worked for the Social Security office in Ashton since 1952, Ruth was finally retired at the age of 55. Determining the eligibility of applicants while working as a Claims Examiner had been demanding, often requiring her to work 10-hour days, though Ruth had never complained. She was kind, caring and went out of her way to help others whenever she could. In fact, Ruth was liked and well-respected by everyone with whom she had ever worked. True, she had never been part of the office gang; she did her job each day and went home. Ruth was a very private person with virtually no social life, and her coworkers knew nothing about the private hell she was going through at home dealing with her son Luke's schizophrenia and multiple personality disorder. To make matters worse, Ruth's mother Daphne had recently been diagnosed with Alzheimer's disease, and it had become necessary to have Daphne institutionalized, a sad fact that had already begun to deplete her savings. Ruth had no desire to see that happen to her son Luke, too, and was willing to do whatever it took to protect him from being put away. Not only that, without Luke, she would be entirely alone, other than the occasional visits from Leticia. Ruth's depression had understandably worsened in the wake of these life-changing circumstances in her world.

Ruth's retirement party took place in June of 1986, on the 12-year anniversary of her final divorce from Willard. Her coworkers had no idea, of course, the day marked such a sad event in her life. It had also been 12 years since Luke graduated from high school, a special event in his life Willard had not bothered to attend.

"Happy Acres called again," Luke informed Ruth when she arrived at her residence with a shopping bag filled with mementos and gifts her coworkers had given her at her retirement celebration that day.

"What now?" asked Ruth as she set the bag and her purse on the kitchen table before sitting down. It had been a long walk from the bus stop. Luke had failed to pick her up as promised in the blue Toyota Corolla she had previously purchased for him.

"They said the police found Grandma Daphne wandering around the neighborhood again," explained Luke while he poured some orange juice into a glass and topped it off with what was left of the open bottle of vodka on the kitchen counter.

Ruth shook her head with frustration and buried her face in her hands. "I can't believe they would simply let an 84 year old woman with Alzheimer's walk out the door like that! Especially with what it's costing to keep her there! Meanwhile, I can't even afford a car!"

"You can use mine, any time," offered Luke as he put a couple of ice cubes into his drink.

"Thanks, but that's *your* car," replied Ruth when she removed her hands from her face and looked at her son.

"You're the one who bought it for me," Luke reminded Ruth as he gave her a compassionate look. "So, technically, it's *ours*."

Ruth merely nodded.

"Perhaps there's someplace else they can put Grandma Daphne," suggested Luke while he guzzled down his drink.

"Like where?" questioned Ruth. "And *why* are you drinking again? I thought you told me you were finished with that stuff."

"Just a little celebration in honor of your retirement," replied Luke with a devious grin.

"Well, I don't approve!" exclaimed Ruth when she got up and headed for the bathroom.

"Sorry I wasn't there to pick you up today," called Luke from the other room, "but I completely lost track of the time."

Before she could return, Luke hastily grabbed the marijuana paraphernalia he had left out near the sink and shoved everything into a small wooden box he kept on top of the kitchen cupboards where his short mother would never find it.

After using the restroom and drying off her hands, Ruth studied herself in the mirror. *How will life be now that I'm retired? Will we continue to make it financially?*

"I've got some good news that might cheer you up," came Luke's voice from the other side of the bathroom door.

Ruth opened the door to face her son. "I could always use some good news."

"Let's go sit down in the living room," Luke directed her. "*21 Jump Street* should be coming on."

Ruth sighed deeply. She did not care for the show, but it was one of Luke's favorites.

Luke turned on the television set and tuned it to the Fox channel before sitting down beside his mother on the couch.

"What's the good news?" asked Ruth.

"I applied for a job today," revealed Luke. "They needed someone at the State's Human Services Department who speaks Spanish, and I was the only applicant who met all of their qualifications."

Ruth seemed troubled.

"Aren't you excited?" Luke grilled her. "I think we should go out to eat somewhere to celebrate your retirement and my new chapter in life, too."

"You haven't got the job yet," pointed out Ruth, "but I am hungry. Why don't we walk over to Patty's Diner on the corner? I don't think you should be driving right now."

"Sounds good to me," grinned Luke as he pulled Ruth up and gave her a hug before turning the television back off again.

"You'll need to stop drinking if you do get the job," cautioned Ruth when she grabbed her purse. "Otherwise, they'll never keep you on."

"I know," Luke assured her while he opened the front door for Ruth. "Everything will be fine, trust me. Besides, we'll need some money coming in to pay the bills until your pension kicks in, won't we?"

"That, we will," agreed Ruth as the two of them left the older but well-kept red-brick house and began walking towards Patty's Diner.

It was Easter Sunday on April 3, 1994. Nearly ten years had passed since Ruth's retirement. Her constant battle with depression had worsened to the point where she had gone to stay with her daughter Leticia for three weeks. During that time, it had been necessary to have Luke institutionalized for his own safety, due to his diagnosis of schizophrenia and multiple personality disorder. Luke could not be left alone.

"Are you *sure* letting Luke come back to live with you is for the best?" questioned Leticia as she drove her mother Ruth to the red-brick home where Ruth and Luke had lived for more than a decade.

"They say Luke's just fine now," responded Ruth when they pulled into the driveway. "Oh, look! Several of the rose bushes have buds on them already. They are always so pretty when they bloom."

"Is Luke *really* fine?" Leticia grilled her while they got out of the car and began walking toward the house. "Luke's job at the State's Human Services Department lasted barely two months, and that's the only real job he's ever had."

"Luke did have that mail-order business," defended Ruth.

"For only six weeks," Leticia reminded her.

"You're being entirely too hard on him," argued Ruth while she unlocked the door so they could go inside.

"Am I?" asked Leticia when she picked up Ruth's suitcase and brought it inside. "Luke is *not* well. If he fails to take the medications they've prescribed for him, it'll be just like it was, or even worse."

"I'm sure he'll do as the doctor suggests and take his medicine," assumed Ruth. She paused to set her purse down on the kitchen table. "This was just a little wakeup call for both of us."

"Mother, it wasn't a *suggestion*, it was an *order*," differed Leticia. "That's why they call it a doctor's order."

"I know," nodded Ruth.

"Don't forget *your* doctor has ordered *you* to take the medication for your depression," added Leticia.

"You worry way too much," commented Ruth. "Luke and I will be just fine here."

"I beg to differ," countered Leticia. "Last I spoke with him, Luke honestly believed the Nazis were after him, along with some other cult group he couldn't seem to remember the name of. He even thought you and I were imposters and not real people!"

"That was just his illness talking," responded Ruth as she went to the refrigerator and looked inside. *She would need more groceries.*

"Mother, I don't believe you're thinking this through rationally," continued Leticia. "Luke also thinks he was abducted by aliens who injected him with cancerous warts during that cross-country road trip he took by himself after leaving Bible College."

"Luke just needed some time to himself," justified Ruth. "That was right after he and Denise broke up."

"Well, I have reason to believe Luke was out drinking and doing drugs that summer," countered Leticia. "Maybe even LSD."

"Not Luke," insisted Ruth. "He would never do something like that. No, not Luke!"

"Then how do you explain why the doctor wouldn't even allow him to be here by himself while you were away at my house recovering after a complete breakdown from depression?" Leticia interrogated her. "Luke is not well enough to come back home!"

"The doctor seems to think otherwise," opined Ruth as she filled herself a glass of water from the tap and took a drink. "Don't worry, I'm perfectly capable of handling him now that I'm better."

"You can't even handle yourself," insisted Leticia. "Plus, you have Grandma Daphne to worry about, too."

"Grandma Daphne's on hospice now, which is completely paid for by Medicare," mentioned Ruth while she set her drinking glass down on the counter. "And the new place where they have her seems to be keeping a much better eye on her. That'll be one less thing for me to worry about."

"That still leaves Luke," persisted Leticia. "My counselor told *me* that I need to sever ties with both of you if you insist on having him here. I just can't stand by and watch the two of you do this to yourselves. It's time to cut the apron strings!"

"I don't understand," responded Ruth with a puzzled look on her face. "Luke is my son. He's always welcome here in my home, just like you are, any time."

"Well, I may be your daughter," responded Leticia as tears began to flow down her cheeks, "but I've also got my own family to consider now."

"It's too bad they weren't able to be here today," lamented Ruth.

"Mother, Luke is dangerous, and my family is not here because I must consider their safety," Leticia informed her.

"Oh, poppycock," guffawed Ruth. "Luke wouldn't hurt a fly."

"I've seen him when he's drunk," countered Leticia.

"Luke should be here any minute," Ruth reminded her. "Perhaps if you just talk to him and see how much better he is, you'll see for yourself you've got nothing to worry about. Luke's not going to drink anymore, he promised me."

"If only that were true," responded Leticia while she sadly shook her head.

Just then, the blue Toyota Corolla pulled up in the driveway. Luke emerged.

"Mother, I really need to go, I don't want to see him," Leticia informed her as she started for the door.

"Too late," smiled Ruth when the door opened and Luke came inside. "Luke, how wonderful to have you back!" Ruth ran to her son and hugged him for several moments.

"Leticia," grinned Luke. "Good to see you, Sis! Happy Easter!"

"Happy Easter to you, too," answered Leticia, but without bothering to give him a hug.

"I was hoping perhaps we could all have lunch together today," mentioned Ruth while she helped Luke with his suitcase.

"You really don't have any fresh food in the house," argued Leticia. "But, I do have something for you. I'll be right back."

Leticia rushed to her car and returned with a shopping bag.

"What's this?" questioned Luke as he took it from her.

"It's a new phone with an answering machine on it," explained Leticia. "All you need to do is hook it up. That way, we can stay in touch, even if I can't be here."

"Why can't you be here?" asked Luke when he set the phone on the kitchen counter without bothering to open the box.

"I hope the two of you remember to take the medications your doctors have ordered you to take," bid Leticia as she turned to leave. "Just remember, I love you both," she added while she dashed to her car, got inside, started up the engine and drove away.

It was Christmas Eve, 1994. Rheumatoid arthritis and congestive heart failure had taken their toll on poor Ruth; it was with great difficulty that she walked with her son Luke to the corner market every few days for groceries and other supplies.

"Luke, I really wish you wouldn't do that when you're with me," objected Ruth when he purchased a bottle of vodka at the check stand and had the clerk put it into a separate bag.

"Sorry," apologized Luke while he picked up the bag to carry back with him. "I guess next time I'll just make a special trip."

"There shouldn't be a next time," snapped Ruth. "Don't you think people can tell what's in that bag you're carrying?"

"Too bad for them," shrugged Luke as he opened the bottle and took a swig while keeping it inside the bag.

The store clerk shook his head with sympathy at Ruth when he put the change inside her grocery bag containing milk, bread, eggs and a can of spam Luke would be carrying with his other arm.

"Here, let's just put this on the seat of your walker," suggested Luke as he put the grocery bag on her rollator. "You certainly wouldn't want anybody to see someone like me carrying it, now would you?"

"Ma'am, please let me know if there's anything I can do to help," the concerned Clerk whispered to Ruth once Luke had exited the front door with his bagged vodka bottle.

"Thank you, I will," Ruth assured him while she forced herself to smile and nod before following after her son.

"Any time," added the Clerk as he watched her leave.

Feeling faint from the exertion of walking back from the market, Ruth decided to lie down first before attempting to make dinner.

"Are you alright?" asked Luke before finishing off the bottle of vodka that he'd been drinking while walking home.

"I'm not sure," replied Ruth as she headed for the bedroom.

"I can get dinner started," offered Luke.

"Sure," mumbled Ruth when she parked her walker beside the bed and sat down, unsure whether Luke had heard her response as she started to lose consciousness.

Unaware of the medical emergency going on in the next room, Luke proceeded to open the can of spam. "Mother, how many slices do you want?"

There was no answer, so Luke headed for the bedroom where he found Ruth slumped sideways on the floor.

"Mother!" hollered Luke. He rushed over and gently shook her. "Answer me!"

After what seemed like an eternity, Ruth finally opened her eyes. "I think I'd better rest a while." Her speech was slurred.

Luke rushed the walker to the hall closet and returned. After rolling Ruth onto her back, he removed her shoes, and put a lap blanket over her. "I don't think I'm strong enough to lift you onto the bed."

Ruth merely nodded.

"Let me get you a bottle of water," Luke suddenly offered before racing to the pantry to retrieve one. Even though his mother insisted on drinking tap water, Luke had begun drinking bottled water after hearing on the news that tap water could cause lead poisoning.

"You don't have to waste your bottled water on me," objected Ruth as Luke removed the lid and tried to give her some. "I'll be just fine in a little while."

"You can't stay on the floor," objected Luke. He suddenly seemed to go into a trance. Then, without warning, he abruptly asked, "Just who are you? You're not my mother!"

"Luke!" wailed Ruth as he dashed from the room.

Hours passed while Ruth lay on the floor, drifting in and out of consciousness. She could feel a draft from the open window, and it had begun to rain. *Thankfully, the large bush outside the window is keeping most of the rain water from coming inside,* thought Ruth, who could no longer feel her limbs. "Where is Luke?" she mumbled.

Morning light was streaming through the open window by the time Ruth opened her eyes again. *How long have I been unconscious?* she wondered as she tried in vain to get up and was unable to move.

Entering her room without a care in the world was Luke, who was carrying a tray with toast, fried spam, orange juice and eggs. "Good morning, Mother," he cheerfully said when he placed the tray on her dressing table. "Let's get you into bed."

"Where have you been?" asked Ruth in a slurred voice.

"Fixing you something to eat," responded Luke, who seemed to have no comprehension of the passage of time that had taken place.

"Something's wrong," muttered Ruth. "I can't move."

Luke tried to help her up, but quickly realized he was not going to be able to lift her on his own. "Mother, your hands and feet, they're all swollen!"

"Help me," pleaded Ruth.

"I'm calling Grandma Bell," Luke informed her as he hurried to the other room to place the call.

After what seemed like another small eternity, Luke finally returned with three plastic kitchen garbage bags filled with brand new rolls of toilet paper.

"What are those for?" asked Ruth.

"Bell says I should elevate your limbs," explained Luke while he placed a bag under each of her feet and one under her left arm. "Sorry, we only had three of the plastic garbage bags left, but you'll probably need one arm to drink your water with," he added as he placed the water bottle by her right hand. "You still need to drink something."

"I'm so hot," mumbled Ruth. She pulled off the blanket Luke had placed over her the previous evening and was feverish.

"I have an idea," mentioned Luke as he hurried to the other room to retrieve the oscillating table fan normally kept in the living room. Luke then made another trip to retrieve one of the kitchen chairs on which to place it before plugging it in and turning it on. "How's that?"

Nearly incoherent, Ruth began making moaning sounds and from the look on her face it was clear she was in excruciating pain.

"Mother, please," begged Luke. "Please tell me what I can do. There's no way I can lift you onto the bed by myself, and it's nearly freezing in here, yet you keep telling me you're hot. What should I do?"

With her fever soaring, all Ruth could think of was removing her clothing and with considerable effort began tugging at her blouse to try and take it off.

"Here, let me help you," offered Luke as he tried to assist.

Ruth moaned in pain. "I'm so hot!"

"The bedroom window is wide open and it's nearly freezing outside," Luke informed her when he glanced outside. "At least it's not raining anymore."

"Please help!" screamed Ruth while she clutched at her chest with one of her swollen hands. Her breathing was labored; each breath she took had a gurgling sound; bubbles began to come from her mouth.

Just then, there was a knock on the front door. It was Bell.

"Where is she?" questioned Bell when she came inside.

Luke led her to the bedroom where his mother lay helplessly dying on the floor.

"Should I call an ambulance?" asked Luke as Bell bent down to examine her former daughter-in-law more closely.

"Bring me that roll of paper towels from the kitchen," Bell instructed him. She carefully removed her right glove and put it in her purse before feeling Ruth's neck for a pulse.

Luke dashed to the kitchen to retrieve the paper towels and hurried back to the bedroom.

"Leave the roll with me," commanded Bell as she hastily put her right glove back on. "Right now, I need to get her clothes off, she's burning up, and the paper towels will keep her covered for modesty."

"Let me help," offered Luke. He forced himself to watch while Bell set down several paper towels before pulling off Ruth's pantyhose and slip.

"Very well," agreed Bell. "You prop her up while I take off her blouse and remove her bra. She'll be able to breathe a little more easily."

Luke knelt down on the other side of his dying mother to assist but then flushed with embarrassment upon seeing Ruth's naked torso.

"Are you going to help me or not?" Bell grilled him.

"I'm sorry, it's just that I've never seen her like this," explained Luke. Tears began to stream down his cheeks.

"Set her back down," Bell directed him while she unrolled several more paper towels to put down on top of her. "Now, we need to get her bottoms off. She's wet herself. Think you can handle it?"

Luke seemed for a moment to go into a trance but then continued to assist Bell in removing the remainder of Ruth's clothing.

Bell silently wiped away the urine and covered the remainder of Ruth's body with paper towels, wadded up her wet clothing, and tossed it onto the floor by the door. "You can put that stuff into the washer."

Luke complied immediately and hurried to the garage to put Ruth's soiled clothing into the washing machine. *I'll run it later,* he decided.

"Just kill me," begged Ruth when she opened her eyes and looked at Bell. "Don't let Luke see." The garbled words were difficult for Ruth to enunciate.

Bell sadly shook her head as she grabbed one of the pillows from the bed beside her and slowly held it down over Ruth's face. It took only moments for Ruth's body to stop convulsing. Bell immediately put the pillow back onto the bed where it had been before Luke returned.

"I think we should call an ambulance, shouldn't we?" questioned Luke when he came back into the room.

Bell sadly shook her head while she used her right gloved hand to close Ruth's eyes. "It's too late."

"What do you mean it's too late?" questioned Luke. He suddenly collapsed to the floor and began to sob, rocking back and forth with grief; the vodka bottle he had grabbed from the kitchen counter fell from his hand onto the floor by Ruth's feet. "Mother!" he yelled.

"Get up," Bell instructed Luke while she grabbed one of his arms, helped him up, and led him from the room. "Let's just think about this first. If you call the authorities too soon, they'll think you did it."

"No!" exclaimed Luke when Bell helped him sit down on the couch. "This can't be happening!"

"Not only will they think *you* did this," cautioned Bell, "but they'll no doubt haul you away to the looney bin, where they'll keep you for the rest of your natural life. Is that what you want?"

Luke seemed nearly catatonic when he shook his head in the negative.

"I'll be right back," Bell informed Luke. She went to the hall closet for a fresh pillow case and headed for Ruth's bedroom to replace the one that had been used to smother her. *Luke's are the only fingerprints on anything in here,* she realized with relief. *Thank goodness for gloves!* Bell then carefully perused the room one last time before wringing out and wrapping the dirty pillow case with dry paper towels. *I'll burn the pillow case in my own incinerator at home,* she decided. She carefully stuffed the incriminating wad into her black clutch purse.

"What am I going to do?" wailed Luke when she closed the door to Ruth's room and returned to the living room. Luke pitifully looked up at Bell with tears streaming down his cheeks.

"Maybe nothing," suggested Bell while she adjusted her gloves. "At least for now. Give it some time."

"How much time?" asked Luke as he began drinking from another bottle of vodka that had been sitting on the coffee table.

"I was never here, do you understand?" Bell interrogated him while she headed for the front door. *At least they won't find my fingerprints anywhere,* thought Bell when she turned the doorknob to let herself out.

More than two years passed since that fateful Christmas Eve in 1994. It was January of 1997, and yet no one else had missed poor Ruth. The next-door neighbors had assumed Ruth was now in assisted living somewhere, that the house must be vacant due to the declining condition of the yard, and that the son must certainly be getting ready to put it on the market.

Next-door neighbor Marlena Sanchez had searched everywhere she could think of in the neighborhood for her missing cat Felix, calling his name and knocking on nearly every door in the area. All but the empty house next door. Her husband Danny had helped her put up fliers and an ad in the Ashton Times.

"What about the house next door?" he finally asked her. "Sometimes cats do go into vacant houses."

"That's not a bad idea," agreed Marlena. "I probably should search all the flowerbeds, just in case. It is pretty overgrown over there. Can you help me?"

"Of course," agreed Danny as they made their way next door and carefully opened the front gate of the overgrown yard. "Just look at those roses, all out of control."

"Over there!" exclaimed Marlena. "There's an open window over by the front corner."

"Huh," commented Danny. He began pushing back the thick camelia bushes to get a better look inside. "You'd never know there was an open window here with all these shrubs growing over it."

"Can you see anything?" Marlena anxiously asked while she tried to help hold back the branches for him.

"Oh, my God!" yelled Danny as he suddenly turned around and dashed back out of the bushes. "There's a skeleton in there! I'm calling the police right now."

"Did you see Felix?" questioned Marlena while she followed Danny back to their house next door.

"No," replied Danny as he hurried inside and picked up the phone. "And even if Felix is in there, the only thing I managed to see was someone's skeleton laying on the floor."

"As horrible as that is, I'm going back," Marlena informed him while she grabbed a flashlight from their kitchen drawer and started for the front door. "I've got to know if Felix is in there."

"Let's wait for the police," insisted Danny as he grabbed Marlena's arms to stop her. "It's already dark outside and there's obviously no electricity over there. For all we know, a burglar or some other criminal could be hiding out inside that house. It's just not safe. I'm sure if Felix is there, the police can let us know."

Detective Maxwell Klinger and Lieutenant Richard Hernandez had just finished working a double shift. They were busy eating a well-deserved meal at the Old Ashton Hofbrau in downtown Ashton. Being only six blocks from the Ashton Police Department, the establishment had long been a favorite hangout for off-duty police officers, particularly since it was open 24/7. It was well past midnight during the early morning hours of January 23, 1997.

The delicious aroma of whole rump and shoulder roasts of both beef and pork, German sausage, bierocks, and beef-stuffed cabbage rolls with rice, emanated from beneath the glass overhang where they were being served cafeteria style. Customers would grab a clean tray, plate and silverware packet before going through line. Usually, at least two chefs wearing white coats and tall white hats stood on the opposite side and would slice off thin layers of whatever meat was chosen before piling it onto mouth-watering homemade subway rolls with a special savory dipping sauce on top. Optional servings of coleslaw, French fries, and sauerkraut, sat at the opposite end of the serving line. A bowl of fresh apples, bananas and oranges were offered, as well.

Waitresses in tight blue jeans and lowcut black tank tops bearing the logo of *Old Ashton Hofbrau* in bright yellow letters were most efficient in making sure those seated in the booths had plenty to drink. Many of the customers merely ordered a pitcher of beer which was brought with large drinking steins bearing the logo and name of *Old Ashton Hofbrau* on them. The bartender made sure those sitting at the bar were served, as well.

Max and Richard had chosen to sit in one of the individual booths for privacy while discussing a particular case they had in common. Covered in deep red Naugahyde that looked like real leather, the bar stools and booth seats were inviting and comfortable.

The black Formica bar counter and tabletops in the various booths gave the entire place a relaxing feeling. Soft lighting hung from individual poles suspended above each table and were reflected in the wall-to-wall mirror behind the bar where liquor of every imaginable variety sat on narrow glass shelves in front of it. Rope lights along the ceiling and sides of the giant mirror made it seem even bigger than it was. Several electric marquees advertising leading brands of beer and liquor were suspended from the ceiling in front of it. The remaining walls and ceiling areas of the room were paneled with a highly shellacked knotty-pine veneer. Black-and-white framed photos of long-dead police officers from the early 1900s hung on the walls. The reclaimed oak flooring throughout the establishment had once been part of an old barn.

Even at 33 years of age, Richard Hernandez was already a highly-decorated police officer who had quickly worked his way up from Sergeant to Lieutenant of the Ashton SWAT Team. Richard was very well-built, charismatic, and favored by the ladies, despite the gold band on his left hand. Sadly, for his beautiful young wife and two lovely daughters in grade school, Richard was rarely home.

Max, on the other hand, was tall and thin. He worked out and stayed in shape only enough to meet the minimum standards required to keep his job. In his mid-fifties with sharp German features, pale skin from working night shift and never seeing the sun, Max resembled the stereotype of a vampire. His deep brown eyes and graying temples made him look distinguished, according to his ex-wife, though the only time he still saw her was during seasonal family gatherings where his grown children were included.

"Shall I bring you gentlemen a pitcher?" asked the young blonde waitress in her early twenties who had come to serve them.

Richard gave her one of his flirtatious smiles. "Absolutely."

"I'm not sure if I'm up to helping you finish off an entire pitcher," differed Max. "How about two individual steins instead?"

Richard merely shrugged his shoulders and nodded while he maintained eye contact with the young waitress, literally undressing her with his eyes. *Hopefully, she gets off duty soon.*

"Two steins, then," said the waitress as she broke eye contact with Richard long enough to write down their order. "I'll be right back," she added as she winked at each of them.

"Now, that's what I call service," grinned Richard while he stabbed a beef-filled cabbage roll with his fork and stuffed it into his mouth.

"Can't beat the food," agreed Max with a crooked smile as he shook his head. "Hope your wife isn't waiting up for you?"

"She knows better by now," Richard assured him with his mouth still full while he slowly finished chewing the tantalizing morsel.

Unexpectedly, both of their pocket pagers began to beep at the same time. Max frowned when he pulled his special department-issued mobile phone from the holder clipped to his belt and pressed the speed-dial button assigned to the Ashton Police Department's switchboard. Few civilians could afford mobile phones in 1997.

Richard did the same, learning immediately the SWAT Team was to be dispatched to an older red-brick home in the 4700 block of Grand Avenue to apprehend a potentially dangerous individual inside that was attempting to block police entry into the home to investigate a suspected homicide.

Just then, the waitress arrived with two foaming steins of beer, expertly balanced on the tray she held with one hand. Before she had a chance to set them down, Richard slid a $20 bill onto her tray and apologized. "Sorry, sweetheart, but duty calls. Keep the change," he added with a flirtatious smile when he and Max got up to leave.

"Sure, thanks," nodded the waitress as she quickly tucked the money into her bra before taking the untouched order back to the bartender. "Never even had a chance to set 'em down," she explained. "Shall I just take these to table seven?"

The bartender merely nodded. *Did the customer actually pay her or not,* he wondered as he followed her with his eyes. *I don't want to accuse her of stealing without proof.*

Outside in the parking lot, Max noticed at once someone had slashed the tires of his marked patrol vehicle.

"You just make friends everywhere you go, don't you?" asked Richard as he headed for the sleek black Corvette, a vehicle recently seized during a drug raid that was now available for use by undercover detectives, SWAT team members, and other specialized officers.

"Looks like I'll need a ride," muttered Max while he followed Richard to the Corvette.

"You really should be using unmarked vehicles, now that you're a detective," razzed Richard as he fastened his seatbelt and started up the vehicle, simultaneously rolling down the window and placing his magnetic cherry light on top of the hardtop roof before taking off at an accelerated rate of speed with the siren blaring.

Max hurriedly fastened his seatbelt before grabbing the dash-mounted microphone of the unmarked vehicle. He gingerly pressed the button on its side. "Detective Max Klinger calling from Unit 47, with Lieutenant Richard Hernandez driving. We are responding to the call for backup on the 4700 block of Grand Avenue. Please have the SWAT Team and at least two Detective units meet us there. ETA 12 minutes."

"We read you, Unit 47," replied the switchboard operator. "Dispatching the other vehicles now."

"One more thing," added Max. "The tires on Unit 23 were slashed while I was inside eating dinner at the Old Ashton Hofbrau just now. It's still there. Please make arrangements to have it towed back to the station. I'll do the paperwork when we get back."

"Not again," snickered the operator.

"Like Lieutenant Hernandez says," replied Max, "I just seem to make friends wherever I go."

"No worries, we'll take care of it," the operator advised him. "Switchboard out."

"Thanks, Unit 47 out," responded Max before carefully hanging the microphone back up in its holder on the dashboard.

Richard grinned at Max and shook his head.

Three marked police units were already parked in front of the subject home on the 4700 block of Grand Avenue when Unit 47 arrived. Their cherry lights were still flashing, even though their sirens had been silenced. Richard immediately turned off his siren before slowing and switching off his cherry light.

"I'm sure the guy inside already knows the cops are here," pointed out Max.

"No sense in letting him know more are on the way," replied Richard as he studied the surrounding neighborhood.

Seeing at once that the suspect house was the second house in, next to a corner house with several large oleander bushes beside it, Richard continued past the suspect house, around the corner, and quickly parked out of sight behind the oleander bushes. *A perfect place to park unnoticed,* decided Richard as he and Max exited the car and stealthily made their way toward the other officers who were stationed in front of the suspect house.

"Don't shoot!" teased Richard. He held up his badge while he approached, even though the officers there already knew who he was.

Detective Klinger held up his badge, too, just in case. He wasn't taking any chances, and failed to appreciate Richard's twisted sense of humor. Especially at a time like this.

Patrol Officer Garcia nodded and motioned for them to approach. "There's no power or working phone in the house. We're thinking of waiting until dawn to make another try at it," he revealed to them. He and the other officers were positioned behind their vehicles with their doors open as shields.

"Have any shots been fired?" questioned Lieutenant Hernandez.

"Negative," responded Officer Garcia, "but we believe the individual inside to be mentally ill and dangerous. He's already shouted several threats and obscenities at us when we attempted to gain access by knocking on the front door. There's absolutely no way he's letting us in voluntarily. We're gonna need a paddy wagon ready once we get him out."

"Already called for one, Sir," Officer Chilberto informed him from the next vehicle. "They should be here by the time SWAT arrives."

"Who called this in?" questioned Max.

"Marlena and Danny Sanchez, the people in the corner house," revealed Officer Garcia. "She was looking for her missing cat when they peeked through that open window on the west side of the house and saw a skeleton laying on the floor inside."

"Have you confirmed that?" Richard grilled him.

"Yes, Sir," confirmed Officer Garcia, "but based upon the threats the suspect inside has made, we're going to need to subdue him before investigating the scene."

"Understood," nodded Richard when a SWAT van pulled up across the street. "Wish us luck," he added as he headed towards them.

"Gentlemen, we will be doing a deliberate entry from the back of the residence in stealth mode," Lieutenant Hernandez briefed the SWAT team. "Any questions?"

"Wouldn't a dynamic entry be more effective?" questioned one of the SWAT team officers.

"Negative," responded Richard. "The suspect inside has already been made aware of police presence when they knocked on his front door. He knows we're here. For all we know, he could be armed and dangerous. The element of surprise is what we're going for."

"He's believed to be a Luke Bennett, who has resided here with his mother for several years," came the voice of Officer Garcia from behind them. "We don't know her whereabouts at this time. We must assume the skeleton in the front bedroom may be hers."

"Thank you," Lieutenant Hernandez responded to Officer Garcia. "That's useful information."

"Just like Norman Bates," muttered one of the SWAT team officers while he shook his head with disgust.

"Anyone else?" asked Richard as he looked each of them in the eyes. "Alright, gentlemen, daylight'll be burnin' any minute now; let's do this."

The team surreptitiously moved in and began surrounding the house, with several of them on each side of the dwelling, and two of them remaining near the front door in case of an escape.

Without warning, the lead SWAT team member kicked in the back door and entered. Recalling at once the power was not on, he switched on his helmet light. The other SWAT team members followed suit, systematically making their way through the house until seeing Luke Bennett seated on the living room couch clutching a half-consumed bottle of vodka.

"What in the hell do you think you're doing in here?" questioned Luke as he angrily hurled the bottle at the SWAT officer closest to him, but cleanly missed. The bottle shattered against a wall with pieces of glass and vodka spilling onto the floor. "This is private property! Get out! You have no business here!"

"Luke Bennett?" asked the SWAT officer to confirm his identity while he continued to advance toward him. "Are you Luke Bennett?"

Luke suddenly stood up and began hopping in place, thrusting air punches toward him in a threatening manner.

Just then, two of the other SWAT officers who had managed to circle behind Luke unnoticed moved in, grabbed his arms, and tackled him to the ground.

"You'll never get away with this!" exclaimed Luke while he struggled to escape their grasp.

"In here, Sir," came the voice of another SWAT officer when he saw the skeleton. "You'd better come have a look."

After being handcuffed, Luke appeared to be in a trance for several moments. At that point, the SWAT officers helped him stand.

"Is that your mother in the next room?" the team leader interrogated Luke after returning from the room where the skeleton was located. "Does the skeleton in there belong to Ruth Bennett?"

"Yes," mumbled Luke as tears began to stream down his cheeks while the SWAT officers escorted him from the premises.

"All clear," announced the SWAT team leader over the walkie talkie clipped to his bulletproof vest. "Bring in the gumshoes."

Like yellowjackets swarming barbecued chicken at a summer picnic, all detectives on the scene came into the house, nodding in greeting to the various SWAT team members as they left.

"Forensics, you're in there," commanded Detective Max Klinger. "I want fingerprints and any other DNA evidence you can muster. Even after all this time, there must be something we can use."

"Sir, there's signs of rodent and roach activity," responded Detective Stark.

"Which would explain why there's nothing left but some gray matter with the skeleton," nodded Detective Klinger.

"Detective Klinger," came the voice of Officer Chilberto from behind him. "We read the defendant his rights before taking him to the Psych Unit at Ashton Medical Center for further evaluation and questioning."

"Very good, thank you," replied Max. "Okay, gentlemen, I want dental records on the decedent for comparison by close of business today. Let's question each of the surrounding neighbors and reach out to any possible family members to see what they can tell us."

13. Hillview

After reviewing the notes from his case file on Luke Bennett, Dr. Henry Godspeed was deep in thought as he gazed from his office window at the lush atrium garden on the other side. Even though he was finished with his appointments for the day, he could not stop thinking about the troubling case. It was April 20, 1998, and he had been studying this particular patient for over a year; he was no closer to confirming what really happened to Luke's mother now than during his initial interview with him.

In the atrium abutting his office window, gravel pathways with granite stepping stones led past neatly trimmed boxwood hedges, bamboo, barberry and miniature red-leaf maple trees toward a central koi pond flanked by marble benches. Lily pads laden with blooming lotus flowers provided cover for the fish beneath them. At one end of the pond was a pagoda-style statue from which a continuous flow of water circulated. Colorful prayer flags on fishing line were suspended from near the ceiling where several large skylights were located. Handmade wall hangings with seashell art intended to resemble koi fish and silk-embroidered Japanese writing beside them added a touch of elegance to the scene.

Offices and consulting rooms from all three floors of the Psych Unit at Ashton Medical Center encircled the 30-foot high atrium while sharing equally impressive views of its zen space within.

An unexpected knock on his door pulled Dr. Godspeed from his contemplation. "Who is it?" he demanded. *Certainly, my secretary knows better than to allow someone to come to my office unannounced.*

"Dr. Victor Shelley," came the response. "Ashton County Coroner. I was hoping you had some time to discuss a case with me."

Irritated by the interruption, Dr. Godspeed got up to open the door. "You could have just called," he advised Dr. Shelley as he returned to his overstuffed brown leather chair and sat down.

"I understand Luke Bennett has been a patient of yours for well over a year now," mentioned Dr. Shelley when he sat down in the other overstuffed brown leather chair opposite him. A small coffee table sat between them.

"And you must be the Coroner who examined the remains found at the house where they arrested him," presumed Dr. Godspeed.

"Yes," confirmed Dr. Shelley as he glanced out the picture window at the atrium garden. "Very nice."

"It is," agreed Dr. Godspeed. "I'm sure you're aware of doctor-patient confidentiality?"

"I'm actually here to share information with you," clarified Dr. Shelley as he reached inside his jacket pocket and pulled out a brown manilla envelope stamped *confidential* in red ink.

Both men were in their late fifties with graying hair, receding hairlines, pale complexions, brown eyes, black horn-rimmed glasses, and bulging midsections. Neither wore a necktie, one for fear of it getting in the way while performing autopsies, and the other as a safety precaution should a deranged patient unexpectedly grab it and attempt to strangle him.

Dr. Godspeed had on a white jacket over his white shirt while Dr. Shelley wore a plain black suit jacket. Both men had on black slacks and highly polished black leather loafers.

"Are you sure you're allowed to share that with me?" asked Dr. Godspeed as he frowned at the envelope being held out to him.

"By this time next year, it will no doubt be public record," assumed Dr. Shelley with a shrug of his shoulders.

Dr. Godspeed warily accepted the envelope and studied it for several moments before tearing it open.

"It's my official Coroner Certificate and Verdict," Dr. Shelley informed him. "By law, there's a waiting period before I can officially file the complete investigation report with the Court, of course."

"I see you're ruling the official death date as January 23, 1997," noted Dr. Godspeed while he furrowed his eyebrows. "Even though the body was unquestionably there for quite some time?"

"Actually," explained Dr. Shelley, "There's no doubt it took anywhere from 12 to 18 months for the rodent and roach activity to subside, but discovery of the deceased was the one definitive date that could not be questioned."

"I see," responded Dr. Godspeed as he continued to read the report. "Hmm."

"Previous dental records were used for positive identification," continued Dr. Shelley, "though the dried-up gray brittle powder found inside the skull was still viable for testing purposes."

"I see the toxicology report shows no sign of drugs or alcohol," mumbled Dr. Godspeed while he flipped through the pages until reaching the miscellaneous drug section. "That's peculiar."

"Not at all," differed Dr. Shelley. "Even though there was no mercury or arsenic detected, there was a finding of lead in her system."

"What would cause that?" Dr. Godspeed grilled him.

"It was an older house," responded Dr. Shelley. "Could be lead paint on the walls, or perhaps she drank tap water. The dwelling did have lead pipes."

"Are you saying that's what killed her?" asked Dr. Godspeed.

"If you skip to the end, you'll see where I've ruled the cause of death is officially going to be listed as *undetermined*," clarified Dr. Shelley while he maintained eye contact with Dr. Godspeed. "Unless, of course, there is anything you can tell me that might alter my decision. Perhaps Luke may have confessed to *you* that he did it?"

"Damnit, Victor, you know I can't possibly do that," replied Dr. Godspeed while he pursed his lips with frustration.

"Well, Henry, that's a decision only you can make," responded Dr. Shelley as he took a deep sigh. "The body was so badly decomposed by the time we examined it, that there was no soft tissue left, no ligaments remaining, and no cartilage adhering to the bones. Absolutely nothing to prove or disprove smothering or other soft tissue injury one way or the other. The only thing we can say for sure is that there was no sign of blunt force trauma to the skeleton."

"Even if I knew something," maintained Dr. Godspeed, "I cannot violate doctor-patient confidentiality."

"I'm sure you're aware by now we found medication bottles containing Thiothixene and Benztropine in the house," revealed Dr. Shelley, "though both were prescribed to Luke for schizophrenia and multiple personality disorder. Unfortunately, none had ever been taken. And, absolutely no medication of any kind was found for his mother, though we did locate some paperwork indicating she suffered from severe depression and was supposed to be taking something for it."

"Which she wasn't," assumed Dr. Godspeed as he sadly shook his head. "Let me ask you something."

"Please do," encouraged Dr. Shelley.

"Hypothetically."

"Hypothetically, of course," agreed Dr. Shelley.

"Hypothetically, was there any evidence whatsoever of anyone else besides Luke having been at the scene prior to its discovery?"

"That's a very interesting question," responded Dr. Shelley while he studied Dr. Godspeed more closely. "Am I going to need a Court Order to find out what you're not telling me?"

"Hypothetically," reminded Dr. Godspeed, "let's just say, what if one of the various personalities Luke has exhibited might have been an actual person? Hypothetically."

"Why would you think that?" Dr. Shelley grilled him.

"Exactly which of his family members have you investigated?" Dr. Godspeed suddenly asked.

"His sister and her family, of course," replied Dr. Shelley, "but that's a matter of record. Why hell, it's even in the newspaper."

"Anyone else?" questioned Dr. Godspeed with raised eyebrows.

"Each of his grandmothers," added Dr. Shelley, "but one has Alzheimer's and is in a facility. She knows absolutely nothing."

"And the *other* grandmother?" Dr. Godspeed asked him with a pointed look.

"She was interviewed," Dr. Shelley assured him.

"I'm sorry, but you will need a Court Order to find out what else I suspect," apologized Dr. Godspeed. "Just keep in mind, it's only my suspicion, I have no actual proof whatsoever."

* * *

It had been weeks since Janette and Carolyn each returned to their homes after reaching an impasse with Leticia about whether or not to obtain a Court Order to unseal Luke's confidential file from the Psych Unit at Ashton Medical Center. Leticia had returned to her home, as well. It was already October 6, 2023.

Deciding to go for a walk with her friend Leena on a quiet forest trail nearby, Carolyn drove to the location to meet her. The sun was out, birds could be heard overhead in the forest canopy, and the sound of the creek beside the trail was relaxing.

"Perfect day for it," observed Leena when she and Carolyn met in the parking lot and began their walk.

"Yeah, I needed a change of pace," admitted Carolyn as she deeply inhaled the aroma of the foliage around them.

"Do you still call your uncle every day?" asked Leena.

"Absolutely," confirmed Carolyn.

"I'm sure he appreciates it," nodded Leena while they walked along. "Especially being bedfast like that."

"It's just been nice finally getting to know him," responded Carolyn, "especially after all the years we missed out on. I'm definitely finding out why he feels the way he does about his mother."

Just then, Carolyn's cellphone unexpectedly rang. Upon seeing it was from the Las Flores Memory Care Center in Rosewood, Carolyn immediately answered. "Hello, this is Carolyn."

"Hi Carolyn, this is Sue Ellen," came the voice at the other end. "I'm so sorry to tell you this, but Willard just passed a few minutes ago."

"Oh, no!" exclaimed Carolyn as her eyes began to water. "Uh, thank you for telling me, I truly appreciate it."

"I didn't figure Trixie would bother to let you know," added Sue Ellen. "I called Leticia just now, too. She seemed relieved to know Willard's finally at peace."

"I sure hope so," replied Carolyn while she pulled a tissue from her pocket and dabbed at the tears forming in the corners of her eyes. "And, of course, Trixie must know already?"

"Yep, she just got here and is in there now, gathering up his things," revealed Sue Ellen.

"Of that, I have no doubt," commented Carolyn, rather bitterly.

"We each grieve in our own way," Sue Ellen reminded her.

"Say, has the mortuary at Hillview been notified yet?" Carolyn suddenly asked. "As we discussed before, Willard definitely wants to be buried beside his previous wife at the Hillview Cemetery in Ashton, and **not** by Trixie."

"I know, and they've already been notified. In fact, they're on their way here now to pick up his body," Sue Ellen assured Carolyn, "but it might not hurt to call and let them know you're interested in seeing the obituary when it comes out, just in case."

"I'll be sure and do that today, thank you," replied Carolyn as tears began to stream down her cheeks. "And thank you for all you did to care for Uncle Willard while he was there with you. I appreciate it."

"I'm just glad we were able to do what we did for him," responded Sue Ellen. "You take care."

"Thanks, you too," bid Carolyn before hanging up.

"Your uncle?" guessed Leena as she put a compassionate arm around Carolyn and gave her a hug.

"I'm afraid so," revealed Carolyn when she sat down on a green wrought iron bench beside the trail. "I need to call the mortuary where they're supposed to bury him."

"Take your time, I'm in no hurry," responded Leena as she sat down beside Carolyn to enjoy the view of the creek.

Carolyn quickly did a Google search for the Hillview Cemetery in Ashton and then pressed the number listed to call them.

After only two rings, a woman answered. "Hillview Cemetery, how may I help you?"

"Hi, my name is Carolyn and my Uncle Willard just passed away today over at the Las Flores Memory Care Center in Rosewood," she elaborated. "My father Walter was his identical twin brother, by the way, and I was hoping you could notify me of when there will be a funeral service?"

"That would be up to his wife," replied the woman.

"Unfortunately," continued Carolyn, "Trixie is not exactly on speaking terms with his family. In fact, it was the facility, not her, that notified us of his death. We just want to make sure we don't miss out on his funeral."

"Actually, there's an obituary already here in our computer system that just posted," revealed the woman. "Would you like me to send you a link?"

"Yes, please," answered Carolyn. "I would greatly appreciate that. And what was your name, so I'll know who it's from when I see your email?"

"Lucy," revealed the woman.

"Thank you, Lucy, you've been a great help."

"My pleasure," replied Lucy. "Just let me know if there's anything else I can do."

"Will it say in the obituary when the funeral will be?"

"Actually, as you'll see when you read it," replied Lucy, "there's not going to be a funeral, just a direct burial."

"You're kidding!" exclaimed Carolyn.

"That's what it says here in the paperwork."

"Very well," said Carolyn, "I need to call his daughter Leticia in Ashton to let her know about this."

"Definitely," agreed Lucy.

"May I give her your number, in case she needs to call?" inquired Carolyn. "Especially since I'm not sure how she'll feel about there not being a memorial service."

"His daughter is more than welcome to call, and we're open until 4:00 p.m.," Lucy informed Carolyn. "And we're so sorry for your loss."

"Thanks, I appreciate that. You have a nice day," bid Carolyn when she hung up.

"Are you alright?" questioned Lenna.

"I don't know," sighed Carolyn.

"Is there anything I can do?" offered Leena.

"I wish there was," responded Carolyn. "I just can't believe that witch my uncle was married to isn't even going to allow his family to have a memorial service for him."

"That's awful," sympathized Leena. "Perhaps there's still a way you can have one anyway?"

"I doubt it," replied Carolyn.

"Maybe you and Leticia can just go there later and have a service of your own," suggested Leena.

"We'll have to wait and see," considered Carolyn. "I sure hope so."

Upon reaching home after her walk with Leena, Carolyn quickly checked her email and found the one from Lucy. In it was a link to Willard's obituary.

Everything anyone could ever possibly want to know about his professional accomplishments as a welder was listed first. The obituary went on to say that, "Mr. Bennett is survived by his wife Trixie. At his request there is to be no funeral, memorial, or celebration of life service. Burial will be at the Hillview Cemetery in Ashton."

"Oh, my God!" exclaimed Carolyn out loud. *And worse than that, the obituary makes* **no mention whatsoever** *that Willard even had a daughter, much less a granddaughter, or a great grandson! Nor did it mention he had a niece, either,* fumed Carolyn while she stared with disbelief at the intentional omission.

Dialing Leticia's number immediately, Carolyn took several deep breaths as she waited for her to answer.

"Hello?" came Leticia's voice.

"Hey, Leticia, this is Carolyn, I'm so sorry to hear about Willard. Are you okay?"

"I'm just glad he's finally at peace," Leticia informed her. "And that he's no longer suffering."

"Did you see the obituary yet?" asked Carolyn.

"No, already?" questioned Leticia with surprise.

"The lady at Hillview sent me a link to it and I've just forwarded it to you," elaborated Carolyn. "And not only is there **not** going to be a funeral service, memorial or celebration of life, allegedly at Willard's request, it doesn't even mention he had a daughter."

"Unbelievable," muttered Leticia. "One final slap."

"It had to be Trixie," maintained Carolyn. "There's no way Willard would fail to mention he had a family if he had any part in preparing it. She obviously made sure there was no mention of his family in the obituary."

"At least she bothered to mention his welding career," said Leticia when she pulled up and looked at the obituary.

"Sorry to say this, but it would appear Willard finally succeeded in marrying a woman just like his mother," added Carolyn.

"I don't even know what to think, at this point," admitted Leticia. "We've never been unkind to her."

"Perhaps that's the answer," suggested Carolyn. "We can kill her with kindness by going in and adding comments at the obituary website. In fact, I'm doing that now. There, you should be able to read it as soon as they accept it."

"What'd you say?" probed Leticia.

"I'll read it to you," replied Carolyn. "My condolences to his wife Trixie, and to his surviving daughter Leticia and her family from Ashton, who I know he loved. Reconnecting with my Uncle Willard and getting to know him these past few weeks has meant the world to me, and I am grateful for the opportunity. My father Walter was his identical twin brother and it is my prayer they have peace, love, joy and comradery together where they are now."

"That's nice," approved Leticia.

"I'll keep in touch with Hillview and as soon as there's a death date carved on his headstone, perhaps we can meet there," proposed Carolyn. "There's nothing to stop us from having our own memorial."

"I'll have to think about it," responded Leticia. "I got to see him when he was alive, and that was the important thing."

"Okay," said Carolyn. "Just let me know if there's anything I can do for you. Love you, Leticia."

"Love you, too," bid Leticia as she hung up.

It was on October 13, 2023, when Carolyn finally phoned Jim Otterman to see how his investigation was going.

"Carolyn?"

"Hi Jim, how are you?"

"Still working on trying to get a Court Order to unseal Luke's psychiatric record, but without Leticia's consent, I'm not sure if there's anything else we can do," elaborated Jim.

"Jim, Willard has died," revealed Carolyn. "I just sent you the link to his obituary."

"Wow, I'm sorry to hear that," said Jim. "Are you alright?"

"Jim, what if Luke actually confessed to his psychiatrist that he did it?" asked Carolyn. "Wouldn't a situation like that give the Judge probable cause to grant a Court Order to unseal his record, with or without Leticia's consent?"

After a long pause, Jim finally responded. "That's a tough one. Let me see what I can do on that and I'll have to get back to you."

"Thanks, Jim, that would mean a lot to me," replied Carolyn.

"Hey, what are you and Janette doing next weekend?" Jim suddenly asked. "Perhaps you guys can come out to the lighthouse? Susan and Sheree both have been asking about you. I'm sure they'd love to see you again."

"I'd sure like to come when I can bring my husband with me," explained Carolyn, "but right now, he's in the middle of a project which he's trying to get completed before the rainy season kicks in."

"You're retired, bring Janette," insisted Jim.

"She can't come," Carolyn informed him. "Her mother-in-law has gotten worse and can't be left alone. Janette is doing most of the caregiving for her now."

"That's awful," responded Jim. "Hey, I know, Bart and his wife are going to be up your way day after tomorrow, visiting their daughter. Perhaps they can give you a lift in their helicopter?"

"And just how would I get back home?" questioned Carolyn as she began to smile and shake her head.

"I'd make sure you do," promised Jim. "You know I'd do anything for you, don't you?"

Carolyn was silent for several moments. "I know."

"Then you'll come?"

"Maybe Bart and his wife might have other plans," pointed out Carolyn. "I would hate to impose on them like that."

And yet, I missed the ground breaking ceremony of my new museum just for you, thought Jim, though he would never mention it.

"Are you still there?" asked Carolyn when there was no response after an uncomfortable pause.

"Yeah, I'm here," Jim assured her. "I was just looking on the computer to see what rooms we have available here at our bed and breakfast during the weekend of October 28th and 29th. The tourist season will officially be over by then."

"Perhaps we should wait until you're able to find out something more about Luke first," proposed Carolyn. "Maybe by then, Janette can come with me."

"Well, I've booked The Daisy Room and The Violet Room, just in case," Jim informed her. "Please come."

"I'll let you know," promised Carolyn.

"Call me soon, then," requested Jim.

"Okay," agreed Carolyn. "And Jim?"

"Yes?"

"I'm so sorry about you missing the ground breaking ceremony for your new museum," apologized Carolyn. "I know how much it meant to you, and want you to know how badly I feel about it."

"No problem," Jim assured her. "Talk to you soon."

"Okay, bye," bid Carolyn as she hung up.

Shimmering rays of afternoon sun reflected off the water of the vast but peaceful ocean beside them as Carolyn and Janette made their way up the narrow road in the white Dodge Dart she had rented again. The smell of eucalyptus and cypress trees hung heavily in the air. Seagulls screamed loudly while they circled overhead, searching for unsuspecting prey along the beach below. The hypnotic sound of ocean waves licking the shoreline echoed up the mountainside next to them. It was October 28, 2023.

"Are you sure this is a good idea?" Janette suddenly asked.

"Jim said he has something he wants to show us," revealed Carolyn as they reached the top of the hill, pulled into a parking spot at Killingham Lighthouse Bed and Breakfast, and got out to admire the view. "I can't believe it's almost November already."

"This is quite the place," admired Janette while she gazed with awe through the car window at the lighthouse. "I'd forgotten how beautiful it is."

"Very impressive," agreed Carolyn. "Every time I come here, it's like seeing it for the first time."

"Do you think Jim finally got the Court Order?" asked Janette as she, too, emerged from the vehicle and closed the door on her side.

Carolyn merely shrugged.

The unusually shaped white structure was trimmed all in bright red. The building itself was octagonal in shape and approximately thirty feet in diameter. A long, pointed tower projected upward at least sixty feet from its center that was only about fifteen feet in diameter at the very top, but entirely round. Windows could be seen spiraling their way up its exterior, placed to provide natural lighting to as many interior locations as possible. An octagonal-shaped lookout tower at the very top had large picture windows on all sides, except for a single arched exit door that led to an exterior catwalk which encircled the entire upper tower at that level. The catwalk was about three feet wide, could only be accessed through the arched exit door, and was protected by a sturdy wrought iron railing that had been painted white. The tower's conical-shaped roof came to a perfect point on top and was covered entirely with bright red ceramic tiles. At ground level there was a covered entryway, also covered with bright red ceramic tiles. The cement porch and steps leading up to it were painted bright red, to match the ceramic tiles, and a large brass bell mounted beside the front door was graced with a long brass chain with which to ring it.

In front of the lighthouse was a well-lit freestanding sign that read, "Killingham Lighthouse Bed and Breakfast."

"What are those other buildings over there?" wondered Janette aloud as she and Carolyn finally started toward the front door.

"Those are for the generators and yard maintenance stuff," advised a vaguely familiar voice from behind her.

Janette turned around and slowly grinned. "Jim Otterman, how the heck are you?"

Jim and Janette briefly hugged before he turned his attention to Carolyn and then gave her a lingering hug.

"Nice to see you, too," responded Carolyn when she finally managed to extricate herself from his grasp.

"Let me get your bags, ladies," insisted Jim while he hurried to retrieve them from the car. "And I've already checked you in."

Janette gave Carolyn a questioning look. She responded with a shrug of her shoulders as Jim returned with their bags.

"Follow me," Jim instructed them as he set down the suitcases long enough to open and hold the front door for them.

"Thanks," grinned Janette while she winked at him and followed Carolyn inside.

"My pleasure," smiled Jim before heading for a black wrought iron spiral staircase with their luggage.

"The golf course and ice cream shop next door are his, too," Carolyn whispered to Janette when they began climbing the stairs.

"Here we are, ladies," indicated Jim when he paused about a third of the way up by two tandem crescent-shaped guest rooms built just off the staircase at that level. "This is The Daisy Room. The other room on this level is The Violet Room. You can flip a coin on who gets which room. Each set of rooms shares a restroom." The name of each room was on its door.

"Jim, thank you for this," said Carolyn as he set down their luggage on the landing.

"What are those other rooms above us?" questioned Janette while she shoved her suitcase into The Violet Room.

"Well," responded Jim, "as you may remember, there are two rooms on each of the four levels while you make your way to the top. The rooms are actually named after their original occupants."

"Oh yeah, right," recalled Janette.

"The original lighthouse keeper had several daughters," interjected Carolyn, "all named after different flowers."

"That's cute," admired Janette. "I love the beautiful hardwood floors and the Queen Anne furniture thing you've got going."

"Thanks, and of course, there are no locks on the inside rooms," added Jim, "but these keycards will open the front entrance downstairs." He then handed each of them a keycard.

"Anyone else staying here?" queried Janette as she glanced curiously upward at the other rooms.

"You're it," flirted Jim. "Would you like another tour?"

"Sure," nodded Janette. "It's been a while."

"We do have state-of-the-art security cameras both inside and outside the front door, as well as in the common areas and everywhere else besides the actual rooms," bragged Jim. "Not only that, visitors on tours always have a staff member with them. You have nothing to worry about."

"Good to know," approved Janette.

Carolyn took a deep breath and shoved her suitcase into The Daisy Room before following them further up the spiral staircase to view the other rooms. She had also taken the tour before, many times.

"No doubt you remember the tower room," continued Jim when they reached the top of the stairs. "This is where breakfast will be served each morning from 6:30 until 8:30."

Janette paused to admire the highly shellacked, natural wood siding that covered all eight of the octagonal room's four-foot high surrounding walls and the interior of its conical shaped ceiling above them. Resting above each four-foot wall was a large viewing window made of bullet-proof glass that extended upward to the room's fifteen-foot high ceiling above. "Just as beautiful as I remember it," remarked Janette.

"What I might not have mentioned before is that right here is where the main lighthouse lamp used to be, when this was used as a lighthouse," Jim informed Janette while he motioned toward the perfectly round wooden table in the center of the room. The table was surrounded entirely by a perfectly round wooden bench, both of them made from the same highly shellacked yellow pinewood that covered the inner ceiling and walls.

"What happened to the lamp?" asked Janette.

"The previous lighthouse owner was a Mr. Mark Killingham," revealed Jim, "and it was his idea to have the table put here to fill up this space after the lighthouse was decommissioned by the military at the end of World War II."

"I think she wanted to know what happened to the original lamp," pointed out Carolyn while she glanced up at the expensive looking Tiffany chandelier hanging above the round table, right where the lighthouse lamp would normally be.

"It was confiscated by the military and taken to another lighthouse somewhere else," revealed Jim.

"Why would they do something like that?" questioned Janette.

"Because you can't have a functioning lighthouse without proper approval," explained Jim. "You must have a valid permit to be in compliance with federal regulations. Especially since it was the military who voided the Killinghams' permit and decommissioned the lighthouse in the first place, it hardly seemed likely they would change their minds."

"How sad," remarked Janette.

"Not only that, there's a complete set of installation, validation and operational protocols, as well as on-site inspection requirements necessary to be sure the system complies both electronically and procedurally with federal code. Besides, you'd need the right kind of lamp, and those were pretty hard to come by in those days. Still are, in fact," described Jim. "The special type of compound lens used by a lighthouse lamp is also extremely expensive. It's not like you can just go pick one up at the hardware store. They have to be custom made."

"I see," nodded Janette. She was just as intrigued by the ingenious use of space in the lookout tower room as during her previous visit. Beneath the counter and sink, was a series of wooden cupboards. Some open shelves were filled with dishes and various cooking tools in small wooden boxes with handles on them. On the next wall was a small red refrigerator. Beside it was a bright red, hard plastic trash receptacle with swinging lid, where the very edge of a trash can liner could barely be seen protruding.

Two more of the eight four-foot walls were filled entirely with shelves of rare and valuable-looking old books. The catwalk access door faced due west on the ocean-side wall. The final two walls were located on either side of the catwalk access door's wall, and had bench seats built right into them from the same highly shellacked knotty pinewood veneer that adorned the rest of the lookout tower room. Bright red seat cushions placed on the bench seats bore a striking resemblance to the chaise lounge cushions once manufactured at a nearby lumber mill to accompany its popular patio furniture kits.

"Definitely a room with a view," pointed out Carolyn when she stepped out onto the catwalk to get a better look at the ocean below.

The sound of ocean waves could be heard crashing against the craggy shoreline below, interrupted occasionally by cries from a lone seagull as it circled overhead in search of small prey below, near the shoreline. It was almost mesmerizing to watch the panoramic scene sprawled out around them, complete with brilliant tentacles of sunlight moving across the water's surface and slowly making its way toward the ocean horizon.

"Carolyn!" exclaimed Sheree as she joined them in the tower room with a tray of tuna sandwiches and a pitcher of milk she carefully set down on the table.

"Sheree, so nice to see you again," greeted Carolyn when she returned from the catwalk to give her a hug.

"There you guys are," came Susan's voice as she entered the tower room with a pitcher of iced tea and a bowl of lemon slices. She placed them on the table by the pitcher of milk.

"Susan!" exclaimed Janette while she gave her a hug.

"Hector's out working on the golf course," explained Susan as she hugged Janette and then Carolyn, "and said not to wait for him."

"Well, since everyone else is here," Jim motioned toward the table, "let's have some lunch."

"Sounds good to me," smiled Janette as she seated herself at the table. "I'm starved."

Sheree reached into one of the open cupboards and brought out a stack of plates and placed them by the sandwiches. "The silverware is in the drawer by the sink, please help yourselves, if you need any."

Susan grabbed a stack of Tupperware tumblers and put them by the pitcher of iced tea.

Jim suddenly opened a drawer by the sink. Inside was a small box of sugar and artificial sweetener packets. He gingerly placed them on the table with a roll of paper towels.

"Looks like we're all set," grinned Janette while she grabbed a tumbler and began pouring herself some iced tea.

"Let's bless the food first," insisted Sheree when she sat down at the table with them. "Jim?"

"Sure," agreed Jim as everyone closed their eyes and bowed their heads. "Dear Lord, we thank you for this food and for dear friends you have brought safely to us this day. Amen."

"Amen," repeated the group.

"Tell us about the case you're working on now," requested Susan while she put a slice of lemon into one of the Tupperware tumblers and tore open a packet of artificial sweetener.

"You're supposed to pour the tea in first," grinned Janette.

"This way it mixes better," differed Susan when she began pouring some iced tea into her tumbler.

"Each to his or her own," smiled Carolyn as she took a bite of sandwich. "These are good."

"Thanks," nodded Sheree when she, too, began to eat her sandwich.

"Do you mind if I fill them in?" Jim asked as he turned to Carolyn. "About the case?"

"Go for it," nodded Carolyn while she poured herself a tumbler of iced tea and added a lemon slice.

"Too bad we don't have any chips," wished Janette as she glanced at the open cupboards to see if there might be some there.

Sheree immediately got up and went to one of the closed cupboards, opened the door, and brought out a bag of barbecue potato chips. "This is all we've got, without going to the store."

"Now you're talkin'," beamed Janette as she took the bag from Sheree, tore it open, and put a generous helping of chips onto her plate.

"Susan and Sheree," began Jim, "I want each of you to know how much I appreciate your filling in here while I was away helping Janette, Carolyn and her cousin Leticia try and figure out what happened to Carolyn's Aunt Ruth all those years ago."

"What did happen to her?" asked Susan, who was immediately intrigued. "She's not the one they found in that house, is she?"

"Actually, yes," confirmed Carolyn, "but little else besides her skeleton was left by the time they did."

"How sad," commented Sheree while she took a sip of iced tea.

"If no one's going to drink that milk, perhaps we should stick it back into the refrigerator," Jim suggested to Sheree.

She merely looked at him and shook her head before grabbing the pitcher of milk and putting it into the tiny refrigerator. *Jim could certainly have done it himself,* she thought to herself. To keep the peace, she refrained from mentioning anything about it.

"There were two things we set out to accomplish during our trip to Rosewood," pointed out Jim. "The first was to try and find Carolyn's Uncle Willard. She and Leticia wanted a chance to speak with him and find out what he knew that could help us solve this case."

"We did find him," interjected Janette, "but not until you sent me into that horrible memory care facility to try and locate him first. You know, the one that made me feel like I was on the Titanic."

"My Uncle Willard had a heart attack while he was there, right when Janette located him," Carolyn explained to Susan and Sheree.

"It was awful!" exclaimed Janette.

"Did you want me to tell it?" queried Jim with raised eyebrows.

"Sorry," apologized Carolyn and Janette.

"It was Janette who called for the ambulance and had him taken to the hospital," continued Jim.

"Just how is it again you just happened to be there?" queried Susan with a confused look on her face.

"Jim had me dress up like a nurse's aide to infiltrate the place," revealed Janette with a crooked grin.

"They had a pretty tight security system," Carolyn reminded her. "There's probably no other way we would've confirmed his location."

"What about when they took him to the hospital?" asked Janette. "We could have just waited and found him then."

"We had no way of knowing what would happen," argued Jim.

"He's right," agreed Carolyn. "But, it was there that Leticia and I were fortunate enough to finally see and actually visit with him, though. Sorry," she added as she glanced at Jim.

"That's okay," Jim winked at her. "The sad part was when he was taken from there to a private facility and died a few weeks later."

"Did you actually find out everything you needed to from him?" Susan grilled Carolyn.

"I think we learned everything Willard was able to tell us," responded Carolyn as she sadly shook her head. "I'm just grateful I had the opportunity to finally get to know him. He told me how much it meant to him when I would call him each day after that. He was sorry for all the years we missed out on, and even said he loved me."

"That's nice," nodded Susan.

"The part I don't get," interjected Janette, "is how that awful money-grubbing wife of his wouldn't let them have a funeral, memorial service or even a celebration of life for him."

"You're kidding," said Susan. "Why would she do that?"

"Trixie was his fourth wife and obviously was waiting for him to die so she could take all his money," answered Carolyn. "They met at a retirement community after his previous wife passed from cancer."

"And then she just moved in for the kill," remarked Susan while she shook her head with disgust.

"None of us wanted his money," continued Carolyn. "All Leticia or I wanted was to spend what little time he had left getting to know him, especially after all those years we missed out on."

"How come Leticia didn't come here with you?" Sheree suddenly asked.

Carolyn looked at Jim.

"That brings us to the second thing we hoped to accomplish during our trip," elaborated Jim. "We were hoping to find out whether Willard's son Luke was actually responsible for his mother's death, or not. Carolyn may have mentioned to you how Luke had schizophrenia and multiple personality disorder. He also never married, had no children, and was a 40 year old living alone with his mother Ruth at the time of her death."

"Norman Bates comes to mind," interjected Janette.

"I'm not liking the sound of this," Sheree informed them when she thought of her previous husband, Jon Roth.

"It does hit pretty close to home," added Susan. "Especially since Sheree's first husband had schizophrenia and was a patient at the Ocean Bluff Mental Institution."

Sheree glared at Susan for daring to bring it up.

"What?" asked Susan while she shrugged her shoulders at Sheree. "At least you've got a good husband now," Susan added as she motioned toward Jim Otterman.

"I guess I'm quite fortunate not to be married to someone who needs to take Clozapine in order to function normally," growled Sheree when she got up to leave. "Excuse me, but I've got other things to do." She then hurried from the tower room; her footsteps could be heard on the spiral wrought iron staircase while she descended.

Jim looked at Susan and shook his head. "Really?"

"She'll get over it," assumed Susan as she took a bite of her sandwich. "Tell us more about Luke."

"Carolyn and Janette are already aware of the circumstances," replied Jim. "This basically is for *your* benefit, Susan."

"Hey, I'm sorry, okay," she apologized. "Sheree's always so sensitive about things."

"Like the time in high school when we hid alarm clocks all over her room; they went off every 15 minutes that night," Carolyn reminded Susan. "We were horrible to her."

"Well, we're not in high school anymore, and most of us have grown out of that stage by now," pointed out Jim while he scowled at Susan.

"I'll make it up to Sheree, I promise," pledged Susan as she gave Jim one of her pleading looks that he couldn't resist.

"Make sure you do," he cautioned her.

Susan was quite attractive for her age and had been Carolyn's high school roommate at Oceanview Academy. Susan's exotic facial features and hazel-colored eyes hinted at Latin heritage. Her medium-brown hair was parted in the middle and hung loosely over her shoulders with long bangs hanging down to one side.

"The reason Leticia isn't here," volunteered Carolyn, "is because she and I reached an impasse on whether or not to obtain a Court Order so we could obtain Luke's file from the Psych Unit at Ashton Medical Center."

"That should be easy enough to do," assumed Susan.

"Not when Leticia is Luke's closest living relative and must be the one to appear before the Court to make that happen," explained Carolyn. "And she just won't do it."

"Why?" Susan quizzed her.

"Because the whole thing was a very painful memory for her," answered Carolyn. "She's done. Still, it was a surprise to all of us when Leticia suddenly decided she just didn't want to pursue it anymore."

"Maybe for her, finding out the real truth about Luke would be like reliving the whole thing all over again," speculated Janette.

"The Coroner ruled that the cause of Ruth's death was *undetermined*," continued Jim. "When a body is left somewhere for that long, much of the forensic evidence just disintegrates over time."

"There was no sign of blunt trauma," recalled Janette.

"But they could not rule out smothering or other soft tissue damage," Carolyn reminded her.

"The worst part was that Luke continued to live in the house with his mother's body for almost two years," scowled Janette. "Who would do something like that?"

"Wow!" exclaimed Susan.

"We were hoping Luke might have finally confessed to one of his counselors whether or not he actually did it," said Jim.

"Which is why you need his file," realized Susan as she nodded her head with understanding.

"Luke died back in 2019," Carolyn mentioned. "In my opinion, there should be nothing else stopping the Psych Unit at Ashton Medical Center from agreeing to give us access to Luke's file, especially in a case like this."

"Didn't you say Leticia already gave you written permission?" Janette interrogated her.

"Yes, she did," replied Carolyn. "Apparently, that isn't good enough for those people. It's a Court Order or nothing."

"Will you be posing as a Court Clerk anytime soon?" questioned Susan while she gave Janette a mischievous grin.

"It's someone else's turn to go into the lion's den," replied Janette. "Maybe *you* might make a good Court Clerk."

"No one's going to be impersonating a Court Clerk," interrupted Jim. "Besides, that would be against the law."

"And my pretending to be a nurse's aide wasn't?" asked Janette.

"Technically, you were an employee of a company I own," Jim reminded her, "and were there to substitute for someone who was out that day while training on the job to be a nurse's aide."

"That *night*," corrected Janette. "On graveyard shift!"

"Which brings us to the reason we came here," pointed out Carolyn when she turned to Jim. "You said you have something to show us."

"I do," confirmed Jim with a slight smile.

"Well?" Carolyn raised her eyebrows.

"My partner, Detective Chip Priest, has been helping me try and find out who Luke's counselor was during his extended stay with the Psych Unit at Ashton Medical Center," revealed Jim.

"Don't keep us in suspense," prompted Susan.

"Dr. Henry Godspeed is the man we're after," related Jim.

"Just what does that mean?" Janette grilled him.

"It was back in 1997 when Dr. Godspeed first saw Luke," explained Jim. "The man was in his late fifties at the time."

"I see where this is going," muttered Carolyn.

"That was 26 years ago," calculated Janette.

"He's definitely in his eighties," estimated Susan.

"And retired," Jim informed her.

"Knowing our luck, he's probably got dementia," suspected Janette. "Or dead already."

"Most successful professionals with enough money usually disappear into the sunset when they retire," remarked Carolyn. "I had a doctor once who bought a yacht the day he retired and took off with his family to sail the globe."

"Never to be seen or heard from again," assumed Janette.

"Except in this case," explained Jim. "What we've been able to find out is that the man bought himself an island in the San Juan area and lives there now with his wife and research assistants."

"I find that hard to believe," doubted Janette.

"It's true. Not only was Dr. Godspeed independently wealthy, but he also received a sizeable grant from a private organization to help finance his continued research there," elaborated Jim.

"Maybe he's doing some weird sort of experiments on people, like Dr. Moreau," speculated Janette.

"Earth to Janette," said Jim as he gave her a look of frustration.

"Only four of the San Juan Islands are open to the public," recalled Carolyn. "At least that's how it was when my mother and I went there a few years back."

"Actually," differed Jim, "Lopez, Orcas, San Juan and Shaw are the only four of those islands you can travel to by ferry. There are several others the public can visit, but only if they have their own boat."

"Good to know," nodded Carolyn

"Aren't there hundreds of islands up there?" questioned Susan.

"There are 172 named islands and reefs in San Juan County alone," recalled Jim, "but the San Juan Islands are made up of literally hundreds of islands, some no bigger than a rowboat and others that disappear if the tide gets too high, while many of the small and medium sized islands are privately owned."

"And you somehow managed to find the one owned by Dr. Godspeed," presumed Janette.

"We did," corroborated Jim. "Fortunately for us, it is located on our side of the Demarcation Line."

"What's that?' asked Janette.

"Well," described Jim, "The San Juan Islands are bounded on the west by the waters of Haro Strait and Boundary Pass which serve as the International boundary line. Still farther westward lies Vancouver Island and the smaller Canadian islands which fringe its eastern margin. In other words, Dr. Godspeed's island is in the good old USA."

"You could have just said so," frowned Janette as she finished off her iced tea.

"Meaning we won't need passports to get there," realized Carolyn with relief.

"Exactly," said Jim while he winked at her.

"What's it called?" inquired Susan.

"I believe it's called Godspeed Island," replied Jim.

"When do we leave?" questioned Susan with a crooked smile.

After lunch, Susan and Janette decided to go for a walk along the beach. Carolyn had chosen to remain behind; she needed to call her husband to discuss the possibility of a trip to Godspeed Island.

"This is the safest route down," Susan pointed out to Janette as she motioned at the tiered trail leading to the beach.

"That's gotta be a 100-foot drop without this trail," guessed Janette. "How'd you guys get down there before Jim built this?"

"More like 75 feet," corrected Susan, "but there's another access point over by the school. It's a road cut straight through the cliffs. You can drive or walk on it, right down to the beach."

The far edge of the lowest and smallest tier on the trail stepped down onto a well-manicured gravel foot path inlaid with large slate stepping stones. The path itself was bordered by a hearty mat of creeping succulent ice plants interspersed with sedums. The herbaceous evergreen ground cover would not bloom until early summer, but bright pink and yellow blossoms were expected. Several Hoary Manzanita bushes, however, were already blossoming. Some of them had pink blooms while others were white.

"I'm not sure if I can be gone long enough for a trip to the San Juan Islands," mentioned Janette when they reached the sandy beach.

"Me, neither," sighed Susan as she took off her shoes and decided to carry them.

Seagulls screamed loudly overhead. Susan closed her eyes for a moment to listen to the sound of the surging ocean waves beside them. Breezy fingers of wind blew sensuously through her hair while delicate rays of sun kept her from feeling too cold.

The pungent odors of cypress and eucalyptus trees that grew in abundance along the windswept cliffs above them wafted through the air. "It's beautiful here," admired Janette when she sat down on the sand and removed her shoes, too.

"Oh, look, what's this?" asked Janette when she noticed a translucent blob on the wet part of the sand, close to where the waves were coming ashore.

"I wouldn't touch that," cautioned Susan as she started toward the location to get a better look.

"Ouch!" exclaimed Janette. "I think I just stepped on one!"

"That's a jellyfish," Susan informed Janette while she raced over to assist her. "Let's get you away from the water, over there. You can sit by that piece of driftwood until I get back with Jim."

"It burns," moaned Janette when she noticed how quickly her foot was turning red and how irritated the skin was.

"Well, don't walk on it," cautioned Susan. "The last thing you need is for it to get infected."

"What if it's one of those jellyfish that kills you in just a matter of minutes? I read about 'em in school," recalled Janette.

"Stay here," commanded Susan, "I'll be right back."

"Wait," insisted Janette while she grabbed Susan's arm.

"I need to get Jim," insisted Susan as she removed her arm from Janette's grasp.

"Shouldn't we try to see if there's a stinger that needs to be pulled out first?" Janette quizzed her. "I'm not feeling well."

"You're having a panic attack," diagnosed Susan.

"I hope you're right," wailed Janette.

"That's definitely a moon jellyfish and they don't have stingers," Susan assured her. "It will hurt for a while, and could get infected if you mess with it, but I'm pretty sure you'll live."

"And what if you're wrong?" questioned Janette. Tears were streaming down her cheeks.

Susan paused only long enough to put on her shoes before racing for the pathway leading back up to the lighthouse. *Why in the world did I leave my phone behind?*

Winded by the time she arrived at the entrance of the Killingham Lighthouse Bed and Breakfast, Susan put her hands on her knees, bent over, and tried to catch her breath.

"Jim!" hollered Susan as she gasped for air. She immediately grabbed and yanked on the long brass chain attached to the large brass bell mounted beside the entrance door. "Jim!" she screamed while she continued to ring the bell.

14. Godspeed Island

Anxious to begin a new chapter in his life where he would not be subject to the dictates of governmental bureaucracy, Dr. Henry Godspeed finished gathering up the last of the things in his office at the Psych Unit of Ashton Medical Center. He had taken home his finely-framed degrees, potted plants and expensive oil paintings the previous day. It was June 30, 2003.

The simple retirement party his coworkers and subordinates had put on for him that morning consisted of nothing more than cake, punch and potluck-style finger foods in a break room. After a few well-chosen words of rhetoric from his various colleagues, most of whom he would probably never see again, Dr. Henry Godspeed was finally free.

After returning to his old office one last time to pick up the small box containing what was left of his personal things, Henry paused to glance at the beautiful atrium view. He would miss seeing its gravel pathways and neatly-trimmed shrubs, especially the koi fish pond laden with blooming lotus flowers. He suddenly felt a touch of sadness. *Will this be what I miss the most? Or, will I miss the many patients I was able to help during my 35 years of practice? All except Luke Bennett,* reflected Dr. Godspeed as he picked up the box and departed from the room that had been his office for so many years. *Why am I so troubled by that particular case? Did Luke's grandmother really do it? Did my silence allow a murderess to go free? Is she still alive?* wondered Dr. Godspeed while he walked from the office carrying his box. *I'll have to do a web search to see what I can find out.*

Luke Bennett will most likely remain in custody at the institution for the rest of his natural life for something he didn't do, lamented Dr. Godspeed. *If only I could be sure, one way or the other. Such a tragic life,* reflected Dr. Godspeed while he glanced at the token gold pocket watch his associates had given him. It had been a final retirement gift. Henry gingerly returned it to his pocket when he exited the building and headed for his car.

After putting the box in the trunk of his new Bentley Continental GT, Henry took one last look at the parking lot.

Tomorrow, this space will belong to someone else, he pondered. *Why should it bother me? Is my work here really done?*

Spread out on the passenger seat beside him was an upper-end real estate magazine advertising islands for sale in the San Juan Island chain. Just that morning, his wife Martha had finally agreed to his plan to purchase one of them so they could relocate.

Unknown to his friends and associates, Henry was the recent beneficiary of a rather large inheritance left to him by his late mother.

Henry picked up the magazine and tried to imagine what it would be like to live on the beautiful island pictured in the ad. He then studied the description more closely:

- Once in a lifetime opportunity to procure and build your dream home in a pristine, serene, breathtaking setting.
- Self-sustaining 29-acre private island completely off the grid with independent power/water systems. 4200'+ saltwater frontage with tidelands, beaches & bluffs.
- 60 x 80 deep water dock with 2 slips approved for seaplanes & yachts.
- Guest cottage. Permitted helipad. Commanding views, glorious trees for health, privacy & protection.
- Escape. Breathe. This is Freedom. Your destiny.

This is exactly what I'm looking for, decided Henry. *A place to conduct the kind of research I could only dream of before. Perhaps a chance to help others like Luke Bennett who will benefit from my research.*

* * *

"Susan, what is it?" questioned Jim.

"It's Janette," gasped Susan. "She's been stung by a jellyfish. I told her I would come and get you."

Without waiting for further explanation, Jim raced inside to a small closet in the foyer, pulled out a small red backpack with a white cross on it, slung it over his shoulder, and raced back outside.

"Come on," Jim commanded Susan as he headed for the stepped trail leading to the beach. "I may need your help. Grab the green Army blanket in the back of my Jeep."

Still breathing heavily, Susan complied, though keeping up with Jim was out of the question. *Hopefully, I'll get there in time to help.*

"Janette!" hollered Jim upon reaching the beach and seeing her by the driftwood.

"I'm sorry," apologized Janette when Jim knelt beside her to examine her foot. "I'm guess I'm not much use to anyone now."

Jim hurriedly unzipped his pack and pulled out a bottle of water that he handed to Janette. Next, he pulled out a plastic pill organizer and opened the lid marked Benadryl, gingerly removing four tablets and handing them to Janette. "Take these," Jim instructed her.

"Isn't that too many to take at one time?" questioned Janette.

"These are 50 mg tablets," explained Jim. "It's perfectly safe for children age 12 and up to take up to 300 mg in a 24-hour period."

"But not all at once," hesitated Janette.

"Janette, I'm also a physician," Jim reminded her.

"Of course, you are," Janette tried to force a smile.

"Do you trust me?" asked Jim with a raised eyebrow. "Time is of the essence here."

Janette merely nodded while she put the capsules in her mouth and washed them down with the bottled water.

"That should slow the progression of your reaction," explained Jim, "but I'm going to have to do a couple of things to get that foot cleaned up before we take you to the hospital."

"What for?" asked Janette with a worried look on her face.

"So they can get you hooked up to an IV to help flush the toxins from your system, and to get you on antibiotics," answered Jim. "Sorry, but that's not something I normally carry in my emergency pack."

Janette tried to get up, but Jim stopped her. "You need to remain as still as possible."

"Janette!" hollered Susan when she arrived at their location panting, breathing heavily, and carrying the green Army blanket she had grabbed from the back of Jim's red Jeep Cherokee.

"I'm pretty sure it was a moon jellyfish," Susan mentioned to Jim as she pointed toward the place where it had been.

Jim hurried over to get a close look at it and nodded.

"Definitely a moon jellyfish," confirmed Jim. He carefully picked Janette up and carried her to the water's edge, several yards away from the jellyfish location.

"What about the blanket?" asked Susan.

"Spread it out to put her on after I finish washing off her foot," Jim directed Susan. "We will need to keep her warm if we can. But first, I need you to bring me my pack."

Susan quickly spread out the blanket, grabbed the pack, and hurried over to the water's edge where Jim had set Janette by the incoming waves.

"Thanks," nodded Jim as he pulled a pair of surgical gloves from his pack and put them on. "The first thing we are going to do is wash off any tentacles or venom from the affected area of your foot with salt water. It may burn."

"My butt's getting wet," screamed Janette while she tried again to get up to move further inland.

"Sorry, but it can't be avoided," apologized Jim when he pulled a handkerchief from his pocket and used it to briskly scrub her foot with the ocean water.

"Oh my God, that stings," winced Janette.

"The next thing we need to do," elaborated Jim as he pulled a pair of sterile tweezers from his pack, "is to remove any remaining tentacles we can see."

"Just don't let any more of those awful things get me," pleaded Janette while she nervously glanced at the incoming waves to see if any more of them were on the way.

"I guess the last thing you need is a sting on the butt," grinned Jim while he grabbed a bottle of rubbing alcohol from his pack and poured a generous portion of it over her foot.

"Aaaaah!" screamed Janette. "Was that really necessary?"

"Oh yes," Jim assured her. "It's always important to apply vinegar or rubbing alcohol to the affected area to stop any more firings of nematocysts."

"What's a nematocyst?" Janette grilled him as Jim carried her to the green Army blanket before pulling it around her. Next, he gently picked her back up and raced toward the stepped trail leading to the lighthouse.

"Bring my pack up," he yelled at Susan over his shoulder.

"Am I going to die?" Janette suddenly asked.

"You're going to be fine," Jim assured her while he hurried up the trail with Janette in his arms.

"Then what is a nematocyst?" Janette interrogated him.

"The nematocyst is produced in cnidoblast cells. It contains a hollow coiled thread that secretes a poison to capture prey and protect from enemies," elaborated Jim. "And that's the short version."

"What's a cnidoblast?" questioned Janette when they reached the parking lot by the entrance of the lighthouse where Carolyn was just emerging. It had been her plan to join Susan and Janette on the beach.

"Open the back door of my Jeep," Jim commanded Carolyn. "We need to get Janette to the hospital."

Carolyn immediately complied. "What happened?"

"We'll tell you on the way," replied Jim as he gently put Janette onto the back seat.

"Wait for me!" hollered Susan when she reached their location.

"Sorry, but there's only room for one in the backseat now," replied Jim. "Just let Sheree know we've taken Janette to the hospital."

Susan took a deep breath of frustration and slowly let it out. "If she's even talking to me now."

"Then you'd better go tell her you're sorry," snapped Jim while he opened the front passenger door for Carolyn, who quickly climbed inside without argument.

"Oh Janette, I hope you'll be alright," said Susan as she hurried over to the Jeep to see them off.

"Me, too," Janette assured her from the backseat before Jim closed Carolyn's door and hustled over to the driver's side to get inside.

"Let us know how she is," called Susan as Jim started the engine and drove off at a high rate of speed.

"I stepped on a jellyfish," Janette mentioned to Carolyn, who was speechless at the moment.

"It was a moon jellyfish," explained Jim. "She should be okay with the proper treatment."

"Good thing I'm not allergic to antibiotics," mentioned Janette.

"Unfortunately, you won't be coming with us to Godspeed Island," replied Jim when they reached the narrow, winding, two-lane stretch of road they would need to traverse to get to their destination.

"How far is the hospital?" questioned Janette. Throbbing pain began to shoot through her foot.

"The nearest town is Ocean Bluff and it's 30 minutes away," interjected Carolyn.

Relentless wind began to rivet through the row of cypress trees growing on the bluffs beside them.

"Janette, in answer to your question before," Jim suddenly spoke up, "a cnidocyte is an explosive cell containing one large secretory organelle. It can deliver a sting to other organisms. The presence of this cell defines the phylum Cnidaria, which are used to capture prey and as a defense by the jellyfish against predators."

"What in the world are you talking about?" demanded Carolyn as she gave Jim a sideways glance.

"Janette was asking me about what a nematocyst is," replied Jim. "And I was explaining to her that it is produced in cnidoblast cells. It contains a hollow coiled thread that secretes a poison to capture prey and protect the jellyfish from its enemies."

"I think he's talking about the stingers," guessed Janette.

"I thought a moon jellyfish didn't have any stingers," frowned Carolyn while she glanced at her friend Janette with concern.

"The moon jellyfish differs from many jellyfish in that they lack long, potent stinging tentacles. Instead they have hundreds of short, fine tentacles that line the bell margin. The moon jelly's sting is relatively mild in comparison, and most people have only a slight reaction to it if anything at all," clarified Jim.

"I would beg to differ," snapped Janette.

"While moon jellyfish stings are painful and often accompanied by red marks, itching, numbness or tingling," conceded Jim, "this type is not life threatening. On the other hand, if you'd been stung by a box jellyfish, for example, it could have been fatal, triggering cardiac arrest in your body within minutes."

"Jim, that's enough," Carolyn instructed him. "Can't you see you're upsetting her?"

"Actually, he's scaring the hell out of me," clarified Janette.

"Sorry," apologized Jim as he gave Janette a sheepish look in the rearview mirror. "Everything will be fine, trust me."

* * *

It was Monday, November 6, 2023. Dr. Henry Godspeed slowly made his way toward the guest cottage where his expected guests would soon be staying. Things were so much easier when his wife Martha was still alive, but she had passed the previous year.

Considering who was coming, Henry wanted to make sure everything was in perfect order. He paused to admire the scenic ocean bluffs that surrounded his island. Save for the maintenance man who came out to Godspeed Island when summoned by ham radio or to make regular deliveries, Henry was all alone except for Maria Alvarez, his devoted housekeeper. Maria was in her mid-forties, spoke little English, and seemed content to take care of Dr. Godspeed by herself until a new nurse could be hired; the last one had quit unexpectedly due to a family emergency at home in Seattle. Being 85 years old brought with it the expected health challenges for Henry, but overall, he was in good health for his age. He rarely saw patients in a clinical setting anymore and spent the majority of his time preparing research memoirs for eventual publication.

While generally assumed across the medical community that there's no known cure for schizophrenia or multiple personality disorder, and that symptoms can only be managed using antipsychotic medications, there just has to be an alternative, believed Dr. Godspeed. *Just how long can anyone keep ahead of the inevitable serious side-effects of taking such medications?* Maria had been a patient of his once, but with the proper therapy, lifestyle changes, and a genuine desire to improve and maintain self-management, he had observed her living a relatively normal and drug-free life for the past 20 years.

Maria is one of the lucky ones, reflected Henry while he pulled up the hood of his rain jacket to protect himself from the wind and rain that had suddenly worsened. *Not the best time of year for guests, but I welcome the company.* More than anything, he was curious as to why Luke Bennett's family had waited until now to reach out to him. *And, how did they ever manage to find me after all this time?*

Dr. Godspeed was well aware Luke Bennett had died only one year after being released from custody in 2018. Luke, along with 300 other institutionalized patients the County's budget could no longer afford to house when its funding had failed, had been released at that time. Some had returned to live with their families; others were still out there living on the streets.

Luke Bennett had died homeless and penniless on the steps of Ashton Community Hospital in October of 2019. Henry still kept the one-sentence obituary he had clipped from The Ashton Times in the desk drawer of his island office. Henry always suspected Luke was one of the first COVID patients in Ashton, though identifying the disease or testing for it was unavailable at that time.

"Dr. Godspeed, un helicóptero está aterrizando junto a la residencia principal," Maria informed Henry upon catching up to him on the trail leading from the main residence to the guest house.

"Por favor llama a Hank y hazle saber que lo necesitaré durante el fin de semana," he instructed her. *I'll need to have an extra staff member on hand for the weekend to assist with the expected guests.* Hank Zimmerman had become much more than a maintenance man over the years. He was also a friend.

"Sí, Doctor," Maria replied as she hurried off to place the call on Dr. Godspeed's ham radio to the mainland.

The whir of the helicopter blades spinning while it landed on the helipad nearby would undoubtedly make it difficult for Maria to hear when she placed the call.

"Are you *sure* he knows we're coming?" Bart questioned Jim while he set the helicopter down on the private landing pad. "I've tried all three authorized frequencies for this location and there's absolutely no response whatsoever."

"Perhaps he's not here," suggested Susan. "Seems like his helicopter would be here somewhere if the man was home."

"I just spoke with Dr. Godspeed by satellite phone this morning," Jim assured her. "The guy's in his mid-eighties and no longer flies. He doesn't have a helicopter."

"Then how does he get here?" questioned Susan.

"On his yacht," answered Jim.

"I saw a yacht on the dock while we were flying over it," recalled Carolyn. "It must be his."

"I sure hope you're right," responded Bart as he began powering down the helicopter.

"Me, too," agreed Jim, "but when I spoke with him this morning, Dr. Godspeed seemed sharp as a tack and said he was looking forward to seeing us."

"Hey, thanks again for letting me come along," mentioned Susan, who was seated in the back beside Carolyn.

"It was at Sheree's insistence," Jim reminded her while he gave Susan a stern look of frustration. "Let's hope she's more amenable to your next apology than she was to the last one."

Susan merely nodded. *I'll do what I can to smooth things over with Sheree when we get back.*

"Look at it this way," Carolyn grinned at Jim, "at least this way you can keep an eye on her."

"That's for sure," agreed Bart when he glanced at Jim. *I'm not about to be stuck babysitting Susan again!*

"Hey Bart," mentioned Susan. "Seems like yesterday you and I repelled down to the jungle floor in South America with Carolyn, after you crashed into the canopy there."

"Don't remind me," frowned Bart.

Jim Otterman and Bart Higbee had been straight A students in high school where they had been roommates at Oceanview Academy. Both were from families of means and had been aviation students together, as well. It was one of the courses Oceanview Academy had offered to pupils with an acceptable GPA whose families were able to afford it.

Bart had always taken his lessons quite seriously. He had a natural aptitude for flying and airplane mechanics. In spite of his seriousness about flying, Bart's pleasant Polynesian face usually wore a genuinely contagious smile.

He was now semi-retired from his lifelong career of inspecting and maintaining commercial airliners, as well as propulsion systems for orbiting spacecraft. Though offered an opportunity to take up residency at an orbiting space station recently – to assist with the many ongoing maintenance challenges there – Bart had chosen instead to remain earth-side near his family.

Bored with an abundance of spare time on his hands, Bart often volunteered to pilot small planes during humanitarian aid missions of mercy to third-world countries. Most recently, he'd piloted a rescue helicopter for the Coast Guard following a tsunami off the coast of Sumatra. Fortunately for Jim, Bart enjoyed the challenge of flying during inclement weather and other hazardous conditions.

"The weather forecast shows 100% chance of rain today," noted Jim as he glanced at his smartwatch.

"Ya think?" Bart asked sarcastically while he shook his head. "It also shows 76% humidity and winds up to 40 knots expected by this afternoon when the storm increases."

"We're not gonna be stuck here, are we?" questioned Susan.

"A two-blade, single-engine helicopter like this one has a recommended windspeed limit of 40 knots to safely start her up," interjected Jim.

"That's because a two-bladed system teeters in the wind and might dip low enough to strike the tail boom," added Bart.

"Multiple-blade helicopters are not as restricted," continued Jim, "but a Bell 206 like this one will remain grounded until after the storm."

"Sometimes storms last for *days* here in the San Juan Islands," pointed out Bart with a mischievous grin at Susan before exiting the helicopter. He wasted no time tying down the craft to keep it secure from the expected wind.

"Greetings," called Maria when she approached the helipad to welcome them. "El Doctor está en el cobertizo esperándote."

"She says the Doctor is in the guest cottage waiting for us," interpreted Susan, who was proud of her Spanish-speaking skills.

"We heard," replied Jim and Bart, who were both fluent in Spanish themselves.

"English works for me," commented Carolyn while she reached for her suitcase.

"¿No habrá alguien cargando nuestro equipaje?" questioned Susan as she turned to Maria.

"Maria is the only one here besides Dr. Godspeed," Jim informed Susan, "and **no**, they won't be carrying our luggage."

Feeling slightly embarrassed and humiliated, Susan turned to Maria to apologize. "Lo siento, no debería haberlo supuesto."

"No es nada," Maria assured her, "pero como eres el único aquí con más de una maleta, déjame ayudarte."

Everyone frowned at Susan when Maria grabbed her extra suitcase and headed toward a trail leading into the forest.

"I guess she felt sorry for me," Susan explained to Carolyn, "what with me having more luggage than the rest of you."

"Yours will be the first to get tossed out on the return flight," Bart promised Susan, "should the need arise to lighten our load."

The 200-yard trail leading from the helipad to the guest cottage had become slippery from the rain. Branches whipped in the wind, some of them hitting the guests in the face as they made their way through the forest. Upon emerging into a small meadow where the guest cottage was built, it was easy to see how fiercely the angry waves surrounding the island were beating against its bluffs.

"Let's get inside," shouted Jim to be heard above the wind.

"Stay in lobby," Maria instructed them in broken English before sitting down on a bench to remove her shoes. She then grabbed the last towel from a shelf beside it to dry herself off. "I get more towels."

The large A-framed cottage was 30 feet high with large picture windows on three sides. Its wrap-around deck was devoid of patio furniture at the moment, as it had already been put away for the winter.

Inside, hard-wood floors, walls and ceiling gave the entire place a natural appearance, along with the natural stone fireplace in which an inviting fire was burning, easily visible from the lobby where Jim and his party waited for Maria to return with more towels.

"Aquí," said Maria upon returning with a stack of towels and handing one to each of them. "Sírvete tú mismo si necesitas más," she added as she glanced at Susan before putting the rest of them on the shelf by the bench.

"Gracias," smiled Susan as she nodded at Maria.

"Welcome," greeted a commanding elderly gentleman when he approached from the fireplace area and waited while the guests removed their shoes and dried themselves off the best they could.

"You must be Dr. Godspeed," assumed Jim while he approached and held out his hand.

"And you must be Dr. Otterman," smiled the man when he shook his hand. "A pleasure to meet you. I've read many of your dissertations and am anxious to discuss them with you."

"Really?" Jim seemed surprised.

"You're far too modest," smiled Dr. Godspeed.

"Likewise, I'm sure," replied Jim while he maintained eye contact with Henry for several moments. "May I introduce my long-time friend Bart Higbee, who is our helicopter pilot."

Dr. Godspeed cordially nodded at Bart and then motioned toward a sectional sofa located in front of the fireplace. Its Herculon fabric was maroon with green and beige floral designs on it. Several clean dry towels had already been placed on its seating surfaces.

The large trunk-shaped coffee table in front of it was fashioned from a large slice of Redwood, highly shellacked and mounted on sturdy legs made from thick limbs. Otherwise, the entire living room was devoid of furniture. Light from the fireplace and from small ceiling lights 30 feet above them near two large skylights appeared to be the only available sources of light.

"I'm Susan," she volunteered as they sat on the couch, "and this is Luke Bennett's cousin Carolyn."

Dr. Godspeed immediately turned his attention to Carolyn and made her feel awkward from the scrutiny of his penetrating gaze. "Delighted to meet you."

Carolyn glanced at Jim before responding. "Dr. Godspeed, the one thing I was hoping for while we're here is to find out what you know about my Aunt Ruth's death."

"Before we go any farther, let's drop the formalities," he insisted. "You are my guests; please call me Henry."

"We appreciate your hospitality, Henry," responded Carolyn.

"Looks like you may be here for several days," pointed out Henry while he motioned toward the easily visible storm outside.

"Unfortunately, we're not prepared for more than an overnight stay," apologized Jim when he glanced at the huge empty kitchen on the opposite side of the ground floor.

"No worries," Henry assured him. "My maintenance man should be on his way here now, with supplies."

"In this storm?" questioned Bart.

"Hank will be arriving by private ferry," explained Henry. "Flying in this weather is obviously out of the question. In fact, you're lucky you made it here when you did."

"Indeed," agreed Bart.

"I hope you tied down your craft," mentioned Henry.

"Absolutely," Bart assured him.

"You have a beautiful place here," complimented Susan as she glanced at the giant loft above them.

"Thank you," smiled Henry. "Unfortunately, there are only two bedrooms up there, so you'll have to share."

"Susan and I were roommates in high school, so it shouldn't be a problem," mentioned Carolyn.

"Jim and I were roommates in high school, too," added Bart.

"Just like old times, then," grinned Dr. Godspeed while he studied the group more closely. *How fascinating that they're all still friends.*

"We won't have to share a bed, will we?" asked Susan.

Henry seemed amused by her as he slowly shook his head. "No, each room has two queen-sized beds, but the four of you will have to share a single bathroom in the middle."

"Will you be staying here at the guesthouse with us?" questioned Carolyn. "The storm out there seems to be getting worse."

"I appreciate your concern," responded Dr. Godspeed, "but Maria will be accompanying me back to the main residence shortly. "We will expect all of you there for breakfast at 7:00 a.m."

"Se está volviendo demasiado peligroso ahí fuera," differed Maria. "Not safe for you, Doctor."

Just then a loud clap of thunder could be heard overhead. Heavy downpour and sustained winds suddenly caused a mature cedar tree on the edge of the meadow to topple, narrowly missing the guest cottage when it landed.

"Oh, my God!" exclaimed Susan.

"That was too close for comfort," stated Jim.

"Fortunately for me, this couch also makes into a bed," acknowledged Henry as he walked over to the picture window to get a better look at the fallen tree. He did not seem too concerned about it. "Maria, do we still have extra sheets in the hall closet?"

"Sí, Doctor," responded Maria while she hurried to the hall closet on the landing half way up the large wooden staircase leading to the loft. "Las almohadas también."

"¿Que hay de la comida?" asked Susan.

"There is an abundant selection of canned goods in the pantry," revealed Dr. Godspeed when he walked over to the kitchen and opened a hidden door to reveal the assortment.

"At least we won't starve," noted Jim as he joined Henry in the kitchen and opened the refrigerator.

"Thank goodness we won't be stuck with just canned food," Susan sighed with relief upon noticing the refrigerator was full.

"Surprising there are no kitchen implements of any kind on the counters," commented Carolyn from the couch where she was seated beside Susan and Bart.

"What about my medication?" Henry suddenly asked when he turned to Maria. "I'll need another insulin shot soon."

"I go get," volunteered Maria. She immediately headed for the front door.

"Wait for Hank," Dr. Godspeed instructed her. "Él puede ayudarte a traer la caja de notas de mi estudio que iba a compartir con estas personas."

"What did he say?" Carolyn whispered to Susan.

"He told her Hank can help her bring back a box of notes from his study. Hopefully, he plans to share them with us," replied Susan.

"The acoustics in here are excellent," smiled Henry as he headed back to the couch, "so there's no need to whisper."

"We try to speak English," Maria promised Carolyn while she finished putting on her shoes and coat before leaving.

A gust of wind from the open door made the fireplace flames temporarily increase in size.

"It's cold out there," complained Susan upon feeling the breeze.

Just then, the door slammed shut again.

"You'll live," sniggered Jim as he slowly shook his head.

"What happens when the log you have in there now burns out?" questioned Carolyn.

"Follow me," Henry directed her while he headed for the staircase and pressed a secret panel, causing a hidden door behind it to slide open.

"Nice," Carolyn nodded with approval upon seeing the neatly stacked cord of firewood inside the huge storage space.

"Any other concerns?" inquired Dr. Godspeed as he smiled with amusement at Carolyn.

"Why don't we see what's upstairs," suggested Carolyn.

"Before you respond to my question, of course," grinned Henry. "You are the suspicious type."

"Not of you," assured Carolyn. "Just of responding to any question without all the pertinent facts first."

"You may want to grab your suitcases," Dr. Godspeed suggested to the group when he began climbing the stairs, being careful to hang onto the handrail as he went. *A fall at my age could prove disastrous.*

"I guess I'll have to make two trips," mumbled Susan while she retrieved her larger suitcase first and began pulling it up the stairs.

"Good thing they invented rolling wheels for those things in 1972," laughed Carolyn as she easily pulled her suitcase up to the room in the loft she would be sharing with Susan.

"For those who need 'em," mentioned Bart while he hoisted his backpack over his shoulder. "Never use the things myself."

"Me, neither," snickered Jim, who had also chosen to use a backpack rather than a suitcase for the excursion.

"Gentlemen on the left," directed Henry as he nodded toward an open bedroom without a door. "Excellent views of the ground floor from your railing."

Jim and Bart quickly set their backpacks on the floor by the beds and paused to glance downstairs.

"Ladies on the right," motioned Henry while he led them into an enclosed bedroom with a hall door that closed for privacy. "You should be able to see the ocean from your window, if you wish," he added when he pulled open the blinds on the far end of the room.

"Thank you so much," responded Carolyn as she put her suitcase beside the bed closest to the hall door.

"Oh good, I get the window side," grinned Susan. "Just like old times back at Oceanview Academy."

"Minus the clanky old steam heaters," smiled Carolyn.

"No steam heaters here," promised Henry while he reached for another hidden access button and pressed it. Once the panel slid open, it revealed an opening into the upstairs bathroom.

"Nice!" exclaimed Susan.

"The door on the other side leads to the hall," demonstrated Henry. "Be sure to lock it from the inside whenever you plan to use the facilities."

"I see, like when we shower," realized Susan while she admired the spacious bathroom, complete with shower, lighted mirror, hot tub and white marble counter with two sinks.

"What if they forget to unlock it and one of us needs to use the restroom during the night?" questioned Bart.

"Then you gentlemen are welcome to use the half-bath downstairs," invited Dr. Godspeed. "It's nothing more than a sink and a toilet, but it's right beside the compartment where the firewood is stacked, behind another hidden door."

"This place is just full of hidden doors," remarked Susan as she glanced around. "Any others we should be aware of?"

"None I know of," replied Dr. Godspeed while he headed for the staircase to go back downstairs.

"Will Maria be making dinner for us?" questioned Susan as she walked beside him.

"You have many questions," noted Henry when he returned to the couch, "but it's Carolyn's questions I'm inclined to entertain at the moment."

"Perhaps I should get dinner started," suggested Carolyn. "Just in case the power goes out."

"The backup generator should keep us going for at least three days, should the need arise," described Dr. Godspeed. "I'm sure Maria can take care of the domestic chores when she returns with Hank. Besides, it's only three o'clock."

"How about some hot chocolate?" asked Jim once he noticed a box of hot chocolate packets in the pantry.

"Help yourself," offered Henry as he turned to Carolyn and motioned for her to join him.

"Thank you," smiled Carolyn when she came over and sat beside him. "I've really never talked to a real live shrink before."

Henry laughed quite heartily before responding. "My dear lady, the moment you notice me shrinking, please let me know at once."

"I like him," flirted Susan when she sat down beside them. True, he was an old man, but she just couldn't help herself.

"I'll get more firewood," volunteered Bart as he went to retrieve another log from the compartment to have handy when needed.

"Who wants hot chocolate besides me?" queried Jim from the kitchen while he began pulling large mugs from a cupboard and putting them onto the counter.

"How about some for everyone," proposed Henry.

The others all nodded assent.

"Tell me about the first time you met your Cousin Luke," requested Dr. Godspeed as he focused his attention on Carolyn.

"I actually only met him once in my entire life," revealed Carolyn. "I was three years old and staying at my Grandma Bell's house for the day when my Uncle Willard showed up with him."

"I see," nodded Henry.

"The odd part was," continued Carolyn, "that when I ran up to my Uncle Willard, I thought at first it was my dad."

"Walter?"

"Exactly," confirmed Carolyn. "After I said '*daddy, daddy,*' my next words were '*you're not my daddy, who are you?*'"

"I take it you had no idea you even had an uncle," presumed Dr. Godspeed while he slowly nodded.

"Or a cousin, for that matter," added Carolyn.

"How did Luke react to the encounter?" Dr. Godspeed asked.

"From what I recall, Luke was very shy," described Carolyn. "He hid behind Willard's leg and didn't say a single word. Basically, he was terrified."

"What do you think would have made him so afraid?" Dr. Godspeed quizzed her.

"I have no idea. My Grandma Bell simply told me Uncle Willard was my dad's identical twin brother, and the boy was my Cousin Luke. Then she went on to make a big deal about how Luke was unusually shy around strangers."

"Anything else?" pressed Henry.

"I remember my Uncle Willard handing Bell an envelope before grabbing Luke's hand and leaving," elaborated Carolyn. "That was it."

"At what point did you ask your parents why you'd never been told about your Uncle Willard?" Henry interrogated her.

"Actually, the first person I asked was my Grandma Bell," revealed Carolyn. "Interestingly, all she did was give me some mumbo jumbo about her sons not being on speaking terms. Not once did she tell me why."

"And then?" prompted Henry.

"Once my parents picked me up, I was full of questions, asking them why I'd never been told about Uncle Willard or Cousin Luke," replied Carolyn.

"While you were still in the car on the way home?"

"Absolutely," smiled Carolyn. "I was full of questions as a child, always asking everyone about everything."

"What about Leticia?" Dr. Godspeed suddenly asked. "Were you aware Luke had a sister?"

"Not until I was in high school," answered Carolyn.

"I see," nodded Henry.

"Carolyn and Leticia are actually quite close now," volunteered Susan. "They email and write one another all the time."

"True," confirmed Carolyn.

"If it weren't for Carolyn," added Susan, "Leticia might never have had the opportunity to see Willard one last time before he died last month."

"Huh," sighed Dr. Godspeed. "Was Leticia shy, as well?"

"Absolutely," responded Carolyn. "Leticia was so shy, in fact, that she and the man she's married to now sent notes back and forth to one another for an entire year before finally having the courage to have an in-person date. They worked at the same school, but it was their faculty member friends who passed the notes for them. She was a substitute teacher and he was a janitor."

"Incredible," nodded Dr. Godspeed.

"But the mental illness Luke had did **not** affect her," clarified Carolyn. "Leticia is as sane as you or I."

"I notice she did not come with you," pointed out Henry.

"That's right," replied Carolyn. "After going through finding and becoming reconnected with her father, and then having him die like that last month, it was all pretty hard on her."

"From the autopsy report and the newspaper articles I reviewed back in 1997 and 1998," indicated Dr. Godspeed, "it appears Leticia reached a point where she needed to separate herself from the entire situation."

"Yes, for her own well-being and for the safety of her family," recalled Carolyn. "Though we were certain at first she was on board with finally finding out what really happened to her mother."

"Until she changed her mind," interjected Susan.

"That's right," agreed Carolyn. "Without Leticia filing for a Court Order to obtain Luke's psychiatric records, the only thing we're left with is guesswork as to what really happened. Did Luke do it?"

"That truly is the question," agreed Dr. Godspeed as he slowly nodded his head.

"Do *you* know the answer? What really happened to my Aunt Ruth?" questioned Carolyn while she maintained eye contact with Henry.

"Tell me about your Grandma Bell," requested Dr. Godspeed.

"Seriously?" asked Carolyn. "I could write a book about that woman. According to my Uncle Willard, she was an *evil woman*. That was something he told me over and over again. To his dying breath, he blamed her for everything that happened between him and my dad."

"How close was Luke to Grandma Bell?" questioned Henry.

"I have no idea," admitted Carolyn.

"Thank you," acknowledged Henry as Jim brought over a coaster with a mug of hot chocolate and set it on the table in front of him.

"Nothing like a mug of hot chocolate on a cold, blustery day," smiled Carolyn as Jim hurried back with a mug and a coaster for her.

"My pleasure," Jim assured her while he gave Carolyn a longing glance that did not go unnoticed by Dr. Godspeed.

Susan and Bart each hurried to the kitchen to retrieve their own mugs of hot chocolate when Jim went to get his.

"Did you ever know your Grandma Bell to be physically violent in any way?" Dr. Godspeed unexpectedly asked.

"Absolutely," responded Carolyn without hesitation. "I couldn't even begin to tell you how many of those wooden yardsticks she broke over my back end for supposedly *goofing off* when she caught me taking a break while cleaning her house or doing chores in her yard."

"Guess you're not spoiled, then," grinned Henry. "As per the old adage about sparing the rod and spoiling the child."

"Not in my opinion," answered Carolyn. "In fact, my dad was so afraid of spoiling me that I was forced to take sewing classes and make all my own clothes starting in the eighth grade."

"Carolyn's an only child," volunteered Susan.

"That may or may not be correct," differed Jim.

"How so?" Dr. Godspeed grilled him.

"When Carolyn first came to me with this case," explained Jim, "finding out about what happened to her Aunt Ruth was only one piece of it. The other was to try and find out whether she and Leticia were actually half-sisters, or not."

"Even if they are half-sisters," responded Dr. Godspeed, "DNA tests provided by most commercial ancestry testing companies in the market today do not analyze enough markers to distinguish the genetic markers in a way that can adequately establish paternity."

"That was why we needed samples from each of them to test at Otterman Laboratories in Ocean Bay," Jim informed him.

"Did you manage to obtain them?" asked Henry.

"Not from Willard," lamented Carolyn as she sadly shook her head. "Everything happened so fast with finding him, visiting him, and then him suddenly passing away."

"Unfortunate," commented Dr. Godspeed.

"Perhaps we could get a Court Order to exhume him," suggested Jim. "Otherwise, there would be no way to look beyond the 15 standard markers analyzed in most paternity tests."

"At this point, we can't even persuade Leticia to get a Court Order to unseal Luke's psychiatric file," Carolyn reminded him. "There's no way we'd ever succeed in getting an Order to have Willard exhumed, plus it would involve obtaining permission from that horrible woman Willard was married to at the time of his death."

"Trixie didn't even acknowledge in the obituary that Willard had any family," volunteered Susan.

"That's right!" exclaimed Carolyn as her eyes began to water with anger at the thought of how Trixie had treated them.

"The test we'd hoped to have done at my laboratory includes the entire genome sequence," described Jim. "As many as six billion markers would be examined, and normally such a test can identify at least a single mutation in one of an identical twins' genetics that has been passed on to a child."

"There still would be no way to determine with 100% certainty whether or not Leticia and Carolyn are half-sisters, or which of the twins was their father," countered Dr. Godspeed. "Even after such an expensive test."

"No charge in this particular case," indicated Jim.

"I see," responded Dr. Godspeed while he glanced at Carolyn and then back at Jim. *Does she have any idea how Jim feels about her?*

"We do know that in the 1970s each of our dads stepped out on their wives," admitted Carolyn as she hung her head with shame.

"I'm sorry," consoled Henry when he put a comforting hand on Carolyn's shoulder. "Sometimes things like that happen. After all, we're each only human."

"I know," nodded Carolyn. "In Walter's case, he repented for his single transgression, pleaded for forgiveness, and was finally reconciled with my mom; she forgave him unconditionally."

"Charlotte was a good Christian woman," mentioned Susan.

"What about Willard?" queried Henry.

"That was a completely different story," clarified Carolyn. "According to Leticia, Willard cheated on Ruth for *years* before finally leaving her for the woman who became his second wife."

"How long did that last?" questioned Henry.

"Until Beatrice died of cancer in 1981," described Carolyn. "But, according to Leticia, Uncle Willard did not like being alone for very long. He turned around and married his third wife Matilda in 1982. She's the one they buried him with."

"When did Matilda pass away?' asked Henry with a troubled look on his face.

"Matilda died in 2016. Shortly after that, Willard moved into an independent living facility where he met and married Trixie in 2017," elaborated Carolyn, "and quit having anything to do whatsoever with the family afterwards."

"Nothing but a gold digger, that one," muttered Susan.

"Apparently, Luke took it pretty hard when his father abandoned his mother and married Beatrice back in 1974," mentioned Carolyn.

"Indeed, he certainly did," confirmed Dr. Godspeed while he considered the information. "And if I recall correctly, the marriage took place on the exact same day Willard's divorce from Ruth was final."

"That's horrible," disapproved Susan.

"It was also the same day as Luke's high school graduation," revealed Dr. Godspeed, "an event his father failed to attend."

"Leticia told me at one point that Luke wanted to become a pastor," recalled Carolyn.

"Among other things," considered Henry.

Just then the front door opened, again causing a cold blast of air to fan the flames in the fireplace.

"Hank no come," explained Maria, who was holding something wrapped in a plastic bag to keep it dry from the weather. "Radio and insulin," she explained when she set it down on the bench beside her before taking off her wet shoes and coat.

"My insulin and the handset from my ham radio," recognized Dr. Godspeed as he came over to retrieve then. After placing the ham radio on the coffee table, he took his insulin to the refrigerator.

"Amateur Extra, General or Technician?" asked Jim.

"Technician," replied Henry with a slight smile at Jim when he returned to the couch. "What about you?"

"Technician," answered Jim.

"I would expect nothing less from a man like you," opined Dr. Godspeed while he carefully looked over his ham radio handset to make sure it was still dry.

"I take it Maria has her license, too?" questioned Jim.

"Amateur Extra," notified Maria as she came into the room to join them. "I start dinner now."

"¿Por qué Hank no pudo venir?" Henry inquired of Maria.

"Coast Guard warn bad weather," explained Maria while she took a large pot from one of the cupboards, filled it with water, and put it onto the stove to boil. "They stop him; not safe."

"There is the box of things I had hoped to share with you while you're here," described Henry, "but bringing it over here from the main residence in this weather is just not possible."

"Perhaps tomorrow when the storm passes," suggested Carolyn as she went to the kitchen to see if she could help.

"Say, Jim, would you happen to have any syringes in your medical bag?" asked Henry when he glanced at the clock. "I probably should have my insulin shot now."

"You're in luck," Jim assured him with a crooked grin.

The morning of November 7, 2023, arrived with an unexpected calm. Tentacles of sunlight reached through the surrounding forest whose moist limbs glistened in the reflection.

Carolyn slowly opened her eyes when a ray of brilliant sunlight reached her face. Disoriented at first, she quickly realized where she was and hurried to the restroom. Thankfully, no one else was there.

The hushed voices of Jim Otterman and Henry Godspeed could be heard downstairs. The smell of bacon, eggs and pancakes wafted upward, causing Susan and Bart to awaken, as well.

"Let me in!" shouted Susan as she banged on the bathroom door.

"One minute," replied Carolyn while she finished her business and flushed the toilet before unlocking the door.

Without waiting for her to leave, Susan hurried to the toilet. "You don't have to leave on my account," she grinned at Carolyn. "We were roommates, you know."

"Okay, sure," acknowledged Carolyn as she went to one of the sinks and began washing her hands and face.

"Will you be much longer, ladies?" asked Bart from outside the hall door.

"We're just getting started," Susan informed him while she finished up and flushed the toilet.

"I'll just go downstairs," volunteered Bart. "Take your time."

Downstairs, Jim and Henry were involved in a deep discussion about KarXT, a new combination therapy for treatment of schizophrenia and multiple personality disorder that combines two different drugs, xanomeline and trospium chloride, into one treatment.

"These drugs target receptors in the brain and body associated with the cholinergic neurotransmitter system – which has a key role in learning and memory, digestion, control of heartbeat, blood pressure, movement and many other functions," described Dr. Godspeed. "In fact, there are two types of cholinergic receptors, nicotinic and muscarinic. In KarXT, xanomeline activates muscarinic receptors in the brain, whereas trospium chloride blocks activation of muscarinic receptors in the body."

"Wasn't xanomeline originally developed to treat Alzheimer's disease?" questioned Jim. "In studies I've read, it was shown to improve cognition and some of the behavioral symptoms of Alzheimer's in trials, including reducing delusions, agitation, and hallucinations, but its development was stopped as some people experienced problematic side effects."

"Yes, those side effects were caused by muscarinic receptor activation in the body," corroborated Dr. Godspeed. "Nevertheless, it was anticipated that combining trospium chloride with xanomeline would reduce those side effects and this new therapy would reduce psychosis in people living with schizophrenia and MPD."

"And it worked?" asked Jim.

"Absolutely," confirmed Henry. "In Phase 1 of the trial, KarXT was shown to be safe and well tolerated with a 50% reduction in side effects compared to xanomeline alone in healthy adults. Results from the Phase 2 trial in people with schizophrenia and MPD were also positive, and in 2019, it was proven that KarXT led to a statistically significant reduction in psychotic symptoms in people living with schizophrenia and MPD."

"Is that what the bulk of your research out here entails?" Jim quizzed him.

"Seven years after our initial investment," elaborated Dr. Godspeed, "results from a Phase 3 trial of KarXT in schizophrenia and MPD have found the treatment to result in clinically meaningful and statistically significant improvements in symptoms of psychosis, such as delusions and hallucinations, compared to placebo. It also improves negative symptoms of schizophrenia and MPD, including lack of motivation, social withdrawal, and cognitive impairment, which often are not impacted by current drugs. Very encouraging was the result of it not being associated with common problematic side effects experienced by current antipsychotics, such as sleepiness, weight gain and abnormal motor movements."

"Very impressive," praised Jim as he pondered the information.

"Historically," continued Henry, "antipsychotic drug treatments have focused on the neurotransmitter dopamine. They work to block some of the dopamine receptors in the brain, which can lead to problematic side effects. These side effects mean some people stop taking the medication, causing them to relapse. Moreover, between 20% and 33% of patients don't respond to dopamine-targeting drugs at all."

"That's always a concern," agreed Jim.

"Not only that," added Henry, "the KarXT trial is the first positive Phase 3 trial for an investigational medicine that does not directly rely on dopaminergic or serotonergic pathways in the brain in approximately 70 years. KarXT works in a completely new way. It was found to be well tolerated and to relieve symptoms of schizophrenia and MPD, providing a potential treatment option for people with psychosis – a key priority for our Mental Health team."

"Who else is on your team besides you and Maria?" questioned Jim. "I would have expected you to have at least half a dozen researchers here on the island with you."

"Five of them were here," explained Dr. Godspeed, "until the conclusion of our tests last year."

"And now you're writing your memoirs," presumed Jim.

"Precisely," confirmed Henry. "Unfortunately, my dream of finding a way to treat patients with schizophrenia and MPD without the use of drugs remains just that. With the exception of Maria."

"She was a patient?" Jim was genuinely surprised.

"A very determined young lady who, with the proper therapy, made lifestyle changes. Maria had a genuine desire to improve and maintain self-management," elaborated Henry. "She's lived a relatively normal and drug-free life for the past 20 years she's been here with me on the island."

"I hate to interrupt you," apologized Maria while she gave Jim a peculiar look, "but breakfast is ready now." *Why is Henry telling him about my past?* she wondered.

"Smells wonderful!" exclaimed Susan as she and Carolyn came downstairs to join the others.

"Do we have any fruit?" asked Carolyn upon seeing nothing but bacon, eggs and pancakes on the table.

"We got jam, butter and syrup," smiled Bart when he placed them beside the other things.

"And orange juice," added Maria while she retrieved a pitcher of it and put it on the table. *Are these strangers a threat to the secluded life I enjoy here with Dr. Godspeed?*

"What about actual fresh fruit, like bananas, oranges or apples?" questioned Carolyn. She normally ate oatmeal for breakfast with blueberries in it, and little else.

"Only at the house," explained Maria. "Not over here."

"We'll have to grab some for you when we're over there later today," mentioned Henry. "In fact, the weather is surprisingly nice outside. Perhaps, after breakfast, we can all go to the main residence."

"That would be great," approved Carolyn as she took her morning pills with the orange juice and began eating a pancake without anything on it.

"No butter or syrup?" questioned Maria while she studied Carolyn more closely. *Is she really Luke Bennett's cousin?*

"None for me," declined Carolyn. "I never eat butter, syrup, or bacon, but I'll take an egg for the protein."

"Well, I'll take some of everything," grinned Susan as she began loading up her plate.

"Me, too, thanks," said Bart while he and Jim both began helping themselves to the breakfast items.

"I be back soon," Maria informed them when she suddenly headed for the door and left.

"Did I say something wrong?" asked Susan.

"I don't believe so," responded Jim, who suddenly seemed concerned about something.

"Maria is an excellent cook," praised Henry while he gave himself an insulin shot before joining them at the table. "Hopefully, I'll be able to find a replacement for my nurse soon, as all of this is far too much for Maria to handle on her own."

"Seems odd your nurse would leave you in a lurch without bothering to find someone to fill in for her first," opined Carolyn.

"What happened to her?" questioned Jim as he turned to Henry.

"Isabel quit unexpectedly due to a family emergency at home in Seattle," explained Henry.

"What was her last name?" Jim grilled him.

"Romero," revealed Henry. "Why?"

"Did you confirm her reasons for leaving?" Jim continued to interrogate him.

Dr. Godspeed seemed troubled. "No, why?"

"Then how do you know why she quit?" asked Jim.

"Maria told me," responded Henry. "She left a note."

Jim pressed a button on his satellite-activated smartwatch, put it on speaker, and waited while it rang.

"Hello?" came a voice at the other end.

"Chip, it's me, Jim," he announced himself.

"How's it going out there?" questioned Chip.

"I'm not sure. Chip, I need you to do me a favor," requested Jim. "Can you please do a background check on a Maria Alvarez for me? She's a housekeeper for the doctor here on the island, and this may be nothing, but I just need to confirm my suspicions."

"I don't understand," objected Henry while he furrowed his eyebrows.

"And Chip," added Jim as he motioned for Henry to be silent, "I also need a background check on an Isabel Romero, who worked here as a nurse until quitting unexpectedly to deal with a family emergency at home in Seattle."

"You got it," agreed Chip. "Anything else?"

"Call me with the information as soon as you get it," requested Jim. "That's it."

"Yes, Sir," bid Chip when he hung up.

"Is all that really necessary?" asked Henry.

Jim glanced at Carolyn. *I'll never forgive myself if anything happens to her.*

"Answer me," demanded Henry.

Jim turned to Henry. "There was something peculiar about Maria's behavior this morning, and it's just a feeling I have. It may be nothing, but what if it isn't?"

"I don't understand," admitted Henry.

"You told me yourself Maria is a former patient of yours and you believe she is cured," elaborated Jim.

Bart mouthed the words, *Oh my God!*

Carolyn and Susan exchanged a concerned look.

"Maria is fine," Henry assured Jim.

"Then you should have no problem with me following up on a hunch I have," described Jim. Jim could not shake the uneasy feeling that persisted since Maria had given him the peculiar look.

Dr. Godspeed was clearly upset by the implication. Maria had never given him any reason to suspect her schizophrenia or multiple personality disorder were active again. *Could his earlier conversation with Jim have somehow triggered the reemergence of her symptoms?*

"Henry, I need to be sure we're safe here," insisted Jim as he turned to Bart. "Bart, can you please check on the helicopter?"

"I shouldn't be too long," announced Bart when he set down his fork and wiped off his mouth with the napkin. "I need to make sure there was no damage to it from the storm last night anyway. Hopefully, no trees fell down on it."

"Have you tried to use your ham radio this morning?" Jim asked Dr. Godspeed.

"I was planning to do that at the house," Henry informed him.

"Wouldn't Hank have come over here to check up on you, if he didn't find you at the house?" Jim grilled him.

Henry merely nodded while he retrieved his ham radio handset and attempted to place a call. "I don't understand it, there's absolutely no reception at all."

"It is 9:00 a.m. already," pointed out Bart as he finished tying his boots in the foyer, "giving Hank plenty of time to get here by now if he were coming."

"Didn't you say Maria was the one who called him yesterday?" Carolyn suddenly asked. "What if she didn't?"

"This can't be happening," muttered Henry while he carried his ham radio handset to the foyer, put on his jacket, and stuffed it into his pocket. "Bart, hold up. I'm coming with you."

"We'll all go," insisted Jim as he went to the foyer, put on his boots, and began tying them.

"I probably could stand to lose a few pounds, anyway," commented Susan when she joined them in the foyer.

"I'll just get his insulin," offered Carolyn before dashing to the refrigerator to retrieve it.

"Carolyn, before you put your boots on, can you please go upstairs and grab my first aid pack," requested Jim. "It's inside my other pack, small and red with a white cross on it."

Without comment, Carolyn hurried upstairs to retrieve it before coming back down.

Just then, Jim's smartwatch began chiming. "Hello, Chip?"

"Jim are you alone?" Chip immediately inquired.

"I'm on speaker, and you're free to talk," Jim advised him.

"Jim, the body of an Isabel Romero washed ashore on Orcas Island six months ago," revealed Chip. "That's not too far from where you are. Apparently, she was strangled, and the case remains unsolved."

Henry appeared as if he'd been struck by lightning when he sat down in the foyer and began lacing up his boots. *Wouldn't Isabel have been missed before now? Surely someone must have known she worked on the island, yet Maria was the one to hire her.*

"Was there anything about Isabel's family having an emergency during that time period?" Jim interrogated his fellow detective.

"She had no family," answered Chip. "Her parents were killed in an automobile accident over ten years ago. Isabel's husband Ken died of cancer shortly thereafter; they had no children."

"What about Maria Alvarez?" asked Jim while he maintained eye contact with Henry.

"I've got a whole file on her," replied Chip. "Apparently, Maria was under investigation for the unexplained death of her father about 21 years ago, though nothing was ever proven. Do you want me to send you the file?"

"You bet I do," requested Jim as he sadly nodded his head.

"Please let me show you what I have on her," offered Henry.

"I insist," agreed Jim while he pulled his 45-Colt revolver from the concealed belt holster at the small of his back. He quickly checked to be sure there was a bullet in the chamber.

"Hopefully, this trip won't turn out as badly as the last one," muttered Bart as he pulled out his Ruger Security-9mm pistol to check the status of his ammunition. He, too, kept his weapon concealed in a belt holster.

"Gentlemen, please!" exclaimed Dr. Godspeed. "I cannot believe you would bring weapons here."

"And I cannot believe you would fail to warn us about Maria being a former patient of yours," countered Jim.

"What are you planning to do?" questioned Henry.

"Hopefully, we won't need 'em," responded Jim when he re-holstered his gun, "but you can thank me later if we end up saving your life. Right now, there's a potentially dangerous patient of yours loose on this island who may perceive us as a threat to this idyllic life of seclusion you've provided for her."

"Even if her schizophrenia and multiple personality disorder have somehow been triggered," qualified Dr. Godspeed, "I know she'll listen to me."

"You'd better hope so," responded Jim as they departed from the guest cottage and made their way toward the trail leading through the forest to the helipad.

"Perhaps I should take the ladies to the helicopter first," suggested Bart. "And run 'em to the mainland?"

"We stay together," insisted Jim. "Let's all go to the helicopter. And, provided it's in one piece, we'll proceed to the residence."

"The trail can be slippery," cautioned Henry while he carefully made his way down the trail with them toward the helipad.

The group traveled in relative silence for several minutes as they walked through the forest. Even with rays of sunlight and the sounds of seagulls in the distance, there was an ominous feeling in the air.

"I don't believe it!" exclaimed Bart when they emerged into the clearing where the helicopter should have been.

"Over there," pointed out Susan upon seeing the damaged helicopter at the far end of the opening by the trees, lying on its side.

"Look at the blades," gasped Carolyn upon seeing how impossibly bent they were.

"Someone had to have untied it," deduced Bart as he inspected the ropes that he'd personally secured the previous day. "The tail boom's broken, too."

"Even if they hadn't, the windstorm would still have done some serious damage," opined Jim.

"I had a storm take out the boom on my helicopter once, when I had one," recalled Henry.

Jim glared at Henry for a long moment before taking a deep breath and shaking his head. "Is it salvageable, Bart?"

"I doubt it, but either way, you're not leaving me here alone," Bart advised Jim. "Even if I had the needed parts and could repair the damage, there's no guarantee it would get us safely to the mainland. Not with this kind of destruction. We're gonna need to call for help."

"Agreed," nodded Jim when he turned to Dr. Godspeed. "Which way is the residence?"

"Follow me," directed Henry as he headed for a fork in the trail they had just taken and began walking in another direction.

The sound of waves crashing against the shoreline below were a constant reminder of the unpredictable nature of the sea. Today the sun was out; tomorrow could bring another storm.

"Ever have a tsunami here?" asked Susan while they trudged along.

"They predict a 30% chance of another one happening within the next 50 years," answered Henry, "though I don't believe there has been one here since 1965."

"Aren't earthquakes what causes them?" queried Carolyn.

"Indeed, they are," confirmed Dr. Godspeed. "For example, in a recent simulation done by the Department of Natural Resources, it was predicted an earthquake with a magnitude of 9 on the Cascadian Subduction Zone could cause 10-foot swells within about 15 minutes."

"No way!" Susan could not believe it.

"Actually," corrected Jim, "the simulation done by FEMA showed the first waves in their model reaching the *outer coast* in about 15 minutes. The hypothetical tsunami then traveled through the Strait of Juan de Fuca and into Puget Sound, finally reaching the Tacoma waterfront about 2½ hours after the initial earthquake."

"Which would put the worst of it here after about an hour and a half," described Henry.

"How long would you have to get out of here if you knew one was coming?" Susan grilled him.

"Probably 10 minutes, with a certain means of escape handy," clarified Henry. *Hopefully, my yacht is still intact.*

"If we were to die in a tsunami of that magnitude, would they ever find our bodies?" pressed Susan.

"They'd most likely wash up on Orcas Island," interjected Jim. "Assuming the water currents are consistent around these parts," he added as he thought of poor Isabel.

"A very real possibility," realized Henry while he pursed his lips. *How could I have been so careless as to let my guard down with Maria? Will all of us pay for my mistake?*

"And, here we are without a helicopter," muttered Jim. "I suppose we'll get a look at your yacht when we get to the residence?"

"I certainly hope so," replied Henry, "and the boat dock, too."

"Would Maria be able to sail out of here on her own?" Susan suddenly asked. "She wouldn't just leave us here, would she?"

"We're here," muttered Henry when he paused at the edge of the clearing surrounding his residence, relieved to see the boat dock still there, along with his yacht.

The elegant mansion was painted in colors of brown and green, visually blending into its surrounding forest environment, even with the fire clearance area around it as a precaution.

The entire center front of the three-story mansion jutted outward at a 30-degree angle. Its second and third floors came to a point where each side met at the angle, supported by a massive round column. Beneath them at ground level was a large inset porch, allowing access to the triangular-shaped porch from either side and giving it a futuristic appearance. As many picture windows as possible dotted the exterior of the building, allowing stunning views of the well-kempt yard, bluffs, and ocean below.

"It's like something out of a storybook," admired Susan as she studied the beautiful home and yard.

Several yards behind the home stood a smaller building with a giant radio tower above it. "Let's go there first," decided Henry.

"Maria wouldn't have a weapon, would she?" Jim asked when they stepped into the open area surrounding the home.

"Absolutely not," Henry assured him. "Other than the weapons you gentlemen have, there are absolutely no guns on this island."

"Lead the way," nodded Jim while they followed Dr. Godspeed to his ham radio shack.

"The house appears dark inside," observed Bart as he put his hand on the butt of his gun for easy access.

"You both look like you're ready to draw and shoot at any moment," objected Henry.

"Would you rather we approach with our weapons drawn?" questioned Bart. Just to be prepared, put his thumb on the safety.

"I promise you, she's not armed," Henry assured him. "There's absolutely no way."

"Not with a gun, anyway," responded Jim.

"I'm still hoping you're wrong," mentioned Dr. Godspeed when they reached the door to his ham radio shack. "That's odd."

"What's odd?" questioned Jim as he tightened his grip on the butt of his gun.

"She must have forgotten to lock it back up after placing the call yesterday," assumed Henry while he started to open the door.

"Let me go first," insisted Jim. "Just in case."

Slowly and cautiously, Jim opened the door to the structure.

"There's a light switch inside the door," described Henry.

Jim carefully turned on the light and went inside, stunned at what he saw next. The sledge hammer used to destroy the unit beyond any hope of repair was still laying on top of it.

Unable to wait any longer, Henry came inside. "Oh, no!"

The others quickly crowded in behind him.

"Bart, I want you to take Susan with you. Go check out the yacht," Jim instructed him. "Be careful to check out the dock, too, before you try to walk on it."

"Here's the key," offered Henry as he pulled out an orange boat-float keychain with a single key on it. "It's the only one I have."

"You don't have a backup?" asked Bart when he took the key from him. "That seems odd."

"Lost it a while back," admitted Henry. "Always meant to get another one made, but I hardly ever leave the island."

"We'll wait for you guys there," Bart promised them while he and Susan made their way towards the boat dock.

"How about we go over to your house and see if we can find the box you wanted to show us," suggested Carolyn.

"That's the plan," muttered Dr. Godspeed.

Carolyn and Jim cautiously followed him to the back door of the main residence.

Jim continued to keep one hand on the butt of his gun, ready to draw it from the holster at any moment if necessary while they followed Henry into his home.

"Where did your research assistants stay when they were here?" queried Carolyn as they made their way through his galley-style kitchen.

"Some of them stayed at the guest cottage, others here," he revealed when they reached the formal dining room.

"Nice table," admired Carolyn upon seeing the solid oak table with 12 matching chairs around it.

"Thanks," replied Henry while they continued to the living room. Refurbished Queen Anne style furniture, Tiffany lamps and a natural stone hearth gave the entire room a mid-eighteenth century feel. Hardwood floors with a large burgundy area rug on top seemed to transport visitors into another time.

"I often use this room for hypnosis," revealed Henry when he glanced about to see if Maria was there.

"Let's try upstairs," suggested Jim.

Henry merely nodded as he returned to the main foyer and began climbing the stairs. Each of the five bedrooms and three bathrooms was empty, other than the expensive furniture inside them. Commanding views of the coastline from every room were impressive.

"The only place left to look is in the basement," deduced Henry. "That's where my research laboratory is."

"Do you really think she'd go there?" questioned Carolyn.

"She might," believed Dr. Godspeed. He gingerly pressed a hidden panel on the hallway wall upstairs. Without warning, an elevator door opened. "Hopefully, this will be our element of surprise, if she's there."

Jim repositioned his grip on the butt of his gun when they entered the tiny elevator and waited while Dr. Godspeed pressed the button marked R.

"What happens if the power goes out while we're in here?" asked Carolyn as they slowly descended.

"Now you sound like your friend Susan," teased Henry.

"I'm sorry," apologized Carolyn while she forced a smile and shrugged her shoulders.

"No worries, the entire place is on a backup generator," Dr. Godspeed reminded her when they reached the lower level and waited for the elevator door to open.

Inside was Maria, seated at Dr. Godspeed's desk with an open file in front of her.

"Maria," he greeted her as he stepped from the elevator. "What are you doing here?"

"I don't know," she replied in the frightened voice of a scared child. "I'm not sure how I got here."

"Sweetheart," he said while he approached and put a hand on her shoulder, "I'm afraid your schizophrenia and MPD may be active again."

"But how?" Maria asked as her eyes began to water.

Henry then used her shoulder to turn her towards him in the swiveling chair. With his hands on both her shoulders, he came close to examine her more carefully. "First, I want you to know how much having you here has meant to me."

"You're going to send me away, aren't you?" questioned Maria while she gave Jim and Carolyn the peculiar look again.

"Never," promised Dr. Godspeed. "This is your home."

"Then *why* are they here?" asked Maria as the expression on her face seemed to change.

"Their presence here has absolutely nothing to do with you," assured Dr. Godspeed. "Carolyn is Luke Bennett's cousin, and she came here to find out what I know about him."

Maria glanced at the box on Henry's desk. "Are you going to show them the videotape?" she interrogated Henry while she gave Carolyn a suspicious look.

"Not without popcorn," replied Henry. "No movie is complete without popcorn. Does that sound like a good idea?"

"Sure," agreed Maria. She seemed to relax, but Jim and Carolyn were obviously confused.

"Jim, there are some packages of popcorn in the cupboard above the sink by the coffee station," described Dr. Godspeed.

There must be a reason why Henry is suggesting this, hoped Jim while he walked over to the cupboard and pulled out a packet of microwavable popcorn.

"Please make some for each of us," requested Henry as he joined Jim by the microwave and pulled four large serving bowls from the cupboard. "I'll get the extra salt," he added with a meaningful raise of his eyebrows. "Maria likes extra salt on hers."

Both Carolyn and Jim immediately understood; Jim quickly unwrapped and put the first popcorn packet into the microwave.

"Just 2½ minutes or it will burn," cautioned Dr. Godspeed while he pulled out his keys and swiftly unlocked a drawer beside the sink. *Hopefully, Maria will not realize his plan.*

Jim watched with interest as Dr. Godspeed opened the drawer. Inside were various compartments filled with capsules and pills. Henry gingerly grabbed a capsule from the bin marked Loxapine.

Of course, realized Jim. *Loxapine is one of the few medications for schizophrenia and MPD that comes in a capsule form.*

"If only I had *that* kind of salt handy," whispered Henry when he pointed toward the bin marked Clozapine.

"Do you have a mortar and pestle?" responded Jim in a hushed voice. "Perhaps for dessert," he added in a normal voice.

"My thoughts exactly," approved Henry as he handed two of the Clozapine tablets to Jim, along with a small mortar and pestle that he normally kept in the medication drawer.

Jim managed to surreptitiously put them into his pocket as the microwave beeped.

"Allow me," offered Henry while he pulled out the bag, carefully handling it by the edges, and dumped its contents into one of the serving bowls. "Smells delicious!"

"I'll get the next one started," indicated Jim.

"Thanks," responded Dr. Godspeed as he pulled apart the Loxapine capsule and sprinkled it over the top of Maria's popcorn.

"I'll take it to her," said Carolyn.

"Uh, why don't we all go sit on that couch over there while we eat our popcorn," suggested Dr. Godspeed while Jim waited for the next bag of popcorn to finish popping. "Maria, can you please turn on the television set for us?"

"Sure, I'd be happy to," agreed Maria as Carolyn followed her over to the couch and carefully placed Maria's bowl of popcorn on the coffee table in front of it.

Waiting until Maria's attention was distracted, Jim took out the small mortar and pestle before crushing the Clozapine tablets.

"Maria, do we have any Pepsi down here?" Dr. Godspeed suddenly asked her.

"I can get some from upstairs," replied Maria.

"That would be great," smiled Henry. "Carolyn, perhaps you can go with Maria to help hold open the door and press the elevator buttons for her."

"I can do that," agreed Carolyn while she glanced at Jim.

Jim was not pleased, but understood the need to get Maria out of the room long enough to add the Clozapine powder to the top of her popcorn.

"Sorry," apologized Henry as Carolyn climbed into the elevator with Maria, "but it's the only way."

"Are you sure mixing the two medications is safe?" asked Jim after the elevator doors closed.

"The addition of Loxapine will have no effect on her Clozapine plasma levels," assured Dr. Godspeed. "Loxapine acts by its own mechanism."

"Nothing had better happen to Carolyn," cautioned Jim as he gave Henry an intimidating look.

"Carolyn will be fine," promised Henry. "Tell me, just how long have you been in love with her, anyway? I'm curious."

Without answering, Jim handed the pestle containing the crushed Clozapine powder to Dr. Godspeed, who immediately went over to sprinkle it over the top of Maria's popcorn.

Just then, the next bag of popcorn was ready. Jim switched them out before dumping the second one into a serving bowl.

"Does Carolyn know how you feel?" pressed Dr. Godspeed.

"She knows," answered Jim while he waited for the third bag to pop.

"I take it you are each married to someone else," presumed Henry as he studied Jim Otterman.

"You presume correctly," muttered Jim. He quickly looked away from Dr. Godspeed's penetrating gaze.

"And yet you have carried a torch for this woman for over 50 years," calculated Dr. Godspeed.

"That about sums it up," agreed Jim as he folded his arms in front of him while waiting for the third bag to finish popping.

"I hope I'm not making you uncomfortable," commented Henry when the microwave beeped again.

"I vote for changing the subject," replied Jim while he put the final bag of popcorn into the microwave and punched in the time.

"Whether you may realize it or not, she cares about you, too," informed Henry as he seized the third bag of popcorn, pulled it apart, and dumped it into a serving bowl.

"Look," snapped Jim. "My relationship with Carolyn is none of your business, and is off the table. The reason we're here is to find out what *you* know about her Cousin Luke and whether or not he murdered his mother."

"My apologies," extended Dr. Godspeed. "I did not mean to hit such a sensitive note."

"Didn't you?" questioned Jim when he looked Henry in the eyes. "Carolyn has been married for almost 40 years now to the man she has chosen to spend her life with, and if he can make her happy, great."

"Her happiness is very important to you," observed Henry with a sly smile.

"Yes, it is," barked Jim as the elevator door opened.

"Is everything alright?" questioned Carolyn when she and Maria came into the room.

"Just fine," interjected Henry as the microwave beeped on the final bag of popcorn.

Carolyn noticed with relief the three other bowls of popcorn were still on the counter in the coffee area. She definitely wouldn't want to eat from the wrong bowl by mistake.

"These already cold," volunteered Maria while she set down the case of Pepsi. "From refrigerator."

"Excellent," beamed Dr. Godspeed as he removed the fourth bag of popcorn from the microwave and dumped it into a bowl.

15. For Whom the Bell Tolls

Carolyn watched with great concern as Dr. Godspeed inserted the old videotape into his player. "Hopefully that's not the only copy you have."

"Unfortunately, it is," lamented Henry. "You see, most of the sessions I conducted before the turn of the century were all done on videotape, especially in 1997 and 1998."

"You could easily have them transferred to DVD," pointed out Carolyn. "Most videotapes only have a shelf life of about 15 years."

"I know," replied Henry, "but I honestly had not planned on watching it again." He had not yet pushed play.

Jim's smartwatch suddenly chimed. It was Bart.

"Hello?" answered Jim.

"Everything alright?" asked Bart.

"We're fine," Jim assured him. "Maria is here with us, and we are just getting ready to watch a videotape with Henry."

"I see," responded Bart.

"Tell him about my ankle," called Susan from the background.

"Oh yes," added Bart, "Susan has sprained her ankle. The dock survived the storm and the yacht is functional, but she managed to slip on the rocky path leading down here."

"Of course, she did," muttered Jim as he shook his head.

"Would it be a good time to run her to the mainland?" asked Bart. "We can retrieve our luggage from the guest house when I return. Besides, I shouldn't be too long."

Jim hesitated and then glanced at Henry. "Would that be okay?"

He merely nodded.

"Yeah, that's fine," agreed Jim. "And perhaps Chip can come back with you? You shouldn't be boating alone."

"A great idea," responded Bart. "I'll call him now."

"Thanks," replied Jim before hanging up.

"Is Chip someone we can trust?" Maria suddenly asked.

"Absolutely," Jim assured her. "Chip is my business partner."

"We wouldn't want Bart to try and sail our yacht by himself, now would we?" questioned Henry while he put an arm around Maria.

"No," she answered as she put a handful of popcorn into her mouth and began chewing.

"Again, my apologies that I do not have a DVD of this," mentioned Dr. Godspeed, "but technically it came from a box marked for destruction at the time the Ashton Medical Center finished converting any existing videotapes housed in the Psych Unit over to DVD."

"You seem to have quite a collection here," observed Jim while he motioned toward the hundreds of videotapes stored on the wall behind them. "Are these the videotapes that were allegedly destroyed?"

"Yes, I'm afraid they are," he admitted rather sheepishly. "Technically, none of them exist," grinned Henry.

"Fair enough," nodded Jim.

"This particular videotape is one of the sessions where Luke talks about Bell," revealed Dr. Godspeed. "In fact, *each* of his five individual personalities eventually refers to themselves as being part of Luke. However, all of them refer to Bell as *someone else*, not Luke."

"Huh," muttered Jim.

Just then, Maria began snoring. Her bowl of popcorn was nearly empty. Dr. Godspeed gingerly took it from her and placed it on the coffee table. He seemed pleased with the result as he returned his attention to the video player and pressed play.

* * *

"Today is March 23, 1998," informed Dr. Henry Godspeed on the videotape. "I am here today with Luke Bennett."

"Hello," said Luke while he glanced at the tripod where Dr. Godspeed's video camera was mounted. A red light in the corner of the frame indicated it was on.

"Luke, we've talked extensively about your Grandma Bell," Dr. Godspeed reminded him, "and how she used to beat you with her yardstick whenever she was displeased with how you had done chores at her house when you were a young lad."

"She was not one to be messed with, that's for sure," Luke assured him as he took a drink of water from the water bottle in his hand.

"We've also talked about the time Bell came to your rescue when you appeared before the court on June 10, 1976, to answer for the charge of physically assaulting your roommate Richard Springfield at Bible College," reviewed Dr. Godspeed.

"What about it?" asked Luke while he shrugged his shoulders.

"It says here that you not only punched him in the jaw, but that you made verbal death threats toward Mr. Springfield and his friend Denise Jones, who witnessed the attack," summarized Dr. Godspeed.

"Liars, both of 'em!" shouted Luke, who was becoming more agitated by the moment.

"The court file indicates that neither of the victims were willing to press any charges against you," continued Dr. Godspeed. "I'd say you were quite lucky the matter was dismissed like it was."

"Because I didn't do it," maintained Luke.

"Fortunately for you, your Grandma Bell was there to pay your $250 fine for you," added Dr. Godspeed.

"Big deal," muttered Luke while he took another sip of water.

"Did you live with her afterwards?" asked Dr. Godspeed.

"Hell, no!" exclaimed Luke as he rolled his eyes.

"Where did Bell take you to live?" questioned Dr. Godspeed.

"Home, to my mother," lied Luke. *There's no need to mention my week at Madam Claudia's place.*

"You and your mother were quite close," noted Dr. Godspeed when he studied the file he was holding. "You speak of her often."

Luke became serious and the expression on his face changed considerably. "She was my world."

"Did Ruth ever encourage you to marry or have children?" probed Dr. Godspeed.

"No, why would she do that?" Luke furrowed his brows.

"You mentioned to me earlier your mother became quite ill in 1995," Dr. Godspeed reminded him. "Tell me about it."

Luke began running his right hand through his hair and glancing around in a suspicious manner.

"Tell me about the night Bell came over to help you," requested Dr. Godspeed.

"Don't make him talk about it again," responded Luke in a different voice. "Can't you see how upset he is?"

"I need to hear it from each of you," specified Dr. Godspeed.

"There's nothing more to tell!" yelled Luke in the different voice. "Leave Luke alone!"

"Then, perhaps *you* can tell me what happened," hoped Dr. Godspeed. "Luke doesn't need to know you told me."

After a long pause, Luke's alternate personality continued. "Luke called Bell to come over and help. That's when she made him leave the room while she took care of his mother."

"Was Bell *alone* in the room with Ruth at the time she died?" Dr. Godspeed questioned him.

"Yes, she was," replied Luke in yet another voice, one that was calm and detached. "We've all told you that already."

"Do all of you believe Bell might have smothered Ruth to put her out of her misery?" asked Dr. Godspeed while he maintained eye contact with Luke.

"Without question," responded Luke's alternate personality.

"Then *why* didn't any of you mention this to the police when they came to the house two years later? The night they arrested him?" Dr. Godspeed grilled him.

"Make it stop!" Luke suddenly screamed as he began rocking back and forth, pulling his knees to his chest. "Make them stop!"

"Luke, listen to me," instructed Dr. Godspeed. "You're safe now, there's nothing to be afraid of."

"Yes, there is," insisted Luke. He suddenly began to sob.

"What are you afraid of, Luke?" pressed Dr. Godspeed.

"Of *them*," hollered Luke while his eyes began darting around the room, looking at specters that weren't there.

"Of who?" questioned Dr. Godspeed.

"Of *them*," repeated Luke as he started to hyperventilate. "They made me leave her in that room!"

"Luke, I'm going to give you a shot to calm you down," Dr. Godspeed advised him while he pressed a button on his desk. "Nurse Redding, please come to my office at once."

Nurse Redding hurried into the room to help restrain Luke while Dr. Godspeed gave him a shot of Clonazepam. "I am giving the patient an injection of Clonazepam at this time to calm his hysteria," described Dr. Godspeed for the videotape. "This interview is ended."

The tape went dark.

* * *

"Unbelievable," muttered Carolyn as she shook her head.

"I guess Bell really was an evil woman," opined Jim. "Just like your Uncle Willard kept telling you."

"Is that what Willard actually said about her?" questioned Dr. Godspeed.

"More than once," Carolyn assured him. "According to Uncle Willard, his mother was the cause of everything that ever went wrong in his life, and behind all of the problems he had with his brother."

"Luke did mention his Uncle Walter during one of our sessions," recalled Dr. Godspeed, and said the twins went for most of their lives without speaking with one another.

"That would be correct," corroborated Carolyn, "and it would break your heart if you knew all the things Bell did to those boys."

"Would you care to elaborate?" asked Henry.

"Well, a lot of what happened was never shared with anyone else," began Carolyn, "but what I do know after speaking with both my father and his brother is this. When they were boys, they had a paper route, but their mother kept all the money."

"Why would she do such a thing?" inquired Dr. Godspeed.

"Who knows," Carolyn shrugged her shoulders. "Perhaps to have power over them."

"A possibility," agreed Henry. "Please, go on."

"When my Uncle Willard was dying, he told me the same story, adding to it the fact that Bell finally did use some of that money to buy a left-handed baseball glove for his brother Walter."

"Your dad," acknowledged Henry.

"Yes, but apparently there was only enough money for one glove and Willard was right-handed," explained Carolyn. "Obviously, he never got over it."

"Jealousy is quite common between twins," explained Henry. "Particularly identical twins."

"I don't know whether it was jealousy as much as it was Bell constantly turning them against each other, always telling one of them one thing and then turning around and telling the other one something else," elaborated Carolyn.

"Interesting," nodded Henry.

"There were, of course, the times Bell's older sister Violet sent her daughters Joanie and Verna to stay with them each summer when they were in high school," recalled Carolyn. "Apparently they were romantically involved with their cousins and created quite a stir."

"Let me get this straight," said Henry. "Joanie and Verna were sent to stay with Willard and Walter by themselves, or with the family?"

"With the family, of course," clarified Carolyn. "At Frank and Bell's house."

"Tell me about the stir," directed Dr. Godspeed.

"Well, Willard and Joanie fell in love and planned to elope, but Bell found out about it and put a stop to it," revealed Carolyn.

"I take it her sister Violet might not have been too happy about it, either," assumed Henry.

"That's an understatement," replied Carolyn. "Not only did Bell make sure her boys were sent away to military school at the time, but Violet allegedly made Joanie join the Navy."

"Why allegedly?" questioned Dr. Godspeed.

"According to Willard, Joanie was kicked out of the Navy after about nine months and then sent home," answered Carolyn.

"No doubt a story they told him to cover up an unexpected pregnancy," deduced Henry.

"That was my suspicion," Carolyn advised him. "The only thing I do know for sure is that Willard was still in love with Joanie all those years later. He told me that story on his deathbed."

"Incredible," marveled Henry.

"Even more incredible is the fact that Joanie and Verna were the only relatives from that side of the family to show up for my father's burial back in 2004," continued Carolyn.

"Walter died in 2004?" asked Dr. Godspeed.

"Yes, that's why they buried him then," responded Carolyn with a straight face. *Really?* she thought.

"I'm sorry, please go on," Henry encouraged her.

"I'm sorry, too," apologized Carolyn as she gave him a weak smile. "Believe it or not, Verna came up to my mother and me at my dad's funeral and introduced herself as one of the *kissing cousins*. We thought at the time it was a bizarre thing to say, as we hardly knew the woman, but all these years later when I learned about them from Willard, it finally made sense."

"Like pieces of a jigsaw puzzle falling into place," nodded Henry. "Please, continue."

"Both twins were pretty much on their own financially after that," responded Carolyn. "Sadly, they did get conned into buying the Bennett family car from Bell once they were on their own and had jobs."

"Sad how?" Henry grilled her.

"From what I can piece together between what each of them told me," explained Carolyn, "Bell told each of them the other one had failed to pay their half, so each covered for the other and ended up paying double."

"When did they realize this?" questioned Henry.

"Not until 2004, when Willard came to visit Walter on his deathbed," clarified Carolyn. "Very sad they missed out on all those years they could have enjoyed being a part of each other's lives."

"How well did you know Bell?" questioned Henry.

"Extremely well," answered Carolyn. "My parents used to leave me with her when I was little, and every moment I was there she kept me busy cleaning her house or doing chores in her yard. She certainly believed in using that wooden yardstick of hers whenever she thought I was slacking off."

"Were your parents aware of this?" inquired Dr. Godspeed.

"No, not until the day I fell from her lemon tree and got my arms and face all scratched up," recalled Carolyn. "I was in grade school at the time, so I would go there after school each day. Anyway, that night when my mom came to pick me up, I told her about all the things Bell was having me do. My mom got really upset and informed Bell she certainly wasn't paying her to watch me and then let something like that happen."

"How did Bell react?" asked Henry.

"It wasn't so much how Bell reacted as it was how my Grandpa Frank reacted when he learned Bell had been getting paid all that time, but pocketing the money," described Carolyn.

"Frank had no idea Bell was being paid to watch you?" Henry seemed surprised.

"Just like the paper route money situation with her sons," corroborated Carolyn. "Bell was always making deals and earning money on the side. That's what she did."

"Besides using corporal punishment as a means of discipline for children, was Bell ever physically abusive in any way?" Dr. Godspeed unexpectedly asked.

"Not that I'm aware of," frowned Carolyn.

"Did she have any pets?" asked Henry.

"There were dogs in the family when Walter and Willard were young, but it was entirely their responsibility to take care of them," said Carolyn. "The *only* pet Frank and Bell ever had during my lifetime was an English bulldog named Butch, but they didn't acquire him until after I was grown."

"How was Butch treated?" pressed Dr. Godspeed.

"Grandpa Frank loved Butch with all his heart," replied Carolyn. "Butch had pins in almost every leg, had a glass eye, and was the only canine patient I know of who ever had open heart surgery at Stanford University. Grandpa loved Butch so much he would have done absolutely anything to prolong his life. They were inseparable."

"How did Bell feel about that?" probed Dr. Godspeed.

"I do remember something odd Bell confessed to me once," related Carolyn. "Apparently Butch became so old and sick he really didn't have much quality of life left, but Grandpa refused to have him put down. He believed when it was Butch's time, the good Lord would take him, and that was that."

"What was it she confessed to you?" asked Henry.

"She put an overdose of sleeping pills into a piece of cheese and gave it to Butch as a snack one night," elaborated Carolyn. "According to her, Butch died with his chin resting on Grandpa Frank's leg."

"Frank must have taken it pretty hard," assumed Henry.

"Bell said he never knew about the cheese snack," added Carolyn, "but Grandpa was so depressed after Butch died that he became reclusive for about two years."

"Incredible," muttered Henry. "Believe it or not, Luke told me the very same story."

"Obviously, Bell was capable of putting a living creature out of its misery," interjected Jim, who had been quietly listening to the exchange. "It wouldn't be much of a leap to assume she was capable of putting a dying person out of her misery, as well."

"Anything else you would like to share with me about Bell?" inquired Henry as he turned to Carolyn.

Carolyn merely shook her head.

"I appreciate you sharing what you did," acknowledged Dr. Godspeed. "It does answer some questions I've had about her, though in all honesty, we may never know for sure whether she actually did it. All we have to go on is the video."

"I think it speaks rather well for itself," opined Carolyn.

"Nevertheless, you must keep in mind that this video technically does **not** exist; it was destroyed. In other words, you never saw it," cautioned Dr. Godspeed.

"I understand," agreed Carolyn.

"What did your Uncle Willard believe about how Ruth died?" Dr. Godspeed suddenly asked.

"That Luke did it, of course," replied Carolyn. "That's what we all thought, but after watching your interview with Luke, I'm inclined to believe otherwise."

"What do *you* think?" Jim unexpectedly asked Dr. Godspeed.

"Where is Bell now?" asked Henry, without answering.

"She died in 2005," revealed Carolyn. "The same day Mt. Saint Helens erupted again."

"That figures," grinned Jim while he shook his head.

"I guess it's best to consider for whom the bell tolls," pondered Dr. Godspeed.

"Well, it's certainly going to be tolling for you soon," predicted Jim, "unless you get someone out here to help you. I don't feel in good conscience we can leave you alone with her." Jim nodded towards Maria, who was still fast asleep.

"What is her story, anyway?" inquired Carolyn.

"Very similar to Luke's actually," Henry informed them. "She never married, had no children, and lived alone with her father until the time of his death."

"Please don't tell me she left his body locked in a room for two years," requested Carolyn.

"No," replied Henry. "She actually put him in a freezer in the basement, and continued to live in the house for about a year."

"And now she has *you*," Jim reminded him with a pointed look.

"She will, of course, need to be medicated for the rest of her life," admitted Dr. Godspeed, "but you are correct I am going to need help managing things around here."

"I just happen to own an employment agency," revealed Jim.

"I don't know if I could afford it," objected Henry.

"Consider it a tax-deductible donation," Jim advised him. "Your research is important, and who knows, maybe someday you'll find a way for patients to leave their medication behind."

"Perhaps some sort of neuro-surgical procedure," speculated Carolyn. "You never know."

"They did used to give people lobotomies back when it was still legal," admitted Dr. Godspeed.

"Actually, they are technically still legal," corrected Jim, "though they are rarely performed anymore."

16. Epilogue

Susan's sprained ankle was propped up on a pillow where she sat in the tower room of the lighthouse, gazing wistfully at the ocean horizon beyond it.

"Can I get you anything else?" asked Sheree rather curtly.

Susan looked up at her. "Please know how sorry I am for what I said before. I didn't mean it."

Sheree approached Susan and put her hands on her hips. "Yes, my first husband did have schizophrenia and multiple personality disorder. He also was a patient at the Ocean Bluff Mental Institution, so yeah, it hit pretty close to home."

Susan swallowed hard and seemed to squirm beneath Sheree's unpleasant stare.

"That doesn't mean I feel comfortable having the subject brought up, especially in front of people I don't know," fumed Sheree.

"I'm so sorry," Susan apologized again.

"But you're right about one thing," added Sheree while she glanced out the window and saw Jim walking with Carolyn down on the beach. "At least I've got a good husband now, right?"

Susan turned to see what Sheree was looking at and gave Sheree a look of sympathy.

"Don't you *dare* pity me," added Sheree as tears began to escape from the corners of her eyes.

"Carolyn would never allow Jim to do anything inappropriate," Susan assured her. "She's very much in love with her husband."

"It's not Carolyn I'm worried about," responded Sheree. "But it's no secret how Jim feels about her; he worships the ground she walks on, and I know he'd do *anything* for her."

"Perhaps you're overreacting," assumed Susan when she finally took a sip of the hot chocolate Sheree had just brought her.

"Let me ask you this," countered Sheree while she sat down beside Susan. "How would *you* feel if your husband felt like that about Carolyn, knowing at any time he'd be at her beck and call, ready to leave you for her without a moment's notice if she were to change her mind about him?"

Susan became somber as she blew on her hot chocolate before taking another sip.

"Well?" urged Sheree.

"I still say you have nothing to worry about," insisted Susan. "Carolyn thinks the world of you, and so do I."

"Really?" Sheree appeared dubious.

"Hey, Jim's not her type," insisted Susan with a mischievous grin. "You know that."

"Then how is Jim still interested in her after almost 50 years?" questioned Sheree. "She's obviously *his* type."

"Don't waste the time you have with Jim worrying about what might be," counseled Susan. "Be grateful for what you have."

"That's easy for you to say with all the husbands you've had," muttered Sheree while she continued to watch Jim and Carolyn advancing their way down the beach.

"They're not even holding hands," pointed out Susan with a crooked smile.

"That's not the point," argued Sheree.

"Hey, Hector's been good to me," admitted Susan, "but we all have our moments. It's just life."

"I still can't help but thinking my daughter Ann would be alive today if she hadn't followed Jim and Carolyn down to that awful jungle," lamented Sheree. "And her husband Ted, too, not to mention our unborn grandchild!"

"Sometimes bad things happen to good people," described Susan more seriously. "A lot of people died during the trip."

"Not to change the subject, but did you guys ever find out what happened to Carolyn's Aunt Ruth?" asked Sheree.

"Carolyn was the one who had the private session with Dr. Godspeed," Susan reminded her. "I was the one who slipped and fell on my way to the boat dock, so I missed out on it."

"Wasn't Jim in on the session, too?" Sheree grilled her.

"He was," confirmed Susan as she took another sip of hot chocolate, "but neither of them bothered to fill me in on the details yet. I think we should pin them down on it, don't you?"

Sheree merely nodded when she suddenly noticed Jim and Carolyn were no longer visible. *Where did they go?*

"Maybe this isn't such a good idea," objected Carolyn as she followed Jim over to a driftwood log near the infamous beach cave where Joyce and Veronica's bodies had previously been discovered while solving *The Oceanview Matter*.

"We're perfectly safe here," insisted Jim when he reached for Carolyn's hand to help her climb over a rock.

"Thanks," acknowledged Carolyn while she stepped over the rock before removing her hand from Jim's grasp and sitting down.

"Anytime," responded Jim with an unseen wistful look at her before sitting down on the log beside her.

"I want you to know how much I appreciate all you've done to make it possible for me to find out more about my Aunt Ruth," mentioned Carolyn while she gazed out at the incoming waves.

"Still think Bell did it?" questioned Jim as he raised an eyebrow.

"No question," replied Carolyn while she turned to study the cave entrance and the locked gate just inside. "A lot of bad things happened in there."

"Things we've put behind us," Jim reminded her. "Just like you need to do with your Aunt Ruth."

"You're right," agreed Carolyn as she took a deep breath of fresh salt air before slowly letting it out. "It sure gets windy this time of year, doesn't it?"

"Foggy, too," added Jim while he nodded his head.

"Good thing it's a nice day," responded Carolyn as a seagull landed on the beach nearby and began digging in the sand until uncovering a dead fish.

A second seagull landed beside it and tried to steal its find, the two birds becoming involved in a screaming match until the victor finally grabbed its treasure and flew away.

"Have you had a chance to share what we've learned with Leticia?" Jim suddenly asked.

"Not yet, but I will. There's no hurry," answered Carolyn.

"You don't think she'd be anxious to find out?" asked Jim.

"It's just that Leticia didn't seem the least bit interested in helping us obtain Luke's psychiatric records," explained Carolyn. "I'm not sure how she'd feel about the way we finally got to see 'em."

"*Touché*," grinned Jim as he folded his hands around one knee and drew it up to his chest, his other foot resting on the log.

"There is something else I just thought of this morning," revealed Carolyn while she pulled out a tube of lip balm and applied it to her lips before brushing a strand of hair from her eyes. *The wind is so unforgiving.*

"Tell me about it," urged Jim as he put his leg back down and scooted indiscernibly closer to Carolyn before putting an arm behind her, casually resting that hand on the log.

"I remember when Bell died, it was left to me, my mother and a family friend to clean out her apartment at the facility where she was staying," recalled Carolyn.

"Never a pleasant task after someone passes," said Jim.

"Several weeks before she died," continued Carolyn, "we all noticed something was wrong with her; more so than usual. Her face was often red and her mood swings kept getting worse. She constantly made false accusations and threats toward everyone."

"Perhaps she had the beginnings of dementia," guessed Jim.

"That's what we thought at first, too," replied Carolyn, "until we went through her kitchen cupboards."

Jim leaned slightly closer. "And?"

"I think she was a closet alcoholic," Carolyn blurted out while she shook her head. "It would certainly explain her behavior. Not only did we find multiple half-consumed bottles of hard liquor, all of which we dumped down the sink, but we also found some really old mason jars filled with something we think was moonshine."

"What?" Jim began to laugh. "You're kidding!"

"I wish I were," responded Carolyn, "but there were literally dozens of them, along with a really old log book from the 1940s with a list of customers, dates of sale, and how much she made."

"Bell was certainly an enterprising individual," noted Jim with a crooked smile. "Didn't you say she did all the sewing for a local Madame and her girls, as well?"

"That's right," confirmed Carolyn. "And poor Grandpa Frank probably had no idea about any of it."

"So, between putting Frank's dog Butch out of its misery, and all the other questionable activities she had going on," assessed Jim, "it would appear Bell was quite capable of painting outside the lines."

"Murdering Ruth goes way beyond painting outside the lines," fumed Carolyn. "And she got away with it, too!"

"Perhaps in this life, yes," agreed Jim, "but ultimately she'll have to answer for everything, just like everyone else."

"I'm glad we had Luke buried beside Bell in the Bennett Family plot at the cemetery," commented Carolyn as another gust of wind blew her hair into her eyes again.

"Most appropriate," opined Jim. "Poetic, actually."

"Indeed," nodded Carolyn as she brushed the hair from her face.

"You must be freezing," realized Jim while he took off his jacket and put it around Carolyn's shoulders, deliberately allowing his arm to remain around her as they stared out at the water together.

"We'd better get back to make sure Sheree and Susan haven't killed each other yet," suggested Carolyn when she stood up and headed back toward the wet sand where it would be easier to walk back to the lighthouse.

Jim nodded in agreement as he stood up and rushed over to help her step over the rock again.

"Thanks," smiled Carolyn while she studied her friend. Grateful she could trust him to be a gentleman, she allowed Jim to put his arm around her while they made their trek back.

Unknown to either of them, Sheree was carefully watching like a hawk from the tower room of the lighthouse as they approached and made their way up the stepped trail from the beach.

"Jim, thank you for being my friend," Carolyn informed him when they reached the front entrance.

"My pleasure," assured Jim as he held the door open for her. "I'm always here for you, any time."

"And I appreciate it," Carolyn added while she kissed him on the cheek before going inside.

"Perhaps Leticia can come join us for a few days," suggested Jim when they entered the foyer.

"Actually, I need to get home," declined Carolyn, "but thank you again for everything."

"There's no need to rush off," Jim reminded Carolyn as Sheree descended the spiral staircase and joined them in the foyer.

"I just got a text from my husband and one of my cats has gone missing," explained Carolyn, "so yes, I really do need to get home to try and find her as soon as possible."

"We'll be sorry to see you go," lied Sheree as she forced a congenial smile.

"No, you won't," discerned Carolyn when she took off Jim's jacket and handed it back to him. "And if I leave within the hour, I can get home before dark and still have time to start looking for my cat."

Embarrassed by Carolyn's perception, Sheree's cheeks flushed. "I'm sorry, but it's just that all Jim ever does is go running off to help you solve these cases. I never know each time he leaves with you whether he'll make it back home alive or not. Then there was Ann, Ted and our unborn grandchild!"

"Ted and Ann each chose to go down there when they did," Jim reminded Sheree as he put a comforting arm around her. "I loved them, too, especially Ann."

"Hey, you two, don't waste time bickering over what you can't change," recommended Carolyn when she paused on the spiral staircase. "We'll see them again someday. I know it! Besides, I'm pretty sure they'd want you to get along and enjoy the time you have left. Life is short."

THE END

Made in the USA
Middletown, DE
10 April 2024

52777750R00205